Praise for Sapph[ire]

"[A] highly stylized narrative that portrays J.J.'s fury, perplexity, and passion. J.J.'s voice rises and skids to its own staccato rhythms. Often dipping into sexual fevers or dream states, it seems to nod to the subjective narrators of William Faulkner.... Sapphire has taken the challenges her Kid faces and distilled them into a devastating voice, demanding and raw.... An accomplished work of art." —*Los Angeles Times*

"[Sapphire] remains fearlessly committed to telling uncomfortable truths.... Like *Push*, *The Kid* is deeply moving and unflinching." —*Essence*

"*The Kid*'s unflinching authenticity makes it tough yet ultimately rewarding to read." —*People*

"Sapphire keeps the reader on edge—sometimes, like Abdul, you don't know whether a situation is 'real' or is taking place entirely, or somewhat, in the young man's mixed-up head. As with *Push* the author doesn't gift us with even a semblance of a happy ending, but she does give us hope." —*BookPage*

"Social realism only begins to get at the way Sapphire approaches her work.... Her work confronts incest, abuse, poverty, cruelty, and pain with a steely eyed, full-frontal daring.... In Sapphire's writing, the inner life of her characters is often at odds with the harshness of their experience. In their minds, they progress from defilement to purity, from guilt to innocence, from the present back or forward." —*Philadelphia Inquirer*

"*The Kid* is more ambitious than *Push*." —*USA Today*

"That's the genius of Sapphire's writing: Abdul, like Precious, while not a monster like his grandmother, Mary, is both a victim and an oppressor. He cloaks his occasional casual brutality in denial and in hope. We want to shake him by the shoulders when he is at his worst, but we never want to give up on him. . . . The dialogue in *The Kid* is pitch-perfect and true to the characters. Honestly, though one might wish for less profanity, it could not have been written any other way."   —*Buffalo News*

"This is a greatly textured story, varying mood to mood, line to line; devoted to encompassing the deceptions, placations, and terrors of Abdul's mental landscape. . . . For Sapphire the study of life's accountabilities big, small, and unknown is the whole point. She overcomes the melodramatic nature of her material through the power of her language, rhythmic and poetic."   —*Indiana Post-Tribune*

"[A] powerful, disturbing tale of adolescent angst and the importance of relationships . . . *The Kid* ultimately proves to be a distressing and provocative testimony to the importance of familial guidance to the success and happiness of children. It is a story of love lost, freedom chased, desperation and escape."   —*Desert News*

"Incorporated as well [in *The Kid*] is Langston Hughes's preoccupation with the dream and the desire, à la James Baldwin, for someone to know our names. But it is Richard Wright's autobiographical *Black Boy* that Sapphire resurrects most expertly. She updates the physical and psychological hunger Wright describes growing up black in the Deep South, and captures the continuing confusion about what it means to be a black man in the contemporary world."   —*The Globe and Mail* (Toronto)

"[*The Kid*] gives a voice to the millions of orphans caused by HIV-AIDS, why sexual abuse is so prevalent in her work, and the heartbreaking reality that black children are last in line to be adopted."   —theGrio.com

"Powerful and disturbing."   —*Kirkus Reviews*

PENGUIN BOOKS

THE KID

Sapphire is the author of two collections of poetry and the bestselling novel *Push*. The film adaptation of her novel, *Precious* (2009), received the Academy Award for Best Screenplay and Best Supporting Actress, in addition to the Grand Jury Prize and Audience awards in the U.S. Dramatic Competition at Sundance. In 2009 she was a recipient of a United States Artist Fellowship. She lives in New York City.

THE KID

SAPPHIRE

PENGUIN BOOKS

PENGUIN BOOKS

Published by the Penguin Group

Penguin Group (USA) Inc., 375 Hudson Street, New York, New York 10014, U.S.A. • Penguin Group (Canada), 90 Eglinton Avenue East, Suite 700, Toronto, Ontario, Canada M4P 2Y3 (a division of Pearson Penguin Canada Inc.) • Penguin Books Ltd, 80 Strand, London WC2R 0RL, England • Penguin Ireland, 25 St. Stephen's Green, Dublin 2, Ireland (a division of Penguin Books Ltd) • Penguin Books Australia Ltd, 250 Camberwell Road, Camberwell, Victoria 3124, Australia (a division of Pearson Australia Group Pty Ltd) • Penguin Books India Pvt Ltd, 11 Community Centre, Panchsheel Park, New Delhi – 110 017, India • Penguin Group (NZ), 67 Apollo Drive, Rosedale, Auckland 0632, New Zealand (a division of Pearson New Zealand Ltd) • Penguin Books (South Africa) (Pty) Ltd, 24 Sturdee Avenue, Rosebank, Johannesburg 2196, South Africa

Penguin Books Ltd, Registered Offices: 80 Strand, London WC2R 0RL, England

First published in the United States of America by The Penguin Press,
a member of Penguin Group (USA) Inc.
Published in Penguin Books 2012

10 9 8 7 6 5 4 3 2 1

Grateful acknowledgment is made for permission to reprint excerpts from the following copyrighted works:
"Your Love Is King," lyrics by Sade Adu, music by Stuart Matthewman and Sade Adu. © 1984 Angel Music Ltd. All rights administered by Sony/ATV Music Publishing LLC, 8 Music Square West, Nashville, TN 37203. All rights reserved. Used by permission.
"The Kid" from *Vice: New and Selected Poems* by Ai. Copyright © 1979 by Ai. Used by permission of W. W. Norton & Company, Inc.
"The Negro Speaks of Rivers," "Mother to Son," and "Dreams" from *The Collected Poems of Langston Hughes*, edited by Arnold Rampersad with David Roessel, Associate Editor. Copyright © 1994 by The Estate of Langston Hughes. Used by permission of Alfred A. Knopf, a division of Random House, Inc., and Harold Ober Associates Incorporated.
Wise Blood by Flannery O'Connor. Copyright © 1962 by Flannery O'Connor. Copyright renewed 1990 by Regina O'Connor. Reprinted by permission of Farrar, Straus and Giroux, LLC.
"Have You Ever Been Out in the Country" by Mercy Dee Williams. By permission of Bug Music.

Publisher's Note
This is a work of fiction. Names, characters, places, and incidents either are the product of the author's imagination or are used fictitiously, and any resemblance to actual persons, living or dead, business establishments, events, or locales is entirely coincidental.

THE LIBRARY OF CONGRESS HAS CATALOGED THE HARDCOVER EDITION AS FOLLOWS:
Sapphire.
The kid : a novel / Sapphire.
 p. cm.
Sequel to: Push.
ISBN 978-1-59420-304-6 (hc.)
ISBN 978-0-14-312120-6 (pbk.)
 1. African American boys—Fiction. 2. African Americans—Fiction. 3. Harlem (New York, N.Y.)—Fiction. I. Title.
[DNLM: 1. Bildungsromans. gsafd]
PS3569.A63K53 2011
813'.54—dc22   2011001739

Printed in the United States of America
DESIGNED BY NICOLE LAROCHE

For Angelica

And for the 16 million and still counting

orphaned by HIV-AIDS

And now abide faith, hope, love, these three:

but the greatest of these is love.

—I CORINTHIANS 13:13

BOOK ONE

I'M NINE

Where you come from is gone, where
you thought you were going to never
was there, and where you are is no good
unless you can get away from it.

—FLANNERY O'CONNOR,
Wise Blood

ONE   "Wake up, little man." Rita's voice is coming under the covers at me. It's warm under the covers, smell good like Rita and clean like sheets. I curl up tighter, squeeze my eyes shut, and go back to sleep. In the dream it's Mommy's birthday party and she's holding me in her arms kissing me and dancing with me. Our house is smelling like lasagna, wine, and people, mostly girls sweating and perfume. One girl is smoking weed. Everyone is laughing. Mommy puts me down and goes to open her presents. She's sitting in the blue armchair under the light. All the people have presents in their hands and are holding them out to her. A lady, who looks nice but when she smiles all her teeth is black, is holding out a pretty present tied with a gold ribbon. No! No! NOOOO! I want to say, but no words come out my mouth, and Mommy takes the box. And I want to stay asleep, even though I know it's a bomb and I'm not dreaming anymore, and if I was dreaming, the bomb would be exploding now. And now that it's too late, my voice would be loud. "Abdul." Someone is shaking my shoulder. Rita. I squeeze my eyes shut, 'cause when I open them, when I stick my head out from under the covers, my mother will be dead and today will be her funeral. "Abdul." Rita shake my shoulder again. I try to go back to the music, people dancing, and our house smelling like lasagna again, but I can't. "Nuh uh," I tell Rita. "Five more minutes," she say. The music is all gone now. There's clear plastic tubes stuck in my mommy's nose, they come out her nose and is taped to the side of her face, go up to a clear plastic bag hanging up above her head. Another tube is stuck in her throat, it has tape around it. Her hands got tubes stuck in 'em too and is

3

all swole up. A machine is going *whoosh-rump whoosh-rump whoosh-rump*. The doctor is from Africa. He talks to me in French sometimes and looks at my homework. He tells jokes. But today he is not joking. "She's doing her very best to stay here, little man." He grabs me up in his arms. "But God may have other plans." He hand me to Rita, but Rita's skinny, can't hold me, puts me down. He leaves, comes back with a stool. "Here, stand on this. Come on, little man, your mommy's traveling. I want you to hold her hand." In the hall the nurse say, "I'm very sorry her condition is critical, absolutely no visitors except—" "Let them in!" Doctor say. White lady and lady with long dreadlocks come in and stand behind Rita at the foot of the bed. I'm scared to touch Mommy's hands with the tubes sticking in 'em. I look up at the doctor, frog eyes of his red, but he ain't cry. I ain't crying either. He walk over put my hand on Mommy's shoulder. "Wake up, Mommy." But her eyes don't open, she don't move. Then it's like when you turn down the TV set and can see the pictures moving around but ain't no sound. It's quiet. Mommy cough then go like ahh-ahh. Her head raises up a little but her eyes don't open then her head falls down. "Oh my god!" Rita say. Then the room is all noisy again, nurse in the hall talking, machine going *whoosh-rump whoosh-rump*, somebody drop something. The doctor pick me up like I'm a baby and carry me out the room. I look back as the door swing shut, the nurse is pulling the tubes out Mommy's hand.

I FEEL RITA sit down on the side of the bed. She trying to pull the covers down. I got 'em pulled over my head. "Come on, little man, it's time to get up! We gonna have eggs and bacon, and I let you have some coffee." I don't want to get up. "Come on, I got the space heater on for you and everything. Come on, git up, go pee, and then come back and wash your face and brush your teeth. Come on, Abdul!" I let her pull the covers off me, she's lucky I do 'cause I'm very strong. I hop out the bed, run to the door, Rita swing it open. "Hurry 'fore someone else gets in there. Put on your slippers! The floor might be nasty." I put on my slippers and run down the hall to the toilet. Psssss, feels good to pee. "Close the door if you gotta number two." "I ain' gotta." "You sure?" "No," I say, and close the door, pushing the little bolt through the loops to lock the door. I doo-doo, flush it down, open the door, and run back up the hallway. Rita hand me a washcloth and point to the sink.

That's all that's in the room, really, a bed and a sink in the corner. Rita ain't got no refrigerator, TV, or nothing, but I rather stay with her than Rhonda or any of my mother's other friends. I like Rita, she's nice to little kids. I'm not really a little kid anymore, though. I'm nine. I run the washcloth over my face. Rita come in, wet it, squeeze it out, hand it back to me. "Get your eyes, all that sleepy stuff, then behind your ears! Take off your pajamas and wash your booty and under your arms. Hear!" I nod, she heads down the hall to the toilet. The man in the room next door turn his music on. Tupac. The woman across from us is cussing in Spanish. She ain't got no kids. The lady next door got three. I only been here for a week. Since my mother died.

Behind me on the bed, Rita gots my underwear and socks laid out. I like Tupac, but not that much. Man next door play him every morning. Rita say maybe that's all he got, but I looked inside his door once, he got CDs lined up along the walls up to the ceiling almost. My white shirt and black suit my mother bought me is hanging on the nail on the door. I know everybody on my block miss me, my friends probably wondering where I am. *I* wonder where I am. I know my mother ain't dead like they be saying 'cause I be talking to her all the time just like I always did. But I know we probably ain't going to Callie, to Disneyland, like she said we was. Two more years—*When I get outta school, we're goin' to California, to Disneyland!* Where's California? *Don't be silly, look at the map!* But I mean where is it really? *Whatchu mean, honey?* On the map it's long and orange, near water. *Right, it's on the coast, like New York, but the West Coast. We gotta get on an airplane to fly across all this land,* she wave her hand, *and then wham, Callie! Look just enter: www.google.com, then Disneyland, California.* I do, it's 1,560,000 listings.

"Abdul!"

"What?"

"*What?* Who you talking to? Don't 'what' me! Put those clothes on."

"Yes, Aunt Rita."

Outside the window a train is passing by.

"What train is that?"

"Boy, you be asking some questions 24/7, don'tchu!"

"I only want to know, my mother say if you want to know something, ask."

"Of course, Aunt Rita's sorry." All I gotta do is mention my mother and I can get anything I want. "That's Metro-North going upstate to Scarsdale, White Plains, and Bedford Hills. We'll get a schedule and see all the places it goes and go on a trip one day if you want. OK?"

"OK," I say.

"Now, get your suit on and put some lotion on your face and hands. We wanna look nice." Rita is getting out her perfume and stuff, putting it on her head, under her arms, then out the bottle behind her knees and neck. "C'mere, we wanna smell nice." I walk over to the side of the bed where she's sitting down. She got all her stuff on the windowsill and chair near the window. "Raise up your arms." She laugh and spray under my arms. "Your mom do that?" I shake my head no. "Well, just for today," she say, then she puts stuff from one of the bottles behind my ears. I don't mind, it smell nice. I go put my clothes on while Rita is making her eyes black. I look over my shoulder at her when she get up from the bed and take off her robe. It's not like girls in the magazines. Rita just look like a lady in her underwears, lumpy like. But when she puts on her black dress, what's all shiny and got a ruffle around the bottom, she look beautiful. Now she making her lips red. I like that, my mother do that too sometime.

"Ready?" She finish zipping up her dress.

I get my leather jacket.

"That's nice, your mommy got that for you?" Rita ask about my jacket.

"Um hm."

"So let's go get some breakfast and say good-bye."

Rita put her Bible in her purse, she holding some pretty black beads.

She look at me, nod at the beads. "It's all good—rosary, Bible. Precious ever take you to church?"

"No."

You ever gonna leave me, Mommy? *Well, I can't really say, baby. What I can say is, I never wanna leave you.*

Rita close the door, lock it. Guy next door peep his head out. "Y'all outta here?"

"Yeah, we gonna get some breakfast then hit it."

"Try Bennie's. You know my brother-in-law into delivery."

"Uh, no I didn't know that."

"Yeah, all up and down here; say he deliver more often to Bennie's than any other place, so that mean his shit is the freshest, right?"

"Hey, sound right to me."

"And you, little man, be strong!" He give me handshake on the black side.

Lady across the hall open her door. "*Ay, Dios!* Poor baby!"

"They going to breakfast, then to el funeral."

"You shoulda tell me, I gots coffee here," she say.

"That's OK," Rita say, and we tell 'em bye and walk down the stairs.

It's warm outside even though it's November. I look up at the sign over the hotel, PARK AVENUE HOTEL. We walks down 125th Street past Bennie's to Mofongo's. I order bacon for breakfast, my mother usually don't let me eat bacon. But the waitress ask me what do I want. Rita done already ordered sausage and scrambled eggs please. I say bacon and eggs over easy please, then say no, scrambled. Restaurants ain't like my mother, I don't want no runny eggs. Waitress ask, You said bacon, right? Right, I say, and nothing happens like my mother saying, Bacon ain't good for you. I put strawberry jam on my toast. Taste good. My mother is dead. Rita say one espresso and one café con leche. Here put some sugar in it. Why milk? *'Cause kids need milk, makes bones grow.* Why? *Why what, Abdul? I don't know why milk makes your bones grow. I just know it does! So would you please shut up and drink the damn milk. You gonna be the death of me yet!* The coffee taste good, sweet, like a kinda chocolate or something.

"Finished, little man?"

"Unh huh."

"What 'unh huh' means?"

"Means yeah, what you think it means?"

She laughs, I smile. "Oh, we gots a smart one here," she say, rubbing my head.

"Yeah." I know I'm smart.

"It's only a couple of blocks we can walk or take the bus then walk up Lenox, OK?"

Mommy, who's that man? *A friend of Mommy's. Why, don't you like him?* No. *Why not, he's a nice guy. Mommy likes your friends unless they get you in trouble like you know who! Don't you want Mommy to be happy?* Yeah, with me!

"You thinking about your mami?"

Where was that train going? Beyond the subway, I been on all the subways almost. Metro-North, I been upstate. I look down Park Avenue, tracks overhead as far as you can see. It's busy underneath the tracks, people is getting they dope, ladies is standing around doing the wrong thing, and it ain't even night yet. Across the street from the bus stop is a vacant lot surrounded by a high chain fence with dogs running around in it. The people at the bus stop with us is probably TGIF'ing, as Rhonda would say.

Monday my favorite day, Abdul. I think I'm the only sistuh I know like Monday. Why, Mom? *Jus' do, maybe 'cause the weekends is so lonely.* I'm not lonely, Mommy. *Well, that's good, honey.*

"You thinking about your mami?" Rita ask.

I don't say nothing. The crosstown bus is coming, so we get on instead of walk and then get off at Lenox Avenue. The Black Israelite brothers is standing on the corner, one of 'em is screaming in a microphone. All of 'em got on headbands. They got big Bible pictures set up on the sidewalk. *They can stand up there and holler all day long, but the African merchants had to go.* Go where, Mom? *I don't know where they went. I just know they went.* Why? *Cutting into the white and Korean merchants' profits I guess.*

They complained to Giuliani, so he iced the Africans, Abdul. He can do that? He can put the Africans out of Harlem and let them stay? *They vote, sweetie. We live here, but they own the property.* Ever gonna change? *Yeah, baby, that's you and your little friends' jobs. Do something beside throw water balloons and*— I did not! *I know, Ms Jackson just lyin' on you.* Rita squeeze my hand. "I loved your mami, Abdul! She was a good woman. Come on now, it's almost ten o'clock. Oops! Here, let's get this uptown 102. We can walk home later if you want to walk."

We get off the bus in front of Lenox Terrace. *I was raised up on this block. Right there, see that building, I used to live there.* She's pointing across the street from Lenox Terrace at a raggedy brick building with a black door. I ever been there when I was a little boy? *No, thank God.* Leaves falling from the trees in front of Lenox Terrace, ain't no trees on the side of the street my mother say she was raised up on.

Where *is* she? Rhonda say gone to glory, heaven, sitting at the feet of a king. Her crown is bought and paid for! All she gotta do is put it on! Mommy, a crown? I ask her one time why we ain't had a princess like Diana? *We spozed to be a democracy, Abdul!* What's that? *What's that! You ain't studied democracy and why we vote and all in school?* Nuh uh, I shake my head.

"'Nuh uh' what?" Rita ask.

"Nuh uh nothin,'" I say.

We cross Lenox Avenue at 134th Street. There's a tall guy standing in front the laundrymat on the corner of 134th.

"That's Hamid from Somalia, own the laundrymat. He knew your mami."

"Sorry to hear she pass." He nod at a bunch of people standing a couple of doors down on Lenox between 133rd and 132nd.

Rita squeeze my hand. "This her little son, Abdul."

"You don't say! How old is he?"

"Abdul?" Rita say, squeezing my hand. I don't say nothing. "He's nine," she say. Somali guy reach in his pocket give me five dollars.

"What do you say, Abdul?"

"Thank you."

Africans is where we come from, Abdul, remember that. How come they don't like us? *Whatchu mean?* The ones in the restaurant and stores and stuff. *Well, I didn't say they liked us. I said it's where we come from.* The funeral home gots a cover over the door out onto the sidewalk, like what McDonald's got across the street. "Whatchu call that?" "Huh? Oh, the awning. Is that what you're talking about?" "Yeah, the awning." My mother's friend Rhonda is standing by us now. "Honey," she say, "that's one thing his mother did teach him, to ask questions!" I don't like Rhonda all that much even if she is my mother's friend. God, God, God, that's all she talk about. Bible this, Bible that! Rhonda go in her handbag and hand me something warm wrapped in foil paper. "Eat this before you go in." Ummm, beef pattie! "Whatchu say?" "Thank you." Rhonda not so bad. When I go to put the foil in the trash can, it falls onto the sidewalk 'cause the can is so full. Oh well, I tried. *You gotta do more than try! You gotta do it!* I pick the foil up and put it on top of the heap of trash in the can.

"I gotta go," I whisper to Rita.

"Bathroom?"

"Yeah."

We walk up to the door of the funeral place. Rita tells the guy at the front door, "He gotta use the bathroom." The guy opens the front door for me and says, "Go straight down the center aisle, at the pulpit go right until you see the green doors, that's the bathrooms." I run down the red carpet, then stop. Mommy! There she is! In that black box. Grown-ups lie and lie. Why? My mother is not in heaven. My mother is right here in a box like dead people on TV. She look different. I never seen that dress before, shiny white, silver. *I see the moon and the moon sees me.* I gotta pee bad! *Well, for heaven's sake go pee!* But that's me. Say it to me, Mommy, talk inside my head. Talk! I turn down the aisle and run to the bathroom. Pee and pee, feels good, shake. Put my penis back in my pants. *Your private parts have names. Well, dick is one of 'em, but penis is another. Balls is testicles.* I laugh, that's the funniest thing I ever heard, except for *buttocks.* Ha, ha! *Don't worry about rememberin' all those words, just remember your*

private parts are yours an' no one is supposed to touch 'em 'less you say so, hear?
Hear? I stare up at the ceiling light, squeeze my eyes shut. The light is red-orange through my closed eyelids. I breathe try to smell something, maybe like the smell after Mommy comes out the bathroom sometimes or how her underwears smell. Also that stuff Aunt Rita gots. What's that, Ma? Oh, cologne, you like it?

"Abdul! Come out of there! Whatchu doin'?" That's Rita outside the door. I smile. Ha, ha! Don't move. "Abdul, are you finished? Don't make me have to come in there." I laugh. "Stop playing, silly rabbit!" Together we go, "Trix are for kids!" And I run out laughing. Rita's standing there smiling, her black dress and red lips is pretty. *Marks? Oh, that's acne, probably from when Rita was a teenager. It's actually the scars, she don't have it no more, but she must have had it pretty bad once. But Aunt Rita's still pretty, ain't she, 'Dule?* Rita hold out her hand. I take it, look up at her. "You're pretty," I say. She bend over kiss me. "And you're just a sweet sweet little boy!" Tears from her eyes splash on my cheek. I smell her cologne, smell different from Mommy's.

"Whatchu say?"

"Nothin'."

"You said something about your mommy."

"I can't smell her no more."

Rita look over at Mommy in the box. "Did you try?"

"No."

"Well, don't. You're right, Papi, you can't smell her 'cause it's over. And if you touch her, it's going to be different too. Precious is dead, Abdul, you understand what that means?"

"Yes."

Rita takes my hand and we walk from the bathrooms back to where Mommy is. People coming in the church, down the aisles, sitting down.

"We gonna sit close to the stage?"

"Honey, that's like a pulpit or altar."

"And where Mommy's box—"

"Don't say 'box.' It's called a casket, or some people say coffin."

"I don't understand what a funeral home is. This looks like a church to me."

"This ain't no church, it's the chapel part of the funeral home. And we're gonna sit right here." A big old white lady in a green dress moves down so we can sit in the second row. The first row is empty. Who gonna sit there? No one. Rhonda is sitting behind us. I'm glad no one is in front of us, I can see Mommy better. The black box is long and shiny, curlicues on it, inside is a shiny white quilt. A little lamp is over her head. Everybody think she is dead. I mean *dead* dead. They don't know she is talking to me all the time even though she is in the casket box not talking, not moving. Behind Mommy is a picture of Jesus. Black with curly hair. What's lamb's wool? She go get the comb out the bathroom, try to stick it in my hair. *That's lamb's wool, silly!* she says, pulling the comb through my nappy head. Jesus had hair like us? *I don't know, I'm just showing you what the Bible say.* Is the Bible true? *I don't know.* It's kinda cold in the funeral home even if it ain't cold outside. Flowers is all around Mommy, roses, lilies, flowers I don't know the name of, maybe a thousand. I wonder what earrings she got on. I always like her earrings. I want earrings. *When you're twelve.* I can get earrings? *A earring.* Huh? *One.* I want both! *Stop screaming like you crazy! I tell you what, you can have one when you twelve, then if you still want two when you sixteen you can have two. How's that?* OK, I guess. *Ha! You guess! Listen to you!* Mommy, you gonna stay like that? *Like what?* Like in a box? *Abdul, you know what Mommy being here means?* No, I don't know. NO!

"Shhh!" Rita rocks my shoulder.

I look behind Mommy at Jesus hanging on the cross. Thorns is sticking in his head, drops of blood is coming down his face. He was that color? *What color?* Black like they got him up there? *I don't know, Abdul!* Behind Mommy is the stage kinda, podium, like in school, where the preacher gonna stand, I guess, then to one side of the podium is a piano and a bench. I want to hear some music but not church music. My mother don't like no church music either! A lady in a long black preacher robe get up on the stage.

"Who's that?"

"That's Reverend Bellwether who gonna do the service." A man follows behind Reverend Bellwether and sits down at the piano. Mommy's casket is in front the stage on wheels like.

"Good morning, friends and family of Precious Jones. We're gathered here together in sorrow for one who is no longer in sorrow, one whose pain has ended, one who has passed over to the other side." The guy start playing the piano and singing: The storm is passing ovah, the storm is, the storm is, the storm is passing *ovah*.

I don't know that song, I don't like it. It's sad and stupid; ain't no storm.

"Would the family and friends of the family, starting with the last row, one row at a time, please rise and come forward to view the deceased." Reverend Bellwether wave her hand for people to get up, then she frown. I turn around to see what she's looking at.

"Sit down!" Rita whisper, but she's staring too.

"Is that the mother?" Rhonda ask.

"No, you'd know it if it was the mother. I seen her once, she take up the whole aisle."

A old lady in a dirty orange dress is coming down the aisle moaning, "Oh Lawd, oh Lawd!" She got on a funny hat and her clothes is like from the olden days. She come up to where me and Rita are and reach over Rita and grab me. "Oh Lawdy Lawd, my baby." Ugh! She smell terrible.

"Please!" Rita say.

"What the do-diddly!" Rhonda say, and take the lady's arms from around me. A guy come up behind the old lady, take her elbow, tell her, "Let's have a seat, ma'am." She starts crying more crazy and tries to walk up to the casket. I look up at the Reverend look like her eyes gonna fall out her head. Rita looks back. "Speak of the devil!"

"Is that her?" Rhonda ask.

"Uh huh." Rita nod.

A big big lady is coming down the aisle waving her hands screaming, "My BAABEE, My BAAABEEEE!" She so big she can almost touch both sides of the aisle. She got on a big black raincoat. Her hair is sticking straight up like on the cartoons when they put their fingers in the electric socket. Why is she screaming like that? I start crying. Crying and crying. Snot coming out, my teeth is chattering. She remind me of Channel Thirteen, elephants in Africa. A elephant gets killed, all its friends come out and shake the earth with they screaming.

"MY BAAABEEEEEEEE!"

"You know who that lady is?" Rita ask me.

"No."

"You should tell him, Rita."

"Enough already!" Rita tell Rhonda.

The lady stops screaming. She's wringing her hands like she's washing 'em. Then she turn around mumbling. Her hair is smashed flat in the back, and there's a bald spot. From the back you can see a big tear in her raincoat, look like she ain't got nothing on under it, ugh! Her bedroom slippers going *schlup-schlup* down the aisle.

I look down at my shoes, my "good" shoes. Special occasions. When I was in the play at school, my mother bought 'em. I wore 'em when she took me to see Aretha Franklin at Lincoln Center. *Remember what you seeing, Abdul. She's the greatest.* I wore 'em when we went to see Haitian people's paintings at the Schomburg. At the Schomburg on the first floor there's a circle made of gold stand for the world with blue lines through it for rivers. I read the poem written on the floor, "I've Known Rivers." *Underneath is Langston Hughes's ashes.* I look at Mommy, my shoes. I got these on today 'cause she's dead. Not because I'm going anyplace. Who gonna buy me shoes now? I lean against Rita, I'm tired, I want to go to sleep.

"Sit up!" Rhonda hiss.

"He's tired, he's just a little boy."

PING! go Rhonda upside my head with her forefinger and thumb like a slingshot. "Dis your mother's funeral. Sit yourself up!"

"Would you let him be!" Rita's mad.

"No, Rita, you wrong. He don't need to sleep through this."

"Sit up, baby."

More people is coming down the aisle now. Ladies is crying. One lady is crying so hard she can hardly walk, two guys is helping her. "No, no," she sobbing, "I don't believe it." I stop crying to watch her. Ha, ha.

"Lots of these people is from your mother's job and from where she went to school. Some of them didn't know she was sick."

I knew she was sick, but not sick enough to die. What you do in college, Mommy? She laugh. *Work, work real hard.* I'm going there when I grow up? *Of course.* The old lady in the dirty orange dress who was hugging on me is creeping down the aisle now. Weird. Everybody sits back down.

Reverend Bellwether looks at us. "The family may come forward to view the deceased."

"Deceased?" I whisper.

"Dead," Rita say.

Reverend Bellwether is still looking at us. "Come on, baby, that's what we came here for, to say good-bye to Precious. They gonna close the casket after this." We walk down the aisle to Mommy. I like her dress, white, shiny. Her face looks funny, the way her lips is pressed together make her look like somebody else. Rhonda lean over and kiss Mommy. Then she come behind me. "You want to kiss your mudder good-bye?" Before I can say anything, she pick me up and lean me over the casket. I feel like my lips done bumped up against the water fountain at school, hard, cold. I start crying. Loud. Rita pull me from Rhonda.

"You shouldn't have done that!"

Rhonda go sit back down without saying nothing.

Reverend Bellwether says, "Good morning." I wipe my nose on my sleeve. Rita gives me some tissue. I wipe my sleeve with the tissue. She shake her head. "We're gathered here this morning to say good-bye to someone who has finished with this world," Reverend Bellwether say.

"Yes we are!" someone shout.

"Umm hm!" someone say.

"'For now we see through a glass darkly!' the Bible says."

"Umm hm, yes it does! Yes it does!"

"In this life we don't know God! God is revealed to us but still not known. We think we know God, got him labeled, unh huh! done named that file and saved it under Sunday! Sunday morning ten a.m. to one p.m. to be exact. Or, or"—Reverend Bellwether wheels around and points at Jesus hanging on the cross—"God is a statue dripping with blood. Or a book somebody told us was holy. Same somebody put us in chains and brought us here."

"Uh oh! Tell the truth!"

"Where she going with dis? We ain't paying her for dis nonsense," Rhonda grumble. "Dis spozed to be a funeral."

"Let me tell you, you don't know God and you ain't seen God! The glass is dark on this side. The only time you see God, the only time the light shine bright enough to see is when you doing God's work! We may not know God, but we know what God wants us to do. He has been clear about that. Don't kill. Don't steal. Love thy neighbor as thyself. *As thyself. Love thyself?* Yeah, how you gonna love anybody as you love yourself if you don't love yourself? Jesus was a loving child of God. 'Forgive them, Daddy,' he said, 'for they know not what they do.' That's what he said, not an eye for an eye or a tooth for a tooth. But love! And she—unh huh, who we're gathered here together to wish her well on her journey from this life—she tried to do that, didn't she?"

"Yes!"

Journey? Heaven? How is she gonna be in heaven if she's here? How can she go someplace if she's dead?

"You know she did! You wouldn't be here if she hadn't, wouldn't be people standing here in the aisle for one little ol' single mother as they call us nowadays, nothing spectacular about that. No, you wouldn't be standing in the aisle if she hadn't been filled with love. I know you loved her and I know she loved you. It's love, then. *Then* we see, know, and are known. Death takes everything, and into it you can take nothing but the part of you that is like God—spirit! The part that stands face-to-face with your Creator, who don't care about Gucci, Halston, or Hilfiger! Hair or degrees, color or pedigree—he knows you by the work—not your work, *his* work that you have done. He knows you by the love in your heart. So she's at rest here, now. Finally. And we can rest too, even in our sorrow, knowing God will know Precious Jones and she knew him."

"Yes!"

"Yes he will!"

"We're saying good-bye to someone who loved and who we loved. Faith! Hope! Charity! Charity meaning love. Jesus said, 'I give you these three, faith, hope, and love. And of these three love is the greatest'! Without it everything else is as tinkling brass, paper tigers, and three-card monte. Don't mean a thing if you ain't got love. Hollow, empty, keep your toys, prizes, hold on to 'em, 'cause without love they all you got! No one ever tell me when I'm up there at Harlem Hospital, 'Reverend Bellwether, could you contact my BMW, could you see if my Jaguar could come see me before I go, could you tell my IBM ThinkPad I love her!' You're able to laugh even now in this hard hour at the absurdity of that. You know what they tell me? 'I broke up my brother's marriage in '86, tell him I'm sorry.' 'I haven't seen my mother in three years, tell her everything is OK and what's past is past. She'll know what I mean.' 'My daddy threw me out when he found out I had the HIV, tell Junebug to go by and tell him I love him and ask him would he come see me.' 'I had a son I gave up for adoption when I was sixteen, can you write it down somewhere if he ever come looking I loved him and thought about him every day. I couldn't do nothing for him on heroin. It was the best thing.' Now, that's what they tell *me,* Reverend Bellwether. I don't know what they tell you. But I ain't heard 'em mention they Jaguar Apple laptop BlackBerry BlueBerry yet!

"Twenty-seven years is not much time. But it's all the time God gave our sister, I don't know why any more than you do. It was all the time she had, and she used it well." Reverend Bellwether stop talking for a minute and sigh. "Her friends, teachers, clients, and son can all testify that she used her time well. Some of the people here are going to say a few words about our sister who is no longer with us."

That's stupid, Mommy's right here. I'm thinking sometimes all this is just a game we're playing, ha, ha! Or a story with a surprise ending like at school, they give you a story with no end and you get to write the end, or this is a joke, not that Mommy played a lot of jokes, but she could! She could just jump up laughing and climb out the casket hollering, *Psyched you out! Psyched you out!* Then grab me by the hand and say, *The fun is over. I don't have time for all this foolishness! What do you think I be doing all day, sitting on my butt? If that bathroom is not clean when we get home—I don't want to hear no excuses! The bathroom and taking out the trash are your jobs. You hear me, it ain't no goddamn joke out here. You think it's a joke? Huh? HUH?* No, I don't think it's a joke, I say. We'll go home and I'll run go turn on the TV and she'll come turn off the TV and say, *Do your homework.* I'll stomp my feet and throw my book bag on the floor when she leaves the room, and she'll come back in the room and say, *If you know what's good for you, you'll pick those books up like you got some goddamned sense and do your homework.* She'll go in the kitchen mumbling about I don't know how lucky I am, and I'll be in the living room mumbling about I wish I could go live with my father or by myself! But I'll do my homework, then she'll come and see me doing it, smile, and say the Asian Student Union showing *Return of the Dragon* for free at her school Friday night, we can go and go to McDonald's afterwards if she don't hear no nonsense from me till Friday. I'll smile. And she'll say, *So could we have drama-free homework until Friday?*

"Abdul." Rita's shaking my shoulder. "Let the lady pass." I stand up and a big white lady who had been sitting down the aisle from us squeeze past.

"Hello," she say when she gets up front. "My name is Sondra Lichenstein. I met Precious almost eleven years ago when I was working for the Board of Ed. I won't even try to describe the circumstances that we met under, that's like a book or something, really. But I will tell you I stayed in touch with her, sometimes whether she wanted it or not." She laughs. "Eventually we became friends. Before she died, in addition to being a student in the SEEK Program at City College, she worked as a peer counselor at Positive Images in Harlem, and was a full-time mom of a beautiful little boy, Abdul, who is a wonderful student; and it was Abdul who made the computer graphic design you see next to the Langston Hughes poem in the middle of the program. I'm going to sit down now and let Blue Rain, one of Precious's teachers, speak." She comes to sit back down. Good, I'm glad; it makes me sick to hear people talking about Mommy like she's dead.

Oh, I know her, lady with dreadlocks. I seen her before, she's one of my mother's friends.

"Hi, I'm Blue Rain, I was Precious's teacher and later became her friend." Blue Rain looks down at a little card and says, "I didn't want to forget anything I had to say or go on too long, so I wrote down what I had to say. I remember once Precious telling me, 'What difference does it make whether the glass is half full or half empty? You just drink as much as you can while you can.' Abuse truncated her life and led to the AIDS"—AIDS! What she talking about?—"which finally took it. But she showed me, all of us, what a good game you can still play when the deck is stacked against you."

"Ashé!" someone yell.

"Tell the truth!" someone else yell.

"She learned to read and write at the age of sixteen." Who she talking about? "At twenty she received a GED and began the slow walk toward a college degree. Her achievements were remarkable because of what she was able to overcome and perhaps even more remarkable because of what she wasn't able to overcome. We who knew her watched a child become a woman, a half-full glass spill over, something broken become whole. And in the act of witnessing became more whole ourselves."

If I had been good and done what she said, she wouldn't have gotten sicker and sicker. *Do you have to make so much noise!* My job is to clean the bathroom. When I open the medicine chest over the sink—*Don't bother with that, I'll do that*—I count thirteen bottles of medicine. In the morning in the afternoon at night. Why, if nothing's wrong with you? I know you don't have what they're saying because you're good we're good I'm good we don't have that, we're, I'm a boy who's *going somewhere, gonna be something*. I didn't mean to be making noise I miss my father I wish he would come and get me and make it alright I want to go horseback riding if I had a father I could go horseback riding all the time. But I don't and I won't I wish my mother would get up out of that box and holler (even though it's November) APRIL FOOLS! APRIL FOOLS! I PSYCHED YOU OUT! I PSYCHED YOU OUT! and we could go home again like before I feel so tired and I don't like listening to all these stupid people talking. This is the fourth, no fifth one. Tall skinny woman in blue jeans and a jacket and tie.

"We are all here today—oh, my name is Jermaine Hicks—as we were saying, we are all sad to see our friend and sister lose her valiant—I mean that in every sense of the word—val-lee-ant, fight for life. She was a star, a diamond among rhinestones, a warrior. That's not rhetoric, that's real. I guess there were bad things you could say about her, there's bad things you could say about anybody. But to me this moment is about celebrating the life she did have, as well as pouring out our grief for the one she didn't have and now will never have. Her shit was not easy— Oh, I'm not supposed to talk like that here?" She look over at Rhonda. When I look at Rhonda, Rhonda is staring the girl down so hard her eyes look like traffic lights. "I'm not supposed to mention Medicaid didn't want to pay for her drugs or that the 'fare was threatening her again to leave school or lose her benefits, that there's a padlock on her door and that she died broke and depressed, deeply depressed."

Rhonda mumble behind us, "I done had enough of dis bungee-brain crack addict."

Rhonda get up. The girl is still talking.

"And now we're looking at her laid out in a white dress talking about her like she was an angel. Yeah, well, maybe that's irony or something, 'cause her life sure the fuck was hell!" My mother's life wasn't no hell!

"Excuse me," Rhonda say. Jermaine don't pay Rhonda no mind. "She died broke, depressed but with a heart too mutherfucking big to be bitter." She looks at Rhonda, who's standing next to her now. Rhonda say something to her.

"Yeah, I'll sit down when I'm finished, but I ain't finished yet."

"Hey, let's go!" Rhonda stare at her until she go sit down.

"I think Rita have a few words she want to say before we close out dis part of the service," Rhonda say.

Rita lean over kiss me, then get up in front Mommy's casket. Rhonda come sit next to me.

"This girl was my friend, my sister, and sometimes my daughter. I loved her." She unfolds a piece of paper. "This poem is called 'Mother to Son' by Langston Hughes. The first time I heard it was when Precious memorized and recited it to the class, serious back in the day!" She laughs. "I'm going to read it now." She looks at me. "This is for you, Papi."

MOTHER TO SON

Well, son, I'll tell you:
Life for me ain't been no crystal stair.
It's had tacks in it,
And splinters,
And boards torn up,
And places with no carpet on the floor—
Bare.
But all the time
I'se been a-climbin' on,
And reachin' landin's
And turnin' corners,
And sometimes goin' in the dark
Where there ain't been no light.
So boy, don't you set down on the steps
'Cause you finds it's kinder hard.
Don't you fall now—
For I'se still goin', honey,
I'se still climbin',
And life for me ain't been no crystal stair.

She turns around to Mommy. "I love you, Precious." Then comes and sits back down. I like her poem, I feel good.

"What's next?" I ask. PING! go Rhonda upside my head again. I hate her!

"Dis ain't no show, boy! 'What's next?' I never hear the like!"

"Would you jus' stop!" Rita says to Rhonda, Rhonda jus' roll her eyes at Rita. Rita lean over and whisper, "They're going to close the casket now."

"Huh?"

"The pallbearers, they're the ones who actually carry the casket out the funeral parlor to the car, and then when it's at the graveyard they take the casket out the car and to the grave site."

"So—" I don't understand but I stop talking, one of the guys done turned out the little lamp over Mommy's head. Another guy is moving a hinge on one end of the casket, another guy at the other end is doing the same thing. They lowering the lid over Mommy's face. "She won't be able to breathe!" I tell Rita.

"She's not breathing, Abdul. She's dead. They're closing the casket so we can take it to the graveyard and put her body in the ground."

"No!" I throw my arms around Rita, push my face in her dress, crying. The material of her dress gets all stiff when it's wet.

"It's OK, it's OK," Rita say over and over. Someone picks me up from the bench, I don't know who, I'm still crying. I bury my face in his clothes squeeze my eyes shut. I open them again as a big guy is setting me down on the sidewalk on Lenox Avenue next to Rita. It's gotten colder outside than it was, but the sun is still shining bright.

"Come on, boobie," Rita says, "get in the car." I scoot in next to her. I like riding in cars. We pull out from the other cars and get in back of the black Lincoln with Mommy in it. I don't know where we're going. I'm just reading the signs on the highway. The world is zipping by like when you on the computer playing a game in your car. I feel a little sleepy. I like cars. Mommy, why we don't have a car? Mommy, I'm talking to you, why we don't have a car? *Well,* is what she would say, *because we can't afford one right now, Abdul.* But she don't say nothing now. We turn off the freeway, houses out here got grass and swing sets. I'm gonna live out here when I'm grown.

Coffins? Graveyard? Spooky place from Halloween movies on television. Dracula climbing out the casket with spiderwebs and stuff. Dark, scary stuff. But when the car stops, it's like a pretty park, green grass, sky blue with fluffy white clouds. I lean back on the seat close my eyes, hear car doors open people talking, hear this car door open, open my eyes, get out. Me and Rita walk behind the pallbearers and Reverend Bellwether up white gravel path sparkling in the sunshine. Then we turn off the path onto grass. I like walking on grass. It's like a city out here! Green grass, the gravestones are little houses; a person is under each one? First a person then they turn to bones? We go up a hill, there's some chairs, a big pile of dirt; get up closer see the big hole. I look up at an airplane disappear across the sky.

On one side of the big hole is a big pile of dirt. The casket is on the other side. Reverend Bellwether is holding the Bible but she don't open it. She look at everybody then up at the sky then at everybody again.

"Heavenly Father—" she say.

"Amen!" Rhonda shout. Why? All she said was Heavenly Father.

"Heavenly Father," she say again, "Great Spirit, what we know you taught us, where we are you brought us. And from our mother's body we are brought forth and to the body of the Great Mother we shall return."

Guy in dirty overalls wave his hand and the pallbearers move the casket over the hole on top some ropes and like strips of canvas. Then he go to the end of the grave and turn a handle. When he turn the handle, the coffin go down.

"Ashes to ashes!" Down, down, handle go round and round. "Dust to dust!" Lurch, bump. I look up at the sky. Blue. The sun shining bright. I look for another airplane. None. The man in the overalls picks up a shovel, shove it down hard in the dirt.

"Come on." Rita pulls my hand. "It's over."

RITA ASK THE MAN driving to drop us off on 125th Street at the Harlem State Office Building instead of the funeral home.

"What's here?"

"Some friends of your mother's have cooked some food. People gonna eat some, talk, and then go home."

"Home?"

"Come on!"

"I'm not hungry!"

"Yes you are, stop acting silly!"

"I wanna go to McDonald's!"

She laughs. "I thought you wasn't hungry!" She points across the street. "See that."

"What?"

"The Hotel Theresa, that's where I met your mom. We learned to read and write together."

"Whatchu mean?"

"Whatchu mean, what I mean?"

"About you and my mom learning to write, or whatever, at the Hotel Theresa."

"She never told you about that? No? Well, remind me to one day. We ain't got no time now."

I got time now. Plus I don't want to go in there, whatever it is in the Harlem State Office Building. Rita hold out her hand, I shake my head.

"Come on, stop acting silly and bring your booty over here. People are waiting on us." We go up in the elevator to a room with people walking around smiling and sitting in chairs against the wall eating food and drinking coffee. Rita take me over to a woman in a black and white stripe dress.

"Abdul, I want you to meet Mrs McKnight. She used to be head of Each One Teach One before it closed down." So what was it? Lady leans over to kiss me. I'm tired of people kissing me, I don't want her to kiss me, but she does.

"You eat quiche?" Rita asks.

"I like the mushroom kind."

"Well, try this, it's spinach and cheese." We move down the table of food. I get some ham and potato salad, I stop in front of a whole bunch of cakes, a lot of them. "Go ahead, get what you want." I get carrot cake with frosting and chocolate cake.

"Let's sit over here." She points to some chairs against the wall. I never seen these people before. What this got to do with my mother? My mother said I was the most important person in her life. The quiche taste good, ham too. I don't like this potato salad; I like the way my mother make it.

"After you finish your cake, we go talk to Ms Rain."

RITA CLOSES THE DOOR to the little office. I hear the people outside talking and laughing with their food. Ms Rain is sitting behind a desk.

"Have a seat, Abdul," Ms Rain say. I don't want to sit down. I think I know what they're going to say. I wanna run out the room, go home. But home is with my mother, without my mom ain't no home. How I'm feeling? What she think? I don't talk smart. My mother don't allow that. I look at Rita. My stomach feel funny. I wish they would just go on and talk.

"Well, your mother is gone. And your father too, evidently he's been dead for quite a while. I guess you already knew that?"

I didn't. I look out the window. I don't usually be this high up, what, we on the twentieth floor or something? I look outside see a computer screen instead of the sky for a second. Plane tumbling down first slow then over and over again then whoosh screen bust into flames! Then I see myself tumbling through the air. Headlines NINE-YEAR-OLD BOY JUMPS TO HIS DEATH. They'll be sorry then they lied about my father and saying stuff about AIDS.

"Abdul. I know you're wondering what's next, where you're going to stay and school—"

"I catch the bus to school," I tell her. Rita looks at Ms Rain, then at me.

"I never told you, boobie, I'm a little sick myself." I feel hot, the room, Rita look like a dream, red lips powder face. I run to the wastebasket, almost make it before ugh! Quiche, chocolate cake, grape soda ugh! AHHH!

"It's OK," Rita say. Ms Rain hands me some tissue.

"Are you alright?" she asks.

"Yeah," I say, and sit back down. I know what's coming. Kids at school ain't got no parents live at fosters homes and group homes and stuff. I look out the window see myself tumbling over and over again like the plane. BLAM!!

"Where's all my stuff?" I ask.

"Huh?" Ms Rain seems surprised.

"My computer, my toys, my books, my posters, my bike."

"Your mother sent someone over to the apartment before she died to get her notebooks, papers, legal documents, and stuff. I don't think she believed she was going to . . . to pass away. I think she thought she was going to get better one more time. Rita and I went over there the day before yesterday, and there was a padlock on the door and a sheriff's notice of eviction. I don't know if she had been behind in the rent or if the landlord just is pulling a fast one. He'd been wanting that apartment back for a long time. But we just have the stuff of your mother's that her friend got—papers, books, notebooks, some jewelry. Rita has records with your shots and old report cards, birth certificate, things you'll need at your new school." She turn to Rita. "Did she ever get him a Social Security card?"

"She would have had to because of social services."

"Of course. I'll try to get as much together before I leave today and give it to you to take back to the hotel. I'm going to London at the end of the week. Abdul, you're going to spend tonight with Rita. She's been putting off going into the hospital—"

"Don't say that, La Lluvia."

I start crying. "We was gonna get a dog."

"What did he say?"

"I don't know. *What*, boobie?"

"We was gonna get a dog!" I scream.

"I know it's hard, Abdul. If I could change it, I would. I think this is the hardest part. Once you're settled in, it'll be better. Rita can come and visit you," Ms Rain say. She's looking at Rita, Rita's looking out the window.

"I'm going to a foster home."

"Yes."

"When?"

"In the morning."

TWO Rita hands me a shiny plastic square that opens out to be a garbage bag. "It's clean, new, put your stuff in it for now." She's standing by the bed holding my good shoes. My suit is on the bed folded up and wrapped in plastic from the dry cleaners, my shirt too. My shirt, black suit, good shoes, and leather jacket, and what I got on—jeans, my Batman T-shirt, and sneakers is all I got from home. Everything else I got is at home. My CD player, my mother's but I'm the one use it most, my TV, my mother's but she don't like TV, my computer, my mother's but my school don't have computers for the fourth grade, my jeans, not baggies, my mother don't allow that, my down jacket Triple Phat, Timberland boots, my favorites, what I'm gonna wear when it gets cold. My swimming trunks for when I go swimming, flippers, guy down the hall gave me, even though I can't swim yet. My CDs, me and my mother's, some is mine, some is hers. *All* is hers, she said after I traded one I *thought* was mine, MC Lyte, for Biggie Smalls. My mother attaches to old school. My G.I. Joe men, Indians, Crazy Horse, Red Cloud, Custard and the soldiers, map from the Battle of the Little Bighorn, marbles (I never play with), string, knife (Swiss Army knife that I'm never, NEVER spozed to take out the house), the goldfish, they probably not alive anymore if didn't no one go in and feed 'em. My books. I got a lot of books about black people and Indians. I like Native Americans better than black people. Ain't no Indians stupid like Danny. My play clothes, crayons, paints, my paints but my mother use 'em more than me. On my dresser is a picture of my mom, where's it at? Who got my stuff? I want it.

"Abdul, you ain't moved!" Rita shakes the bag. "Come on now."

She puts my shoes, suit, and shirt in the bag. Everything else on the bed she bought me, elephant and tiger flannel pajamas, slippers, another pair of jeans, two undershirts, briefs, four pair of socks. She reaches under the pillow, hand me a bag.

"A surprise for when you get to your new place. Don't look now."

She takes it from me and puts it in the bag. I sit down on the bed. She puts the bag near the door, then goes to sit on the bed near the window and starts putting on her makeup. She's putting on her lipstick when someone knocks hard on the door.

"Who is it!"

"Mrs Render from the Bureau of Child Welfare for Ms Romero and Mr Jones."

Rita opens the door to a tall white woman in a gray suit like a man's only she has on a skirt instead of pants. She's smiling.

"Are we ready to go?" Mrs Render smiles even more.

Rita looks at her like she's crazy. "He's ready," she says.

"You have the papers?" Mrs Render asks. Rita hands her the manila envelope.

"How long has he been here?"

"Since his mother passed. I brought him home from the hospital. He had been staying in the house by himself."

Mrs Render looks at the bed. "Is this where he's been sleeping?"

"Where else would he sleep?" Rita asks.

"Ready to go, Mr Jones?"

I almost laugh. Mr Jones? Who's that!

"Personal articles?" Mrs Render smiles.

Rita nods at the trash bag. Mrs Render reaches for the bag, I zip to the door and get it, she opens the door, I look down the dark hallway, the bathroom door at the end, closed, someone must be in it; in the middle of the hall, before you get to the bathroom, the stairs.

"You want me to carry that for you, Jamal?"

"No, I can carry it." Down one two three four five six seven eight nine ten eleven, the rug's not even a color no more, just old chewing gum, cigarette burns, twelve, thirteen, drag the bag—

"Sure you don't want me to carry it?"

"Yeah." Pick up the bag, fourteen, fifteen, sixteen third floor. At the Battle of the Little Bighorn I fought side by side with Sitting Bull and Crazy Horse. I was the only black Indian there with my war paint, eagle feather. Me and Crazy Horse are friends, the only dudes who don't smoke the pipe before we fight, we don't believe in all that. My horse is a mighty white steed, stallion? What's the difference between a stallion and a steed? Where's all the people usually be in the hallway, how come nobody got their door open to give me a pastel or a croissant? How come Rita ain't walk me to the door? The man behind the plastic booth near the door buzz me and Mrs Render out the hotel. It's cold on the street, feel like it's going through my leather jacket. My mother say leather ain't nothing but style, it don't really keep you warm.

"Over there." She points, her car is new, a blue Saturn. I get in the backseat, there's a catcher's mitt and some comics on the floor. She must have kids. At home I got comics, the *same* ones. On the wall I got posters of Biggie, Crazy Horse, Sitting Bull, Michael Jordan, and Tupac. I got Tupac up because my mother don't like him. Ha, ha. *It's a bunch of mess, all that gangster shit.* But it's my wall, I can put whatever I want on the walls in MY room. *No you can't.* Why! *I pay rent here, you're a little boy and you can do some things and some you can't. You can**not** do everything you want.* I hate you! *You know what, it's time for you to shut up 'fore I let my hand do the talking!* No! *I said—are you crazy take that fucking poster down!* How come you get to curse! *I will knock your silly—* Leave me alone (I run around the room and slide under the bed.) *Stop screaming, fool!* I'm not a fool! *You acting like one!* You was gonna hit me! *I was not!* You was! *Would you stop all that damn screaming and come out from under there.* No! *It's not acceptable for you to tell me no when I tell you to do something!* Is it acceptable for you to die and not get me my dog!

"How long have you lived in Harlem?" Mrs Render asks, turning up Lenox Ave.

"I dunno."

"You don't know? Where were you going to school?"

"P.S. 1_."

"All of Miss Lillie's boys go to P.S. 5_. Well, here we are." I can't see her face, but she's probably smiling.

I thought we was going to an office building or something. This building is by itself stuck in the middle of two vacant lots. Dusty bricks and garbage. Ashes to ashes? I still don't know what that means. We seen a video of a baby getting born, ain't no ashes.

"Well." She leans over and opens the door for me. I follow her, trying not to drag my bag on the sidewalk. A little crack vial with an orange cap reminds me of Tyrese: TV, screen, Asian guy next to yellow-haired woman. "We're happy to bring you this evening's news." (I'm not paying no attention.) Then she says, "There have been no new developments in the case of young Tyrese Knight, kidnapped last Monday from the school yard of P.S. 1_." (My school!) "The kidnappers, supposedly rivals of young Tyrese's older brother, an alleged drug dealer in Harlem, are demanding one hundred thousand dollars for the seven-year-old's return." On the screen behind her big head is a note made from pieces of newspapers: "LEAVE MONEY AT PICKUP PLACE U KNOW WHERE SNITCH & BOY DIES." Until then when I would hear people talking about Tyrese got snatched and all that, I didn't believe it, it was like something on TV. But seeing it on TV made it real for me. My mother says, *Danny can't count to a hundred thousand, much less come up with it.* The lady says, "Police are still testing a finger found in a paper bag under a table at a McDonald's on Broadway and 125th Street last week after the kidnappers directed Tyrese's brother, Daniel Knight, to retrieve a bag from the fast-food restaurant." They show Tyrese's picture on the screen behind the lady, then a recording of his voice screaming: "Danny please I love you, you're the best I'm sorry Pleeaase give them the money. I'll give it back to you when I'm grown up PLEASE. They're going to cut off all my fingers Danny PLEEEZE."

"Well." Mrs Render smiles at me. "You sure you don't want me to carry that?"

"No."

"No?"

"No, I *like* to carry it."

Nothing like that is ever going to happen to you. You and Tyrese are two different people. Plus you don't have a fool for a brother like Tyrese has. I don't have nobody. *Don't worry about it, just be a good boy and get in there and do your homework please.*

I follow Mrs Render up the sidewalk to the front door of the raggedy building. She pushes at the front door. "This door is usually locked. I'm over here a lot. Miss Lillie has a few boys who are doing quite well. Where did you say you went to school?"

"P.S. 1_."

"All Miss Lillie's boys go to P.S. 5_."

You told me already!

"Miss Lillie's apartment is on the top floor. Ever lived on the top floor before? You don't talk much, do you? Here, honey, give me that bag now."

She takes my bag and starts walking up the steps! One two three four five six seven eight nine ten eleven twelve thirteen fourteen. She got big veins like wrinkled blue straws sticking out the back of her legs. Ugh, wonder what they feel like seventeen eighteen nineteen twenty twenty-one twenty-two twenty-three twenty-four twenty-five twenty-six twenty-seven twenty-eight twenty-nine—

"Here we are, Mohammed. I mean, Jamal."

Mohammed? She walks out the stairwell into the hallway, I'm looking at the split in the back of her gray skirt, the backs of her white giant legs, the blue veins. She's a giant, way taller than my mother and my mother is tall. The hallway smells like Pine-Sol, my mother use that to clean our kitchen. Pine-Sol smells like Christmas trees and motor oil together. The hallway is dark, only one light working and that's the one when you're coming up out the stairs. Somebody's tagged the walls big time **BB** in big black letters. She stops at a door at the end of the hallway. I hear what sounds like a dog rush up to the other side of the door. His toenails scratching on the floor, I can hear him panting, I can almost see his tail wagging. Another, two dogs? The number on the door is 6-F. I want to snatch my bag back from Mrs Render and go home. She rings the bell.

"Git back, y'all!" a lady hollers from behind the door, and then opens it. Smells like dogs, I can't see nothing except pink polka dots. When I step back from the pink, I see this big light-skinned lady in a polka-dot housecoat and two big collie dogs.

"Well, don't just stand there, come on in!"

"How are you, Miss Lillie?"

"Fine, fine, if I do say so. How about yourself? Coming in?"

"No, no, I have two more pickups this morning, I can't stop." She looks at my envelope, then hands it to the lady, "Miss Lillie, this is Mr Jones, Jamal Abdul."

"Howdy, honey."

"Say hello," she tells me.

"Hello," I say.

"Miss Lillie is going to be your foster mother."

One of the dogs plops down by Miss Lillie's feet, the other is dancing around shaking himself, his tongue is hanging out. The one laying down is looking up at me with nasty eyes with snot in 'em.

"Well, come on in, honey. You ain't scared of dogs, is you?"

I shake my head no.

"Well, come on then."

Mrs Render sets my bag down inside the door and I step inside the apartment next to it. Then she turns her back and rushes away, it's like her giant legs and blue veins is what's saying, "Bye, bye now, I'll be back to see you, OK?" as she hurries away.

"Come on in, you can call me Miss Lillie, or Mama, whatever. You like dogs?"

"He looks old," I say. I don't say his eyes look like some kinda disease.

"He is, honey, he's fourteen if he's a day. You know how much that is in dog years? That's almost a hundred! How old are you?"

"Nine."

"You gonna be a big one, yep you is. Well, don't just stand there, pick up that bag and git on in here. Don't none of us bite."

I don't like her.

"Fox," she touch the dog laying down with her foot. "He's part collie. This one," the one dancing around, "is all collie."

I don't like these dogs.

She closes the door. "Come on in here. OK, let's see what these here papers say. What you got in the bag?"

"Clothes."

"I figured that, big talker, but what exactly? I need to know so I can make sure you got everything you need."

"My suit and stuff."

"OK and stuff, let's take a look in this envelope and see what we got here. Hm, uh huh Jamal A. Jones, nine years old alright."

"My name is Abdul Jamal Louis Jones."

"Well, sweetie, it say Jamal A. Jones here, and on your Medcaid card it say Jamal Jones. So I guess we gonna go with Jamal Jones, what you say J.J.! Hey, I like that, how about we call you J.J. here on out to save confusion."

The dancing dog is sniffing at my feet wagging his tail.

"Come on out the doorway. That old dog ain't gonna hurt you. You ain' gonna make it here being no scaredy-cat."

"I ain't scared."

"Well, that's good. You had any breakfast yet?" I shake my head no. "Well, come on, I got some Chinese fried rice from last night. They serve breakfast and lunch up at the school, so most of the time the boys eat there during the day. Come on, let's put your stuff up and get you something to eat. Batty Boy stayed home sick today, so he back there in bed, you can meet him. The others be here as soon as school's out. Come on."

I follow her down the hall and she pushes open a swinging door. "That's the kitchen, y'all don't really need to go in there 'cept dinner. See back there." She points to a door in the back of the kitchen. "That door is my room. Don't come in there 'less I call you. OK, that's the bathroom, I keep a little light on all night, no excuse not to get up and use the bathroom." Going down the hall, she opens another door. "This here is the living room." Pretty. The white and gold couch is covered in shiny plastic, white marble coffee table, gold curtains. "You boys don't need to go in there for nothing, really." She pulls the door shut hard.

"Watch yourself!" I look down in time to lift my bag and sidestep a newspaper with dog doo-doo on it. Wonder did somebody save my goldfish. At school we was doing reports, mine was due but that's when my mother died. I step around another piece of newspaper yellow and wet, no dog doo-doo. Miss Lillie stops all of a sudden, I almost walk into her pink polka dots. I jump back from her. *Mama,* my mother would never wear nothing like that.

"This is y'all boys' room." She opens the door and a boy laying on the bottom of a bunk bed jumps straight up and hits his head BAP! on the top bunk. We must have scared him. Ha! Ha! I laugh. He stares at me so hard I look down at the floor, which is like a big checkerboard, black and white squares. When I look up, the boy is still staring at me.

"This here is Batty Boy. Everybody in this house got a nickname. You gonna fit right in, J.J. Wait'll you meet Snowball, that's my baby." She turn to the boy still staring at me. "And you, Mr Batty Boy, since you so sick I suggest you lay your behind back down or git up and go to school. And stop looking at J.J. like you ain't got good sense." I follow Miss Lillie over to a big dresser against the wall. "You can put your stuff in the bottom drawer, it's empty since what's-his-name left, ain't it, Batty?"

Batty don't say nothing, and he ain't laid back down like Miss Lillie said or stopped staring at me like he hates me or something. I start taking my stuff out the bag.

"What's that?" she asks.

"My shoes."

"Well, don't put them in the drawer."

I wasn't going to. Batty Boy is staring at me putting my socks and underwear away. Why? None of it can fit him. I should hang up my shirt and suit but I don't want to say anything to Miss Lillie, so I just go ahead and put them in the drawer. Miss Lillie looks at the bag.

"You got a coat aside from the one you got on?" Miss Lillie asks.

"I got a down jacket, a pea coat, and another coat like a raincoat at home."

"Um hmm." She looks down at me. "And I know you got Mary J. Blige at home to cook your dinner too, at *home*. But I'm talking about *here* now."

I look up at her. Why is she talking to me like that?

"J.J., you just like all the rest come in here, you got to adjust. Whatever you had at home is over and probably never was! I know how you kids make shit up." She opens my envelope, looks in a folder, and starts reading, "'Father unknown, mother deceased November 1, 1997, HIV-related illness.' Uh huh just what I thought, so OK, J.J., relax, you like everybody else here." She looks in the drawer. "Is that a suit?"

"Yeah."

"Why don't you hang it up in the closet. You can hang your leather up too. Landlord keep it warm in here. Y'all don't need to be walking around in no jackets."

She looks around the room, at what? Ain't no toys or furniture except for the dresser and another set of bunk beds in the corner, diagonal-like across from the bunk bed Batty Boy is standing up in looking like a . . . a weird person.

"Well, let me go heat up some of this good ol' chicken lo mein, pork fried rice, and egg drop soup."

The door close and it's like some magic or something, all of a sudden Batty Boy can move. He's coming toward— I— He . . . he's gonna hit me? For what, this is stu— BAP! I step back, look in his eyes, sleepy stuff, he smells like pee, hatred. Fight back, I tell myself just as he slams his fist into my eye, knocking me down. He jumps on my chest, pinning my arms down with his knees.

"Who you laughing at!" he screams

Oh, man, this dude is crazy. "Stop! Stop!"

"Shut up, you fucking baby! I said shut up, stupid!" He hits me again, and I see orange polka dots, then nothing.

"WAKE UP, STUPID!" A gray shadow smell like pee-the-bed is over me shouting, "Faker! Faker!" It grabs me by my shoulders and raises me up and slams my head into the floor. No air. I can't scream. Rita's gonna be mad at me. I'm gonna die. Someone hit you, you hit 'em back. I try to raise myself up. My head burns, *burns*. I try to say something, spit blood on the checkerboard floor. My mother dead. Rita. Please please.

"You can have it," I finally say. That must be it, my jacket, he wants my jacket. "You can have my jacket." My suit? shirt? What he want?

"Fool I got that jacket! It been mine, asshole!" Blood from my nose in my mouth. My head burning.

"I'm thirteen!" He raises me up and slams me into the floor again. "You better do what I say." I ain't gotta do what he says. I gotta get home to my mother.

"I ain't gotta do what you say! I only gotta do what my mother and the teacher say."

"Nigguh, shut up! You ain't got no motherfucking mother! She's a crack-addict ho died from AIDS!"

"BATTY!" Miss Lillie's voice bust through the door. "Batty! Nigger, is you crazy! Get up off that boy! Get up off J.J. Is you *crazy*! You done lost your motherfucking mind. He got to go to school! I said git *off* him! Well, I'll be damned. He can't go to school looking like that. Come on, J.J. sweetie, sit up. Batty Boy was just playing with you. He didn't mean you no harm! I know how rough you boys are. Rough, honey! Yes indeed. Let me go get something to clean up this mess. And you FOOL! You better not lay a hand on him while I'm gone neither."

She come back she got latex gloves on like the hospital. "Come on, let me wash you up so you can come eat. You ain' had no breakfast. Neither has Batty, that's probably why he's so irritable." She wipes my face with a warm washcloth. "You alright, you got a little bloody nose and a black eye. If Batty ever ever lay a hand on you again, they won't have to take him out of here, I'll kill him myself! Don't you worry, that's why he's here 'cause I'm one of the few that can handle him."

She pulls my hand for me to follow her in the kitchen. Everything seems red or maybe everything is red, at least the tablecloth and chairs and kitchen cabinets. I can feel my eye swelling shut. My head is . . . feels like it's broken or something.

"What you staring at? You done seen a roach before. Good thing is they only in the kitchen. Some people got 'em all over. I gotta get the man back in here to spray.

"Sit down, sit down."

She places a plate in front of me, it smells good. I didn't know I was so hungry. It stings the cut on my lip! I push the plate away and lay my head down on the table and start to cry. "I wanna go home! I wanna go home! I wanna go home—" The tears is burning my eye and the cut in my lip.

"Hush up, J.J., it's over."

"I wan—" I can't hardly talk. "I . . . go home."

"Hush, J.J., you is home."

I put my head back down crying. I don't know where to go. If it was the olden days, I could run away to be with Crazy Horse, be a great warrior. Walk in moccasin shoes. I feel cold, I got my head down. I don't see him or hear him, but I feel Batty Boy in the room.

"Look at him! He can't go to school like that! Goddamn you, Batty! Put your hands on him again and your simple ass is going to a group home or Spofford, hear! HEAR!"

Loud as she's screaming, he oughta be able to hear. Heeeaaar! HEAR! I raise up to look at Batty, like those dogs, can she control him. I'm surprised, he looks like a different person from a few minutes ago, bright and cheerful, smiling, not weird.

"Soup," he says.

"What!" Miss Lillie says.

"What! Smut! Some soup, that's what!"

"Good idea, Batty! You smart as a whip when you wanna be. Put him some soup in a bowl."

I'm looking at him, then it seems like he disappears, like everything disappears. The cabinets is turning from red to rainbows.

"Here, drink your soup, J.J. It ain't gonna burn you." Batty Boy's voice comes through the colors, sounds nice like a mother almost.

Miss Lillie is putting some ice in a plastic bag against my eye. "You can't go to school like this. I do know that. Lord have mercy! What you say to Batty to make him so mad? Here, hold this ice on your eye and finish your soup. Then when you finish you can come in and watch TV with me."

I look up at the wall, the clock is all twinkly with stars, but I can't tell what time it is.

"What you looking at? I swear you is the peculiar-est chile I done seen in a while."

"I'm looking at the clock. What time is it?"

"Ain't no clock up there." She looks at her watch. "It's twelve o'clock."

"I wanna lay down." My head really hurts.

"OK, you can finish your soup later."

I gotta get outta here, go home. Go back home. I'm hungry. My shirt and jacket is all messed up—

"Come on."

My mother's there, back home. Follow Miss Lillie to her room.

"Don't you want to take your jacket off before you lay down?"

"No."

I'M CONFUSED when I wake up. I think I'm Mommy. But if I was her I wouldn't be thinking I'm her, I would just be her. Then I think like on TV, that cartoon, the magic genie, or that TV show where you get another chance, get a wish, make it better, do it different. Mommy is not dead but in bed and like in the movie gonna change and she gonna get up and we go home or to have pizza and our life be good. We win like the

Indians winned once, we win like that, I'm so glad to be in the hospital with my mother. Huh? Huh? I don't think this guy understand, he keep asking me stupid stuff. Nothin' happened! Me and my mother, we getting ready to get out of here. You can't keep us here we don't want to be here. We well. My mom is well, I won the show, I get to go back, my wish? Today is not today, it's yesterday.

"Come on, I think you do know. Can you tell who did this to you?"

Me and my mother gonna get pizza and go to the Apollo. Don't nobody in my class go as many places as me— "Did what! What you talking about. Leave me alone! *Nothing* happened."

"J.J.? J.J.? J.J.?"

My name ain't no stupid J.J. and I'm not a little boy—

It seems like all the light's whiteness is pouring in my eyes and I honestly don't remember. I'm a little boy a little boy a little boy I'm a little boy! No I don't, don't have to, don't wanna remember I don't remember. I told you once! He banged my head on the floor. The floor was black and white squares on the linoleum. I don't remember I don't remember. It didn't happen.

"What didn't happen?"

"What you're thinking didn't happen. What you thinking—"

"Somebody hurt you, J.J."

I forget all I don't know. Sink further down in the bed even though I'm already flat on my back.

Home, home. How do I feel? I feel like I want to go home. Turn off the lights, Doctor.

so I can go to sleep

night in the hospital is light.

so you know what happened to you

so you know what happened to you?

Batty Boy jumped out of his bed and jumped me

for my jacket

I don't know Batty wanted my jacket so he beat me up.

orange juice please

you like orange juice

yes I

yes I

five dollars

I had five dollars from the laundrymat guy

Star Magic Kaleidoscope from Rita

He hit me

"Where?"

I

Batty Boy hit me?

"Anything else? Did he do anything else?"

Nothing happened, really, I fell and hit my head at school and my head hurts bad I wonder can you fix it. In my dreams I'm not black, and if I am I'm only half black and an Indian. I'm a warrior riding across the plains, in my dreams we drive the Europeans back into the ocean, in my dreams sometimes I am black, blacker than I am now, the blackest black man, Hannibal riding an elephant over the Alps, a ruler of a kingdom of a land where my father's picture is like George Washington's on the dollar bill, in my dreams I have not been beat. Or left alone. My dreams are mine, I do 'em with my eyes open. When I close my eyes my dreams belong to the boogeyman, the devil. They are the devil's *lies*. But my dreams were not lies before my mother died, or, except, maybe that time just before Mommy died was bad dreams. Before that my dreams was very good, like I was clear who I was gonna be when I growed up, I was like Michael Jordan. Like how my father must have been.

My mother says everyone even the ones who go to the same church have different ideas of what's God. *It's different for every person, Abdul. I don't know exactly how to describe it to you, Mommy's learning herself. Sometimes I feel you know more than me. But how I see it—I dunno. OK, see that apple, tell me about it.*

It's green.

Yeah.

It's shiny.

Is it?

No, but apples can be shiny.

How big is it?

Little.

Littler than a ladybug?

No.

Littler than a golf ball?

I never seen a golf ball.

Are you crazy—Tiger Woods!

But that's on TV.

Is it littler than a basketball but bigger than a golf ball?

Yeah!

OK, see, that's like they tell us in school, you and I have agreed upon reality. You and I look at the apple and see some stuff about it and say OK, but ain' nobody seen God. Bible say he had skin like copper, hair like wool. I read it! One professor brought us pictures of Venus of Willendorf from ancient days, big ladies, said they was goddesses. I'm not down on the white people's God, but then when I think about my life I ain't down with it either, at least I don't want to be.

You don't have to be, Mommy.

Whatchu mean?

What we think can be God. We can think anything.

You get so programmed, baby, in spite of yourself, you get so programmed.

WHEN I CLOSE my eyes I fall down without moving, like I'm tumbling through space, like astronauts but I'm not weightless and keep tumbling down to a dark place and my breath feel like fear in my throat. In the hospital I been dreaming one thing. One thing that didn't happen. Batty did bad. Batty hurt me. They ask me questions over and over. I wanted the tubes out my nose and hands. I don't have AIDS. I don't have pneumonia. Stupid questions. When will I get my computer back, go someplace that's not here? To Michael Jordan, to training camp. To the Indians. I don't want to talk.

"In the three weeks you were there—"

Stupid guy! "I was not there no three weeks!" What's he talking about. I was only there for one day. It hurts to turn my head.

One day an extra-stupid lady comes with dolls. She holds up one of the dolls. I hate her. She has flakes of dandruff.

"What happened to this little boy?"

She leans toward the bed. I feel like I'm swimming on the white walls, the air, like I can go anywhere. Just float. I'm anybody. I could be God if that was the agreed-upon reality. In the dream I have a bad headache for two weeks and we've finished dinner and I want to do my homework. In the dream Batty is sitting across the table from me. Snowball is on one side of me, he's a little albino boy. He doesn't like to be called Snowball but that's how it is. I forget his name anyway. My head hurts all the time. Bobby and Richie Jackson are sitting next to Batty, across from me. I'm hungry. Everybody's eating, I'm not. I'm hungry but sometimes my head hurts so hard I can't do nothing not even eat. Miss Lillie say it will go away. I just need to eat and drink plenty of water. I do. Miss Lillie says shut up crying or I'll give you something to cry about. But she doesn't. She's nice sometimes lets us watch TV in her room. Miss Lillie doesn't ever hit us, none of us, not even Snowball when he doo-doos in the bed. Batty hits us. Until my head echoes like a bell. In school I can't remember nothing. I sit there. They talk about dinosaurs. I go to the library and check out books I had at home: *Bury My Heart at Wounded Knee, Indian Chiefs, Sitting Bull and Other Legendary Native American Chiefs, Michael Jordan: The Athlete and the Man*. In real life if real life was real I am not here. My father came and got me the minute he found out my mother died and they had put me in foster care. Not my son! My head hurts so bad. All the time I vomit. Inside I feel like Chief Joseph of the Nez Perce. (My mother had got her nose pierced.) "My heart is sick and sad. From where the sun now stands, I will fight no more." My mother said he probably didn't say that, they probably just wrote it that way to make him sound like a fool. Mommy, do you hate them? *White people?* Yeah. *No, why, does it sound like I do?* Yeah, sometimes. *I . . . I, but I don't, I really*

43

don't, but they hate us, and they hated the Indians and the Asians, but now it seems like it's us they hate the most. Why? *A lot of reasons, none of them good.* BONG! BONG! My head. I'm scared he's going to hit me again. I look down at the hot dogs and pork and beans on my plate.

Miss Lillie orders Chinese food for herself. We eat breakfast and lunch at school. It's different every day. Here, we eat the same thing for dinner every day, hot dogs and pork and beans or leftover Chinese food, every day. Miss Lillie always talking, not *to* us, just talking.

"I useta cook. I don't mind cookin' but why should I? These damn kids don't appreciate nothin'! Uh huh, I useta cook, broccoli, mashed potatoes, meat loaf, the whole shebang, you know what I mean. And these stupid niggers be passing the meat loaf to the dogs! Balling up they vegetables in they napkins, sticking toy soldiers in the mashed potatoes. Yeah, baby, the Battle of Bull Run at the dinner table; this one got the whole damn infantry stuck in the mashed potatoes, that one got his cornbread on top the toy tank delivering it to the wounded and shit. Honey, these niggers is crazy! So finally I said, 'What do you niggers want to eat? 'Cause y'all wasting my time and money. This little bit of money they give me for y'all ain't shit. Damn sure ain't enuff to be throwing away. Well, tell me something!' I said. So they said, 'Hot dogs!' And another one said, 'Yeah! With pork 'n beans.' So, honey, it's been hot dogs ever since."

Our plates have big red roses on them. It's seventy-five of 'em in the cabinet. Snowball counted 'em once. Miss Lillie got 'em in the soap powder before we was born, in the olden days, those were the days.

"I done had these plates thirty years if I had 'em a day! Got 'em in Tide, you hear me. They useta give you something for your money when you went to the store, honey, but all that done changed. Ain't like that no more! Bidnesses is in trouble nowadays, whole economy is in trouble! Too many people on welfare and this dope messing shit up. And Clinton, that calm freak we got for a president, boy, was that a goddamned mistake."

Except she's not talking to us, she's talking to the TV or the wall or something. Something that don't talk back, or like if she had a boyfriend or a sister that's her own age, like a friend. We're not her friends. She don't like us or hate us, except Snowball. She likes Snowball. When we get home she takes out two packages of hot dogs and two packages of hot dog buns from the freezer and sets 'em in the red dish rack. Then she get two big cans of pork and beans out the cabinet and sets them on the kitchen table and goes back in her room to watch TV. Then Batty Boy is like our mother, puts the hot dogs in a pot of water to boil and warms the beans up. He gets the mustard and ketchup out the cabinet and puts them on the table and always remember that Richie likes mayonnaise and gets it out the refrigerator. He turns on the oven and puts the hot dog buns in the oven. Then he puts our beans on our plates, four hot dogs and two buns that are always hot on the outside and cold in the middle. Then he sits down, folds his hands, and bow his head and mumble:

Bless, oh Lord, and

dese die gifts

If my head don't hurt too bad I eat my hot dogs, 'cause I want to grow big and strong and get out of here and go find my father. Tonight Batty leans over across the table toward me, puts his hand right into my plate, and grabs one of the hot dogs on my plate in his fist.

"You and me." He laughs, shaking the wiener, orange sauce from the pork and beans is running down his arm. "No, you. Ha ha ha, you!"

I can't figure out if Batty laughs like a grown-up or a maniac. Sometimes I look at him and see that first day, the black and white bedroom floor like a checkerboard or chessboard, blood all on it, then taste blood in my mouth. You and me? What's he talking about, a book, a game? I have so much homework. I tell Miss Garnet at school my head hurts. "Your behind is what oughta be hurting! Don't come in here with a bunch of excuses, we got kids in here who've been through more than you could dream possible and you know what, *they* do their homework." Batty tells everyone at school that my mother died of AIDS. I say it's a lie. It is, a *big* one. Number one, my mother ain't dead. Number two, my mother didn't die of AIDS.

in the dream he ties my hands

in the dream Batty is bad and

my head hurts more

HE IS A BAD BOY

the eyes of Richie and Bobby

is floating around without they heads or bodies

in thick clouds

i have never done this. i never kiss a girl

except my mother

but my mother don't put her tongue

inside my mouth

in the dream i wake up and Snowball and Bobby is wrapping
wire around my wrist. i try to move my other hand but it's tied to
the bedpost. i try to sit up but i'm laying on my stomach. it's hard to
breathe i open my mouth breathe go back to sleep

"J.J." SHE HOLDS UP one of the dolls. "Tell me what happened to him."

I look in her eyes. Go away, go away.

"I never saw that doll before. How'm I gonna know what happened to
it?" She puts the puppet doll away and asks the guy who's cleaning the
floor if he could bring us a dinner tray. I'm not hungry. She takes some
toy soldiers and toy Indians and line them up on the tray.

"Of course you don't know the doll, but we're *pretending*. So let's play
with these little guys here that we know aren't real. What we can do, what
everyone playing does, is give some of our own feelings and thoughts to
the little toy soldiers. OK? OK, J.J.?"

The Native Americans are yellow plastic and the soldiers look like
they got on Civil War uniforms or something like it, they got silver sa-
bers, they're blue.

She holds up a yellow man on a horse with a war bonnet. That bonnet
is eagle feathers like One Who Is Not Afraid of Horses. "Who do we
want this to be?" she asks.

"Curly."

"Can you tell me a little about Curly?"

Hey! While she's talking, the African doctor from when my mother was here puts his head through the door, but when he comes in the room he walks over to the baby in the crib way across from where I am. I sit up. He reminds me of my father. He loved me. He's black.

"Hi, Doctor," I say.

He doesn't hear me.

"What's up, little guy?" he says to the baby.

Stupid thinks I was talking to her stupid self.

"You can just call me Kate, J.J."

I hold out my arms to the doctor, but he doesn't see me and walks out the room.

"Are you O.K.? Do you know Dr Ngugi? No? Well, O.K., J.J., tell me a little about Curly. What's he doing?"

"He's high on a rock dancing and singing to God."

"What does he feel?"

"He feels sad."

"Why, J.J.?"

"Because he does."

"What is he singing about on the rock?"

"He's *dreaming,* not singing, he's dreaming of the day he will kill all the white people, shoot arrows through their eyes and send them back to the sea. He'll lead a army of warriors and kill the white people with rifles, knives, and arrows."

"How long has he been dreaming like this?'

I put him down.

"What's happening here?"

"He's tired. He hates stupid people. He wants to go to sleep."

if my father

if my father

if my father

If my father wasn't dead he would come get me from here for sure for sure my head hurts and I can't go to the bathroom right so I can't eat stuff like I like in the dream a boy that looks like me but isn't me goes into the kitchen lightning in his brain he will fight he will drive the Europeans back to their ships he is different from the other boys of the tribe he lays naked on the mesa under the moon he puts sharp rocks between his toes he sees a vision the war cry shut up in his bones flies out his mouth he draws lightning bolts with mustard across his cheeks his nose is pierced like my mother's. He opens the kitchen drawer and gets the big butcher knife. "Here, Fox, here, Fox." He stabs the nasty-eye old dog over and over and over again and again. That dog is really Custard and he is Crazy Horse. His head stops hurting and he laughs and laughs.

WHY AM I in the hospital? What's a concussion? How do I feel? No, I don't know anything about the dog. I'm sorry for the dog if it's dead. No, Batty never hit me. No, I didn't know he hit other kids 'cause he know not to hit me. No, no one ever hit me. No, I told you, I wasn't so upset I hurt the dog. I don't even like the dog. No, that's not why I did it. I never did it. How do I feel? No, I never thought of hurting anything! How do I feel? Stop asking me, please. I think of hot dog buns hot outside frozen together on the inside.

"We think you're ready to go home now, J.J."

I don't like being in the hospital, but I don't want to go home.

"Your injuries were very serious, but you've really done a fine job of getting well. Do you remember my name?"

"Dr Spencer."

"Yup, that's my name. You've seen a lot of different doctors and people since you've been in the hospital. Do you remember any of their names?"

"Yes, Dr Zachariah."

"Right! He did the surgery that drained the fluid out of your head. You're fine now, you know that, right?"

"Dr Zachariah also repaired the tear in your sphincter muscle from where you were hurt. That's a lot better too and soon is going to be all better."

"When?"

"Well, you're such a good boy, pretty soon I would say. For the next couple of months you're going to take stool softeners and drink lots of water so you don't get constipated and strain and reinjure yourself and keep coming back here where I'll be glad to see you and be checking up on you to make sure you get well. Who else do you remember?"

"Kate."

"Right, Kate Cohen, the play therapist. Did you like her?"

"No, she's dumb."

"Why do you say that, J.J.?"

"In school we say Native American and she doesn't. And then one time she came talking about what the doll did and stuff—'What did this little doll do to that little doll?'" I mimic her dumb self how she talks. "Stupid stuff like that."

"Well, I certainly won't tell her who said it, but I sure will tell her someone thinks she needs to learn some things."

"I don't care."

"Don't care about what, J.J.?"

"If you tell her who said it."

"What do you care about, J.J.?"

"Nothing."

"That's not true. You care about the Native Americans being called by their right names. Who else do you care about?"

"The Africans, birds, and sea mammals dying from pollution."

"See there, you care about a lot."

My head doesn't hurt anymore like it did. "How long I been here?"

"A few weeks. I know Kate told you you'd be going to live in a new place."

"Uh huh."

"You're going to a new facility for boys in Harlem called St Ailanthus, run by Catholic brothers. It's a home and a school for boys where they've already had tremendous success academically with the youngsters there. Well, look here! Right on cue, here's Kate!"

Kate walks in the room with a big man dressed in a long black robe with a white collar like a preacher.

"Hi, J.J." She smiles at me. I close my eyes. "This is Brother John from St Ailanthus School for Boys. Tomorrow, when you leave the hospital, you'll leave with him, so I wanted you to meet him beforehand."

"Hello, J.J., I've heard a lot about you. How are you?"

"Fine."

"That's cool."

Brother John talks funny.

"So I'll be back for you in the morning to take you to your new home."

"St Ailanthus is a temporary placement," Kate says. "We hope, of course, that we'll be able to find another placement soon. A foster family or adoption situation. Do you understand?"

No, I'm not sure I understand.

BOOK TWO

FALLING

I'm fourteen. I'm a wind from nowhere. I can break your heart.

—AI, "THE KID"

ONE

I rise slowly and start to glide toward him. My pajamas are too short for me, way above my ankles, but they're the largest boy's size. I need man size, I think. The room is dark and filled with the sound of breathing. I float past bed number five, Malik Edwards; four, Omar Washington; three, Angel Hernandez; two, Richard Stein. Bed number one, Bobby Jackson, is at the opposite end near the door. Across the aisle is the other row of beds; start with number fourteen, Amir Smith; number thirteen, Jaime Jose Colon. Number thirteen supposed to be unlucky, like black cats. Brother John say we lucky, all of us, to be here.

"Jaime," I whisper, sit down on the edge of his bed, lean over place my lips on his neck. His silk hair brushing against my lips cause my balls to itch. I'm rubbing my dick slow think, scratch. I touch his shoulder. He stiff up. I rock his shoulder gentle like a memo, a note, that says wake up, I'm here, don't go to la-la land on me, dude. *Please,* I say to myself, like the sound of steam hissing, please don't make me mad-dog you. Jus' be a good boy, Jaime. Just be good. I pull at the skinny blue blanket. He grab the blanket tighter around his shoulders.

"Jaime," I whisper, "you not sleep." I pull the blanket and sheets out from where they tucked in at the foot of the bed and throw 'em up in his face where he grabbing the sheet and blanket. He's shivering with excitement. I'm hard. I grab him with both hands, raise his little booty to me. I jam him. Thrust, I like that word, in him. It's so good, tight. He squeal, I slam his face in the pillow, kill that. OOOHHHH this shit feel good! Feel good to him too. In out, in-out, in-out, in in in. I'm someplace else same time as I'm thrusting in him. Bed creaking turn me on more. The in-out creak music. I hear that sound in the dark, turn me on, I know somebody getting it on. Fucking him I wanna sssscream but I don't. I go in an ultra-sweet whisper aaaaahhhhhhhhh! It's like ice cream and cake, blowing out all the candles at once! I pull out him, my seeds like a . . . a king! I feel like a king. I want him to suck me now, make me come again. I lean down whisper, "Show me some luv, Papi, show me some luv!" He don't get it, what I'm saying. I grab his head, push it down, "Suck it," I'm saying, "suck it!" Pleeeaaase, I made him feel good, do me, little Papi, do me. I try to push his head down. He start to cry. Stupid! Stupid mother-fucker. I get up pull my pajamas up over my privates.

I'm flying now like Michael Jordan across the aisle, over those beds, number one, two, three, four Omar, five Malik, six my bed. Why I'm so stink panicked I don't know. Ain' nobody gonna hear that stupid little motherfucker. Shit, nobody never heard me.

I lay down go to sleep. Huh? Huh? What happened? Are you crazy, motherfucker? Nothin' happened. From inside my sheets I shout, "Shut up, asshole! We tryin' to sleep!" And I really do wish he would shut up, his crying getting all mixed in with my good feeling of . . . of being a king.

SUNDAY WE SIT in Mass by dorm assignment. Same thing after in the cafeteria for breakfast. What I'm getting at is, you just do as you're told, sit where you sit, 'cause that's it. So anyway, I carry my tray of cornflakes, orange juice, milk, and pancakes ('cause it's Sunday) over to the nearest of the tables we spozed to sit at. Like plunk, I put the shit down. I'm not scheming or nothing. I just sit down. Across from Jaime.

The pancakes are one of the few really good things here. On every table is a little stainless steel pitcher of maple syrup. I put some butter on my pancakes, pour some syrup, look over at Jaime who act like his eyes is chained to his plate or some shit. He's grabbing his fork tight. Not moving.

"Eat up, dude," I tell him, cut my pancakes, they tastes good. What's wrong with this dude, he ain't eating his pancakes. "Come on, dude, you don't want your food to get cold." My plate's empty. "Shit, give 'em to me you don't want 'em. You can have my cornflakes." He pushes the plate toward me without even raising his head. "You sure, dude?" I say. "These some good motherfucking pancakes. I don't know why you don't like 'em."

He push the plate the rest of the way across the table. I push the cornflakes in front of him. I'm not really that hungry anymore, but I put some butter and syrup on the pancakes. Jaime raise his hand. To be excused from the table we gotta raise our hands, then one of the brothers come over and we say some shit like, I'm finished, Brother So-and-So, may I be excused to go to the gym or the library, or wherever it is you wanna go.

Brother John come over to the table with his big weird-looking ass. "What's going on here?"

"Huh?" What's with this motherfucker, ain' nothin' goin' on. Brother John look at the plates in front of me, Jaime's plate of pancakes and my empty plate with just a few drops of syrup on it. Then he look at Jaime's simple ass sitting there holding on to his fork like it's money with two little boxes of unopened cornflakes in front of him.

"I said what's going on here?"

I don't know what he's talking about.

"Nobody's got a tongue here?"

"I gotta tongue." Fuck this faggot.

"So use it to explain how it is you have two pancake plates in front of you and Jaime doesn't seem to have eaten at all."

"He didn't want his pancakes, so he gave 'em to me," I say, "and I gave him my cornflakes."

"Is that right, Jaime?"

All of a sudden, Jaime start crying like some bitch. Drop his fork and just you know start boo-hooing. His little curly head going up and down. His whole body is shaking. What's wrong with him! Brother Bill comes running over to the table and scoop Jaime up in his arms. I wish it was me. I don't know Brother Bill, everyone say he one of the "nice ones," whatever that means.

"There, there, Jaime. It's alright," he says, and walks out the cafeteria with Jaime in his arms. Brother John and everyone else is just staring at me.

MONDAY WE'RE REVIEWING Unit One in earth science.

"J.J." Brother John always calls on me. I'm the best in the class, I don't know if I'm the smartest, there is a difference, but I *am* the best. I look in Brother John's blue eyes that sometimes remind me of the sky but this morning remind me of the painted turquoise bottom of the swimming pool that time I was wading through the warm chlorine-smelling water right left right left step step. And I went too far and the bottom disappeared. I screamed panicked, gulping down water. Panic. I feel panic now hearing Jaime sob. But when I blink and pull my eyes away from Brother John and glance over at Jaime, he's not sobbing, he's smiling at me, waiting for me to answer the question, staring at the board where Brother John has written:

THE FOUR MAJOR BRANCHES OF EARTH SCIENCE:

1.
2.
3.
4.

I remember my first day here four years ago. Brother John was holding my hand. I wasn't that scared but I *was* scared, sad too. I thought about my mother every day back then. The class was quiet, it was different from public school, everybody had on a white shirt and a black tie and black corduroy pants. No girls, just boys, who cares, I don't like girls anyway, no one does until you're grown up. I never had a girl who was my friend. And it was *bright,* all the lights was on, not like in public school, half the lights out. Everybody was doing something, a lot was going on, but it wasn't noisy. "Attention please!" Brother John hollered. "I want every-body's attention. We have a new boy today, Jamal Jones, J.J." He turned to me. "What do you like to be called, Jamal? J.J.?" J.J., I told him. "OK, everybody say hi to J.J." Two or three kids say hi and then everybody goes back to what they were doing.

"Omar." He calls a fat kid almost as tall as me. "Show J.J. around the room, why don't you."

Omar immediately goes over to the rabbit's cage, which is in the back of the room where the sink is and where some boys are doing some kind of experiment with potatoes and some other boys are looking in microscopes.

"Come on!"

I'm afraid of rabbits but more afraid Omar will find out I'm afraid. Omar reaches in the rabbit's cage where LeRoi Rabbit—that was his name, he's dead now—is sitting surrounded by pale green lettuce and pellets of doo-doo, or maybe that's his food, I'm not sure. His eyes are red. Omar grabs him by the neck like you do a cat.

"Here," he says. "Touch him. He likes people."

I was sweating, but I made myself touch him. His fur looks fat and fluffy but underneath he's skinny and trembling. He's scared! Somebody gonna jump me, maybe all of them, or slap me like Batty Boy. Thinking about that my ear inside my head start ringing. Are they laughing at me?

Omar puts the rabbit back in the cage. "Wanna see the turtles?" he asks, looking at the turtles, reaching back to latch the rabbit cage shut, but before he can do it LeRoi jumps out the cage! Then Brother John leaps from his desk, swoops down, and grabs LeRoi by his ears, and it seems like in one step he goes from the front of the room to the back and throws LeRoi in the cage and locks it in one motion! The class giggles nervous all together like they're one boy instead of twenty.

Omar don't pay them no mind and tries to hand me a turtle.

"Show him the wall, why don't you, and then come back to the turtles and then go over to the rocks."

I didn't know then Brother John was a geologist. This school didn't have reading groups like my old school—High Alligators, Beavers, and Cobras. Everybody was in a cluster depending on what their class project was and everybody read hard stuff and easy stuff too, the same. Omar told me later he was keeping up for the first time in school. Omar hands me the turtle and takes me over to the mural.

"Jaime, Amir, you want to come over here and help Omar tell J.J. about the mural."

The mural takes up half the wall. Amir, who turns out to be Omar's cousin, is one of the biggest kids I ever seen in fourth grade, he's fatter than Omar and taller than me. And Jaime is one of the littlest kids I ever seen to be in the fourth grade.

Amir points to the mural. "We painted that. The building is the Schomburg Library, and the man in the middle"—he points to a face in the middle of the building, a dark, heavy man with wavy hair—"that's Arthur Schomburg, and all the faces floating in the sky around the building is famous people that's in the Schomburg."

Amir starts reading the words underneath the mural:

CIVIL RIGHTS JOURNAL
Premiere Edition
published by the U.S. Commission of Civil Rights

Arthur "Afroboriqueño" Schomburg

By Robert Knight
© 1995

Arturo Alfonso Schomburg, a self-described "Afroboriqueño" (Black Puerto Rican), was born January 24, 1874, of Maria Josefa and Carlos Féderico Schomburg. His mother was a freeborn Black midwife from St. Croix, and his father a mestizo merchant of German heritage. They lived in Puerto Rico, in a community now known as Santurce. Young Schomburg was educated at San Juan's

Instituto Popular, where he learned commercial printing, and at St. Thomas in the Danish-ruled Virgin Islands, where he studied Negro Literature. (He reads good!)

While his education equipped Schomburg with tools essential to his extraordinary bibliophilia, it was also in school that he encountered the flame which burned throughout his career. By Schomburg's own account, it was in fifth grade (that's what I'll be in next year!) *that a teacher glibly asserted that people of color had no history, no heroes, no notable accomplishments. Young Schomburg embarked on a lifelong quest to refute the mythology of racism in the Americas.*

"That's how the Schomburg Center got started, man!" the little guy Jaime screamed. I didn't know then he was gonna be my friend. I wanted to say back, *I know,* but I just ask, "What's bibliophilia?" I wanted to ask, *What's the mythology of racism?* too, but I realize they probably don't know either. What's on the Internet is complicated and true. I know they got this from the Internet, that's how we did at my old school, we got a name and then went to Google and read it and then print out what's the best for our reports.

"A bibliophile is a person who collects or has a great love of books," Brother John answers my question. "Do you love books, J.J.?" I shrug my shoulders. What kinda question is that, what kinda school is this?

Omar takes me over to the turtles. I'm looking at the faces floating in the sky on the mural, Charles Drew, Zora Neale Hurston, John Perry, and Crispus Attucks. I heard of them before. I even been to the Schomburg before, I think, I'm not sure. Omar hands me a turtle. That's where they got Langston Hughes. I know stuff, these boys better not be thinking I'm dumb. I was in High-A reading group in my old school. Batty Boy thought I was a girl, dumb. I'll show these boys. My ear does its funny buzz buzz. They better not mess with me. Nuh uh! Not here!

"J.J.!" Brother John has grabbed my arm. "Open your eyes! Let the turtle go! You're going to squeeze him to death! What's wrong with you!"

Confused, I look up at Brother John and open my hand. Omar is making little circles with his finger and pointing to his head.

"I . . . I was just holding him."

"So tight!"

"I didn't know I was holding him so tight."

"Why did you close your eyes?"

"My ear was hurting me—"

"J.J.!"

"Huh?"

"Huh! We're waiting for you, and you're daydreaming!"

I look up and Brother John is tapping a piece of chalk on the board beneath where he's written *The Four Branches of Earth Science.* OK, OK, I get it.

"Oceanography, geography, meteorology, and astronomy," I snap.

"And describe two events that occur in each branch."

In the seat in front of me, Bobby Jackson looks at the clock, shifts in his seat, and closes his book. What he do that for?

Brother John looks at him nasty and mean. "Well, Mr Jackson, since you seem so impatient today, perhaps you can answer the other half of the question."

Bobby looks at him, real pain on his face, he is not faking. He couldn't answer the question even if he *had* been listening, he's like, DUH, stupid for real. The silence Bobby should be filling with the answer gets big. Way past big. But I ain't gonna say anything, I ain't gonna dis Bobby.

"Well, Mr Jackson, let me ask you where it is you're in such a hurry to go to."

"The bathroom," Bobby says. Everybody laughs.

"While you're there, read chapters one, two, and three and have the answer Wednesday when I call on you. Class dismissed!"

On my way out the door, Brother John asks me to stop by his office before I go out to next period.

THE PICTURES HANGING in the halls here is mostly dead niggers or fag-gots like Martin Luther King and astronauts and shit. But Brother John's office got pictures of Alonzo Mourning, Shaq O'Neal, Dikembe, Michael Jordan, Dennis Rodman, Magic, Kareem, and some other back-in-the-day dudes I can't name, motherfuckers way way before my time. For a fraction of a second, a thousandth, no, a millionth of a second, I see Brother John's pale pink penis shining in the fluorescent light coming from the window over my bed. It's the only window in the whole room, only thing it looks out onto is the parking lot. He's sitting on my bunk and someone who looks like me is on his knees in front of him. "Gimme some luv," he's saying. I exhale hard, nothing like that could happen in front of everybody, why asinine shit like that is even in my head to think.

Brother John is supposed to be a special guy. He was abandoned at birth and raised by a black foster mother in Harlem. La-di-da, how about that! He get up, cock his head to the side in assembly, and say shit like, "I know these mean streets." To himself he sounds like a nigger, to me he just sounds wacko. I don't hate him like I do Brother Samuel, but I don't like him either. Sixteen, I'm outta here if I make St Ailanthus Boys' Prep Program upstate. Brother John said I probably would. Five from out each junior class from each school in the diocese get picked. I'm gonna be one of them, I think.

Brother John is sitting at his desk in his maroon leather chair. He has a collection of jazz and hip-hop CDs lined up on one side of the little ledge by his window. I look out his window at a wall of nothing but bricks. What does this chump want with me?

"Have a seat, J.J." I sink down on the sofa facing his desk. The sofa is the same color as the chair. I get my own pad, I'm gonna hook it up like this. I look over Brother John's head and below Jesus on the cross is a picture of Dennis Rodman in leather pants sitting on a motorcycle. You know like I repeat what does this chump have to say to me.

"How are things?"

"Cool."

"Cool?" He echoing me or mimicking me? I can't tell. I realize I have no fear of this freak. Freak? Why is he a freak—'cause he got Dennis on the wall? He has Dennis and them guys on the wall 'cause he's black inside, right? He know these mean streets, right? Gimme a break!

"Um hum." I nod. "Cool."

"Well, your class work is outstanding so far. Good things, man, I'm hearing really good things about you. So you dig Shakespeare, huh?"

"I read 'im," I say cool.

"Mrs Washington is very pleased with the work you're doing in that class. Ah—I told her when I recommended you for accelerated English studies you'd be great. You like your math class?"

"Yeah, I like it a lot. I wish I could get into the Computer Programming I, though."

He gets up from behind his desk and comes over to the sofa and sits down. I can smell Irish Spring, the soap the whole school uses.

"Well, that class is packed and is reserved for the 8A students. Don't worry, you'll be right in there come January." He presses his knee against my knee. I look at him. He's looking at our knees touching.

"What's this about Jaime?"

"What do you mean?"

"I know," he says in a voice more colored than usual. "It's all a m-f-ing lie. I know that. Just a little asshole of a kid trying to get some attention. But I had to tell *them* that I talked to you. Be careful." He squeezes my knee. "It's so easy for a little . . . I don't know, a little-little kindness, a little luv to be taken the wrong way."

"I didn't do nothing."

"I know you didn't." He takes his hand off my knee. "Well, you've read *Hamlet*. What does Mrs Washington have lined up next for you guys, *Macbeth*?"

"Yeah."

"That should be fun," he says.

I get up.

He looks at me funny, then says, "Yes, J.J., you can go now."

GO WHERE? Next class has already started, and they know I was in there with Brother John, so I'm marked Excused, not Absent, and next period is lunch. So where? The park? Naw. Maybe 125th Street, over the bridge to the Bronx? Go where, do what? It bugs me about Jaime. I don't want no weird shit on the wire about me. I ain' did nothin' to that stupid kid.

Go to the library, get started on *Macbeth*. Like shock Mrs Washington. What had happened in *Hamlet*? How come he stuck ol' Polonius like that? For nothing, really, and he ended up not really killing the king, or did he stick the king? His moms drank the poison. But everybody ended up dead? He just shoulda took ol' Uncle Kingie out when his father first came to visit him. He should have believed his dad's ghost right from the start.

Where's my father? Dead? I don't even know who he is, so how I know if he's dead? My mother said she didn't know who my father was. What kinda shit is that? You don't even know who the father of your child is. I ever have a kid I'm gonna be there, hang out with my kid. But shit, I ain't never gonna have no motherfucking kids, least not none I know about. If I pop one of these hos from the neighborhood, it'll be hit-and-run. Maybe my father was like a basketball coach that cared about kids. Naw, that can't be true or I wouldn't of got put in an orphanage when my mother died. But maybe my mother had me and didn't like my father so she never told him I was born and he don't even know I exist? That's what happened to one kid whose father came and got him.

Ophelia lost it 'cause of her father being killt? The sun is the cause of rivers, all moving water, really, Brother John had said. I could go to Countee Cullen on 136th Street, but I actually like 124th Street library better, plus it's close to the park. I'm gonna major in computers when I get in high school, get a job with some real ducats. I like Mrs Washington, but I can't see being no English major like she suggest. I don't need to think about that shit now. What I need to think about is Jaime's ass, man. What that motherfucker go stupid on me and he know I ain' did nothin' to him. I'm gonna go to the dorms.

We ain' spozed to be in the dorms before bedtime, but fuck that, because ain' nobody spozed to be there, it's where I can be alone. It's three big rooms on the same floor, one for the little kids, one for the eight- to eleven-year-olds, and then one for us, the big kids. Two rows of beds in each dorm, feets facing the center aisle, heads toward the wall. Lotta space between the beds, wide aisle between the two rows. The main thing you feel here is loneliness. Separated in your bed by yourself. Before you was here you was together, and after you leave, when you are grown, you know, you will be together always like on TV or in the movies. When I think of being a little kid, it's like I'm in a dream in a dark room with a big table and on the table is a bunch of pictures, I hear some music or smell something and a light comes on and the picture comes alive like a movie, like life, and I see myself in my life before and it hurts me even if the picture is a happy picture, so I look around for the light and smash it. The dark feels good. I've never been afraid of the dark like some kids. But the whole thing, the pictures, the light, makes me mad. Thinking about Jaime right now makes me mad. Tonight I'll be waiting on him. No, he'll be waiting on me. The return of J.J. He knows he likes it.

Underneath our beds we have chests for our clothes and stuff. Then behind the cafeteria room we have a locker we can lock. They're small and the brothers have all the combinations and can go in them if they want, and they do if someone has something stolen or if there's rumors of someone with drugs, or a knife, or nasty pictures. But you can keep stuff in there and it won't get stolen. Guys keep stuff like letters, awards, jewelry, and stuff in their lockers. I don't have no jewelry, but I have my kaleidoscope which no one else at school has, some of these guys didn't even know what one was. I have a picture of people at a party or something after my mother's funeral, ain't none of them her of course. I don't get no letters. I waited a long time for a letter. I have two letters in my locker now. I took them. One is in Spanish. The other ain't about nothin', a lie, some grown-up talking about they gonna come get the kid. They always say that. I ask guys, "What your letter say?" It's always the same shit, We love you, be good, we gonna come get you as soon as Mommy gets out of the hospital, we gonna come get you. But they don't, it be a lie. It was nice to open the envelope, take the letter out. Sitting watching other people open their mail and stuff made me wanna do it too. That's all I got in my locker—my letters, kaleidoscope, spelling award and science team award, two rocks and some shells I got at the beach. The rocks look beautiful wet. Really, I could keep my things in my chest under my bed, don't nobody mess with my stuff, really. Some guys here, even in Dorm Three, the big-kids' dorm, our dorm, look like they six years old. I guess they gonna grow later. I'm six feet. How scared other boys are of you is demonstrated by your chest. I mean if you are bad, don't no one rip you off. They don't want no type of retaliation if you see them with your shit. Most of the time, that is, 'cause some of these little kids got larceny in their hearts. They will steal even though they know when you catch them with your shit you are going to beat them to death! They can't help it. It's like trying to stop a cell from undergoing mitosis or stop a cat from climbing on shit, it can't *not* do it, that's its trip—to climb, it's inherent! Some kids born to steal. That's why I lock up my shit. Me, J.J., I'm no thief. I'm a lover, I guess. A born lover. I feel warm, good, when I think that shit! J.J. and Jaime, J.J. and that girl look at me in the park, J.J. and lots of people. Then a main-squeeze girl I'm gonna marry. After dinner we do cleanup, study, and then go to the lounge and watch TV till ten minutes before lights-out, then ten minutes before lights-out we run to our room, change into our pajamas, line up in the bathroom, brush our teeth, hit our knees, pray all of us real loud:

> *Now I lay me down to sleep,*
> *I pray the Lord my soul to keep.*
> *God bless our parents, here or departed,*
> *God bless the Brothers of St Ailanthus,*
> *God bless all the children of the world,*

including myself, God's dearest lamb,
and God bless the sweet little Lord Baby Jesus.
In the name of the Father,
the Son, and the Holy Ghost.
AAAhhMMMmen!

"God"—one of the brothers stand at the end of the room, his fingers on the light switch, reciting same time as we praying—"author of all heavenly gifts. You gave St Ailanthus both a wonderful reverence of life and a deep spirit of compassion. Through his merits, grant that we may imitate his sympathy. Amen." When we say, "Ahh," he flicks the lights off, by the time we got "men" out, he turn in his robes and is gone. That's when the promises and shit start: "I'm gonna get you tomorrow, motherfucker!" "On the court, nigger." "Say some shit to me again in history and I'll knock your eyes out your head!" Don't nothin' ever really start or get too loud 'cause Mr Lee right down the hall if shit do, and he run his old ass in, throw on the lights, and blink 'em till the brothers bust in like police in long robes.

After the lights go out, I lay there, I'm thinking, why shouldn't I? I mean, it's not wrong. I'm no faggot. I just wanna do this, have fun for now. The sheets feel like concrete laying up on top of me. How I feel is like a basketball after it hits the ground and is flying up! But I'm laying here trying to pretend I'm asleep. I shift under the covers. I don't know what I know. It's wrong? It's how we live, whether anybody talk about it or not, man! This shit common as H_2O, man. Don't make you no freak. His hair is like the collie dog's hair I had at the foster home once. His eyes is like that too, big and brown. But he moves like a little kitten skittering down the hall with his backpack bouncing over his butt.

I'm pulling the covers back now. The only relief from darkness at his end of the dorm is the glow from the exit sign, the clock face, and a crack of light from under the door. I grab him in my arms. He's like a little child. I'm like the big father. He's such a small boy, a faggot child, I guess. Jaime, what kind of name is that? I'm hard. I hold him in my lap, put my hand on his chest, his heart is beating, beating.

"Don't," he says.

That makes me sad. "OK." I feel bad I just sit there. I don't know why, but tears well up in my eyes, fall, drop off my cheek onto his chest. He touches my cheek.

"I won't hurt you, OK?" I say. "OK." I ease him out of my arms back onto the bed. Brother John's voice is in me now saying, *Show him some luv, show him a little luv.* I open his pajamas and kiss him there. His skin is like a baby, he smells like the spaghetti we had for dinner and a little like pee. I'm like in earth science, the gentle winds caressing the earth's surface. I want him to love me. I take his penis in my mouth. He's like a little boy, but I know he's not. He's thirteen, his thing is as big as mine. I go round him with my tongue, then suck and suck like I'm going to die if I stop. He comes in my mouth. I swallow him, he's mine now. I get up, fly down the aisle. I didn't hurt nobody, do nothing bad. I'm not bad. I'm a good king. I think about flying out the window over my bed, but it's too high up. The light breaks in through cracks in the curtains and slashes me.

The night sounds are like zeros that add up to nothing. Silence. I like that. And the dark. I slide quiet back to my own bed. We have a test in earth science tomorrow. See can I hand Jaime some answers. Tired of seeing my boy fail. He's the same as me even though we look different. We are both boys, thirteen years old. I know what he feels. Only our skins, our hair, and our sizes are different. I'm six feet, he's four feet, I'm dark brown, the mountain, and he is the color of sand on the beach with curly hair like a doll's. I never played with dolls, I never will. I stretch out my feet and they touch the metal bar at the end of the bed. I wonder where he's from, the Dominican Republic, I think. His father got killed in a taxicab accident? His mother, it's weird to ask about people's mother, but if he's at St Allie's he probably ain't got one. I dream about birds flying over water, water, water that don't end.

SCHOOL IS OVER, we're on our way to the swimming pool, the 135 City-Rec, following behind Brother Samuel. Me and Jaime are bringing up the back of the line. I ain't said nothing to him. He ain't said nothing to me. Brother Samuel done turned and looked back at us a couple of times. Good, bear ass, see, ain't nothing going on. Lies, you done heard.

"How'd you do on the earth science test?" I ask.

"A lot better'n I been doing, thanks."

We turn the corner on 135th Street. I look over at the blood-red brick projects.

"You from the Dominican Republic?"

"No, man, I'm from here. My parents and shit was from the Dominican Republic."

Was. I look at him and ask, "You like me?" I'm scared what he's gonna say.

"Yeah, man, but you come on so loco and shit at first, what's with you?"

"I'm sorry, you know, I jus' couldn't help myself."

"Why you couldn't?"

"I don't know, man, I just, you know, *feel* you that much."

"When I get grown, I'm gonna go with girls," he says.

"Of course," I say. "Don't all guys unless they're gay or some shit? We're friends, ain't no one gonna fuck with you, ever."

We at the door of the 135 City-Rec, everyone else has gone in. "Let's go over to Vee-O-Game on Fifth Avenue!" I say, and dash down the steps and head toward the street, waving for Jaime to follow.

He's panting. "We spozed to go upstairs with Brother Samuel if we wanna be on the swim team!"

"You wanna be on the fucking swim team?"

He giggles like a girl. "No!"

"Then let's get the fuck outta here," I say.

"Wanna get some smoke?" he says.

"Where? I ain't got no money."

"I thought that was what you was going to Vee-O for, that guy who get the coins out the machine—"

"Retarded-looking guy?"

"Yeah, him!" Jaime say.

I ain't never smoked before, but I don't want him to know that. I stop point up at the red bricks of MLK homes. "See that," I say.

"The motherfucking projects," he say, bewildered-like.

"No, man, the swimming pool."

"Man, you must already be high. We just left the swimming pool."

"No, man, my swimming pool. My mansion, green grass, and society-cool people sitting around the tables at the pool like in Miami, Florida." I feel like I'm rapping almost. "Get me?"

"I got you at half pass a monkey's ass. I wheeling out the driveway in a freak-ass Ferrari," Jaime says.

"I tell my little snickumpoo come here and take care of me and my friends. My friends dudes, so she don't be jealous."

"She got a banging body?"

"BANGING!! White minidress—"

Jaime starts to move his hips and tugs at an imaginary minidress.

"She say what you want, Papi? I roll the Royce out the garage to go to the store go get some champagne and Old English 800. She hop in the car beside me rub me up rub me down!"

Jaime sticks out his tongue at me sweet, then says, "Let's go get a jay and we can smoke it later on. But we better go 'fore they go 911 on us! All I got to do is let ol' retardo touch it and he give me what I want."

I look at Jaime with new respect and pride like I feel when I get the right answer in class.

"What we gonna say when we get back?" he says.

"Don't worry," I say. "Let's just hurry up."

When we get to Vee-O, it's like Jaime says, only the dude wants to touch both of us for the joint. We go ahead and smoke there. He says it's Black Thai, which is even badder than Chocolate Thai. I only took two hits, but I'm HIGH!

"What we gonna say when we get back?"

"I'll figure it out when we get there." I feel good, like lightbulbs is turning on in all my cells. They ain't gonna fuck with me, I think but must have said out loud 'cause Jaime says, "It's me I was worried about."

"Look!" I shout over my shoulder running up the stairs two at a time, stopping on the third-floor landing, looking through the door of the pool balcony at the St Ailanthus swim team bodies still splashing in the water below. "We'll just come walking down the stairs innocent-like after they get out the pool, you know, and say we was waiting for the team upstairs in the gym 'cause we thought that was where the team was gonna meet. You know, we been up there all the time, ain't left premises or nothing. Nada!"

"Will he go for it?"

"They ain't gonna fuck with me," I say, believing myself.

"They fuck with me," he says. I don't know what he mean.

"Can you think of anything better?" I say.

"I'm not the one who said let's leave premises!"

"Can you think of anything better?" I repeat.

"No."

"Then come on," I hiss.

"But we way late, man."

And I'm way high for the first time. Fuck this scary dude, no plan but complain complain! I ain't scared of them stupid-ass motherfuckers. Usually if ain't no guys playing basketball, the gym is empty, but when we get up the stairs, I stop short. All kinda people in here today dressed in bright-colored tights, leotards, and sweats, some got on African clothes. On one side of the room like trees growing up from the floor are four shiny drums sitting in front of four empty chairs. A big guy, taller than me, in a long white African robe, sits down behind the biggest drum. Then three more dudes sit down behind the other drums. They go BAP! BAP! Tee dee dee BAP BAP! Another guy picks up a flute and starts to blow. It's so beautiful it *hurts,* feels like someone just kicked me in the balls! Then wild, man! Wild! Maybe it's the Black Thai. Maybe, but it's still real. Something stops screaming in my head. In one fucking second I know my life, it's this sound.

"What's up, man?" Jaime is looking at me weird. I shake my head. Guy blowing on flute is killing now like a tidal wave or atoms splitting or some shit, this is from before Hamlet. Bap dee da dap bap BAP! The drums break and stop.

A woman in a yellow leotard and African skirt steps in front the people and says, "Everybody back! So we can start moving across the floor."

"Man, let's get out of here," Jaime says. "These people is dancers or some shit."

"No!" I groan. I ain't goin' nowhere.

"Get in lines of six," she says. Everybody does what she says, including me. Jaime is staring at me stupid. I look at him and go meet what's mine—shit, like I went to him when I wanted. I get in the back line behind a fat Spanish-looking girl in a brown and blue African skirt who is stepping from side to side bobbing her head to the beat.

"Why don't you take off your shoes?" she says, bending from her waist till her torso is over her knees, still stepping side to side.

I take off my shoes, start stepping side to side right behind her. The drums start up, and the woman in yellow hollers, "Aiiii deee laaaay ohhhhh!!" The people start moving, and I move with them.

WE TRY TO inch up to the two lines of lucky Ailanthus boys. Brother Samuel's back is to us. *Was* to us. Just when we think we're over, he turns around and screams at us like the mad dog he is, "Where have you two been!" But he's looking at me like I'm a snake ain't allowed to crawl. I pull back and look him dead in the eye, fuck him! Faggot, want a showdown, let's have one.

Then Jaime surprise the shit out of me by saying in a loud voice, "We was upstairs with the African people."

He looks Brother Samuel in the eye. Brother Samuel clouds over, he wanna say something mean, but he would rank himself now.

Bobby Jackson says, "You was where the African drummers was?"

"Yeah," I say, cool.

"Cool," three of the other guys say at the same time. Everybody is looking at me and Jaime. I see him different, to break on Brother Samuel with no fear. Brother Samuel is not one of the nice ones. Shit, I know.

"Get in line," Brother Samuel tells us, even though we're already in line.

Now it feels like firecrackers is going off in every motherfucking cell of my body! Nothing's gonna be the same for me ever. I know it.

MONDAY, I ALREADY BEEN to Brother John, now I'm in Brother Samuel's office. I already get that African dance and St Ailanthus School for Boys ain't gonna be Kool-Aid and water, but I didn't think it was gonna be this stupid.

"Yeah," I repeat. "Dance class. I want to go to the African dance class at the 135 City-Rec on Saturday."

"African class?" He swivels around in his chair so he's directly facing me.

"African *dance* class." I stress "dance." I hate this stupid motherfucker, his stupid office, his stupid black leather furniture, stupid fucking crucifix over his big head. He tries to make me feel like I ain't shit, like I'm a little kid! I rub my forehead, close my eyes for a second, see myself pulling a sawed-off shotgun out a briefcase. I put it to the side of Brother Samuel's head. *Kneel down, cocksucker. KNEEL DOWN! Faggot.* Then I tell him, *Pull up the skirt, bitch! You heard me, bitch, pussy! Pull that goddamned skirt up and let me see them cupcakes—*

"I'm afraid that won't be possible, J.J."

"Why?"

"Well, for one thing our insurance doesn't cover you outside the home unless you're with an adult from the home."

"But we go places by ourselves all the time." I hate how my voice is sounding all high.

"Yes, but supposedly places where minimal risk is involved. This African thing sounds risky, like gymnastics or something. Also, I don't know whether this thing is something St Ailanthus supports for you boys. None of us here have ever been to the class, observed the content of the class or it's modality of instruction to see basically if it's even suitable for young boys."

"So what are you trying to say?"

"J.J., I am saying no."

"No don't mean nothin' to me."

"Well, it had better start, young fella."

"'Young fella'! Who are you talking to!" I'm screaming at him I'm so mad.

"J.J., I'm talking to you!"

I turn and walk out the door. I'm going to African dance class on Saturday same as if this bear-ass motherfucker had said yes. That's that. Fuck that old bastard. Try to do the right thing and they disrespect you, treat you like a child. Fuck him Fuck him Fuck him *Fuck him*. I'm gonna do what the fuck I want to do. Saturday I'll be in that class, fuck him.

WHAT THE FUCK I want! What the fuck do I want? The clock over the door glows 3:25. I want to go back to sleep. I close my eyes see red. I'm still crazy mad. I can't sleep. I feel like my own shadow. That's stupid, "my own shadow," where that come from? Too much Shakespeare. These covers feel like fire on me. I don't know whether I was dreaming or what, but Brother Samuel was on fire, standing at the altar like he was giving Mass, the chasuble, then the robe underneath it, going up in flames, burning off him, but his body isn't burning, it's pink and naked, his dick rising up like a short pink Hitler salute. I never done this before. What? What am I talking about? I ain' did nothin'. I never done this before Ineverdonethisbefore. What! I do what the fuck I want. Hear that, Faggot Samuel! The light from the parking lot coming in my window has always disturbed me. If I complain, maybe they would fix the curtain so no light comes in I could sleep better. I peel the burning sheets off me. You never done this before. Shut up! Shut the fuck up! Does the floor feel cold because I'm so hot? I'm sweating. Am I pretty, beautiful, handsome? Whatever boys are? No, I'm ugly. I hate it when I can't get Brother Samuel's face out of my head, when he is just dangling in there, his pink face like clak-clak balls kids bang together driving you crazy unless you're clak-claking too. But this is the loudest noise maybe because I can't hear it no place but in my head. It just bangs in my head *CLAK CLAK CLAK CLAK* fucking with me and fucking with me *CLAK CLAK*. Big bear-ass motherfucker pressing down, balls in my face, hair red wires in my mouth, the quiet loud like in science-class flicks where time-lapse photography amplifies sounds you don't usually hear like silk being ejected from the spinnerets in the spider's belly. The floor is sticky, I pad past Malik, Omar, Angel, Richard, Bobby, Amir, Jaime. Behind me the aisle is burning. I'm moving like in a dream now.

Maybe I am in my dreams. Maybe this is not real. It is a dream. I dream I'm walking toward the exit sign, I push the door open and walk out into the hall. The lights are very bright. To the right are the stairs and the little office where Mr Lee the night attendant sits sleeping in a chair, *Always there if you boys need me.* I don't need the motherfucker. I turn left.

In the dream I'm naked at the end of the hall in Dorm One, the little kids' dorm. There are things here I like; some kids have teddy bears, dolls, or stuffed monkeys. There are no windows here. In the dream I sit on Richie Jackson's bed, quietly. You would think I'm a king the way I sit so nice and quiet. I sit here like the world is mine and I do what the fuck I want. Richie is Bobby Jackson's little brother. Why don't I have a little brother? When you're king, you rule the world. I slide off the foot of the bed down to my knees. I pull the covers over my head. I'm playing a game, it's fun. I sniff his little toes. My blood is electricity surging through me. Hey, I'm all lit up! He is sleeping on his side, his breath is going in-out, in-out. I pull his little pj bottoms down, pull his little butt down to me. He's like a little doll. I close my mouth around his little penis. I know he loves me. I'm sucking him, sucking him! At the same time going up down up down on my penis, dick! It's so good. He doesn't wake up, I want him to wake up even though I'm scared for him to wake up. OOOhhhh! I come like one of Mr Lee's mousetraps *SNAP!* surprising myself. I groan quiet, get up off my knees. I never felt so happy in all my life! I float back down the hall to Dorm Three, glide past fourteen, one, thirteen, two, twelve, three, eleven, four. I climb back in my bed, stretch out flat on my back, the light from the parking lot still in my eyes. But the dream is over. I can finally go to sleep.

WHEN I WAKE UP, it's like, Yo! I know where I'm going and I don't care who likes it. Every morning the lights go on with the sound of Brother Samuel ringing the brass wake-up bell. We get up at six on weekdays, seven on Saturdays, and eight on Sundays. We go to bed 9:00 p.m. regardless. Boys complain and shit, me too, but I don't mean it, deep down I like the regularity.

Boys is groaning and pulling the covers over their heads. Brother Samuel is still ringing the stupid bell. I pull my trunk out from under my bed. I gotta wear something besides jeans so I can move. These past couple of days been feeling almost like summer so I just grab my red athletic pants and a T-shirt. We don't have to go to morning Mass on Saturday, so we don't, except for the little altar-boy punks. I'm not really a Catholic. I don't care how many times I say I am, go to Mass, genuflect, sign of the cross hail Mary full of cum the Lord done had thee or you wouldn't be having a motherfucking baby! Ha! Ha! First communion, confirmation, shit!

This is a home for Catholic boys who are orphaned, and if anybody calls up here willing to adopt older kids, it's Catholic people. So you know, fuck it, I ain' really thinking about shit like that no more. But just in case, I'll be a Catholic. Religion is about believing, and I don't believe nothin' I can't see. And anyway if they was so all that, then why shit goes down like it does. *CLAK CLAK CLAK*. It's a toy. There's these two strands of nylon cord tied together at the top, at the bottom of each cord is a hard clear plastic ball, smaller than a Ping-Pong ball, bigger than a boulder marble. The object of the game, the fun, is spozed to be getting the balls to bounce off each other nonstop real fast. The sound is *CLAK CLAK CLAK* over and over and over, loud. That's the real object of the game—driving grown-ups crazy with the noise. I used to love doing it. The little kids here all do. I hate it now; everybody hates it unless they're doing it. It's not just that I hate the noise, it's that the stupid shit noise is like part of my brain now, in there, I can't get it out.

I gotta piss. I pull on my T-shirt and head for the door. Bear Ass is at the door.

"J.J., make up your bed, please, before you leave the floor."

"I gotta go to the bathroom."

"Um hmm, hurry up and make up your bed so you can relieve yourself."

Fuck this fool, I think, and go to push past him. The next thing I know, he's grabbed me and flipped me over his shoulder and I'm flying through the air WHAM! Flat on my back. I try to kick up, he gets me in a choke hold and slams me back down.

"Now!" he growls. "You make up that bed now!"

I scream, he cuts off my air, slams my head to the floor hard, it hurts like fuck. I feel like shit as I piss all over myself. I squeeze my eyes shut to all of Dorm Three looking down on me in pity.

Brother Samuel lets me go. "Well, don't we both wish you had obeyed orders and done as you were told? Now, get *up* and make up your bunk immediately!"

I don't raise my head while I'm making up my bed. I pull up the dingy wrinkled sheets, then the skinny pale blue blanket, reach under my bed in my trunk and get another pair of shorts, pull off the red athletic pants and put on a pair of jeans. I kick the wet clothes near the foot of the bed. Walking down the aisle, I look up at Richard's half-breed ass gawking at me, turn around, and shove him back on his bed.

"What are you looking at!" I pass Jaime, his eyes on the floor. Mr Lee is near the door, mopping up the urine.

Brother Samuel is standing right next to Mr Lee. "After breakfast be in my office. Be prompt."

I walk past him.

EVEN THOUGH I KNOW he can beat me, it's not fear I feel but something else I can't describe. I just stare at the cornflakes. Saturday breakfast is always the same, dry cereal with fruit, bananas or canned peaches. Then they bring scrambled eggs, bacon, and toast with little square things of butter and jam in little plastic tubs—strawberry, grape, or marmalade. I usually take the strawberry from whoever has it. But not today. Today I eat my cereal without looking up. No one says nothing to me, I don't say nothing to nobody. Brother Samuel Brother Samuel *CLAK CLAK CLAK CLAK* step on a crack and break that bear's fat back. Hey! Hey! I'm gonna kill you one day. I look at the eggs the KP boy put in front of me from off the steam cart. I can't eat no motherfucking eggs. I can't eat no fucking eggs! I pick up my fork and jam it HARD into my left hand. The blood seeps out like steam out a valve. I feel relieved. Look up and Brother Samuel is standing over me.

"Come with me *now*," he says. I get up follow him down the stairs to his office. I'm big, he's bigger. I'm sweating. Funky. Tired of following him into his black hole. Office *CLAK CLAK CLAK* English Select *Macbeth* next semester computers last semester biology. Brother John. I got no fight in me, flight either. Fight or flight, instinctual mechanism for survival in animals. I'm thirteen I feel like I'm ninety. Mrs Washington liked my idea for my midterm paper. Time flies flies of time lord it seems like school just started but it's almost two months now.

"HALT!" he barks. I stop. He unlocks the door to his office. Hole. I follow him in. "Don't let me tell you what to do—for God's sake take that damn fork out of your hand, are you crazy!" I remind myself this isn't real. It's a dream, a *movie*! In the movie I'm always naked. A white man pulls me to him rough. I obey. I must. I must obey him. Be a good boy. He kisses my neck. He reaches behind him and puts in a CD, the famous actor, James Earl Jones, reading from the Bible. He tongues my ear. You're pretty. You know I love you. His robes flow like black water his belly is pale whitey white with blue-green veins and red hair like copper wires. The bass voice fills the room with the Bible. He kisses me groans. *My soul has grown ancient like the rivers* I like that poem he pulls me down on my hands and knees his KY jelly is a cold splash on my asshole *my soul has grown deep like the rivers*. I love you I love you, black boy! Don't you know it hurts me to hurt you. Why do you make me hurt you, black boy! I love you! Unh! Unh! I feel his tears hot falling on my back. It hurts. Do you do you love me do you love me. I wish he would get off me. I wish he would get in deeper it feels so fucking good like God I hate myself I hate him I hate him Our Father who art in heaven hallowed be thy Ahhhhha ha!!! I hate GOD! Ahhh! OOOhhhhhh! Get up, get your ass *up* and *out* of here. I don't want any more problems out of you today, young man! You hear? You hear!

I pull on my jeans and T-shirt. Ten minutes after nine. Someone is crying like a bitch, but it's not me. Not me not me oh Holy Mary mother of God in the name of the Father *CLAK CLAK CLAK CLAK* bam a bam goddamn! Bam! I slam my fist on the arm of the sofa.

"Do not leave the grounds today, hear?" He grabs my chin with his thumb and finger and pulls my face to his, tries to stare me in the eyes. I'll put 'em out first, my eyes mine. "Do you hear me? Do you hear me!"

I try to squirm and twist my chin from his grip, look out at the door. He pinches harder. His smell, my smell, sweat, the smell of leather climb up my nose.

"Do you hear me? Do you hear me!"

I nod.

He drops his hands from my face. I walk out the office hear his big bear ass plop down on the couch. I'm going where I been planning on going all week, then I realize how early it is. The Africans don't start till one-thirty. It's not even ten o'clock yet.

I jog down to Marcus Garvey Park. Quiet. Bare brown dirt where the grass has died. Bushes green. It seems like nothing is going on, but it's really like a split movie screen, on one side of the hedges cars is zipping past. Other side, other world—park people, waiting on dope dick ducat. I back into the high green hedges, sink down on my knees. A pair of jeans walks past with a big belly. "Five," the jeans say. "Ten," I say, unzipping the jeans, putting the bill in my pocket.

I got time to kill before class. I run up to the watchtower. No one has rung the bell since 1850 when New York had thatched roofs, I can't imagine that! I love it up here, don't nobody usually come up this high. Don't need the watchtower no more, just let people, niggers, burn up. Who can I tell, where can I go? Brother John said the technology to record CDs was there when they brought CDs on the market, just like two-deck tape recorders, but wouldn't have been no money in it. "Money is the motivating force for almost everything."

"Almost?"

"Yeah, almost, not everything can be bought and sold."

"What can't?"

"What can't is so insignificant in the eyes of the world—"

"What about *us*, the Catholics, St Ailanthus?"

"Yeah, we're different. That's why I'm here. I'm not of the world."

Sometimes I like Brother John. Most times I don't. I like earth science, though. This park is here 'cause they couldn't cut down the rock. I'm a Capricorn, climb the rock. Right now I'm going to Bake Heaven to get some donuts. There's a fracture in the earth's crust that runs across 125th Street. I pull out my ten in Bake Heaven and it's a one! I start back in the direction of the hedges, what the fuck, shit even if he ain't gone which he is, I didn't even see his fucking face.

"CLASS IS FIVE DOLLARS," says the girl sitting on the floor writing people's names on a sheet of paper attached to a clipboard, putting their money in a big manila envelope.

"All I got *today* is a dollar." I stress "today." The girl looks up at the teacher, who has on a deep blue leotard, same style as the yellow one she had on last week, and has appeared like magic by the girl's side.

"Next week," the teacher says.

"OK."

"What's your name?"

"J.J."

She writes my name down and puts my dollar in the big manila envelope. She points to a door down the hall. "That's the men's locker room. You can get dressed in there."

I'm already dressed, though. I slide my back down the wall, sit on the floor, check things out. It's a nice-size gym but not huge. Above us is an indoor track. Some niggers is hanging over the railing looking down at us. Mostly women in the gym. All kinds—young, hip-looking, dark, light, one old white woman. Some is fat, some look like athletes, almost all of them, even the old white one got on some kinda African shit. I wonder how many of these niggers is real Africans and how many is just dressed like it. Against the wall, under the windows, are four chairs with a tall drum sitting in front of 'em, no guys drumming, just the chairs and the drums. These people in the gym seem different from the niggers walking up and down the streets. I try to figure out how and what it is, where or how I fit in, can't—just know this is where I want to be and where I am, and I don't really give a fuck about anything else. Four guys in long white African robes file in and sit down in the chairs in front of the drums. I'm so busy scoping them, wondering what country in Africa they come from if they *are* Africans, that I don't notice Jaime has slid up beside me! His earlobe is swollen and got a little drop of blood on it where he has pierced it with a silver hoop that has a seashell on it. It's like the shells some of the girls have sewn on their belts and African bra tops. Around his forehead he got a band like Indians wear around their heads. I think he thinks it's African. More, I think in some way he's sorry about this morning. Whatever! He's here. That makes something swell up in my throat, I can't even talk.

"Whew!" he whispers. "Man you stink."

I flip back through the dollar scene in the park, back to me flying over Brother Samuel's shoulder in Dorm Three this morning. But I laugh at how funny beautiful Jaime looks and how embarrassed I am to be so glad he's here. The girl near the door with her clipboard hollers to Jaime, "Five dollars!" He walks over to her. I never seen any of the St Ailanthus boys in the park. How do they get money? Rob? They got it, I can see that. I don't strong-arm kids for cash even though I could. Jaime's grandmother be bringing him dust, talking about she gonna break him out when she gets back on her feet. But according to Etheridge, who is a KP, not an office monitor, meaning I don't know how he know everybody's business, she ain't getting back on her feet no time soon. She got AIDS—SIDA, the Spanish people call it. Most of the boys in St Ailanthus is there because of that even though they don't say so. Jaime got on white sweats and a blue sweatshirt say SYRACUSE HIGH #7. Next week I'm coming in here with some African shit on. The woman teaching the class, she's tying a beautiful piece of blue and white cloth around her waist. You could see her stomach is flat, and she got big muscles with definition like dancers do in her legs. Her face is dark smooth chocolate, no wrinkles. But her hair, which is pulled back in a braid and that she's tying a piece of African cloth around, is all white. Weird. It don't compute, she ain't old enough for no white hairs.

We do a lot of exercises with dance names: pliés, tendue-flex-point-flex. Plié, relevé, roll down 1-2-3-4-5-6-7-8 soften your knees for eight counts, now using every vertebra in your back, that's it, roll up slowly. Then we did stretches and sit-ups and push-ups. The stretches are excruciating for me, but the push-ups and stuff are easy.

"Line up four across," she says, nods at me, Jaime, and three other guys, "men come in the back." Rows materialize with the sound of her voice. I like that. She claps her hands and the drums start.

"*Ba* BAH! *Ba* Bah!" she says, her right foot coming down on the *Ba*, her left on BAH! Her arm comes down from where she has it stretched up toward the ceiling, and she flings her hand open to the ground as she stamps her foot on BAH!

"You're planting seeds. You throw the seed into the earth, then you stomp the earth—BAH!" She brings her foot down on the earth where she has just thrown the seeds. "This movement comes from Congolese dance, which really influenced a lot of Afro-Haitian movement."

The drums funk up! Me, Jaime, and the three other dudes are in the last row bringing up the rear as the girls move across the floor. *Ba* BAH! *Ba* BAH! I'm in Africa or Puerto Rico somewhere, planting my seeds on my land.

I FORGET WHEN he starts that Papi shit, but that's when I start to pull away from Jaime. He has me mixed up with somebody, *something* else. I'm a man, not a faggot. I got an A in my earth science project, an A on my midterm paper in English, a B-plus in math, and an A in art. If I wasn't so old, Brother Samuel told me, I would be a prime candidate for adoption, so old and so big, you scare them, they want little boys. If they'll take black kids, they want mulattoes and girls. Whatever they want, they don't want black boys. I guess my question, even though I'm only thirteen, is what kind of motherfucker is Brother Samuel to sit up and tell me some shit like that? I don't know if I want to be adopted anyway. What would I do in a family now? Next month, January, I'll be fourteen. Raven is fifteen. I met her in dance class. I'm meeting a lot of people in dance class. I think she likes me, Raven.

No one says anything to me anymore about dance class. It's been three months now. Jaime still comes. At first it's like he's following me, then it's like he's in this too. He found some shit for himself here. I don't know who we really are. Orphans, I guess, whatever all that means. I'm a regular nigger, I was born in Harlem, Jaime in the Bronx, but here we fucking Africans, everything we are *and* ain't is cool. I don't know about Jaime, but me, I'm going to be a dancer.

BROTHER SAMUEL is standing in the light that comes in through the window above my bed. I look up at the clock under the exit sign over the door. Three o'clock.

"Get up, J.J. I have some gentlemen here who would like to talk to you," Brother Samuel says. The blankets have come off my feet, which are touching the cold metal footrail of the bed. I shiver. I don't know why, but I feel I'm dying, although I don't know how that feels. My life doesn't flash before my eyes, but the dream I had last night does.

In the dream I . . . I feel the light from the window in my eyes, *disturbing* me, the light is saying get up, get *up*. Get up for what, I wonder, and peel off the covers very carefully as if to toss or throw them would make a sound like pots and pans falling. I swing my legs out of the bed and my feet onto the cold linoleum floor and rise. Rise and fly down the center aisle past Malik Edwards, Omar Washington, Angel Hernandez, Richard Stein, and Bobby Jackson on one side, and Louie Hernandez, Billy Song, Etheridge Killdeer, Jaime, and Amir Smith on the other side. I fly slowly, majestically, a flying king I am. I fly under the exit sign and through the door. The lights in the hallway are bright as sun, summer, they make me not able to fly no more. In the dream my feet are on the cold linoleum again, but I'm lucky, I turn into a panther. Real graceful and black, making no noise as I creep stealthily down the hall. One two three four five six seven eight nine ten eleven steps twelve thirteen fourteen fifteen sixteen steps, I push open the door. Slide up slowly, now I'm a trapeze artist flying through the air? A gymnast twirling down the beam? No? Yes! Beam! I'm a beam of light visiting the dark. A daddy to my boy. His teddy bear has fallen to the floor, I pick it up, sit it gentle next to me at the foot of the bed. I pull the sheets and the blankets out where they're tucked in at the foot of the bed. I see his little brown feet white on the bottoms like the belly of a fish. I lean down kiss his toes, run my tongue under the arch of his foot, roll the covers back some more, kiss his calves, bite his calf muscle gently. I feel like the king! Rich instead of poor. I am here to give him something. Everything is like soft music, the low notes on the flute.

Then I don't know what happens. I know I'm hard full of love, a good person, the king here to love him, and he starts to whimper. Whine. It makes me furious, in the dark I see blood red! I slap the shit out of him for being stupid! You know BAP! Like shut up, motherfucker! Then I climb on top of him and fuck him. Fuck him, pushing his little whiny mouth into the pillow, he wants it, I know it, I feel strong like a warrior king, umph, umph, UMPH! Planting my seeds, riding my horse! I throw the covers back over him and slide out the room to the blind light of the hallway. I am not seen in the presence of light, being light I am absorbed and the brightness of things increases and you can see more but you still can't see God like I am. I float through the door, past the boys, bed by bed, to my bed. Now I lay me down to sleep I pray the Lord my soul to keep Bless us all at St Ailanthus Bless all the children of the world AAHHHHHhhhhMennn. And bless me.

Someone is shaking my shoulder. "Come on, get up, J.J.!" In dreamland there's always some kinda crazy mistake. It's not even time to get up! When it's time to get up is 6:00 a.m. on weekdays, 7:00 on Saturdays, and 8:00 on Sundays; one of the brothers, usually Brother John or Brother Samuel, pushes open the door, throws on the overhead fluorescent lights, and starts ringing the bell DING DONG DING DONG! And we get up one by one all of us. But something is wrong now, the clock says 3:00, and Brother Samuel is saying, "J.J., I have some people here who want to talk to you."

"Whaa . . . huh . . . say what?" I'm still all sleepy and shit.

"Say get up! That's what, J.J.!" says this mean voice, then a stick bangs on the metal post at the head of my bed.

"Stop playing games, J.J.," the voice says. "You heard us—*get up!*"

I open my eyes. Brother Samuel is standing with two men in suits and ties next to my bed. "Does he have a robe?" I don't hear what Brother Samuel says, but I don't have a robe. That's extra, only kids who have family still on the set or have sponsors or Big Brothers and shit get extra.

"Get dressed," one of the men in suits says. My blood gets chilly. This motherfucker is a cop. I reach in the trunk under my bed, pull out a pair of briefs, snatch my jeans and a T-shirt from a hook on the wall at the head of my bed.

"Got a jacket?" the cop asks.

"Does he have to go downtown, Officer?" Brother Samuel asks.

It's two cops, one tall skinny don't say nothing, one short mean-looking. The short one looks at Brother Samuel weird and says, "Downtown? No, Father, the station is around the corner."

"I'd like to minimize any unnecessary, unnecessary . . . oh, I don't know . . ." Brother Samuel's voice trails off.

"We just want to ask him a few questions. Put your shoes on, J.J."

"Is he under arrest?"

"No, but we can do it like that if you want."

Brother Samuel doesn't say anything. I look at the clock, 3:10. That's two hours fifty minutes before wake-up time!

"May I come with him, Officer?"

"Yeah," the short cop says. "Be our guest."

AT THE POLICE STATION, the cops walk one on each side of me, they hands on my elbows, not hard or hurting me but serious, like if I do move they'll kill me.

Behind me Brother Samuel says, "Well, gentlemen, I don't quite understand what's going on here. I mean . . . ah, it does seem as if J.J. is . . . ah, I don't know . . . under arrest or something."

"We just want to ask him a few questions, Father."

"Brother," Brother Samuel corrects him.

"Should I seek legal counsel?" Brother Samuel asks. Why does this big Frankenstein motherfucker who been terrorizing me all these years all of a sudden sound like a pussy and even more confusing, like he's in my corner?

"Well, that's up to you, Brother." The short cop seem like he does all the talking. "We'd like to keep this as simple as possible." At the door of a room that looks like every room on TV I have ever seen where they slap the shit out of you and accidentally kill you, Brother Samuel rushes up to me. He puts his hand on my shoulder and looks in my eyes. I let him in, notice that his eyes are not really blue the way Brother John's are but are some kind of deep purple, the color of the sky when the sun's been gone an hour.

"J.J." His eyes widen, he squeezes my shoulder. "You must tell the truth, do you hear?"

I nod my head. I know this big-ass freak is telling me to *lie*. Lie my motherfucking ass off. I feel old, real old, and real smart.

No, I went to bed at the same time I always go to bed. What time is that? Nine o'clock. Did you look at the clock? No. Then how do you know it was nine o'clock? 'Cause that's the time we always go to bed. Did you get up at all during the night? No. Do you usually get up at night to go to the bathroom? Yes, I mean no. What do you mean, J.J.? No, I mean sometimes I do, sometimes I don't. Did you get up tonight and walk down to Dorm One? No. You got up tonight and walked down to Dorm One, didn't you, J.J.? No no no no! What are you getting so upset about, J.J.? You touched Richard Jackson, didn't you? No. Was this the first time you touched him? No, I mean, no, I never touched him. You know what sexual intercourse is, J.J.? Did you have sexual intercourse with Richard Jackson tonight? NO no no I never had sexual intercourse with nobody! I start crying, I'm scared, but my middle name is *no*. Don't be scared, I hear somebody say. I look up, it's Brother Bill, but he's not talking to me. He's talking to Richie Jackson. Is that who hurt you, Richie? I don't know. You said— The cop cuts Brother Bill off. He looks at Richie Jackson. Is that who touched you tonight? It was dark, I couldn't see, Richie says. Get him outta here, the cop snaps like a pit bull. How old are you? he asks me. He just turned thirteen, Brother Samuel says. I didn't even see him come in the room. He must have come in behind Brother Bill and Richie. Let me take the poor lad home, Officer. This is all some kind of terrible mistake. We run a tight ship at St Ailanthus. I'm sure J.J. didn't do anything wrong. Alright, let's call it a night, the cop snaps, then, looking at me, Get him outta here.

I know I'm a good boy. Ask Mrs Washington, ask Brother John. Richie Jackson is a liar. A big liar. If he wasn't a liar, I'd be in jail. Brother Samuel and I walk down the hall when we get back home. His black skirts go *swish-swish* as we walk past the eyes of the photographs on the wall staring down on me. Brother John is waiting for us at the door of the dorm. The three of us walk to my bed. It's stripped down, no sheets, no blanket. Just the black and white mattress covered in plastic even though I'm not a bed wetter. On top of the bed is a big brown suitcase, open and empty. Brother Samuel looks at Brother John, then he turns and walks out of the room. It's still dark outside, but the light from the parking lot is coming in through the cracks in the curtains of the window over my bed. I can hear the breathing of the boys still asleep and the strained silence of the boys not asleep, laying still, trying to hear what the fuck is going on. Which is what I'm wondering myself, what the fuck is going on?

"Pack," Brother John says.

"Huh?"

"Pack up your things and don't be all day about it."

I look at him, but he has turned his back and is facing the window. I pull out my trunk from underneath my bed. I got on my basketball shoes, reach for my loafers, which are right beside my trunk and next to my rubber shower thongs. I put them in the big suitcase. Next I put in my other two pairs of jeans, my sweat pants and NYU sweatshirt, and my Nike jogging suit. I'm trying to put everything in neat. I never knew I had so many socks. Put in my briefs, pajamas. "Get your suit," Brother John says. I straighten up and walk over to get my suit from where it's hanging on a hook on the wall near the window, then I reach for my school uniform, jacket, vest, and pants that's hanging on the hanger behind my suit. We give Mr Lee's wife our dirty uniform once a week, she give us back a clean one for a dirty one. She talk like Mrs Washington: *J.J., boy! If you get one inch taller, it's gonna be all over! Ain't gonna be a uniform in the house'll fit you.*

"Leave it!" Brother John says.

"Huh?"

"You don't need to take the uniform. Get a move on! We don't have all day for this nonsense!"

I put my blue suit in with the rest of my clothes and my miniature chess set in a box that opens out to be a chessboard. Mrs Washington gave it to me even though I don't know how to play chess. I put my calculator that runs on solar energy, red purie boulder marble, and my toy clown Gonza in. Against the wall in my milk crate is all my books. You don't have to lock books up, nobody steals them. I look at my *Norton Reader, Earth Science for the Intermediate School, The Complete Works of William Shakespeare,* which is loaned to me without me asking from Mrs Washington, *Twentieth Century Art*—

"Just"—Brother John's voice sound funny now, less black, like, I don't know—"just take *Hamlet* and your other paperbacks."

I put *The Call of the Wild, Narrative of the Life of Frederick Douglass, An American Slave. Written by Himself, Bury My Heart at Wounded Knee, Crazy Horse, Black Boy, David Copperfield, Indian Chiefs,* Donald Goines's *Dopefiend,* and *Hamlet* in my suitcase along with my loose-leaf binder. Brother John hands me the brown leather bomber jacket he got out the donation box for me.

"Do you have anything in the bathroom?"

The long glass shelf under the mirror appears in my head, the little section that's mine with my name written on a piece of masking tape taped above the glass, with my toothbrush, toothpaste, and Mennen's underarm deodorant and Vaseline lotion from Mrs Washington, *Don't walk around all funky and ashy.*

"Yeah, I got some stuff."

"Well, go get it."

When I push the door open into the hallway, I hear Brother Bill shouting, "How'd he end up here in the first place if he has family willing to take him!"

"Brother John liked him—"

"Brother John *liked* him! Brother John *liked* him! What the hell is that supposed to mean, Brother Samuel?"

"It started out as an emergency placement—"

"This kid is here *illegally* because someone liked him! Are you crazy? Do you know what could happen if this harassment thing gets in the air and they find out the perpetrator is illegally living on the premises because someone liked him? For God's sake, there is a thing called the law!" Brother Bill is screaming like hysterical.

"Well, he *was* an orphan. Three years ago we had a different—"

"I don't believe this—"

I open the door and step out into the light and walk down to the bathroom to get my stuff. I don't believe nothin', everybody's a liar. I hate Brother Bill, he cares about everyone else, not me. I get my toothbrush and other things from the bathroom and head back to Dorm Three. I almost bump into Mr Lee, who's coming through the door too. He looks over his shoulder at me, shakes his head like he's sleepy, then walks up to Brother John and hands him a manila envelope and a plastic bag. Brother John hands me the envelope.

"These are important papers—your birth certificate, your parents' death certificates, immunization records, and other papers. This"—he hands me the plastic bag—"is the stuff from your locker."

It's my picture of my mother's friends and my two letters, kaleidoscope, and other stuff.

"Make sure you put them in a safe place when you get to . . . to where you're going."

I put the bag and envelope on top my loose-leaf binder and close the suitcase. Brother John picks up the suitcase, and I follow him out the door staring at his big ass, then the floor. I don't know where I'm going, but at least I won't have to hear his fake nigger accent anymore.

It's still kinda dark outside. At the end of the sidewalk, a car is parked. The driver sits up like he had been sleeping. Brother John asks him to open the trunk.

"I'll get it," the driver offers.

"Don't bother," Brother John says, and puts the suitcase in the trunk, then opens the rear door for me, and I climb in the backseat. Brother John looks like a giant old lady in his long black robe. I pull that robe up and jam my dick up her old asshole like it's paper! Cut her throat! I fall back in the seat look away from Brother John at the back of the driver's nappy head, then out the window at the swish of Brother John's black robe up the sidewalk walking back into St Ailanthus. The car pulls away from the curb.

WHY? WHERE I'M GOING? I ain't did nothing wrong. I'm a good boy! I'm not a homo, I didn't do nothing to Richie Jackson. They, *he,* even said he couldn't see who it was. I know it wasn't me, and now because of that bitch I'm being sent away? Where's this car taking me? I'm gonna run up on him one day and like kill his ass! I . . . I get so . . . so depressed when I think about motherfuckers telling lies on me I don't know what to do—

"Here we are," the driver says, pulling up alongside the curb in front of a big tree.

"Huh?" We ain't been riding ten minutes. It's just barely light out. I look out the window. The tree has grown so big it has grown into the protective iron gate surrounding it, the stakes of the gate sticking out like a barbwire crown. Broken glass and a big pile of dog shit so big an elephant could have dropped it is on the ground in front of me when the driver swings the door open for me to get out. I don't move.

"Come on, man," the driver says. "This is you."

He walks around to the trunk, takes out the suitcase, my suitcase, I guess it's mine—a present from St Ailanthus? He sets it on the sidewalk. I, a part of me, still don't believe this shit done happened. How could anyone believe I did some weird shit to Richie Jackson? They're crazy.

"Come on, man." The guy yanks the door handle, pulling at it even though the door is already as open as it can get. Cool, cool, I try to respond cool like a man. "Hey, man, where you taking me?"

"I done already took you, little brother, you is here."

"What *here,* man?"

"I don't know *what* it is, all they tell me is *where* it is and *who* it is. So, you know, 805 St Nicholas Avenue, man. This is your new crib."

I don't know what I'm going to do, but I know I gotta get out this dude's car, which I do, stepping over the pile of shit onto the sidewalk. I go to pick up my suitcase, he tells me chill out he'll carry it. The streetlamps blink off by the time we get to the front door. Morning. I look at the words over the numbers on top the door, ST NICHOLAS ARMS. What's that? The driver touches the iron-gated glass door, and it swings open, ain't no lock, nothing, we just step inside like Yo! Ho! Ho! Hello. The lobby is like a huge dirty white cave covered with graffiti from the filthy cracked used-to-be-white floor tiles on up the marble walls tagged NEMO, Ja Rule, someone on the fifth floor named Bettie is a ho who will suck anybody's dick, even the high domed ceiling is tagged, how they get up there?

"You goin' to your folks?" the driver guy says.

"My parents are dead," I say. What's all this "folks" shit? I hate niggers talk all corny.

"Say here 'St Ailanthus temporary emergency placement. Permanent placement with grandmother Ms Mary Johnston and great-grandmother Toosie Johnston—' Say your grandmother currently in hospital and when she returns home you are to be placed with her—umm ..." His voice disappears in the lobby, then comes back even more confused. "Hmmm, she musta been sick a long time."

I look at him, stupid shit! I feel like I'm out on Coney Island in the House of Mirrors, where every real shit comes back distorted. *You're* real. The distortion is an inaccurate reflection of you caused by the use of fucked mirrors. Bent mirrors, elongated mirrors, wiggly mirrors—but shit ain't *you*. Or is everybody all of a sudden on fucking acid or E? He looks at me stupid like he is, big-lipped black motherfucker. I stare at him with as much hate as I can muster up. Man, if this jigaboo stupid ol' motherfucker say one more word—

"Yeah—" he says.

"Yeah WHAT!" I scream, and rear back to leap on his ass.

He drops the suitcase and whips out a gun. Whoa!

"Yeah *this*, motherfucker. You move on me, kid or no kid, your black ass is dead. I don't know what your problem is, but I get paid to drive people, get it? Drive motherfuckers, deliver 'em to the door of where they going, stand there until someone open the door—someone whose name is the same as the one on the piece of paper they give me, then stand there until the door closes behind the motherfucker. You dig? *You dig?*"

"Yeah."

"I ain' done nothin' to you, brother man. *Nothin'!*" He looks at me like I'm that pile of shit that was in front the car door. "You done got use to pushing people around, ain't you? The world ain't a bunch of little kids, my man." Then his face changes back into the face it had been before he pulled the gun and he picks up the piece of paper he had been reading from.

"Now, like I was saying." He sticks the gun into a holster under his shirt. "She must have been sick a long time, 'cause, OK, you was supposed to go to your grandmother's house when she came out the hospital—naw, must be a typo or some shit, that was four years ago—I'm just telling you what it says. Well, you all can straighten all that shit out, the details, later.

"Go on." He nods toward the elevator, signaling me to walk in front of him. In the elevator he slides his back up against the wall, still holding on to the suitcase. "Press six, we're going to Apartment 610." He stops, looks at me. "You alright, buddy?"

"Yeah, I'm fine." You asshole.

"This is it," he announces as the elevator stops on the sixth floor. He follows me out the closing doors. Everything seems slowed down. I look at my feet. They're moving. I hear the feet behind me moving. It's not that I'm dragging my feet but that the air, yeah, the air is providing so much resistance. I feel like I'm walking through water. I see her face in it, ripply but clear. Funny, I been trying so hard to remember, so long nothing, and now everything is so clear.

"Come on! Get a move on, brother man!"

It's not me, I want to tell him, it's the thickness of the air, or water, or whatever's rising. "I don't know where I'm going!" I shout back at him. Fuck his gun. Hallway stinks, pee. I wish he would shoot me! If I had the gun, I'd shoot myself. The hallway looks like it's been painted with blue snot. She's so pretty. Her hair smells like perfume.

"Six-ten, this is it. Stop! Ring the bell!"

I look down at my shoes, bigger than the driver's. I should jump him, let him kill me, but all of a sudden I never been so tired in my whole life. I'm too tired to jump him. Plus I never had a fight with a grown man before. I'm only thirteen. The place where the bell should be is a bunch of wires, painted the same weird color as the hallway, sticking out a hole in the wall.

He knocks on the door hard. First nothing, then I hear some feet, not walking but dragging, shuffling like scrape-step scrape-step *stop*. Hear the thing over the peephole move back, feel the door get ready to open. Remember the snotty-eyed collie at Miss Lillie's. Shit, I had forgot all about that. Hail Mary Mother of God blessed art thou among sinners and blessed is the fruit of thy womb Jesus. The door opens. The driver reaches in his pocket! But it's for the scrap of paper, not his stupid gun.

"Is this the residence of Mary Lee Johnston and Toosie Johnston?"

"Who wanna know?"

"Ma'am, the Black Star Car Line, driving for, doing pick up and delivery for the Bureau of Child Welfare, Services for the Mentally Retarded and Lincoln Hospital Outpatient Services in the Bronx. Are you Mary Lee or Toosie Johnston?"

"Who you?"

"Oh, man!" The driver is getting pissed. "I ain't got all day. Lady, is this your grandson or great-grandson?"

"Gotta be, he look jus' like his daddy, jus' like his daddy."

She's short, real short. Bent over, if she wasn't looking at me, I wouldn't be able to see in her face, which is dark and deep-lined with wrinkles. Ashes to ashes. She's old. Do old people like that fall asleep and die when they're asleep? Miss Lillie said that about somebody once. *How y'all? Come on in, you ain't scared of dogs?* Big tall yellow ugly fat in her pink polka dots. I hate dogs! Old Batty Boy, I kill you now, dude! I feel a surge of anger. No living relatives! Smell funny in her house. Her eyes are yellow. It's obvious she ain't my relative. But if the brothers lied about this shit, maybe they lied about my pops. But this bitch ain't none of my nothing! Grandmother or anything else.

"OK, now I'm gonna ask you again one more time, ma'am, are you Ms Toosie Johnston or Ms Mary Lee Johnston?"

"I tell you what, one of de somebodys you talkin' 'bout is dead, so shut up!"

The driver look like he want to shoot her now. I hope he does. He don't say nothing, though. She got on an old no-color dress, like a rag almost, like something from slavery movies in Black History Month. Air coming out the apartment stinks, old fried chicken grease, mothballs. *What happened to this little boy doll here?* Ophelia floating down the river, STUPID!

"Ain' nobody but me—"

"Me who!" the driver shouts.

"Toosie Johnston!" she shouts back, and he shoves my suitcase inside the door.

"I wanna go back!"

"No happenings, man. I got things to do. This done already took me twice as long as it was spozed to! You know what time I was there to pick you up? Git inside, man. Adjust yourself. Stop acting stupid. These are your peeps."

She pulls the door open wider. I walk in past her. She shuts the door. The driver's footsteps are disappearing. She gets in front of me, I pick up my suitcase and follow her down a vestibule, then we turn into a long dark hallway lit by one dangling lightbulb that reminds me of the cartoons where the giant opens his mouth to swallow you and his tonsils is dangling. The hallway is painted the same blue as the walls outside of the apartment, the linoleum floor looks like black and green paisley flowers or something. Some places the layers of linoleum is worn through to the wood. Doors on either side of the hallway are closed tight. Five doors. The old lady walks slow dragging a leg, this is slow like erosion, Brother John always teaches about erosion, the slow gradual wearing away of the earth's surface. I can't imagine myself as old as her, maybe she's sixty maybe she's a hundred? The rank smell is getting stronger.

"Come on!" she says. I look down at her, her hair is in snowy white little braids. I start to laugh, the laugh gets caught in my lungs somewhere. She drags her leg 'cause it's swollen like an elephant leg, the rest of her is crunched and dark. Come on *where*? On my right are three doors, on the other side of the hallway are two more closed doors and an arched open doorway that's probably the kitchen. She pushes open the first door on the right.

"Dis yourn." *Yourn?* This is THE HOUSE OF MIRRORS! Goddamn! "I'm yo muh'deah. Call me Muh'deah or Toosie, your mama useta call me that steadda Gran'ma." Mine? Toosie? Muddy? "I don't rent out this room no mo', I never really did. It useta be mines, ya know." No, I don't. How the heck would I know? I look down at her, her dress look like she cleaned a bicycle chain with it. I— This is all a weird mistake. I ain't staying here with this . . . this witch.

The room looks like it's for a lady or old people or something. There's a big old four-poster bed and a large wooden wardrobe. And in front of the bed up in the corner is a tall oval mirror and next to it like a vanity table with a skirt around it. There are two windows with the shades pulled down. Everything—the bedspread, the linoleum, the skirt around the vanity table for putting on makeup—is this ugly green and black color in different designs: the curtains and bedspread is like green and black forests, and the floor is green and black paisley linoleum. Two chairs are upholstered in the forest. A roach is crawling out a big crack in the linoleum toward me, ain't even afraid. I don't get this, I got a home, a bed. I feel like someone cut my heart out and is eating it in front of me. I feel stupid, wild, lonely, like after my mother die everything just fall apart.

"Gone put yo' stuff up." What time is it? I put my suitcase on the big bed. *My* bed is a kid's dorm bed. Today is like when my moms died, only it *ain't*, today ain't that day, and there's been a big mistake and—what time is it? I really should be in school. Another roach crawls toward me, like to show me who rules. It's what, about seven, eight o'clock? 'Bout this time I usually be in school. I run over to the window, try to lift one of the dirty brown shades and it comes a loose crashing to the floor! Outside, the sun is shining. Yeah, by the time the sun is up like that, I usually be in school. Yeah, eight o'clock I usually be in school, but I'm here in this dingy-ass room. Look like the green and black forest is alive or some shit, advancing on me. What am I doing here instead of school where I should be. Goddamn, this is a horrible-ass mistake! Brother John said himself he was very pleased with my progress and that I would for sure be in the computer class next semester. For Chrissakes! Holy Mary Mother of God! Today is what, Thursday? My first class is English Select, which I'm already late for! I'm never late to class. I love that class, school. If I don't be a dancer, I'm gonna be a computer programmer or something when I grow up. I better not have missed class! Select is very special, it's a privilege to be in it. We're a group of boys that read ahead in our English text, *The Norton Reader*, which is really for high school and college kids. We select the text we want to read, discuss and write about it. (We never pick anything easy.) *We* picked *Hamlet,* not Mrs Washington, even though she's a fucking Shakespeare freak. Also what "Select" means is we're selected from the pool of students based on our ability and previous performance to be in that class. I must be fucking bugging, BUGGING! To be sitting up in this . . . this roach hole when I got a class, *classes.* I open the suitcase and snatch out my brown leather bomber jacket. Even if I missed English, I can still make earth science!

I bust out the room into the dim hall, the lightbulb dangling like it's gonna drop grabs me for a second. Then I breathe in the last of this funky hole and break out. Out the front door and down the hall. It seems like by the time I exhale I'm on the street. Running! I'm fucking flying! On my way to school! I strike out down St Nicholas and don't stop for air until I hit 135th Street. I turn on 135th Street, run past the old elementary school, the Jehovah's Witness Church, the police station, YMCA. Everything's a mistake, what was I doing there, wait'll I tell Jaime and them about the roaches! I zip past the Schomburg, the whole shit there with all that dope shit because one mean old white lady told the wrong Puerto Rican he didn't have nothing to be proud of. Spic, nigger, whatever he was, spent the rest of his life showing that shit up. That's what I should have done to Brother Samuel's ass when he raised his freak-ass eyebrow when I said African dance class. I shoulda said, Yeah, motherfucker, *Af-*

rican, like the beginning of the world, motherfucker! But I just reacted childish. That's probably why they feel they can pin a false rap on me now, like I can be the fall guy for someone else's shit.

I turn on Fifth Avenue, slow down, look down the street at the bricks, concrete—St Ailanthus. Shit yeah! I ain't crazy, this is where I'm supposed to be—school. Some kids are coming out the main entrance, first-graders. Preemies, we call 'em. Brother Bill is the teacher for the little kids. He looks up from the preemies, who look like a bunch of penguins in their black vests and white shirts. He stares at me, glad to see me! All I can think is, where's my *Norton Reader* and my loose-leaf binder? I don't even have a pencil! Mrs Washington told me once, "How *dare* you come to my class without a pencil, talking about you serious about learning and you don't even have a pencil!" I brush past the preemie penguins make me laugh to call them that, and Brother Bill, who turns and runs in the opposite direction from me. What's up with him? I turn and run up the stairs, Room 206, 8B English Select! I sit down in my seat. Mrs Washington is looking at me stupid, but she's not stupid. She's a doctor, Brother John told me once, but not a medical doctor—an academic doctor. Her dissertation was on some of Shakespeare's shit. We lucky to have her. She could be at some big university instead of here with us. Mrs Washington is standing in front the blackboard, which is green. She has on a gray skirt and a white blouse. In the front of the room in one corner is an American flag and opposite it in the other corner, white with a gold cross in the center, the St Ailanthus flag. Jaime turns and looks at me, his eyes scared. He mouths, *Papi,* without making no noise. I get open. Bobby Jackson is looking at me stupid, I stare him down. He turns around.

On the board is our work for the day:

1. Pre-class writing to be done in your notebook; take ten minutes to write . . .
2. Review your notes and prepare for a short quiz on . . .
3. Today is the last day to hand in the topic for your term paper.

Brother Bill, Brother John, and Brother Samuel are at the door just standing there like long white shadows in black robes, perfectly still, not moving even one little bit. More light than I ever seen is coming in through the window; light like paint spilling over everything, everyone— Mrs Washington, the boys, spilled over with light. It's a circle of white light rising up all around us. I feel warm and good like I do when I'm dreaming.

Maybe I am dreaming, 'cause just above my head I think I see Hamlet, he looks like Kurt Cobain. He's so beautiful. But his voice sounds like, *just* like my mother's. He's telling me something important, *very* important. But I can't hear it because of stupid shit. J.J.! J.J.! LEAVE THE PREMISES IMMEDIATELY! What premises? That ain't Hamlet. COME ON! NOW! UP AND OUT! What kinda shit is this? *You're really doing great stuff in English.* AAAAHHHHHHH! You're HURTING ME! Hurting me! STOP twisting my arm! You hurting me! Brother John! Help me! Don't! Don't! Don't let them! It's an animal screaming, not me, 'cause only animals or girls scream that loud. AAHHH! My arm! Oh, oh God, my shoulder my fucking shoulder. Now a flash of red in front my eyes, then black, black. Falling. Everything black.

"WHERE AM I?"

"You're in the emergency room at Harlem Hospital." That's Brother Samuel's voice. It sounds flat like it's cut out of paper and each word is floating through the air. A white square. Blank. I feel high.

"What's wrong with me?" I whisper.

"That is just what I was going to ask you."

GUY IS DRIVING SLOW. It's gonna be dark soon. My shoulder is numb frozen, but whatever they pumped into me is starting to wear off already. I'm gonna be hurting soon. I haven't even enjoyed the good feeling of riding in a car, which is something I almost never do, 'cause I know where

I'm gonna end up. I'm thinking exactly that as the car pulls up in front the same dark heap of bricks I was at this morning. Shit! I don't want to go back in there. I feel deep down sick. Deep. I see the nasty little white braids on her head like crawling insect larvae, the swollen dragging leg, greasy dress, and all I can think is, what is going on here, what the fuck is going on? I should be home, we'd be through with rec period, eating dinner, then homework. TV till 9:00 p.m., then bingo—bed! But I'm here.

I'm waiting on the driver to get out and come open the door for me. My shoulder is starting to get a tingling feeling like lots of ants is walking around in it, running up and down my arm, stingie stingie. Try to make 'em disappear by closing my eyes, and the green and black linoleum appears swimming in my head and turns to a mass of teeny little green and black spiders teeming inside the paisley shapes. I'm still waiting for the driver to open the door, so I won't get out. I won't move. I will just sit here with these spiders and ants crawling over me. But the driver doesn't move. He just sits there. I'm so tired, and the stuff they gave me for my arm—

I'm drifting off when the driver says, "You know what time it is?"

Huh? I don't know what he's talking about, but I know that voice, it's Mr Lee! Janitor at St Ailanthus.

"You know what time it is?" he say again.

"Huh?" I say.

"You know which way is up, boy!"

He's almost shouting, what's with this gray head? He must be bugging, I don't know what to say.

"Answer me, boy!"

Boy. Excuse me—

"Answer me!"

"I . . . I don't know, Mr Lee. I don't know whatchu mean."

"You done did bad." *Done did bad.* Mr Lee another nigger from the slave movies—yes sir, no sir. He even call the brothers at St Ailanthus "sir." *Yes sir, Brother John, sir.*

"I ain't did nothing!" I holler at his stupid ass. Then I remember him not looking at me like I'm shit when they call him to mop up the piss, urine—whatever on the floor after Brother Samuel attacked me.

"Don't make no difference," he says. "They say you did, and that's how the bricks fell! Ain' nothin' you can do about it now. You kicked outta school. All the way out. You almost brought the police down on the place whether you did or not! So you back to your peoples—"

"What peoples! My people dead, man!"

"Well," he said in his stupid country-sounding voice, "you tell me, sonny."

"My name ain't Sonny!"

Fed up with me, Mr Lee leans over the backseat to open the door. I say fast to stop him from putting me out, "My mother died when I was nine and my father when I was real little. I don't know who my father was. I just know he's dead. I'm an orphan," I say to him, you know like *duh*, "that's why I'm at St Ailanthus."

"*Was* at St Ailanthus."

What's he talking about? He gotta know all this shit is some kinda joke or one of their weird behavior-changing modules or some shit. I know they gonna let me back in St Ailanthus. They probably just want me to say I'm sorry or some shit. Any minute Brother John'll be here with his big ass talking about it's all a mistake or *I hope you learned your lesson this time, dude!* and take me back.

"You may be an orphan, boy, but you got people! I don't know why you was put in St Ailanthus. Maybe didn't no one come forward when your mama died. But you got family, according to this, this here say you going to kin—grandma, sister, great-grand. Anyway, you here. So gone and git on wit' it."

Grand? What kind of shit is this fossil trying to run on me, and why? He don't even know me, nothing about me. He oughta stop talking shit. I oughta . . . oughta . . . I don't know what.

"Nobody never told you you had people?" It feels like there's no oxygen or something in the car. I'm getting tireder and tireder! I wish Mr Lee would shut up and leave me alone. But I don't want to be left alone. I want to go back home. I must have thought aloud, 'cause Mr Lee says, "You *is* home, sonny. You may not like it, but this is it, for the time being at least."

My arm is really tingling now, feels like all these little ants have thorns on their feet. Feels like when this shit wears off it's gonna hurt, hurt like fuck.

"You musta knowed your mama had a mama?"

"No," I finally answer when I see that the question is not going to disappear but swirls in the air in a green and black paisley-patterned question mark teeming with teeny-weeny spiders.

TWO I get out the car. It's almost dark. Streetlamps glowing like white pumpkins. Walking through broken glass, that's how I feel—shattered, fucking shattered. This ain't spozed to be happening to me. It's not. I'm a good kid. This feels like a long time ago on 125th Street after my mother's funeral and some stupid lady is telling me, *You're going to a foster home.* When? *In the morning.* It was like the movies or cartoons, where the guy is standing and the trapdoor opens and he falls out from under his own feet screaming down to hell or someplace where he gets drowned. I don't get life until I get to St Ailanthus. Now I'm standing here falling screaming through the world again.

"Come on, J.J."

My arm feels weird, my stomach too. I ain't going back in that foul house. I wanna run, but where, where I'm going? Kill myself? Jump in front a bus or some shit? Then it's like I'm back in the cartoon again, but I'm through falling. The water's in me. It's over, I'm drowned. So what difference does it make?

"J.J.!"

OK, OK, get off my back. "I'm coming!"

"Well, come on. I'm goin' up there witchu. Lord knows I don't want to see you get in no more trouble."

Feel like I'm disappearing with every step I take, like my bones radioactive, like in cartoons, glowing. A light is pouring out from inside me, like God. *God!* God or . . . or Crazy Horse. Crazy Horse riding, killing, kill Custard or Custer whatever that motherfucker's name was. Ahhh! Shoot a arrow through your heart! Ahhh! Tomahawk your ass!

Whew! That shit's crazy, man, I know it. Mad crazy! But I'm glad to get mad. Mad, I can feel my feet on the concrete. Mad, I remember a little boy thought he was a Indian, got hurt by other boys. I didn't like that and I don't like *this*. I don't like being kicked out of school behind no motherfucking lying-ass kid! And the brothers? Liars! LIARS! Anybody ever know the shit they do! What Brother John and Brother Samuel did! Please! I'm just a kid, a *boy*!

I look at Mr Lee walking beside me, shuffle, shuffle. I'm glad I'm not old. What's the use? Easier to kill old people. Old people so fucking mean. All they care about is theyself. Kids wouldn't be so fucked up if it wasn't for them. How could this be happening to me!

Mr Lee stops when we get in front the lady's door. "Go on, now." Like I'm spozed to knock. Hell no, I ain't knocking on shit! Why should I? I hang my head down. I'm staring at the dirty floor. This is a big building, it looks like the blue-snot—turquoise, I guess you call it—painted hallway goes on almost to the next block.

"Must be nice to meet up with your folks after all this time. I seen it happen before. A kid be around a year or two, then they peoples get it together and come git 'em. Lucky thing to have happen."

Lucky my butt! *Draw a timeline of world events during Shakespeare's lifetime, 1564–1616. What was happening in the Songhai in 1591 (hint: see,* Africa in History *by Basil Davidson), Jamestown, Virginia, in 1607. What was the first Chinese dynasty to leave behind written records? Reread Gertrude's account to the king of the killing of Polonius. Does it square with the facts? Compare what happened with her story.* What for? Who gives a fuck? *Creep is a slow imperceptible downslope movement of soil. Less than 25 precent of the earth's surface can be used to grow crops.*

Mr Lee knocks on the door. "I hopes they ain' gone to bed."

I'm looking at the splashes of turquoise paint the sloppy painter left on the floor, almost the same color as the swimming pool at City-Rec.

Marijuana smoke coming from somewhere and around five feet away a puddle of strong-smelling piss.

"What time is it?"

"When you gonna learn how to say please, boy?"

"Please." You know please, please, *please*. What does he want from me? Mr Lee knocks again.

Same old lady as before opens the door. Now what?

"Boy! Whar you was at?"

Whar you was at? I just stare at her. "Who are you?" Who does this bitch think she is calling me "boy"?

"Shit, you don' know who I am, you don' know who you is."

Mr Lee shifts his weight from one big dirty work boot to the other, clears his throat. "Well, guess we'll come in."

"Whatchu want?" she spits out at Mr Lee.

"I jus' want to get the boy settled in. I'm Mr Lee, the custodian—"

"Janitor!" She snorts.

"Custodian and night attendant down at the school."

"I don' know nothin' 'bout no school."

"Well, it's been a long time, leastwise looking at these papers it's been. Whatchu say your name was, ma'am?"

"I didn't say. You go on 'n git outta here."

"Naw, I ain' gittin' nowhere. I came here to drop the boy off wit' certain people. If you ain' the people, I'll take him round to the Bureau of Child Welfare."

"Oh, fo' land's sake, come in! Stretch yo' eyeballs out yo' head, see if I care."

"Your name?"

"Toosie Johnston."

I follow Mr Lee, who's walking down the hall behind the lady. I feel grateful to him and shit but don't know how to say it. She stops in front of the door of the room my stuff is in. Mr Lee pushes the door open, and I follow him in the room. The old lady stays out in the hall.

"Well," he says, sticking his head out, slow jerking it around like a turtle. "This ain't too bad. If it was me, I'd take a bucket of water and ammonia to it 'fore I lay my head down. But I done seen worse, this here is alright."

Then he turns and walks out the room. I hear his footsteps on the creaky hall floor, the door open and close. I feel like running behind him and kicking his old ass down the stairs. But I'm tired beyond being alive. I feel like I died and am my own ghost instead of me. My suitcase is on the bed, I don't remember leaving it open like that—oh, yeah, to get my brown bomber jacket out. Only I'm back here, no jacket. All this shit is wack! They wouldn't do this shit to me if I was a girl or a Spanish or white kid. I sit down on the bed shaking my head. My arm is tingling needles and pins. Why they do that shit? Jumping on me twisting my arm like they never seen me before. I'm tired, I want to lay back on the bed, but I don't let myself, I can't. I gotta *do* something. Maybe Jaime gonna break me out, come find me. He's my friend. Maybe everything gonna be the same. I could still go to dance class. That ain't gotta change. We useta have so much fun. Like back in the day at my old elementary, we useta have mad fun. The guys always doing crazy shit. Steal stuff from the bodega, the fat Spanish guy be chasing us down the street, stomach going flop-flop. How come I can see the guys' faces so clear, and I can't see my mother's face? My arm is burning now, aches. HURTS. I don't want to cry. I can't cry.

But I do cry, cry my arm burning, my mother dying I want my mommy Brother John I thought you was my friend. How could I be here, be sent here, in a stinky house with a woman if you was my friend? Why is my life happening like this? This like WHAP! Miss Lillie's house, my ear singing, blood in my throat. Now what's going on? Where's my bomber jacket? I never got my black leather jacket back from Miss Lillie's, none of my stuff. What is this shit! Why me? Why me! My head hurts, my arm hurts. I get up, fuck this shit. FUCK this shit! My head, my arm. I go to the mirror hurting. Look at myself. I see someone big tall dark almost pretty but like a man. Jaime say I look like Denzel Washington. I don't know. I look like a man 'cept I ain't got no beard. I got jeans, regular fit, not baggies, we not allowed to wear baggies, white T-shirt that's dirty, and I'm crying. Tears is coming down my face. I don't feel myself crying, but I see it. I am hurting. My head my head my mother my mother! *You ain't got no fuckin' mother!* SHUT UP! *Your mother is a dope-addict ho died from AIDS! Na na nana naa naa!* Batty Boy's big head is floating in the mirror his long arms sticking out my black leather jacket turn into Brother Samuel pulling the black leather hood over his pink face. EEH EEEHH NO! NO! NOOO! Shut up fucking assholes! I see myself grab the sides of the mirror slam my head as hard as I can into the glass, breaking their faces. *You ain't got no mother.* NO! NO! I ram my head into the mirror again so hard I hear the wood frame crack. A big shard of falling glass slices open my cheek before it falls and shatters on the floor, everything is blood and broken glass now but quiet, no voices. I fall down on the pile of broke glass and sob, like people in movies. Moan, like Hamlet.

"You done broke de mirror!" Ol' bitch hollering at me. "You know how old dat mirror is!" I can't get with her voice, like it don't really connect to me but float over me, like it ain't real, maybe none of this shit is real, me laying on glass in the salt-metal smell of my own blood, this old roach room.

"Go away!" I holler at the old nigger slave.

"Git up 'n sweep dat glass up, Abdul!"

"My name is J.J.! Not no fucking Abdul!" I scream back. I can tell I'm gonna hate her. Have to, for pretending to be my relative. I already do hate her.

"Fool, number one better learn yo' name! Number two git ready fo' seven years of bad luck unless de old folks down south is lyin'! Git up 'n stop actin' stupid, you might have to go back to de hospital. Go wash yo'sef."

I get up and walk down the hall to the bathroom, press my body against the sink, and stare at my face in the mirror. Blood is dripping from the top of my head. I put my hand there. It's wet. I pull out a big sliver of glass red with blood. It cuts my hand. I drop it in the sink. There's a jagged pink line where the falling glass sliced open my cheek. I think of Crazy Horse riding into battle with lightning bolts drawn across his cheeks. How I know that? We never study Indians at St Ailanthus. My face hurts bad, but I feel good. The pain and blood make me feel hot. I put my hand in my pants, touch my dick. Hard. The piece of glass laying in the sink looks like a bloody sword. I feel like taking that piece of glass and carving my new name on my forehead. CRAZY HORSE! Goddamn it! Niggers know not to fuck with me, see I been in battle! I will kill! I want to get on a horse and like ride out to St Ailanthus and kidnap Jaime. Then ride on out of there. I drop the piece of glass back in the sink.

"Git in dere 'n sweep up dat glass! I done had dat mirror since befo' you was born. Is you crazy!" The old bitch is hollering outside the bathroom door.

Am *I* crazy? *She* must be totally bugged out to be talking to a total stranger who would be happy, *happy* to kill her old ass because he gonna be a dancing star and don't come from this stinking shit! I am very intelligent, Brother John said so, *It's just that you're so . . . so grown-looking, or it would be easy to get someone to adopt you. The people want little children, but they like intelligent kids too, winners. You're a winner, J.J. Did anyone ever tell you you're beautiful? I was raised in Harlem, J.J. I know what's going on. You're special, real special. Now, come over here. . . .*

"'N when you git through sweepin', report to me!"

Yeah, she's crazy, crazy as one of these roaches on crack. I look down the dingy-ass hall. Time to break out of here. Perfect day to die! This is the third time my life been shaken like my kaleidoscope. God or somebody just pick it up—broke pieces of glass, mirrors at right angles, shake that shit, twist the lens, whoosh! A different picture. God don't care how it hurt you. It's a done deal. Can't go back.

Flipped like cook do pancakes. Flip Flap Clik Clak. I remember sticking a fork in my hand. Was that yesterday? Last month?

As I stagger back down the hall, I look at the ugly linoleum floor decorated now with drops of my blood. I look at the holes worn through to the wood, the weird black and green paisley pattern. The place before St Ailanthus, what color was the floors? I don't know, something weird.

At St Ailanthus? I can't think. Oh come on, I was just there today, or was it yesterday? Fuck it, what's the point in thinking about that shit now? I don't get it no matter how I try, how could a kid be normal? Normal! Have friends—everybody at St Ailanthus love me, my mom love me. How could I end up tossed salad? Thirteen? How I'm gonna be put out of school, my bed? My house. St Ailanthus is my home! I live there. And some assholes can just call me in a room and tell me to pack! And send me to some ol' nasty house like this. Shit, I ain't staying here. I slam the door.

I look around at the bedroom walls. I'm used to a clock, knowing what time it is. She knocks on the door. Opposite the door on the other side of the room are two windows. I could just charge the window, jump the fuck out and end this wack shit now. But that's stupid! I'll never get a chance to dance I do some triple-stupid shit like that. I keep forgetting about my dancing. She pushes the door open.

"Abdul—"

"Stop calling me that!"

"Telephone!"

"My name is J.J., you old witch, remember that shit 'fore I kill your ass!" I'm screaming right in her yellow-eyed, black-prune face. She don't move. She don't blink. I feel like a rock sinking to the bottom of the sea. *Topsoil is irreplaceable.* I'm so far away from anything that makes sense. Old bitch, let her call me Abdul again. I feel enough hate to kill her. I feel wasted. I collapse on the bed. She shuffles out the room. I'm not sorry to be talking to the old bitch like that. I'm sorry for *me* because I'm not raised like that. At St Ailanthus we don't talk to grown-ups bad. I'm a St Ailanthus kid, I got a future. I don't usually scream at people, threaten 'em, but I don't usually feel like I'm losing my mind. Can the brothers just put me out my house overnight like that? Can Brother Samuel and Brother John do that shit to me they did and then put me out for nothing? I squeeze my eyes shut to not cry again. I see Brother John black robes flowing like water his dick pink. My first day they look like Batmans, the brothers. I'm only nine years old. *We'll take care of you. It's a shame you've lost your mother and father. But you have a mother and father in us here at St Ailanthus. We love you and will take care of you until you're a man and can take care of yourself, J.J. All the boys here go on to college or trades—would you like that?* What's a trade? My mother wants me to go to college. I want to go to Callie, Disneyland.

I gotta talk to Jaime. Maybe he knows what's happening. Why I got lied on. Busted. Kicked outta school. Shit, what time is it? I'll have to sneak back to see him. Where is he now? *What's up, dude?* I'll say. My arm hurts, this is the second time Brother Samuel done fucked me up. I try to shake the scene of me on my back that giant pink-ass freak pinning me down while I piss on myself. But then he had my back at the police station. Brother John was nowhere around.

The door creaks, Slavery Days sticks her head in. "Look, nigguh, somebody on de phone waitin' to talk to *J.J.*"

Nigger? Who do this bitch think she is, calling me a nigger! She ain't no kid. I ain't no grown-up. I gotta go see Jaime. I turn to check myself out in the mirror, forget it's on the floor in pieces. Good. Better that damn mirror than this whole fucking place!

"I said, telephone."

She's still standing there? Jesus! Best to ignore her, obviously she's crazy. Somehow between St Ailanthus, Harlem Hospital, and back here, I lost my bomber jacket. And that was a dope jacket. Where would Jaime be right now? I don't even know what time it is. I don't want the brothers going crazy on me like, shit, yesterday? Or was it today? Time? I'm not even sure of the fucking day! It's like a hallucination instead of my life.

So, OK, what now? I'm representing for myself, by myself—a false victim of a crime of lies told against me by people who don't like me. If I knew what time it was, I could figure out where Jaime would be. I look out the window. Are they gonna leave me here for long? I can't stay here. This is insane. I rather sleep in the subway. What Mr Lee mean with his "You musta knowed your mama had a mama" shit? And the other guy, the driver, with his shit! Motherfucker pulling a gun on me! I should kill Richie Jackson. No, everyone'll think I'm a punk laying on a little kid. Kill his fucking brother! He's little, but he's my age. Their lies done caused all this shit. I almost got killt by police, then Brother Samuel twisting my arm around my back like that. I look at a spot on the wall where a roach is climbing out a crack, then at the pile of broken glass on the floor, the dried blood. I can't stay here. I look out the door down the hall with the lightbulb hanging cheap-looking, dim. Sad? I start to holler at her, like, Hello Looney Tunes. What time is it! Then it's like fuck it, lemme just get the hell on out of here.

Air on the street smells good. Fresh. FREEDOM! I wonder who was calling me. Maybe I should have answered the phone? Could have been Brother John telling me the shit is worked out? I doubt it. Yeah, I doubt it. Jaime? How would he have the number? And ain't no use going by St Ailanthus unless I want them to kill me with their crazy asses. I get Jaime on Saturday at dance class. Now lemme get with what day it is. Wednesday? Three o'clock, 5:00 p.m.? I ain't never been around this neighborhood before. I ain't that far from St Nicholas Park. More trees around here. Blue sky over broke-down apartment buildings. Head toward 145th Street?

Twenty-four hours? A day ago? I was living at home, my home, a Catholic home for orphans. St Ailanthus School for Boys. Get up at six, make bed, wash, pray, eat breakfast, go to school. My life was ahead of me. Now, a day later, I been waken up out of my bed, taken to the police station, falsely accused of bullshit, made to pack my bags and driven to a hole in hell in the middle of the night. Then I go back to my home and they attack me! I get taken to the hospital, then *back* to the Slavery Days Roach Motel.

I see this old lady coming toward me on St Nicholas Avenue. "What time is it?" I ask her.

"Time for your butt to get a watch!"

Damn, what's that all about? Now I be a monster if I snatched that shit off her wrist. I run down to the subway. The side of my face is in crazy, stupid pain, mad pain. Between my shoulder and my face, I don't know which hurt worse. What can I do? I can't go back to St Ailan-thus and request to see the nurse, tell her, *Oh yeah, I'm here 'cause Brother Samuel, Brother Bill, and Brother John jumped on me, twisted my arm till I passed out, put me in emergency.* No, I can't say that, I can't say I'm tired and hungry and kicked out my home. That don't make no sense. Nobody thirteen is spozed to get kicked out their home, especially not for no lying bullshit. I remember hot piss, Brother Samuel throwing me on my back. One minute my feet was on the ground. Whap, next minute I'm on my back! Whole dorm looking on. You tell me that big faggot should get to do shit like that and walk! That's not all he did to me, that's just what people seen. So all that they do is just peanuts and popcorn, just par for the golf course! OK 'cause we kids? Brother Samuel did mean things to me, *mean,* I think, running down the stairs.

Clock on the wall next to the token booth says three minutes after four o'clock. Jaime's checking the salt and pepper shakers, setting the table for dinner. He got KP. I wonder who was calling me on the phone, some kinda way I got to see Jaime, get a message to him. I ask the guy in the token booth.

"What day is it?"

"Thursday."

I stand, blink. Thursday? That's dance class, maybe I catch him at the door before class start.

"You OK, buddy?" the token-booth guy ask me, his voice strange com-ing through the microphone behind all that Plexiglas.

"Yeah, I'm OK," I say slowly. I touch the top of my head lightly, and when I look at my fingers they're all bloody. Then I flash—BING!—*my jacket's at Harlem Hospital!* I run for the stairs. Token-booth guy probably really think I'm crazy now. My T-shirt all bloody. Something's sticking me. I got a piece of glass from the damn mirror in my jean pocket. I didn't even feel it. Just lemme go git my fucking jacket! Whoa! Glass in my fucking shoe, now, well, it's really my sock, which makes shit easier, I just take 'em off. So I'm leaning against the wall next to a bodega on 145th Street taking off my shoes and socks. People coming home from work

111

stare at me, but only for a minute. They life probably ain't no cupcake either, even if they is grown up and got a job.

I, SHE? No, it's me I think, make the nurse in Emergency crack up laughing. I look at her, she look at me, we both say at the same time, "Wasn't you here yesterday?"

Even though I was out of it, I remember her: black black skin, blond afro, and a pink metal nose ring hanging down to her blue lipstick. Forget that? I don't think so.

"I left my jacket here."

"You got a hole on the top of your head," she says. "What's your name?"

"I jus' want my jacket."

"Well, I need to know your name, people leave stuff here every day, we put it in a bag with their name on it and hold it here thirty days, then we dispose of it."

"Jones."

"Jones *what*?"

"J.J."

She comes back with my jacket and a big bag. "Jamal Jones?"

"Yeah."

She points to the top of her head, then slides her finger across the side of her face like a knife cutting it open. "Who did that to you?"

"I just want my jacket."

"OK, OK, big man! No more questions! Do me one favor, pleeease!"

OK, she did get my jacket. She look like Village people. I listen for her program.

"No questions, no problems, no nada! Let me get one of the students to sew up your head and put something on the side of your face."

"I'm getting my face tattooed where that shit is!"

She looks at me like I'm crazy. *I* don't even know why I said that.

"No, no! Honey, you let that bad boy heal, you hear me. Give that three or four *months* before you get any damn tattoo." She looks both ways, then pulls the short sleeve of her white uniform up and shows me her tattoo, one of those Maori kind. "Is it phat or what!"

It is.

"When your face heals— Oh, here come gonna-be-a-doctor-one-day Wang. Don't say *nothing*, hear? Just let him do his thing. I'm gonna spray some stuff on your head and face, numb you up a little, OK? And I'm gonna wipe some of that dirt off the side of your face, OK? Then I'm gonna have Wang give you a little shot. He's cool."

"What do we have here?" Wang look like he could be my age.

"Just do it, Wang. Look at his head and hurry up. J.J.'s in a hurry, ain't you, J.J.?"

"Yeah."

"I was telling him where to get his tattoo. I got mine at Hades in the Village. Where'd you get yours?"

"Same place," Wang say. "I got my piercings there too."

"Cool," Blondie say.

"We gonna do the right thing, stitch you up and stuff—"

"Give him some of that time-release."

"Don't worry, Williams. I got my mojo working." They crack up laughing!

The whole shit, stitches in my head, shot, seems like it don't take but ten minutes. I don't know how I look, but I feel better, my face feels better, my shoulder too.

When I go to leave, Blondie hands me my jacket and says, "This nigger won't be needing this no more!" and hands me the bag she had brought out earlier.

When I hit the street again, I'm right on Lenox Avenue and 135th Street around the corner from dance class. I open the bag. Whoa! A pair of black leather pants and like a leather jockstrap or some shit? I'm not sure. I open a sealed manila envelope, there's a watch, two little gold hoop earrings, and a gold chain in it! Well, whatever, Blondie! I wanna run back and give her a hug, thank her, or do something! But I don't want to get her in trouble. Shit, probably everything she did was illegal! But shit, it was *right*.

I was gonna warm up for class if I was early by running around the track upstairs, but when I get there I scope Imena sitting in a little circle with some of the students. Some blue-black dude in African clothes is in the middle of the circle with some statue or something. Everyone's eyes is on him. I go over to see what they're looking at.

"Nkisi is a religious power object," the guy is saying.

It's horrible-looking, whatever it is! It's about two feet tall, a statue kind of. Of a . . . a African? It has real big lips.

"This is from the Congo peoples."

He's carved from wood and has nails stuck all over him! They should keep that shit in the Congo. I look upstairs at the track I could be running around. Poor little thing even got nails in his head! Beads and rags is hanging off him and in his chest it looks like a—

"Yeah." The African guy notices me scoping. "That's very old, but it's a mirror in his chest. I guess if it was made in America nowadays we would put a TV screen in his chest, that's how we see ourselves reflected in this culture? But this is a nineteenth-century art object."

Art? Please! I hope Imena ain't paying this dude to talk to us. She don't need this, she already got a bunch of people taking class for free. Blondie say the spray will wear off in an hour, the shot won't wear off until tonight.

"When was the nineteenth century?" one of the girls ask. *Stupid bitch,* I think.

"From 1800 to 1899," Imena answers, but the girl still looks confused.

"So yes, it was in the 1800s, I'm pretty sure, late 1800s. Wood objects are now known to have a much longer life than we thought. But what you see here is not the original sculpture. A lot has been added to it since it was first created. Each nail was driven in by a member of the community, or 'tribe' as you like to call it here. Beads, bits of birds' nests, feathers, and scraps of folks' clothing were added during the time the object was residing with the tribe. Each nail driven in or scrap added speaks to some moment in the life of the owner or owners—some of these objects were owned collectively."

"How does the Nkisi speak?" Imena asks.

"Well, some of this is conjecture. But I imagine that the power of the Nkisi is one of transformation. Think of Jesus on the cross, his suffering for the people. Instead of them dying for their sins, he died for them. Nkisi absorbed and transmuted the pain and suffering of the tribe. So when starvation or the suffering and dislocation that came as members of the society were either attacked or put on the run by slave traders, the people drove a nail into Nkisi, because Nkisi could take what they no longer could."

Dope! Dope! Dope! I believe it! But, "What's 'transmute'?" I ask. Mrs Washington say ask questions, even if you feel like a fool asking 'em. Don't ask and you'll *be* a fool! Ha! Ha!

"'Transmute' means to change from one form to another," Imena answers me.

The African dude looks like he's getting ready to cry. He leans over and hugs Imena. "This class has been like a refuge for me while I was studying with those depraved people. Every day was a psychological genocide. You think you can imagine that shit down there, but it's unimaginable how they hate us. They have projected their evil onto us and institutionalized it. What's worse than white people?"

What the fuck is he talking about! It feels like the shot is getting stronger in my body, not weaker. I got to move! Imena looks like she don't know what to do—the guy is crying now. He gives her the thing. "I leave Nkisi with you. It means what you make it mean." Then he stand up over it. "It can't take any more real nails, so I drive in a metaphoric nail." He raises his hands like he got a hammer in one hand and a nail in the other. "I won!" He comes down with the hammer. "NYU, you didn't kill me. I won!" He comes down again and again. "This nail is for all the crazy shit, four fucking years of it, then the internship and the residency! Nkisi!"

"Well, let's thank Brother Abubakar and wish him strength on his journey." Everybody claps except me. I just wish he would get his crying ass out of here so we can dance. What kind of kid wants to see a grown-up cry? I look at Nkisi. Imena is looking at me, at the side of my face. I look at the piece of glass in the creature's center, the mirror. He's scary. I blink at the faded mirror in his chest, think of my kaleidoscope revolving, the picture changing. An illusion Brother John said was created by mirrors at right angles. Fuck it! Fuck it! *FUCK IT!* NYU, Nkisi too! Forget all that shit! I came here to dance. I get up, take off my jacket. Lay it casual against the wall, put my bag from the hospital next to it, and like nothing has happened begin stretching out. I look up from the floor where I'm spread out in second position and Imena is staring at me again. I look down at my T-shirt, spattered with blood. I pull it over my head, ball it up, and throw it in the corner with the rest of my stuff. A lot of guys dance without shirts. Imena is saying something to the drummers, meaning we're gonna start in a minute. I get up, roll up the legs of my pants, and go get in the back line with the rest of the men.

"This is a dance for Xango," Imena says. She raises her arm. "He got the *oshe*, that double-headed ax. He's the Orisha of lightning, dance, and passion." She looks at us. "That's what a dancer does. We're like lightning rods, channels, for God. African dance ain't about kicking up your leg, African dance is about spirit!"

I listen to the beat, bah dah dah DAH! One two three FOUR! I don't care what it's about, I just wanna do it! I start to move across the floor, the drums seem like my own heart beating. A guy has a long string instrument, it's pure fire! The music rocks, my body turns into an ear hearing it. My body is not a stranger, not a traitor tricked by white homos in black robes, not a little boy in a hospital bed, not a *man*—big, shiny, and black that makes the brothers look at him. Here my body is my own, here I am a Crazy Horse dude who never gave up. Here I am like that dude Brother John told us the Schomburg got started by, here I am music, I never been to no police station for lies about little kids, here I got a mother and she ain't no ho die of AIDS. Here in the beat is my life. The flute shrieks and I come again and again and can't nobody stop me.

Sweat is pouring down my bare back. I could do this forever. Some of the niggers here is professional. What's that? They do they shit for money that's supposed to be better? Shit, I rob if I have to, beg too, as long as I can do this. Sound wreck me it's so beautiful!

"Shit, man, what the fuck is that?" I ask the dude next to me.

"Oh, man, that's a Brazilian instrument, the berimbau! It's out there, ain't it?"

I never heard a sound like that before in my life. It gets me open. I want to get the fuck out of these jeans. MOVE. Shit, I'm dressed, it ain't like I ain't got on no drawers. The sound cause me to float. My head opens up, and I go with my heart. I feel so sad I could cry, but I don't. I just listen harder to the music, the sound between the one, try to move my body more better like the professionals, like some of the big sisters who ain't professionals but dance better than them dance like . . . like Crazy Horse LIGHTNING! I am too gonna get a tattoo across my cheek like zigzag lightning. A picture like of a finger with a gold ring, no hand, just a little finger, a gold ring on it, bleeding, floats through my brain. Why that? That shit Blondie spray me with ain't no joke! What it be like to stick someone like Blondie, lick Wang boy's tattoos? What I'm gonna get pierced? I seen a picture of this dude what got his joint pierced once. The berimbau music is slowing down even more strange and beautiful. And I feel like Cinderella one minute to fucking midnight, except it's my head gonna come off, not no fucking glass shoe, and instead of a mean stepmother I'm gonna have a psycho slave walking around talking about, *Boy! Whar you was at!* Or I'll be fucking homeless. January I'll be fourteen years old. A man if I wanna be. Who's to tell me different? Before I hear the last drumbeat, I know it's gonna happen—that *when* I hear the last drumbeat, I'm gonna collapse. That all of a sudden my body will feel like it's been arrested, jumped on, arm twisted, run all over Harlem twice, chemical sprayed, sewed up, and drugged up—that when the music stops, the room will go round and round and I'll fall like broken glass.

"My jacket!" I point, falling.

"Get his jacket!" I hear Imena say. "Is that bag yours too, J.J.?" I nod. I want to get up, run away, but can't, I'm tired, real tired. I feel my heart beating. My head is beating too—bong! bong! Shit it hurts! I turn my head—Jaime! He looks away from me and runs out the door.

"Where you live, man?" one of the drummers asks me. I think of the roaches crawling out the cracks in the green and black linoleum, sigh, think, just for the night, just for the night.

"805 St Nicholas Avenue, man."

"Avenue or Place?"

"Avenue." I guess. My head is going BONG! BONG! now. My arm feels like it had a thousand little needles in it that was asleep, that's starting to wake up and prick me. I feel like shit, but I feel OK too. Yeah, I hurt, I got to go back to the roach motel, but I danced! I never danced before like I did tonight. Brother Samuel, pit bull police, my mother checking out, my father dying in the war, none of that, nothing, *nobody*, no-fucking-body can take that away from me. Fuck Jaime! Fuck everybody! I take my jacket and bag from Imena, let the drummer put his arm around me and help me up.

I follow him and Imena, who I assume is his girlfriend by how she's acting, out the gym and down the stairs. I'm holding on to the railing as I go down. Fifteen minutes ago I was like a god, my body was under my control, like Jaime. I was like . . . like Xango throwing lightning bolts or Crazy Horse at the top of the hill. Now my knees fucking Jell-O.

Of course I realize when I get in the car Imena done made her boyfriend give me a ride. I get ready for the third degree. And sure enough—

"What happened to you?" she starts to grill me.

"Nothing."

"Come on, J.J., that shit on top of your head and on the side of your face is 'nothing'?"

"It's OK," I say.

"Tell me what happened, J.J."

Boyfriend gotta put his two cents in. "How long you been coming to class now?"

"A few months." What's that got to do with anything?

"Well, you wanna keep coming to class, you gotta talk to Imena here."

"Don't tell him that, Ibrahim. He doesn't *have* to tell me anything, *and* he can keep coming to class. Have you been messing around with drugs, J.J.?" She looks at Ibrahim. "Where you going? It's only around the corner, at the Boys' Home."

"He said St Nicholas Avenue."

"You moved, J.J.? You not at St Ailanthus anymore?"

I feel seasick even though I'm not in a boat. I'm too tired to cry. I just want to be left alone.

"J.J.! Did those freaks do this to you? Answer me!" Imena is really upset.

"Look, man, we just wanna help you. Imena is not gonna call the pigs or nothing. We . . . well, look at you, man, you had blood on your T-shirt, stitches on the top of your head, the side of your face sliced open. You was dancing all . . . all erratic and shit, man, and then you fall out! We brothers and sisters, man! You wanna be an African dancer, then you wanna be part of a community."

"Artists stick together, J.J. If you can't tell us, who can you tell?"
Nobody.

"How old are you, man? Believe me, the ball is in your court. We ain't gonna say nothing to those Catholic freaks or nobody else. Them homos make a move on you? Them freaks beat you up?" Ibrahim is all beside himself now.

"How old are you, J.J.?" Imena asks.

"Thirteen."

"Whew! You know you look older, man? Way older!"

"It's true, J.J., you look older than thirteen. If . . . people . . . I don't know. So what happened with the Catholics? They move on you and then kick you out or something?"

"Something like that," I tell her. "I fought back, they fucked me up and brought me to Harlem Hospital. Then from there to my relatives, who is real old."

"Real old? Where's your mother and father, J.J.?"

"My mother died in a car accident, and my father got killed in the war."

"Uh, what war?" Ibrahim asks.

"I'm not sure."

"Well, who are these old relatives?"

"I don't know."

"You don't know?"

I wish Ibrahim would shut up and not ask me no more questions.

"Well, J.J., just tell us who these old people are before we take you there," Imena pleads.

"Imena, take it from me, we ain't getting the whole story. I don't know what it is, but we ain't getting it," Ibrahim says.

They're talking about me like I'm not here or three years old.

"Look at him, it's obvious he's been traumatized. It's not his fault. J.J., *please* tell us, to the best of your ability, who these old people are." Imena sounds like in the soaps or something.

"Well, after my mom and dad died, I got took to St Ailanthus 'cause my only living relatives couldn't be found. Then after I got kicked out of St Ailanthus, they found 'em, 'cause they had to have somewhere for me to go."

"Imena, we ain't hearing the full story."

"And we're not gonna tonight. Let's just take the boy home."

It's dark already. We pass everything again, the school, the Y, police station.

"This is it? You said 805?" Ibrahim asks.

"Yeah," I say before I even look. I was starting to fall asleep.

"Want us to come with you?" Imena asks.

No, I want you to leave me alone. I can handle this. "No thank you." It's just a ol' slave, weird stink. Ain't being whatever St Ailanthus was. A lie is what it was. "St Ailanthus Home for Boys"! Ain't no fucking "home." I'm sleepy, I'm tired, I'm cold.

"See you Saturday. Don't worry about money, hear? Just come to class. I don't want you to stop coming to class, OK? *OK?*"

"OK."

"Good night, J.J."

"Good night."

"Lil' bastard didn't even say thank you," I hear Ibrahim saying as the car pulls out.

"For God's sake—" Imena says. I don't hear the rest of what she says.

Well, if I'm gonna stay here, I gotta have a key. I can't believe— Oh, fuck it! I got kicked out of St Ailanthus for knocking one of the brothers out when the faggot moved on me. So big deal, here I am. It happened. Next!

She—I guess her—*somebody's* cleaned up the glass when I get back in the room. I ain't gonna say nothing to her, just keep it like it is, like when I came in the house, I didn't say nothing. She ain't my mother or nothing. I ain't staying here too long. No use in getting all buddy-buddy when my being here is just a mistake. I'll soon be outta here. Soon.

Some towels on the bed. What's that spozed to be, a hint? Can't be, the way she look and how this place stink. But I take 'em and walk down the hall to the bathroom. I need to shit, but I'm all constipated. Laugh, think maybe ain't none in me, maybe the police scared it all outta me at the station. Be good to take a shower or bath.

All I got in the world is in that suitcase back in the room and that bag what I got from Blondie, leather pants, watch. I know I got a couple or at least one pair of pajamas in my suitcase. I go sit on the toilet, grunt, groan a little, feel like at first I'm full of the glass I broke earlier. Then finally whoosh, I shit, shit. Feels good, like the past twenty-four hours is coming out my asshole. Like it's over, outta me. Smells horrible, though. Open the window, night sky black computer stars dots of light. The night air smells clean. I never felt so old in my life. Shit, actually, I guess I never *been* so old in my life.

I turn on the water, all the way hot. Even though I got all these cuts and scratches, I want it hot. The washcloth is soft dark pink, the new bar of soap sitting in the soap dish say Camay. It's *pink,* a girl's soap. I wanna be disgusted, but I'm not. It smells nice. St Ailanthus, Irish Spring, is that a man's soap? Or the House of Faggots soap. Do they fuck each other or only us? Not do, *did,* 'cause I'm gone, past tense. Here now, a free motherfucking kid. If they fuck each other, they homos, if they only fuck us, they dudes. The water is hot. I stick my foot in. Burns almost. I plunge my body in. I wanna be clean. Like after confession. Brother John says you're in a state of grace, if you die right after confession with no sins on your soul, you go straight to heaven.

The opposite of grace is *dis*grace, dirt, polices, lies, sperms. I want it off my body. Off my body, my body of a free boy, felt good to shit. My body of dance, felt good to dance. Fuck them! Fuck all that shit 'cept dance. The water feels good now. I feel my lips on Jaime's neck. I feel so warm, like on ganja or some shit. Don't make no difference if I had one leg, then I be a one-leg dancer, if I was two feet tall, then I be a midget dancer like at the circus, but I'm not a midget dancer, I'm more like God. God see through walls, eyes big and dark pools like Brother Samuel's. I see outside the walls now, a door is opening, the elevator door is opening and a big, fucking lion is walking out the door, spraying shit from his dick like territorial markings. Lion roar AAAAAHHHHHHHH!!!! I'm there, feel scared. Shit, I must be fucking bugging, for a minute I think this shit is real, forgot I'm sitting here tripping. Ain't no lion out there. So why do I think wack shit like that? Shit, 'cause I'm wild! A wild child! A free fucking baby! I'm black! I love to be black. I'm a boy, I love to be a boy! I'm strong six-pack all that! The hot water feels good, burns my scratches, but feel good on my shoulder. I wash like Crazy Horse rode, don't care if it hurt, I like to hurt. I wash my face, splash water on top my head, easy now on them stitches Wang Wang give me.

I wanna be loved. I want someone to open me up like I did the kids and Jaime. Ram me up with love like useta be Brother John and me? *Love,* not like fucking dickhead stupid Brother Samuel. But warm like water. How come don't nobody like me? That's stupid! A lot of people like me. A lot. I'm rubbing the pink soap all over me, thinking about love and jamming and what it be like being a dancer, a professional, what it takes, and the water is good and fucking hot, we only take showers at St Ailanthus. I ain't there no more, thinking that, I get to feeling all creepy, all alone, and it's more than I can deal with, long stupid I don't know. What the fuck, shit, what the fuck I'm thinking is stupid, I got to *do* something. I don't think but see myself like a movie slicing my dick off. Then I'm burying my own body, but it's not me, it's a girl, little storybook girl golden. Rape her. *Something*. I should be in a house getting everything I need, getting good clothes, good food and things and places to go, and I should have a mother and a pops, I should have good shit, I should not be coming apart inside. It should not feel like the cracks in the plaster is me going *crack eeek errrecch* down the wall driving me stupid. When I put my feet on the ground, the ground should not move I should not feel this way I don't understand how a good kid like me could have a mother die of AIDS. Why my mother. Why my mother. Turn on the hot water *hot* that makes me feel good yeah I feel good the hotter the better water feels so good I want to go to sleep I want to dream, call Imena and her drummer-ass boyfriend to come back back back and save me like on TV a parachute outta burning plane getting ready to explode open in rainbow colors. I wanna fall down slide down down deeper in the tub into the warmness of the water and feel how good it feel to have Jaime kiss me there *kill* me there my dick dick dick penis penis how it's a fire a big fire that don't burn you but freak you. I got that feeling, those feelings, let me love you let me love you let me love you I can hear drums break like waves along my balls down low down low it's aching me aching me I need together a place a suitcase pack pack pack a car is waiting a car is waiting to take me away like I was never there never there like I never was there like I never was.

Creepy quiet here. But it ain't quiet like when you really all alone. *Somebody* is here. So where's the old lady? Behind these doors. What's behind all these doors? It's like three on the same side of the hall as the room my suitcase is in, including mine. *Mine?* Then across from me is another door, and down from it the kitchen doorway. So where's her room? Who is the old broad and what am I, a rubber ball or some shit? Hit the ground and I be bouncing up somewhere else next week? This is a nice bathtub, big. This is a weird old apartment, feel like it got ghosts or monsters. One time we seen a BIG cat. Ugly like a monster. *Pregnant,* Jaime said. Jaime threw a brick at it, I threw one too. *Bad luck,* Amir said. Why? *It's pregnant,* Amir said. *It's black, bad luck,* I said. *You ain't spozed to hurt nothing pregnant!* What's pregnant? I wondered. *It was black!* Jaime said. If I was grown up, I would expose St Ailanthus as a camp of terror and cruel shit. Catholic school spozed to be so much better than public school, but they forgot a few little shits! Like beating up and fucking kids. And this shit here, you know, like pack up and get out, J.J., nice knowing your black ass. I can't just let that shit go. What would Crazy Horse do— what would my father do? If somebody did some shit like that to him? The water's getting cold 'cause I been sitting up here with the window wide open. I run the water hot, like a hot spring coming from the earth's interior; in school we learned about people going out in the snow sitting in hot springs. Due to volcanic activity, the rock near the surface is still hot enough to boil water! The water comes up hot even in the snow! I'm gonna stop going to school? I mean, what's up? Can school teach me how to dance? If I was a professional, I could run away somewhere and be a dancer, get paid. Water warm, I'm sleepy again. Nod, see a walled city like in photographs of China, ancient and all green, tigers, which makes me open my eyes and get out the getting-cold-again water, I got enough problems. I dry off and head down the hall past doors harboring big pregnant black cats.

My pajamas are big maroon and white stripes, just like all the other boys at St Ailanthus, unless their parents or relatives buy them something different. Some kids in St Ailanthus got parents that's alive. Most of 'em ain't. Now, it's not no whole row of striped pj's getting ready to bunk, it's just me alone, one boy, one bed, one striped pajamas.

> *Now I lay me down to sleep,*
> *I pray the Lord my soul to keep.*
> *God bless our parents, here or departed,*
> *God bless the Brothers of St Ailanthus,*
> *God bless all the children of the world,*

including myself, God's dearest lamb,
and God bless the sweet little Lord Baby Jesus.
In the name of the Father,
the Son, and the Holy Ghost.
AAAhhh MMMmen!!

In the dream I'm paying attention to Imena, not just waiting for her to shut up and the drums to start. "Nkisi," she says, holding up the ugly thing with its lips like a black duck. Why is she showing us this shit! Are niggers ugly? Or are we beautiful? The walls of the gym change to dazzling white. Blondie appears out of nowhere in her nurse uniform and nose ring. She's holding this big jar. I think she's trying to psych me out, but she can't, can't no fetus in a jar blow my mind. I already seen that shit in don't-do-IT-until-you're-married-because-IT'S-a-mortal-sin abortion videos. But it's not a fetus. It's my penis in the jar!

"Hey, how'd you get that!"

"It's OK, J.J., I'm just going to pierce you, then you get it right back. Right, Wang?" Wang nods his head. He's looking at her big beef nipples poking out from underneath her uniform. Wang nods again, and she sticks a corkscrew into the jar, which has turned into a dark green champagne bottle. It pops open and my penis shoots out of the jar spraying!

"What's that!" I scream.

"Champagne, silly rabbit!" she says in a TV voice, and disappears. I feel my crotch. I'm all there, hard as shit. Wang is down on his knees in front of me. I'm worried the class won't know he's a doctor and will think he's sucking my dick.

"This dog's skull on its head—" It's the African from NYU.

"Ugh!" one of the stupid girls screams.

"The serpent's vertebrae around its neck—"

"UGH!"

"—the sheer size and placement of Nkisi's head speaks to the dominance of the senses in the transmutation of spiritual desire—" He's saying the same shit he was saying in class. Blondie is gone, Wang too. I try to wake up, move, make sure they ain't got no part of me in their jar, but I'm paralyzed. I feel like I'm falling. My body is so heavy, it doesn't hurt, the falling isn't scary, it's sweet dark, down low I feel so good falling I just spread my arms and flying I'm flying back to where it's all green grass and the sky is so blue like the park when I was little. She's saying something I can't hear. I'm little running around and around in the grass. She has a gold ring in her nose. I hold out my arms, I'm opening and closing my fingers like gimme gimme. Everything is aching like when you wanna come, but I'm just a little boy. "Mommy! Mommy!" I sob. I hear birds like seagulls, but I don't see them. The sound moves something wild down deep in my gut. I open my arms wider. Light fills me. Everything is suffused with light. I never seen so— I never *been* so much light before. I'm a STAR born for my mother. I want to put my tongue in her mouth, kiss her. She opens her arms to me, and I start running in the grass. Squirrels that I'm usually afraid of don't hurt me. Trees is singing songs, have faces, leaves tongues, *everything,* even the flowers is singing. "You don't listen, Abdul," she says. "Listen." The trees is talking. She gathers me up in her arms and says something I can't hear. "What, Mommy, what?" She laughs kisses me. "You don't listen, Abdul," she says. "Listen." I'm running again. I know so many things, the brothers taught me how fast sound travels, that God is an indivisible entity known through Jesus Christ his only son. I'm only a little boy, but I know the name of things, rocks—igneous rock, basalt, granite, obsidian, sedimentary rock, calcite, halite, gypsum, metamorphic rock, marble quartz, garnet, and diamonds—and how fast light travels. I'm light traveling she tells me who I am what I'm supposed to do but I'm running so fast I don't hear it except to hear her say it but I don't understand how I can hear her and not hear her. I'm getting confused the sun is going down it's changing here. I look for her but she's gone and I'm falling again. I'm in assembly at Culture Night and the brothers is reading their poetry to us. We don't like it. Brother John howls, "Terror is the gravitational pull toward nothing!" Oh, no! I run behind my brain where the gravitational pull can't get me. Then all of a sudden I'm in a subway car hurtling through an endless dark roar. The clock in the ceiling of the car is blinking 3:00, 3:00, over and over. "SAY WHAT?" a voice blares over the loudspeaker. "SAY GET UP! THAT'S WHAT, J.J.!"

"Git up, nigguh! You gonna sleep yo' life away!"

Huh! The train stops, I sit straight up! In front of me a cracked wall paint peeling? Where's the other boys? I turn my head see old Slavery Days bent over in the doorway. Oh, no! The vanity table, the dried-out oval of wood where the mirror used to be glued to, the bench, open suit-case. Oh, no! Dull hurt throb my cheek. I touch the open cut on my face. Wet but not blood, clear ooze. I squeeze my eyes shut the train is pulling out the station! I look up at the ceiling, the lightbulb dangling, paint roll-ing back from cracks. Oh, Holy Mary Mother of God, No! NOOOOO!

"No my ass! Git yourself up and come git some breakfus'."

I smell bacon think of Rita, sitting next to her in the diner, her silky dress, perfume, she's stirring milk and sugar in my coffee. A big dude says something in Spanish and sets a plate of scrambled eggs and bacon in front of me. Rita's drinking coffee looking at me with her eyes big like a baby. I'm awake but I close my eyes I don't want to let her face go last face in my life loved me I want to go back to sleep.

"I said git up! Git some clothes on! You know how long you been sleep?"

Who cares? I look at the floor, my maroon and white stripes is laying there by the side of the bed. I don't remember taking them off. I close my eyes see the last car of a subway train disappear into black with my dreams and memories. Why do I like the smell of bacon so much? It's just the best fucking smell in the world. I wish this bitch would get out of here so I can go on and get dressed and get something to eat. I turn and look at her.

"Git up!"

"Well, I would if you would get out of here and let me get dressed." I try to talk to her like she got some sense, rationally.

"Like you got somethin' I ain' seed." She laughs. "Simple big-head boy! Git on up!"

Now, how I'm gonna get my pajama bottoms off the floor, under the covers, and back on? I lay there a second, then it's like what the fuck! I get up let it hang. She don't bother me. But she does, she gives me the creeps, the fucking willies, man, staring at me. All I want is some fucking breakfast and for things to get back to normal. She turns and walks out the door. Mission accomplished? If I ever had a doubt about this whole thing being a case of mistaken ID, I know for sure now, this old bitch ain't none of me.

Friday? Yeah, last night I was at Thursday night dance class. Before that? Here, then Harlem Hospital, then St Ailanthus, then here—805 the first time? Then hospital again? I don't know. I do know I started out at St Ailanthus. I had thought I was gonna be there until I was eighteen, then go to college for computers or English or something, maybe come back and teach at St Ailanthus if I didn't become a famous dancer. Now what? Same shit, different day, that's what. Well, whatever! Moving right along. My jeans and briefs is on the floor by the bed. I don't want to put that dirty shit back on. How my clothes gonna get clean now without no Mrs Lee and laundry like St Ailanthus? I got all these little cuts on my chest, rub my nipples, think of Blondie, getting pierced, and I am gonna get tattooed, maybe not my face but something. Where those leather pants? Shit, they fit! Shoes, and let's see what's for breakfast.

The kitchen is a big cruddy rectangle, two refrigerators next to a double sink, and the stove all against the long wall opposite the doorway. Up against the far wall is a table with two chairs and one place set. This is where I sit. She takes a plate from the stove and sets it in front of me. Bacon, eggs, toast, grits.

"What you want on yo' grits, margarine or jelly?"

"I don't eat grits," I tell her, then I feel bad like I ain't got no manners, but I don't—eat grits.

"Well, you got 'em on yo' plate now. Eat around 'em." She laughs.

Hah! Hah! yourself, bitch.

"Social worker was here Friday. She be back on Monday."

Social worker? Friday? She must be bugging.

"Today is Friday," I tell her.

"Naw, fool, today Saturday." She looks at the clock on the wall over the stove. My eyes follow hers. Eight o'clock? "You slept through Friday. Clean through it. Social worker was all in dere tryin' to wake you up, askin' was you high, did you have a history of sleepin' hard. All dat shit. She put 'monia under yo' nose, but you jus' near 'bout killt her slappin' at her. But you didn't wake up. She kept askin' he ever done this befo'. How I'm spozed to know, I ain' seed him since he was a little boy. Quiet is kept I ain' seen you den. But I don' tell her dat."

Her talking like this gives me the fucking heebie-jeebies, like her lookin' at me this morning like I'm a dog show, and now this shit—ain' seed me since—like she know me or some shit.

"But you wadn't wakin' up no kinda way! No sireee! I tol' her go on 'bout her business to somebody else's house. She don' want no one walkin' in on her sleep. She said she wadn't a child under supervision. I tol' her go on, just go on."

Maybe the social worker is gonna come get me outta here. "How long I gotta stay here?"

"How long? You home, Abdul. You cain't go back to de Catholic peoples. Whar else you gonna go? Don' nobody wanna adopt you. Thas why dey sendin' you back, plus you don' need to be adopted. You could go to a foster home or group house, she say, if this ain' fit fo' you. But why do all dat? I tol' her it was fit fo' yo' sister—"

Sister?

"At least whatever little bit of money I gits for you, I gonna give some of it to you. You ain' gonna git dat in no foster home."

I seen this Jamaican kid get hit once with a baseball bat by some black kids. WHAP! All the air knocked out of him. Shit too.

"Eat yo' eggs."

I do, six slices bacon, toast, and the grits too. Ain't nothing wrong with grits. I must of not been hungry before or they must of tasted funny 'cause I was a kid. But I'm a man now, and I'm so fucking hungry I could eat the plate. Where she get this weird plate? Blue and white with a rabbit in the middle of tall grass.

"Ain' no mo' eggs," she says, looking at my empty plate. "You want some mo' bacon 'n grits? Coffee gittin' cold, want some mo'?"

No! Shit, what about milk, old bitch? My bones gotta grow. I take a sip of the coffee. Why people drink this shit?

"Any milk?" I ask her.

"Jus' fo' de coffee, you don' put no sugar in yo' coffee?" She takes the cup and dumps the cold coffee in the sink and pours me some more. I put three teaspoons of sugar in it. She fills the cup the rest of the way up with Pet evaporated milk. Taste better, good.

Guess I'm grown up, what the fuck. I wanna ask her what's going on, tell me something! But then I'm not sure I want to hear what she gots to say. I think I just want the social worker to come take me away.

"Yo' grandmother—"

My grandmother? I'm on my knees, my nose is pressed into, breathing, the black leather of the armchair. Brother Samuel is sliding his dick into my asshole, everything opens up, my toes feel like lightbulbs turning on—one two three four five six seven eight nine ten! I love it. My scream gets caught in the black smell and how good it feels. Nkisi, the nails driven in—the Fon people—it feels so good to come—wheee, me and Britney. Then he takes it all away, sticking a nail clipper cutting my navel the pain. I'm convulsing. Tell, if you want to die, he always says that shit right before he puts that black hood over his pig face. Then he says, Tell me if you want to die. Kings and queens? J.J., maybe we were slaves of kings and queens. All we got is the art, and they steal that. Maybe it's our karma because we're a bought and stolen people. I don't understand. Don't try to. All you, we, got is Basquiat, Billie, Bojangles, and Bird! Bah dee bah dee bah dee dance if you wanna, J.J., gimme some love gimme some love. When the drummer uses the sticks on the outside of the drum, it adds another rhythm to the existing rhythm. This is not disco, J.J. What's disco? Don't worry about bullshit, just listen, *listen.* Listen to the rhythm, then move. *Abdul?* Old witch called me Abdul. You're moving to the rhythm. So did *she.* The rhythm is not moving to you. Submit. You're dancing to the heartbeat of the earth. Five billion years ago the solar system was a mass of whirling gasses. *Big-headed boy?* Excuse me! Who is that old witch talking to? What about Macbeth? Then the cloud shrank or was made to collapse by the explosion of a passing star. What about computers in 8A? French? Haiti, all of Africa, Puerto Rico, Cuba were all affected by the slave trade, the presence of the African in the New World created a new kind of dance. Jaime, Jaime! Come on, bite my nipple! Compression of the cloud's core material heated its interior—

ABDUL!

I look over at the stove where she's standing.

"Believe it or not, yo' mama useta do de same silly shit you doin', stare out in space fo' hours you don' knock her upside de head or somethin'. Like some kinda damn voodoo."

I wipe the egg off my plate with my toast, something a St Ailanthus kid ain't spozed to do. It lacks refinement and we're gonna be out in the world one day. *You don't want people to think you were brought up without—*

"Go to show blood is thicker den mud," she said.

Mud? Grandmother? Abdul? I get up go back to the room. My room? Who's my grandmother? And who is this old bitch? I thought *she* was my grandmother or something? It's Saturday? I went to sleep Thursday? Slept twenty-four hours away? Weird, fucking weird. I look in the wardrobe I guess you call it, the "where you hang clothes," hangers, a lot of hangers. My stuff is still in the suitcase, it's mine. I'm not sure about no grandmother and shit. I look from the wardrobe back to my suitcase. I'm gonna stay here or not? Simple question if you eighteen. Deep-shit question if you fucking thirteen. I don't wanna be no runaway sleeping under no bridge like some of the kids that split from St Ailanthus or fucking a whole bunch of faggots and shit for a Big Mac. Get AIDS for a shake and fries. I'm trying to have a future, like a normal life, go to school, college, be a famous dancer, why is this weird shit happening to me? Messes with my mind to even think about being connected to ugly shit like ol' Slavery Days bitch talkin' like a movie and roaches coming out of cracks. Should I hang up my clothes? You wanna dance? Imena say. Class and practice, J.J. You got to practice. You can't just depend on taking class, that's not enough. I start taking my clothes out the suitcase and hanging them up. I'm gonna keep on my leather pants today. I gotta get more stuff to dance in, like what the professionals got, shit like what everybody got! I'm the only one come in there looking all wack 'cause they ain't got the right shit to dance in. *You gotta take what you learned in class home and P-R-A-C-T-I-C-E. I don't know how to get that into your heads. Dance may be fun, but it's hard work too. Dance is greedy, it's like that, it wants everything! You have to get off your ass! You have to open up!*

Yeah, nigger, I tell myself, you gotta get open. I stand in front where the mirror was before it broke. I don't need no fucking mirror, I can feel my body. I pull my stomach in, my muscles. I ain't got no stomach. But even your muscles can hang, Imena say. Just 'cause you not fat, doesn't mean you don't have to work your body, J.J. Warm up first, J.J., then stretch. You're strong, which is good, but you're tight. You need to stretch. You should spend an hour every day just stretching, and then work an hour on your technique.

I sit down on the floor in second position. Leather pants too tight to stretch in, I put on my sweats. I need some new gear, that old bitch better give me some money. "I gonna give some of it to you. You ain' gonna git dat in no foster home." I know I want more than some of it, shit! I spread my legs out in second again. My inner thigh muscles, adductors, and hamstrings are so tight they feel like bands of iron. It'll happen, J.J., she says, not overnight, but it'll happen. Just breathe into your body and gently sink into the stretch. You'll be surprised at what happens. It hurts. I'm kissing Jaime. I never kissed no guy before. *Kissed.* Shit, I never kissed nobody before. I want to jack off, not stretch. Stretch, then jack off. Brother Samuel bit my nipples. I hated that, the way I couldn't help but scream, but once he did it, I knew I wanted Jaime to do it to me. Now Jaime's afraid of me like everybody else, 'cause of all the lies and shit they spread on me. I look at my watch, right on, Blondie. *Rolex,* I want to fuck her too. Twelve o'clock. Shit, if today is really Saturday, then that means class at 135 City-Rec at one o'clock. Imena said, Don't worry about money, just come. So I'm gonna stretch out another second or so, then I'm outta here. Only thing I know for sure is to get to class and dance! Don't let nothing get in the way of that shit, and maybe this other weird shit will all be over in a little while and I'll go back to school. But maybe that ain't gonna happen? The brothers is some fucked-up people. Why I wanna go back there anyway? Because I like it, because, shit, it's my home. Well, I don't know what happened to make the brothers go off on me, but ain't nothing I can do about it now. I'm gonna finish stretching out, then run to class. I try to grab my ankles, tug a little. My back makes a right angle to my legs stretched out to the side of me. I wonder will I ever be able to just grab my ankles and lay my stomach down between my legs like the professionals do.

I look around the big, square room. I feel like I'm in a green and black box. A roach races from his crack in the linoleum. Fuck roaches, I ain't no screaming girl. As much as I can forget—I want to, and move on. If I can't get back in St Ailanthus, then I just want to move on. I look at my watch, hey, time to go!

Warm out, I got time to walk. I could have left my jacket. My shoulder feels way better, but it still hurts. This is a whole new avenue for me, St Nicholas, but I also think this ain't too far from where I used to live in that foster home with Batty. I'm not sure. Well, whatever. I don't know, it should look stupid—high-tops and leather pants—but it's phat. I see how I look by peeping in other people's eyes when they scoping at me. Old lady looks at me as I pass, she's looking at my chest *hard*, then her eyes come up to the scar across my face. I guess I look like a hood or some shit all scratched up. How old would my mother be if she was alive, I wonder, turning my head back to look at the old lady scuffling down the street. I shift my bag to the shoulder that hurts, make it work. When I think of her, which I don't do a lot, it's like something on the other side of a door, stuck, pushing to get in. I don't know what it is. Gives me the creeps, like a fingernail down a blackboard. I'm glad I'm tall. If I was Jaime's size, I'd have to be dodging pigs all the time. Some kids at St Ailanthus was runaways. I never experienced nothing like that, really, just the foster home. When I think of the foster home, I think of Batty Boy,

WHAP! I feel that shit like it's happening again, whap! like a tennis ball my ear screaming but don't make no noise. Pain. Pain that makes me feel like fucking, why I don't know. Brother John was spozed to be my friend, his big ass was spozed to be on my side. Always talking about how smart I am, how most boys can't stay hard as long as I can, how Mrs Washington said this or that good thing about me, I could be an English major or could go to medical school like Asian kids. About the Schomburg, he been there, done research on things. Nurse say I have 20 percent hearing loss in my left ear. A part of me can't believe this minute right *now*—I'm walking down the street in a freak pair of leather pants that fit me perfect. I just left out of a old woman's house I ain't never seen until a couple of days ago. I'm just out here! I ain't got a dime in my pocket. I'm not sure where I'll sleep tonight.

Why does looking at the blue of the sky seem like it's murdering your heart? No clouds, hot perfect day. I pass the Harlem School of the Arts on my right. What do they do in there? How do you get in? Your school? Parents? I don't have either right now. On the corner of 141st Street, St James Presbyterian Church, big light orangish stones, I don't know what kind. St Nicholas Park begins across the street. It's different from Marcus Garvey Park, which is one big square. This park is blocks and blocks long. First you see just like a regular park, picnic tables, benches, handball courts, then your eyes are drawn up to the huge granite boulders cracking through the green grass bending the trees sticking up maybe a hundred feet in the air. Way on top of that mountain of rock is City College, its gray buildings like Hamlet's castle. Brother John said that's why New York is so strong, because of granite bedrock. Everywhere you look walking down St Nicholas Avenue you see huge glittering slabs of granite. Brother John showed us all this on our Rocks of Harlem earth walk. But these trees, I forgot them; he told us some of them. Everything on earth has a name. Imena said every muscle in the body has a name. They've cut into the earth to build these cement steps that wind up through the trees, rocks, and grass. I don't know where they go yet. Ha! Look at the kids on the swings! What I'm gonna do now? Stay with the old lady? Five years?

Two years? I could hang anywhere except jail for two years? Could I learn enough about dancing in two years to be a dancer? I could. I look at the steps rising out of the rocks up to the castle, at the blue sky—blue blue? What exact color? I don't know, I wasn't good enough in art to be one of the boys got a sixty-four-color Crayola box to keep. Indigo? Cerulean? That's all I can remember from the box right now. My life is just the opposite of that clear sky right now. What could be worse? Being dead or locked up. Well, definitely being locked up would be worse. Dead? I don't know. Maybe I'm lucky I got out? The plan, I think, was for me to be a fall guy like in the movies. Or did they think like in earth science I was the catalyst precipitating the fall? Does that make sense? A catalyst is a substance that changes things in a chemical reaction but isn't changed itself. No, it doesn't make sense. They wanted their life to go on nice and quiet, no one ever know, so that would mean them not wanting me to get in trouble or be in any kind of situation where I might come in contact with anyone and tell. That's why Brother Samuel had my back at the police station. He wanted me out of there before I started talking, which he didn't realize I wouldn't have done. Never, ever would I have told anyone *anything*. He didn't know that I'm loyal to St Ailanthus, him, them, *us*. I believed them:

> *Despite the trauma of some of your lives, each boy comes to us from a different situation, situations that without exception would be better if they didn't exist—missing parents, parents who have passed away, parents who were abusive, or parents who dearly wanted to fulfill their duties but were just too sick or despondent to do so. We are here to fulfill those abdicated duties. We exist here in a community to serve God. And we have chosen to do God's work by serving orphaned and abandoned children. We will not let you down again for a second or third or even fourth time in your short lives. For some of you it would be even more than that. You have arrived at St Ailanthus as result of a string of tragic events; others, as I said earlier, come to us placed by parents and relatives who,*

knowing they can no longer care for their children, you, leave them here in a supreme act of love and trust.

We are committed to providing you with an optimal Catholic education. An education in mathematics, literature, and religion, social studies, foreign languages, and science as well as tracks in auto repair and carpentry. You will be able to enter the world on equal footing, we hope, with the children who have had the benefit of uninterrupted parental care. All we ask of you is you study hard and remain as wonderful and positive as you are now. Your future, which may have been up in the air, so to speak, before you came to St Ailanthus, is now on solid ground. If you put in the effort here at St Ailanthus, your future is assured.

I look up at the sky again as I'm walking the forever blue of it. Vast. Shit, ain't nothin' assured except the sun gonna rise like it's been doing for a zillion fuckin' years and it's gonna go down and the earth is gonna keep spinning around on its axis as it rotates around the sun. *That's* assured. The rest is shit. Spruce trees? I never noticed them before, the spruce trees near 135th Street station, the park benches along the sidewalk painted the same color as the trees. At the red light I close my eyes for a second and I hear what I been trying not to, the old bitch's scratchy voice. She says, I hear it clear, her voice is not scratchy now, her voice is not her voice, it's another voice, clear and gentle, "Your name *is* Abdul." I open my eyes, the light is still red, I look at the oncoming cars, dash out, beat them across the street. I knew I could. Slow down as I pass the Jehovah's Witness Church, cross at the next street on green, keep walking, then, oh shit, I almost trip, I'm in front the police station. My instinct is to break and run, but I keep walking cool. I'm doing the exact right motherfucking thing, innocent people don't run. I ain't did nothing. I ain't no runaway, ain't nobody looking for me. I ain't scared of the police, fuck them! But ah, I think I will walk a different way—home? Back, I'll walk a different way back.

Coming up on the corner of Lenox and 135th Street, I always feel, I don't know, such a *sigh*, yeah, my breath just pisses out and I relax. I feel like I'm home or not far from it. St Ailanthus is around the corner. It's not "home" anymore. Everything around here is familiar to me, Harlem Hospital, the Schomburg, the fancy apartment buildings of Lenox Terrace. Harlem Hospital is big takes up a good part of the block. I remember the emergency room and the nurse—was I born there? I don't remember. Of course I don't remember being born! Who's alive who does? Where was I born? Exactly? How could I find out? Who was my dad? Really? Why does everyone say he's dead? Old bitch said they said something about AIDS. But I don't believe that. That's some of the foulest shit in the world, AIDS and welfare. What could be worse than that shit? I could have AIDS? How you get it? Fucking? But I wasn't really fucking in the park, just getting my dick sucked. And with the brothers that was different—how it happened as a kid and all. The brothers is clean people, the kids clean. I don't have it. I could have it? Just see if I get sick? See if my sores don't heal? Cough, get spots on you? What if I did have it? What difference would it make? Then I would just have it and that would be that. Wonder if I went back and asked Blondie about it. Spoze she ain't in the emergency room no more? How could I find her? Forget about it. I don't want to know. If I got it, I got it. If I ain't got it, I ain't got it. Welfare and AIDS, that's what Brother Samuel said is wrong with African Americans, we're disproportionately represented on the welfare rolls and our lifestyle predispose us to criminality. Brother Samuel's a sociologist. He thinks he knows what's wrong with everybody. Brother John says that's a mistake, just a mistake, he shakes his head, Brother Samuel is wrong, just wrong, most of the people on welfare is white, and he said white people commit more crimes but they go to jail less. He never contradicts Brother Samuel to his face, though. Who's right? I'm not a criminal. Why was I taken to the police station and kicked out of my house? If I am a criminal, well, I ain't. But even if I had done that shit they say I did, how am I different from Brother Samuel or Brother John? I'm not. They're not criminals, and neither am I.

The corner of 135th Street and Lenox is great! It's big, clean. It's modern. I don't see how this is a ghetto. I don't see nothing wrong with this. A library, a hospital, apartments, stores? Nobody's shooting anybody. I don't want to shoot nobody. I want to become a dancer, get married and have kids, have a nice apartment. I don't want to sell dope or be in a gang. How do you get in a gang? Where are they? Would they like me? Probably not. So many people are ignorant, Brother John said, and they don't go past first impressions. I don't know if I like other boys, and I ain't got no friends that's girls. How do you get to be friends with girls? How do you get to fuck 'em? Giving them stuff? Do they like gang members? Yeah, gang members and rappers. The streets here are wide. Brother John said some of the widest in the city. I like watching people's heads come out the subway like they're busting out of some dark body being born.

When I get up the stairs to the door of the gym, I look around for Imena. I walk past the girl at the door with the clipboard, tell her I'm a guest of Imena's. The girl knows that, but I do it anyway, I don't want no static. I'm tense, real tense, it's like something on the other side of the door in my head is pressing. A headache? Panicky, I run over to Imena. Perspiration breaking out under my arms, it's hot, I can smell myself, I'm out of breath, don't know what I'm going to say until I lean down. Imena's about a head shorter than me, and I say it, whisper.

"I can't hear you, J.J."

"Don't call me J.J. no more, OK? From now on call me Abdul."

"What?"

"My real name is Abdul, call me Abdul from now on, OK? *OK?"*

"OK." She tiptoes to kiss me on my forehead. "OK, Abdul."

I go to put on my sweats and T-shirt and warm up for class. I try not to look at the other people, but it's hard. Some of them just sit on the floor in second and lay their stomach down or lay on their back and pull their legs up to their ear like they ain't got no bones or ligaments attached to them. My body ain't like that. Imena says I have strength, ballon—and when flexibility comes, I'll be glad for what I have. Sitting down on the floor with both my legs straight out in front of me, I can't reach my toes or my ankles. It's no better in second, I grab my calves and stretch. I guess

THE KID

if I was older I wouldn't even be here, I'd be someplace trying to fix shit. But what can I fix? What's fixing? A foster home, I'm too grown up to be adopted, but I'm not a man, I don't know how to get out and get a job. My shoulder still hurts, but I know once I get warmed up and moving I'll get over the pain. All these scratches and the cut on my face from the mirror hurt too, but so what? I just put the focus on what I'm doing. One of the drummers is playing the kalimba and singing African words soft like a breeze while we warm up.

"Reach, one two three four." I extend my long arms over my head, try to touch the ceiling. "Soften your knees, contract your abdominals to protect your back, and roll down two three four." Sometimes I have this feeling everything in my head is on a computer screen and the brightness of the screen is turned up sometimes and it's all luminous like how the rays come out of the saint's head in gold on the paintings in chapel. I'm not even on nothing. I just feel happy or hypnotized or some weird thing when the music starts and my juice gets to flowing. Sounds, the *ting-ting* of the kalimba, the flute, woodwind? Wind out of wood! The sounds go through every cell of my body, and I feel it, I *feel* it happening. "*Reach,* two three four." Imena is like my master, I try to be what her voice says. "Feet in parallel." I can smell the girl next to me, sweat pussy smell clean fresh a little like curry powder we had on, or would have, on Thursday, ethnic-food night at St Ailanthus. "Brush your foot out, tendu." The girl in front of me got on lime green tights, she's already sweating, the sweat turning her tights dark in the small of her back and between her legs. Her butt is like two big green apples. Whew! "Rotate your ankle *out,* two three four five six seven eight." I'm starting to perspire. "*In,* two three four five six seven eight." I like my smell. I like how the gym smells, every-body's odor mixed up with the old smell of the gym—wood, sweat, the stink from a million motherfuckers thumping the ball, now us. And the girl's butt like apples. Yo ho ho! My sweat, can the girl next to me smell it? It's not like I feel happy, it's that I don't feel dead when I'm here. I feel I got to do something but I don't know what so I'm doing this. Fuck St Ailanthus's, those stupid kids—

"J.J., pay attention!"

Oops, I thought we was going into pliés, but she's doing hip isolations now warming up for pliés.

When we line up to go across the floor, I get in the back with the rest of the guys—men, Imena calls us. Drummer plays the break, Bee dee dee bah pah dah dah Pah! I almost miss it. Some of the dancers got such good timing, Imena too. She got it naturally or she learned it? "Your hips, torso, and arms are doing this—one, two, three, four in place. Then run—five, six, seven, eight." The drums sound like they're saying, Nkisi boom! Nkisi boom! Nkisi boom! Nkisi boom boom *boom*! My sweat is stinging my cuts and scratches. I check out the guys on both sides of me, their, the whole room's, right foot is coming down on *N*, hips swiveling on *KI SI*, then contract on *boom*! Then run five, six, seven, eight, like you falling, arms going round like you a windmill. I got the step, now I try to dance it!

OK, I got it so now of course she has to change the combination. This step now, funny little catch step after the one, then rotate your hips step together *whoosh,* step together *whoosh,* going across the floor I try to keep my mind on the step, but the rhythm is reminding me, is it a dream? *Whoosh whoosh,* like my kaleidoscope pieces of glass falling into some kind of picture *whoosh* the picture my mother the blood spurting like a geyser the nurse snatched the tube wrong out her hand. I'm so angry that they're all just scared of getting blood on them they ain't trying to help her. But I ain't scared of no part of my mother. Step together *whoosh* I don't know how to tell the doctor, he thinks I'm scared to touch my mother, but I don't want the tubes to break loose again. He think I don't love my mother? The machine by her bed is going *whoosh whoosh* with its mechanical rhythm, quiet horrible sound like a train you can't see that disappears anyway. I see the moon and the moon sees me, Mommy! Step together—oh!

"You're off, J.— Abdul! Listen to the drum, come in on the *one!*"

Shit! I get back on the beat put everything out my head except the drums. She's doing some hard-ass steps today—Haitian, Congolese. It's the Congolese that trips me up, even though she say one come from the other. I forgot exactly where Haiti is. She motions for us to form a half-moon circle in front the drummers. She does this sometimes near the end of the class to give us a chance to work it out doing solos to the drums.

"Listen up! I'm going to tell you a little story," she says. "And I want you to think on it and let the story inform your solos today. Keep moving! Keep moving while I'm talking. You don't have to retell the story or act it out—in fact, I wish you wouldn't. Just let the words in. Way way back *before* 'back in the day' from Father Sky and Mama Earth and rain came the first life on the planet. Father Sky breathed into the dirt, had Sun shine into the dirt, but no life emerged. When Father Sky saw that, he upped the ante and started to blow Wind hard into the earth, tearing its soil asunder, and when that didn't work, he sent Thunder and Lightning down hard into the Great Mother. No dice! Father Sky was so angry and sad with his failed efforts because he really wanted life, and great as he was, he couldn't do it alone. He began to cry. When his warm, salty tears rained on the Great Mother she said, 'Shit yeah, this is smooth, I like it,' and she opened up her body and Life came, and the earth, which had been gray and barren, turned *GREEN*. Grass and grapes and apples, lush greens, collard greens, mustard, avocados, mangoes! The earth turned greener than the mighty ocean. At that time the people had been living under the ocean; in fact, all creatures had been in the water at one time. Now old crocodile, one of the first creatures to really stick his big nose out of the water and talk about what was going on out on earth, came back to the people and told them it was very, very green on earth, greener than down on the floor of the ocean where the people lived. There are mangoes, cherries, and avocados, he told the people. But the people were afraid ol' crocodile was just feeding them a line to get them to come up so he could eat them. Under the ocean they were safe; on the way to land, they might be eaten by crocodiles. One of the old first people had already lived three hundred years and had great respect among the people for her potions she made from seaweed. Potions that gave you immunity from disease and protection from danger. People drank them, but nobody was a hundred percent sure they worked, because there really was no danger or disease deep down under the sea where the first people lived. In all her long life, she had never drunk the guts of the shark potion designed to give . . . well, guts. One day old first woman—Lucy was her name—decided she had to eat this mango, crocodile or no crocodile. So she drank the potion, guts, she walked up from the bottom of the ocean right past ol' crocodile. She was the color of the rainbow when she stepped onto earth. All people were once all colors—how they got separated into different colors is another story. But Father Sky and Mother Earth saw Lucy standing alone. They knew that under the ocean both men and women could give birth. But when they saw Lucy's guts, they gave the job of birthing to her."

Imena turns around, claps her hands at the drummers, and the *ting-ting-ting* of the cowbell starts, and the drums roar. Imena moves her back like she has the ocean in it. She looks around for someone to step out; this freak-ass fine Asian chick jumps out in front the drum. FIRE! FIRE! A lot of the time, I'm the first one out there, I feel like an asshole sometimes, but that's better than standing there watching everyone else and getting scareder and scareder, wishing I had jumped on out there. At least when I get on out there, I feel like I'm, you know, a dancer. These girls here ain't shy, I seen them do a lot of stuff . . . well, not seen but heard the boys, "men," say stuff; it's four "men" men in the class. They gets the girls. What am I? A boy.

The drums is hot now, the Asian girl moves back in the line. I move on out, dancing fast. One of the drummers has a jembe drum, I love its sound. And when they open up with sticks beating on the side of the big conga drum feeding in another rhythm, it takes me out! I go with what I feel; you ain't got to be no professional to do that. I don't care about being no beginner or having tacky clothes, this is Crazy Horse in the house, dude! Wild horse be running past me and stop on the high tabletop on the Great Plains, they call it a mesa. I got scars. Scarification like Africans. I got a eagle feather. I drag the arrowhead across my chest blood drop the lightning is flashing but no rain and my horse is dancing in the sky, jack! *Dancing!*

THE KID

It's that way when I get to moving like a gate opens and buffalo stampede, everything comes rushing out of me at once. It's like I remember everything that ever happened to everyone. My body is not stiff or tight, I'm like my mom, soft, dark, and beautiful. It last about a minute, hah! I feel her kiss, kiss her lips, she's like African. The top and the bottom—Africans got the worst of everything, Brother Samuel say. Nonsense! Brother John would say. I'm so mad at them! Fuck them, right now I'm a warrior walking from the bottom of the ocean to plant my seed! A *man* man! A man! Amen! Our Father Who Art in Heaven—

"Yeah!" People are screaming. "Way to go, J.J.!" "Dance, boy!" "Work that shit OUT!" "Yes, Abdul! Yes yes *yes*!" I look over at Imena shouting at me. A couple of people run over to where I am press both hands over their hearts, then kneel down and touch the ground at my feet. That's like mad respect for another dancer's effort; no one ever did that for me before. I back back into the half circle with the other dancers next to Imena. She hugs me, then dances out in front of the drummers herself. Fast birdlike movements but sexy, she got that. Sexiness! I want to move like that too, yeah! I start winding my hips like she's doing. Another of the guys standing in the circle is doing the same thing. He sashay out to her and they start winding down together! Their pelvises music together. Bah dee dee bah dah dah PAH!

I WALK UP Lenox Avenue to 145th Street, totally bypassing the pigs. I hate them. So what now, it's almost four o'clock. I ain't got a dime in my pocket, and where am I going? Back to 805 St Nicholas. Do what? Just hang out in that room. What about school, ducats, grub, riding the train? I don't get it, I really don't get it.

I hardly ever used to come up this far, 145th Street. Interesting. What guys, kids, do for cash? Sell crack, ass, strong-arm. Rob? I never really robbed before, maybe I hit somebody tried not to give me something like that old guy once in Marcus Garvey Park, gave me ten dollars to blow me up near the bell tower, I wanted twenty, he had *said* he was gonna give me twenty. I didn't hit him hard, I don't consider that robbing. Little as Jaime is, he is doing that shit all the time *and* pretending like he got a piece. Then he wanna act like he's scared of me now.

I get up to the old brick face of the building. What? *What* am I spozed to do? I look up the street, nothing. Behind me dance class, but that's over. Go back inside, just for the night. Tomorrow? I don't know.

I knock no answer try the doorknob it's open! I walk in the vestibule turn left down the hall. All the doors are closed except the bathroom door at the end of the hall and the door to the room with my suitcase in it. Out the bathroom window you can see the city lit up like Christmas, cars crawling across the bridge from far away look like bugs with headlights for eyes. Bronx, Manhattan, I been in every borough except Staten Island. On one side of the hall are two closed doors and the kitchen, which doesn't have a door. On my—the side of the hall where the room is that has my stuff in it—are four doors, all closed except for the one to the room with my stuff. Looking at a hole in the linoleum, the layers of linoleum, um—four, five, six, look like rings around a tree, the bare wood shining through the hole. I think of St Ailanthus, clean, clean, floors like on TV.

I stick my head in the kitchen, go in, pull the light string, and stare at the swimming-pool-colored walls, two refrigerators, probably a lot of people used to live here? Everything—the walls, clock, stove—seems covered with a film of grease, there's a old, I mean *old*, smell of fried chicken hanging in the air. A long table pushed up against the wall is covered with a blue and white plastic tablecloth with birthday hats, whistles, and HAPPY BIRTHDAY written in different spots in big letters. On the table there's an unopened loaf of bread, a big can of peanut butter "USDA Grade" something I can't make out, "Smooth Style," and a plastic container with . . . um, let's see, bacon, about eight slices of cooked bacon, smells good. And next to the container two keys. To the front door? One says "Medeco," the other "Jet U.S.A. SE1." I dash down the hall to the front door and out. Try the keys, bet! Come back in, now for bacon and peanut butter sandwiches? I almost laugh; this shit is funny in a way.

Well, I like peanut butter and I like bacon. I open one of the refrigerators, the olive green one, on one shelf are four trays covered with see-through plastic wrap. The top tray has a plate with grayish string beans, a scoop of mashed potatoes with a pool of gravy in the middle, and brown cubes of something with more gravy poured over it. Next to the plate a bowl of lettuce with orange stuff on it and on the other side of the plate, a perfect pink square of cake. Written across the clear plastic wrap on a piece of masking tape: "WHEELING MEALS senior." On the bottom shelf a carton of eggs, two big packages of bacon, half jar of spaghetti sauce, square stacks of yellow cheese slices. The freezer is full of what looks like hamburger meat and bags of turkey wings, and a can of coffee and a Sara Lee cheesecake that takes, let's see, three hours to thaw.

In the other refrigerator is a big box of grits, a can of look like grease, five, no six more packages of bacon, and a giant jar of grape jelly, a sick-looking head of cabbage, and some looks like water in a pitcher and a liter of orange soda. I grab the soda, I could just go with the jelly and have peanut butter and jelly. But I'm gonna go with the bacon, I think, looking around for a knife as I close the refrigerator door.

There's one in the sink. I rinse it off, the only towel I see is dirty-looking. I shake water from the blade, causing the light from the bulb overhead to dance off the blade and make it sparkle. I was a kid standing by the bathroom door looking in at my mother staring at herself in the mirror, a knife in her hand, the light dancing off the blade and making it sparkle. What she doing? Quiet, no breathing. She raises her wrist to the hand holding the knife. Slice. Blood dribbles down the white sink. I SCREAM.

"What you doin'! What you doin'!"

The sound of the knife clattering to the bathroom floor, her screaming back, "Get out of here! You spozed to be in bed!"

Bap! Not hard, but she never hit me before. I hate her.

"Stop crying, silly rabbit. Mommy's sorry. Mommy's so sorry." She's kissing me now, wrapping a towel around her wrist.

"What you was doing?"

"Nothing, nothing. I was just tired. Go back to bed unless you *don't* want to go to the movies Friday."

"I wanna."

"Well, then get back in bed and go to sleep."

Hmm, weird shit to be remembering now. I walk back over to the table. I don't want to put the bread on the table, got little roach shits here and there. I end up taking the bread out the bag and open the inner cellophane, take out four slices and lay them on the bread wrapper, spread the peanut butter and then lay the bacon on top the peanut butter. Cool, lunch and dinner. Shit, it tastes great! I drink the pop out the bottle. Good, I love orange pop.

Now what? Homework? TV? Bed? I look at the stove, little roaches crawling out the stove door, the greasy blue wall, clock over the table, five o'clock. Read a book? What I got? No TV, nobody to play with. Practice my dancing, stretch out? Jaime always thinks of things to do. I touch my face, feel the scab starting to form on the side of it, my fingers want it. I look in the bathroom mirror, squinch my mouth to one side, which draws the skin tight around the other side of my face where the scab is, and start pulling and picking the scab off. Little beads of blood pop like red pearls as I pull. What's a scab? Blood and dead skin cells? I forgot; what I remember looking at my blood is sliding into Jaime, him calling me Papi, Papi! But quiet real quiet so don't nobody wake up. I don't like it here. Alone. Till? This can't go on forever, peanut butter and bacon sandwiches, roaches. The earth, fuck the earth and Brother John's stupid class, what was all that shit for? The Great Wall of China, crop rotation, erosion—the gradual wearing away of the earth's surface, killing the earth is what they mean! Where I pulled the scab off, the line of little sparkling rubies is starting to drip down my face in red lines. Like tears. If I was good in art—I'm not, I suck—I would draw a black boy's face, the skin crying crying. Our skin do make us fucking cry. I would make it like a Frida Kahlo. When Brother John took us to see her at the Met, Jaime didn't like her. I did. She excite you, gets your freak on. I wish I had a book on her. Jaime said all she paints is pain, who needs it?

THE KID

I think about what I'm going to miss, but maybe not, maybe things will still work out. I never even got to do computers, French either. Spanish, what for? Brother John said, learn Italian, you can't use Spanish as your second language in college. Is that true? But anyway, who you gonna talk to? The ones that hip speak English. Jaime speak English. He don't even speak Spanish. In the bathroom mirror, I see the city lights starting to glitter outside in the twilight. Beautiful. I turn to the window, the lights look like little seeds growing brighter as it gets darker; make me feel small, lonely, and mad horny. I unzip my pants, squeeze myself, I love me, start jacking off, while my hand is working, I feel no pain, fuck Jaime that lame! I see myself pulling a razor across my chest while I'm riding; my blood sprays red in the wind. The other warriors know I am the one! I cut myself to show courage, yeah ooh, ooh. Motherfuckers, Custer included, will know I mean business, know I'm not playing, know ooh oh ohh! Shit! Ump humph! Goddamn fuck! I shake myself, run my hands down my dick, take the semen, sperms—sperm or sperms?—not sure, rub it on my hands, rub my hands together like it's lotion, power potion, Brother John says.

For a second I think I heard something. Did I hear something? Maybe one of the doors? When I look behind me, the hall is still a dark tunnel of closed doors. I turn to the mirror, the lights, the lines of blood drying on my face, and then all of a sudden I'm mad, slam my fist in the mirror. It doesn't shatter but cracks in a pattern like a spider's web radiating out from where my fist struck. I feel so full and totally empty at the same time. My hand don't even hurt. I wonder what kind of glass that old mirror is made from. I could tear up everything in here, but I don't really feel like it. I just feel sleepy now. I go back to the room, I don't even take off my clothes, just climb in bed with my leather pants on, without even wiping the blood from the side of my face. Yeah, go to sleep, that's better than sitting up here going berserk.

WHAT I DO REMEMBER is getting up to take my pants off. They're too tight around the waist to sleep comfortable, no give. It's too cold to be naked, so I look around and try to find my maroon and white stripes, but I don't see 'em, I thought I left them on the bed. I open my suitcase, empty except for my books and manila envelope with my papers in it. Say what? Where's my shit? I wheel around on my heels. The old wooden wardrobe is right in front of me. In there? But how? I open the doors, and the dry smell of dead roaches I've already gotten used to here hits me in the face with the smell of my own stuff. It's all there, sure enough, everything, even my underwear and socks on a hanger. On the floor of the closet is my shoes, the Sunday black loafers we wear to Mass, sitting in a graveyard of roach bodies and droppings. Ugh! Who did this? Her, Slavery Days, of course. I pull one pair of pajamas, I got two, off the hanger and go back to bed.

That's what I remember. I don't remember walking down the hallway, opening up all the doors, talking about, "Hey, hey, it's J.J.!" That's what she said, fucking fossil. She woke up, and I was standing over her, butt-nekkid, talkin' 'bout, "Hey, hey, it's J.J.!" Yes, you *was*, nekkid as the day you was born! Johnson hard as a rock talkin' 'bout, "Hey, hey!" I tol' you, you don't git yo' butt back in bed, you gonna wish you hadda. Then you sat down talkin' 'bout, "Heinie, Heinie," or some shit. I hit you good as I could with this damn lupus 'n all the other shit I got. Hittin' you cost me! Boy, when I lay down even thinkin' about gittin' up damn near kill me. You pulled up my gown. Yes you did! I ain' had a stitch on under it, nuthin'. That woke yo' ass up, and you went on back down the hall—"

I don't remember no stupid shit like that. Why is she even saying some crazy shit like that? What I do think is when I be dreaming I remember shit, but I know it is not a memory but a "dreaming," which I can't control. Memory you can control, at least I can, and I have decided not to remember nothing no more. Her shit included, I don't even know her. It just gets in the way of everything, remembering. Like I don't remember walking down the hall, I'm sure I didn't unless it was to go to the bathroom. I know I'm not crazy. I don't walk in my sleep, so someone is a liar. And it ain't me. I ain't got no cause to lie. I ain't did nothin' to nobody. Why would I go do some weird shit like that after all the trouble I'm in, you think I'm fucking crazy? Crazy? No, I'm not crazy, not at all, at all, *at all*. Sometimes I think, shit, I remember so much, even things that didn't happen, why can't I remember her? I want to remember her, that's different from Brother John, Samuel, the fucking cops, lies, lies, lies! How come I can't forget what I want to forget and remember what I want to remember?

I'M LAYING IN BED trying to go back to sleep when the social worker comes. What's she doing here so early? I was laying thinking about yesterday in the park, climbing up the concrete stairs, thinking about how the green grass can break through concrete and how the water can get in, freeze, crack it. I got ten dollars. On the way down pass the basketball court, one of the guys hold up the ball, do I wanna play? No, I like basketball and handball and all that OK. Yeah, I like it, but I don't want to be bothered with it right now. Right now I'm scoping my environs, wino on the bench, bitches with baby carriages, trash, why people always throwing trash. Broke glass, dog shit. On top the hill, the college, City College. My mom used to go there? October, November, December, January I'll be fourteen. What's that? What the fuck is that! I'll still be a kid. Fuck it.

I'm pulling the covers over my head, my eyes closed seeing all the trees in the park rustling, leaves fluttering in the wind, falling falling, when she came in my room. That still sounds so funny, my room. This ain't none of mine, and if it is I don't want it. But I can't have St Ailanthus back, or my mother, or father?

She flicks the light on. "Come on, git up. You ain't hear me calling you?"

Yeah, I heard you, I think, squeezing my eyes shut to see the green leaves, leaves turning to money. I hate her nasty-sounding voice.

"Come on, Abdul, yo' caseworker here to see you."

Caseworker? Caseworker! Shit, maybe I'm out of here. I throw the covers off and jump into my leather pants. I jump out of them just as fast when I see roach crawling out the leg. I turn them inside out and shake them motherfuckers good. One reason to hang up your clothes at night, even if ain't no Mrs Lee or one of the brothers hollering at you to do it. OK, yeeow! Finally some help, some money, school, a way out of here back to St Ailanthus, maybe I'll get adopted, I heard they got some movie stars who want to adopt black kids. Jaime said, no, Asian, most white people want to adopt Asian kids, not niggers, black or Spanish. In the bathroom I slide a stick of deodorant under my arms, splash some water on my face, and go meet social services as they say at St Ailanthus.

Smell of coffee and out the corner of my eye a pale-haired thin woman staring at the wall as I pad barefoot to the bathroom. While I'm hitting my face with water, eyes closed, I see the trees again, but this time the leaves are disappearing, gone. All gone. I dry my face, wipe my eyes. Yeah, all gone, dude—don't get your hopes up, I tell myself, and head for the kitchen.

She has the coffee cup raised to her lips taking a sip, she almost spits it out when she sees me.

"JJ.?"

Like she don't believe it.

I look at her like she's stupid.

"Excuse me, you must think I'm crazy. It's just I was expecting a much younger boy. And, my goodness, you look so much like my son—he's eighteen, though. Well, sit down, sit down."

Like it's her crib or some shit.

"I'm Mrs Stanislowski from the Department of Social Services." She's skinny, got on jeans, not pretty.

"You're, ah . . . well, Stanislowski is my married name. My husband is African and Jewish. So my son's black, and that's how come you could look like him, not that you couldn't look like him if he wasn't."

It would be hard, I think.

"But you know what I mean. He's in college, my son."

Slavery Days is standing near the stove with her coffeepot. When I sit down, she advances like some kind of fog, coffeepot in one hand, cup in the other.

"I'm actually Irish," Mrs Stanislowski says. "My son is Irish, Jewish, and African."

She says this like she won Lotto.

Oh man, I sigh without making a sound. Good we got milk, I think as Slavery Days plops a carton of milk on the table. Whoop whoop-de-doo. I look at the carton: Marissa Samuels, four feet nine inches, last seen December 9, 19—, that's over ten years ago. I look at Marissa's pretty face, coal-black eyes, gold chain. She probably got kids herself now, ran off with her honey. The feeling I had yesterday climbing the corroded cement steps in the park that ended in a patch of dirt green with wine bottles and crack vials, sun blocked out by overhanging branches, the bushes smelling of urine. Marissa's probably in some space like that by now, bones. I wanna snap Mrs Stanislowski's stupid neck, that's how I feel right now. My hand is shaking a little bit as I set the milk carton back down on the table. *You done got used to pushing people around. The world ain't a bunch of little kids.* I wonder what she knows, thinks she knows.

"Well, J.J.—"

"My name ain't *J.J.*!" I sneer.

"I didn't mean anything J— Jamal."

What's gotten into me? I want to kill her. Crazy Horse, help me! I don't want to hear all this crap about her son in college. Slap her down! But he wouldn't do that. He'd say get out of this one alive.

"Well."

She seems totally tripped out.

"It says here"—she nods at some papers in front of her coffee cup—"I'm to see a thirteen-year-old African American named Jamal Jones, who is referred to as J.J., that's in parentheses, and his legal guardian, Toosie Johnston."

"I don't care what that bitch says." I nod toward her papers. She turns red red. "My name ain't no fucking Jamal, J.J."

I never talked to the brothers like that, no matter what they did.

"Call me out of my name again . . ."

I stare her down, all this shit I been through for nothing. Shit, I may as well do something if I'm gonna be treated like a criminal. Bitch, I don't say it but I kind of *breathe* it.

"Well, er . . . um . . . ah . . ." She clears her throat. "I thought J.J., Jamal Jones, was your name, so I called you that. Just so we'll be clear from now on, what is your name?"

"Abdul. Abdul Jamal Louis Jones," I say. She writes something on her pad.

"And my name is Mrs Stanislowski. Some of the kids call me Stan."

"I don't care what they call you," I tell her, sucking my teeth like Amir at St Ailanthus.

"Well, maybe you should, J— Abdul, maybe you should."

"Why?"

"Why? Because you're thirteen. You may look eighteen, but you aren't. You're thirteen. Somebody's gonna control your life for the next five years. It could be the two of us working together with the Bureau of Child Welfare, or it could be you against BCW, duking it out until we have to lock you up!"

"Lock me up for what!"

"J— Abdul, you're thirteen."

"That's not a crime."

"No, but it's a state of extreme vulnerability—"

"What does that mean, you got me by the balls?"

"Like I said, it could be us, by that I mean you and us. Or it could be *us*—an arrangement with you totally out of control can't be a very pleasant prospect, can it? Can it, Abdul?"

I want to shit in her fucking face, then flip her over and rub her face in it while I fuck her.

"You gonna lock me up?" I sneer.

"Well, if it comes to that . . ."

"You and who else?"

"If it comes to that, whoever else it takes."

Hearing the words "locked up," it's like Brother Samuel throwing me, everything happened so fast, the walls moving; losing control. It's not until

I'm flat on my back I realize the wall wasn't moving, that it was me flying through the air. But right now nothing is moving, it seems like even our breathing, mine, Stanislowski's, Slavery Days', has stopped. Until I shout.

"You think I'm just gonna follow you to jail!"

"No, I don't. You'll run away or fight—hurt yourself or somebody else. But we'll find you—"

"You'll find me! For what? I haven't done anything! You guys fuck up. Send me to some . . . some . . . whatever, then send me to some shit like this! I was just a little boy! A little boy!"

"You're still a little boy!"

She's crazy. I get up. She gets up.

"Look, look, we got off on the wrong foot. I'm sorry. I'm really sorry. All this is totally unnecessary. I'm sorry. I wasn't trying to lay a power trip on you. I was just trying to make sure you knew how serious your situation is and what for no godly reason and through no fault of your own could happen to you. Let's back up some. I'm here to help, supposedly. I can't fix it, but I think I can at least help."

"Help?"

I feel the blood rushing to my face. What would Crazy Horse do to a ugly white bitch like this? A woman with a prison in her mouth. Perfect day to die? But I ain't ready to die. I sit back down.

"Some mistakes have been made, and it's terrible, the situation, the mistakes. You're not a mistake or terrible—that's what you have to remember. It's not your fault. I mean, just erase all that nonsense that just happened between you and me. All I'm here for is to ask you some questions and to determine if your present circumstances are acceptable and to get you back in school. I don't want to make it harder than it already is." She looks at me. "Especially after all you've been through. I want you to win. I'm on your side, if you'll let me be, really."

After all I been through? I hate the sound of her voice. It irritates me, it bugs me. Sounds like the voice that killed Crazy Horse, voice of the lying treaties. If she don't shut the fuck up, I may receive a message from Crazy Horse to kill her. How do you stab someone, like in the movies? I want to get my joint pierced. Nipple too. I wanna jam. I wanna be able to get my leg up! Be able to split. Stanislowski, or whatever this shit's name is, ain't worth my wings. I'll see her, yeah, I'll see her one day in the park, or subway. Yeah, one day I'll catch her coming out the subway, she don't know it's me behind her. I'll say, "Hey, Stan," real nice, and when she turns around—*slice!* Her fucking face open.

"What's going on in that brilliant head of yours, Abdul?"

"Nothing."

"Nothing? I know it's been rough, especially these last few days, week or so. If you decide to make a statement about what happened at St Ailanthus or about any of the brothers, Brother Samuel . . . I mean, you won't be the only one. You know what I'm talking about?"

"No, I don't." I don't want to bust nobody at St Ailanthus. I'd never be able to go back then. I sit there saying nada.

"Ah, Abdul, still here?"

Wishing I wasn't.

"Did you hear what I said about the brothers?"

"I said no."

"Abdul?"

"Could we talk about something else?"

"Like what?"

"Like where I'm gonna be staying on the permanent side, school, money, clothes. Could we talk about that instead of—"

"Instead of what?"

"Instead of bulltwinkie."

All this time we been talking, Slavery Days ain't said nothing. She's standing by the coffeepot on the stove. I've never seen anybody make coffee on the stove. Stanislowski looks at her like she's crazy, then, duh, she gets it. There's only two chairs, what else is she supposed to do?

"Mrs Johnston, did you want to sit down? I could—"

"Thas alright. Once I'm up, it's easier to jus' gon' 'n stay up."

"Well, what do you think about all this?"

" 'Bout what?"

"Well, Abdul has some pretty strong feelings. You haven't said—"

"Forgit 'bout all dat ol' stuff 'n jus' gon' git his butt in school."

Stanislowski persists. "Well, how do you feel about . . . ah, what Abdul has to say? I mean, you are the guardian."

I guess she trying to give Slavery Days a little test? Is she all there? But what if she ain't gonna be my guardian? That's my question, but I'm scared to ask. I been listening to kids talk for years about foster homes, group homes, residential facilities—THE SYSTEM, and none of it good.

"So what shit happened in de first place, thas what he wanna know. Why he got tooked dere is wrong. But people like y'all don' nevah admit nothin'."

Tooked? But she's right.

"So what happened?" Slavery Days says again and picks up the coffeepot and shuffles over to the table and fills up our cups like she's a robot programmed to pour coffee whether we want it or not. Stanislowski is staring at her like she just stepped out of a flying saucer. In my head a picture of a little boy, not me, some little boy like the prince of England, running across grass, no dog shit, no condoms or broken glass, just green. And his yellow hair is blowing, he's laughing, holding a balloon red against the blue sky. But there's something in the grass, a board with nails, knives, snakes? Watch out, stupid boy! Watch out! He loses his grip on his balloon—

"Hey, J.J., what's going on?" Mrs Stanislowski snaps her fingers in front of my face, which makes me mad.

"I told you my name ain't no fucking J.J.!" I slam my hand down on the table, sloshing coffee all over. Slavery Days comes scuffling over with her dirty rag.

"OK, OK, I forgot, forgive me. Now, where were we on this little home visit?" Stanislowski is looking kinda bugged out. I think I scared her.

"School, we were talking about school, clothes, and money," I remind her.

Stanislowski has a kind of help-me-out-here expression on her face when she asks Slavery Days, "How do you feel about the language Abdul uses to express himself, Ms Johnston?"

But before the words are out her mouth, she looks like she knows how stupid she sounds. What she wants to ask is what kind of foul shit is going on here or there where he came from, and are you crazy, or just old, or retarded? She wants to ask shit like that, but instead she says something like the language Abdul uses. Slavery Days is ready for her.

"How you gonna fault him? You gotta look at de peoples who was keepin' care of him all dis time. He ain' learnt dat all by his lonesome," she says sounding almost normal. It's like she got sense enough to know what someone with sense would say. But I know she ain't got no sense. Slavery Days is as empty as my pockets.

Stanislowski stares at her papers. "For now, your grandmother, Ms Johnston, is your legal guardian."

Whoa! Slavery Days ain't my grandmother. Even if she was related to me, she wouldn't be my grandmother, I don't think. They ain't got this shit right at all.

"She'll receive money for you and, of course, see to it that your needs are met as far as transportation, food, lunch money for school, and things like that. You'll get a clothing allowance from us—everything that you need. I think school is the most important thing. Since you were doing so well, I'd like to get you in Boys' Catholic High downtown, no use in you throwing away everything—the good part, at least—of what you got at St Ailanthus."

She stares at my face again like she's been doing. I know she can't hold herself back from saying something much longer.

"What happened?"

I was right.

"I fell in some glass playing basketball."

"You fell in some glass playing basketball? Where?"

"What difference does it make?" I press my lips together. I mean it, what fucking difference does it make?

"Well, in another vein, are you Catholic?"

Hell no. "Yes."

"Was your mom Catholic?"

"No." Slavery Days jumps in. "She was crazy, is what she was."

Check out who's talking!

"Thas another reason you cain't fault him."

Stanislowski look at her like she's got antennae growing out her head rag.

"J—Abdul, trust me, I'll get it right. I mean that in more ways than one. There's a lot wrong here. A lot. I don't know all of what it is, but I'm trying to get it right. I mean, I feel terrible about all this shit that has happened to you. It's not right! You deserve better. I think of my own son. God! At thirteen he needed help tying his shoes, damn near, and you're just— I don't know what to say. I mean, this is more than just a . . . a job. I really want to help. I mean, it's my job, of course, to help. And I want to and am going to, really, really." She says this in a new sweet voice and looks up and stares in my eyes. "Where was I?"

Making a play for my feelings. A minute ago she was gonna lock me up, now it's "really, really." I'm spozed to wag my tail like a little puppy.

"Oh, yeah! The YMCA. You dance. Brother John said you were a dancer. We have kids down there in ballet and jazz classes in an after-school program, and I think they have hip-hop and tap on Saturdays. Would that interest you?"

She fucking knows it would. Wag my tail now, show a crack in the ice. Give her something to write in her report.

"Cool, that would be cool."

She's happy. Before it's all over, another half hour or so, she calls me Abdul three or four times with no J.J. shit, and I make her day on the way out when I tell her at the door, "See you, Stan."

I close the door behind her. Same shit, different day, like Jaime say, Bureau of Child WellFART! They don't give a fuck about you. He's the same age as me but been in the system since he was six. He's right, don't nobody really care about you if you ain't got parents. Like Mrs Washington said, the serfs was fodder for the kings and shit, we fodder for the dickheads like Brother John and Brother Samuel or feel-good fodder for shit like Stanislowski. You ain't got blood, you ain't shit! Would she

leave her kid in a place like this? Hell no, cunt-ass ho! Remember my
mom? What for? It hurts to remember a home, somebody who loved
you, maybe it would be better if it was always shit. 'Cause this shit here
makes me want to kill something, Mommy's little boy going to be something one day. What? My whole life turn to shit because she die. Shit
shit SHIT! I go to hell because she die. That's fair? Right? Brother John
say forget about the world being fair, learn to work with what is. He
say that 'cause he's big and white and got his CD player and his dick
creaming kids' asses. He got the unfairness working for him. I am a
normal boy. NORMAL. They take that away from me? I am a boy. I am
intelligent. When all others in the crowd lose their head. What crowd,
Mommy? I'm all alone. You said I was gonna be something. What I'm
gonna be, police asking me questions, kicked to the curb like dog shit,
roaches crawling up my pants? Where am I going? I hate you, Mommy.
I hate you.

If I—what it be like if I had a dad? Alvin Johnson said his father really loved him before he died in the army, but Alvin's mother wouldn't
let his father see him because she wanted child support from him. That's
what Alvin said. What kinda shit is that? What kind of shit is this here?
Stanislowski, lousy! Ha, ha! Stanis*lousy*! So what's going on, Stanislousy
thinking Slavery Days is my grandmother? When she find out she ain't? I
probably be out of this motherfucker soon. Maybe not. I just want to stay
in Imena's class. I don't know if I'm even down with school, how I feel now.
I feel like in earth science. I done changed, a new compound, not a mixture,
but like when we put silver nitrate in water with salt, sodium chloride, and
first it got cloudy the white stuff, then the silver chloride sunk down to the
bottom. Created from the silver nitrate and sodium chloride. A new thing.
Changed. Fast. Milk when it's sour, that's lactic acid made. Fuck school unless I can go back to St Ailanthus, but even there, what? I be having to slap
the shit out of dudes every day for saying stupid shit, niggers be running
from me like I'm some kind of faggot or shit. I know everybody done heard
all those lies by now. Public school? Jungle, Brother Samuel said, a bunch
of blacks running around like monkeys with guns. Shit! I jump in the air

and hurtle myself around! Imena is screaming, Step, step, LEAP! I wish I could just leap over childhood and be grown!

THAT NIGHT I DREAM I'm lost in a crowd on a busy corner in a city. It's winter, snow is just beginning to fall. People are hurrying to get home from work, I guess. I have the feeling I'm trying to be in a hurry too, but I don't know where—where to or where from. I look around me, there're no street signs. When I look at the faces, they seem more like masks than faces, perfect beige and black faces without lines or big noses or glasses. I look in one man's eyes. His irises are like a fan going round and round. They make a whirring noise. How am I going to get where I'm going? Back. He's an android.

The four corners of the street are ice floes now, the one I'm standing on starts to crack. I see the face of a girl in dance class. Her eyes don't have the fan in them. The piece of ice I'm on breaks off, separating me from her. "Jump!" I feel scared, I should have jumped. I'm going to lose her, I'm here looking in the mirror, my face is a mask, my eyes hollow holes fans going whir whir—

"Telephone!"

Huh?

"Git up! I ain' nevah seed a child sleep as much as you do!"

I'm sweating, my heart is beating like the time Jaime and me was rolling and damned near OD'd. I got so dehydrated, I was having convulsions and stuff—

"Telephone!"

Oh, who cares if this bitch is calling, but I go ahead and get up anyway.

"May I speak to Abdul Jamal Louis Jones?"

"This is me," I say.

"I know it's you. Look, Abdul, you're only thirteen—"

"I know how old I am."

"Let me finish, Abdul. What I have to say is hard enough as it is, OK?"

"OK," I say.

"I've only been with the Bureau of Child Welfare six months. I'm actually a sculptor. You should see my stuff one of these days. I make these life-size sculptures of people, I mean, they are the people. I cast the people in plaster, then make a mold, then voilà! It's amazing! At least that's what people tell me. I've done ten of my son, one with his arm up, getting ready to dunk a basketball. You still with me?"

"You said to let you finish."

She sighs, exasperated-like. I feel not what she's going to say but the . . . the *suffering* that's going to come with it. In school once we saw a picture of a girl in some magazine from Sierra Leone. They had chopped off her arms. I forgot why. Both arms.

"I'm going to tell you this even though maybe I shouldn't, and I don't have to. But then, I have to since I know. At least that's the way I look at things."

I haven't been here a week yet. I avoid the old lady as much as I can. Tomorrow I start dance classes downtown, and Monday I go to school. That's all I need to know—how to get there, some money, and some clothes.

"Well, a big part of what happened to you is . . . um, uh, I guess what you could call a kind of reverse synergy. Do you know what synergy means?"

"Yeah, synergy, when two things act together to make more happen than they could by themselves?"

I'm sick of her, just do your job, lady.

"Well, yeah, that's exactly right, when two events happening simultaneously create more, in your case, havoc, than they would have alone. Not only did these two events make a disaster, it seems likely they, along with just plain, old indifference, worked together to create a bizarre cover for each other. You'll see what I mean when I explain it to you, if it can be explained.

"Well, the first thing, and probably the most significant, the brothers or a brother—or a 'paperwork mistake,' they're saying now—essentially didn't *know, forgot,* or *ignored* the fact you were a temporary emergency placement, and they processed you as if you were 'in-domiciled, an orphan, permanently placed in the care and custody of St Ailanthus School for Boys until the age of eighteen.' *Someone* signed papers to have you placed as a permanent placement. That's currently being investigated—"

Shit, I'll never get back in now!

"The second incident that conspired, I guess you could say, against you—and by the way is *not* being investigated—is that someone, some people actually, it had to be at least two people, and one of them had to have worked for or had some kind of in with the Bureau of Child Welfare, as far as I can get it—and by the way it was me that got all this dope—"

Stan is all fired up. I see that girl's face in Sierra Leone; it was a black-and-white picture. Her skin is even darker than mine, shiny. I'm breathing fast, starting to sweat, I have the feeling if I was talking, it would be in the voice of a little boy, high. I'm the opposite of Stan's happy excitement. I'm filling up with a black panic. Do I want to hear this shit?

"You know what it was? Your name. When you kept going off about you know, 'My name ain't no J.J. My name is Abdul,' it just . . . I don't know. At first of course I was mad, reacting, and then it hit me, there's something in this. I don't know how I knew, I just did—"

Whoop whoop-de-doo!

"So anyway, some woman in the Bronx, who evidently went to school with your mother, a 'friend of hers'—believe me when I say 'friend,' it's with quotation marks around it—anyway, she got all your mother's papers, assumed her identity, and continued collecting your mom's SSI checks. She started out receiving AFDC for you in addition to a Social Security check for permanent disability for ARC, as they called it at the time—"

What does any of this have to do with my mom's car accident, finding my father, or going to school? I didn't ask to hear all this shit; I don't *want* to hear all this shit.

"Maybe because AFDC requires a different kind of record keeping and reporting, and this woman just plain old knew the system! And she didn't want to be—*couldn't* be—bothered with face-to-face appointments, home visits, and all that, and this woman had to have access to or was in the social service system. She actually got possession of your mother's death certificate—don't ask me how—copied it, and altered it to say a . . . a little boy, *you,* had died. This false certificate was actually filed with us, and you went on record as dead.

"So none of this is an excuse for what happened, just some insight into *how.* How we, as you said, and I agree, 'fucked up'! No one looked into what was going on with you because they thought you were dead. Which of course you weren't, aren't. You were . . . were, you were lost. Lost. I don't know. Like I said, when you said that thing about your name, I just got chills. When I got back to that office, I got on the computer, I started worrying people, making phone calls, digging in file cabinets and stuff. 'My name ain't no fucking J.J.!' That's it! That's it! I said to myself, 'His name. Why are those men over at that place calling him by a nickname as if it was his real name?' Then I said, 'You're crazy, Marie,' but I don't know whether I had picked up a discrepancy before this or what and just never made the connection, but whatever, it just hit me in the gut. Go for it, I thought, what do you have to lose?"

She's all excited now. I'm supposed to be too? For what, finding out somebody said I'm dead? What am I gonna get out of this? Like, does that girl in the picture in social studies care why someone chopped off her arms?

"So, like, can I sue, get some ducats or something?" You know, like get my life back, bitch.

"I don't know what you mean, Abdul."

"I mean why you tell me all this . . . this *injustice* if it ain't gonna help me or change nothing?"

"Because it's the truth, and you should know it."

"So why can't it help me, get me a different house, some people aside from this to take care of me or adopt me?"

"Abdul, oh, Abdul, honey, honey, it's . . . yeah, I hear what you're saying. It's not going to be like that. What's done is done. I just thought you might want to know what had been done. Abdul?"

"Yeah?"

"You ever been walking on the beach?"

"Uh, I guess."

"You know how your feet leave footprints in the sand?"

"Yeah."

"And the water comes behind you and washes the footprints away? Most of what I've told you is being washed away as we speak. They're not going to admit shit, or as little as possible. A lawsuit would take years, access to . . . I don't even know what. Well, for one thing lawyers, information—I had to break a few rules, *laws,* to find out what I did. I got a kid in college, which is hopefully where you'll be in a few years."

"So I just got fucked."

"Don't talk like that. You're a kid. No matter how bad it's been, you're still young. Young, beautiful, and extremely gifted."

Aw, shut up. I start thinking about what I'm gonna get with the money I get from Slavery Days. Gear! A black leather jacket to match my pants, a pair of Timberlands for winter—

"Still here?"

"Yeah." Where else would I be?

SHE SAYS IF THINGS don't work out (and what does that mean?) I don't have to stay here. How many days have I been here now? I wish for that mirror I broke, to see my body. There's no mirrors in Imena's class, I *can* feel myself from the inside. Still, I wonder how I look executing a step on relevé or in plié. I can almost feel myself growing sometimes, it's weird. If I did go to a group home, you know, so fucking what nobody's gonna bother me.

Some addict stole my mother's identity, declared me dead. What kind of wack shit is that and why should I care? Why should I have to? Ain't I a kid? Maybe a group home would be better than this, whatever *this* is, maybe I could just forget everything and go back. I really want to go back to St Ailanthus—at least I was close to my future there. If I went back, I could just put all this behind me—805 St Nicholas, Slavery Days, the police, lying kids—everything. Just forget it and start over again.

Stanislousy said my father is dead. I kinda knew that, or maybe I did think my mother was keeping him from me because he wouldn't pay child support. So Slavery Days? I ain't into that no kinda way. I reject that shit as having anything to do with me; the old bitch gives me the creeps. Why she's still alive if my mother and grandmother is dead? Creeping around!

I could ask her about my father? Maybe he ain't really dead. But I don't know if I want to hear whatever crazy shit she gonna say, she ain't normal. When she talk, it's like fingernails going down a blackboard, I wanna scream!

How do I feel? How am I holding up, she ask? Fuck Stanislousy! *I'm* the one staring at a translucent sac on the kitchen table, watching the teeny baby roaches bust out the sac, transparent little crawling white shits, crawling all over the table, nasty, nasty, nasty.

THREE

"Stand with your feet pointed straight ahead and then without sticking out your butt pull up your gut, and from your hip socket turn out your feet. OK, see that? How much your feet turned out when you did that, that is your turnout for now. If— OK, come back, come back! Turn your feet back in pointing straight ahead. Now, without engaging your gut or your hips, turn out using just your feet. See, you get almost a straight line, a hundred and eighty degrees. But where do you feel it? No, no just stay there for a while and tell me where you feel all that hundred-eighty-degree turnout coming from. Yes, you feel it in your knees because your hips is still turned in, parallel, and the turnout, yeah, it look good on the ground but it's coming all from below your knees, so the knee joint is very stressed. And notice how your butts is stuck out and your guts hanging. Please, please come out of that terrible position! Now stand with your feet pointed straight ahead, suck up your stomach muscles like a straw, suck 'em up, up! Now, without rocking back on your heels, which will release your butt muscles, which is what we don't want, visualize your thighs turning out in the hip socket and turn your feet out as a result of the opening in the hips. See that!"

I look down at my feet splayed open in first position. Good for me!

"For now that is your turnout! You wish for more, you work for more, but right now that is what you got, and dancers we live in now."

I stare at the small man in loose sweats and a black T-shirt, his feet in white canvas ballet slippers. The front of his body is flat as a piece of paper. I can see that even with the baggy sweats he got on. He turns his feet, which were pointing straight ahead out. His heels are touching, but his toes are pointing in opposite directions and form a 180-degree angle. His arches are so high a mouse could run under them. He can't be any taller than five feet three or four inches.

"This, I repeat, is first position, for me, now." He is so perfect. The picture of him I take it into my head, but my body, twice as big as his, can't do what he's doing. My feet won't line up like that, like his. *Yet*, I tell myself. He brushes and points his right foot out in tendu (I know that from Imena's class). Both feet are still turned out, but now his legs are separated.

"This is second position. The butt, the gut is still pulled up. The action is in the hips. Now plié. Plié just mean open the hips even more and bend the knees, not all this here," he says, sticking his butt out.

Some people laugh. I'm not one of them.

"You keep this here pulled up." He pats his stomach. "Now from second position everybody plié, that's it, down two, three, four. Up two, three, four. Learn to love working in second."

Imena says your hip sockets are like a lid on a mayonnaise jar turning, turning, yeah open! Roman's head snaps around to glare in my face.

"What you is smiling at!" Was I smiling? I mean, he was talking about second position, right, loving it?

"I . . . I love second position, like you were saying," I stutter, feeling as stupid as I'm sure I sound.

"You think you cute? You think you gonna be a dancer, huh? Huh? I seen hundreds of boys come through these doors every year just like you! They don't go nowhere!"

I look at the other faces in the class, they're all looking at the floor.

"They gonna show me! They gonna prove me wrong! Little ones, big ones, pretty ones, black ones, white ones—so wipe that smile off your face, big boy. *Parlez-vous français?*"

I don't know what to say, so I say, "Not yet." Thinking he wants an answer. And it's true, I would of, maybe still will take it next year at St Ailanthus.

"Learn, stupid! You here to learn. You can't impress me. You can't hurt me. You ain't got nothing I want. Understand?"

"I—"

"You don't get it, do you? Don't speak. You do as I say. You want to be a dancer?"

I nod.

He steps closer to me I can smell his cigarette breath, feel it on my face. "Say, 'Yes, Roman.'"

"Yes, Roman," I say.

"Good, good, you are capable of learning I see. Those are the only words you'll need for a while, 'Yes, Roman, No, Roman.' Understand?"

"Yes, Roman."

He turns away from me. The class sighs.

"OK, third position. Kapoot! It's over, we don't use it anymore hardly. Don't nobody really use it in choreography or nothing. Some people use third instead of fifth, their knees is damaged, their thighs is too fat, whatever. If you have to use third instead of fifth, do something else, OK? There are enough people out there who can piss through the eye of a needle while they doing triple tours. If you can't jump or do this thing or that thing because you fat or injured or structured deficient, forget it now, before you waste any more time or money. Both is very hard to come by."

Fifth is a bitch. We never used it in Imena's class. My thighs are big. I look around me, I'm the biggest person in the class, the only black person. I never experienced this before, being the only black person. I remember what Imena said, turn out from the top. Same thing he's saying. Always, always from the hip socket, not from your knees. You got a good body, use it correctly. Just envision a stream of warm water falling down your back and another one jetting up the front of your belly at the same time, release in back and pull up in front.

It's fucking shit-ass hell! Everything hurts, and I can't do anything this guy is saying, and he's dissed me in front of the class. But I know sure as my ass is black I'm coming back to this motherfucker. I will return. And return.

"I demand everything from *les étudiants*. I give everything. Eventually you will leave after you have sucked me dry, taken everything."

I look around, not one face seems to disagree. "But you are stupid if you leave before that."

My thighs are burning, my feet feel retarded, they can't do what the little funny man with his accent asks. But I'm pulsating, open, I feel like . . . like a big ear. I hear him. Shit, man, I hear him!

"How old are you?"

"Seventeen," I lie.

ON THE TRAIN back to where I'm temporarily staying, I play the class over in my mind, remembering what Brother John said: *Don't get hung up on what you can't do. My mother* (he's talking about his black foster mother) *would always say, see it, whatever it is, see yourself doing it or having it, and the Lord will provide the way.* I don't know, but yeah, I'm standing at the barre, I plié, my legs opening wide, wide, my turnout is the best in the class—"145th STREET!" I hop to my feet, I didn't even hear the conductor call out 125th STREET. Where was I!

The good smell of hamburger frying hits me when I open the door. Her food usually smell better than it taste, I done found that out. But I'm hungry. "BOY!" she hollers when she hears me. It's more like a dog barking than a greeting. I put my backpack in the bedroom and go in the kitchen. Seeing her small and dark bent over the stove in the greasy smoke reminds me of Batty Boy, his black skinny arm stabbing wieners out a big steaming pot with the long-pronged fork. The wiener buns is damp and cold inside from being frozen. In another room he hits me so hard my nose is bleeding. I put my hand up to my nose, it is not bleeding. If I shake my head, it feels like it would rattle like in the cartoons or like my kaleidoscope. Shake shake turn turn change.

The hamburgers smell really good. She takes out a jar of mayonnaise. OK. Mustard. Jaime useta love cheeseburgers and cheesy fries. I talk about him like he's dead or something, "useta." I miss him, the little guys, the brothers. They miss me too, I know they do. If I'd been a grown-up or . . . or I don't know, white or a girl, I don't know. I can't figure out how something like this could happen to me without a trial or a chance to prove myself as a good person. I am! Look how fast that police officer, pig or no pig, kicked that shit to the curb when Richie's lying ass admit, admit, he didn't see me move on him. Framed like on TV. I didn't understand it then, but I was being framed. It was all a setup to make it look like I was doing the shit the brothers was doing. They knew just like on TV eventually they would get busted, sooner or later, so they decide to try and pin that shit on me. Also, they probably knew I was gonna break sooner or later about all that shit happened to me. And, like, fuck Richie Jackson, that little faggot, he want people to hurt him and shit. I'm not a faggot. I don't want that shit on my ass. So the brothers knew I was getting ready to bust 'em, so they set me up for the bust. But I'm innocent.

I wonder what Mrs Washington think about all this shit. What lies they done told her? I left *Macbeth* on the first page. When Mrs Washington makes a mistake in class, she says, "God ain't through with me yet." Ladies is funny, Mrs Lee, Mr Lee's wife, is like that too, always saying stuff like a grandmother or some shit. I tell you one thing, if there is a God, he's through with the motherfucking brothers! What would I do if I was God, vengeance is mine sayeth the Lord? I bite down on my burger which is not charbroiled like the TV gourmet cook. The TV gourmet cook when they peel tomatoes, they put the long-prong fork through the tomato then "immerse the tomato in boiling water for about thirty seconds. Then peel away the skin with a small knife." That's what I would do to Brother Samuel. Peel his skin off. Take a sharp knife or a straight razor and start with the skin on his fat pink neck, peel slow, then pull slivers of skin off his back, his butt, then his big hairy belly, then bit by bit pull the skin off his dick. His love-a-kid dick, his hate-a-kid dick, his turned-me-into-not-a-kid dick. I hate him. Did I get to be like I am because of him, wanting to do the stuff 'cause of him? If I hadda been left alone, I woulda been a good kid. Maybe I would already be a dancer like that girl in the paper at ABT, thirteen! But them's the kids with parents behind 'em. I ain't got shit behind me except Brother John and them, and they turned against me in their cover-up shit.

Brother John? POW! Bust a cap in Brother John's big almost-a-nigger head—POW! POW! But first bend down Brother John and eat your dog shit! Uh oh, poor baby, you spilled some, come on, Brother John, and eat it. You must be a good little brother or I'll have to slice your balls off and throw them to the dogs that live under the train tracks. You wouldn't like that, would you? Where they go, I ask her, looking out the window at the trains passing, shaking the bottles of cologne on the windowsill. *Connecticut and shit, where white people live.* Her soft skin brushes against my cheek, her black hair silk like Jaime's. She sprays me with cologne. *Come on, we're going to say good-bye to your mami.* OK, Brother John raised up on the mean streets of Harlem by a black foster mother. I pick up my hamburger finish it off in a bite. Brother John, did I ever tell you I get tired of hearing that same old story? Did your old black mammy teach you to fuck little kids, did she tell your big sissy ass to get little nigger boys and stick 'em under your black dress, remember that! Bend down! I said. I'm gonna kick your motherfucking face dead in that shit. And then grind your nose in it.

"You finished?" she says loud. Can't she see? Maybe not, I realize.

"Yeah."

Brother John's nose ain't in no shit. It's mines that's in shit! What is this here but shit! Yeah, Brother John probably got another little kid by now up there talking about you have a future here with us. Is this my fucking future? I look at her, rag tied around her head, bent over, then back at the table where, as usual, a determined roach is advancing toward my plate. I believe she's my relative like I believe Brother Samuel is a man of God and the police is there to protect and serve our ass. Save that for thirteen-year-olds dancing at ABT, they get to believe the world is a good place. Slavery Days, this whole thing is like some story on TV or some shit Mrs Washington give us to read, where the protagonist wake up in another time, or another body, or as a beetle or some shit. Or like the stories where there's like a cave or something and you go in and find the monster or old witch, her, and they tell you something to make you rich or get married. But she ain't got nothing to make me rich. I feel like spitting on her old ass, I feel like shouting, TALK, TALK, TALK! Tell me what you did to get me up in here.

I look around the kitchen. Two big skillets and a big aluminum pot like at Miss Lillie's on top the stove. Hmmm, Miss Lillie's, try to forget that. I shoulda asked her for some cheese, I know she got it. What's she saving it for? I wish I had a Quarter Pounder with Cheese right now. Peeling paint is hanging off the ceiling in dusty gray flaps. It's so smoky 'cause there's no ventilation, no windows, not even a fan. In the kitchen fog, a lightbulb dangles yellow light from a cord hanging from the ceiling. Over the sink is a big clock with a second hand, the cord hanging from it another transit route for roaches. The handles of two of the cabinets on the wall are looped with a chain and padlock. I'm almost fourteen. I got to stay here till I'm eighteen? Four years? Four years! What happens if she dies? She's going to or she could, old as she is, that weird smell come off her, that swollen leg—what's that? I stand up.

"What happens if you die!"

"Well, I'll be damned! All dese days you done sat up here 'n said nothin', 'n when you do open yo' mouf, it's bullshit."

We read about Avi, who was so happy when his grandmother came and got him and then he ended up throwing her out the window. Front page of the *Daily News*. Avi was old, though, seventeen. I don't know if I hate her like that. I know I can't stand being scared all the time, I can't stand that this, this is . . . is my life.

"Yeah." I don't care how she feels. "What's gonna happen to me if you decease?" I want to say it's a legitimate question, like I would in class. I like Brother John, he never makes fun of us when we're trying a new word, anything. Yeah, bitch, decease, die, expire, terminate, delete, cancel, passing death like my mom. Answer me, lady. I don't even know if her ass get what I be saying.

"If I die? Boy, I believe you got a serious problem. Serious." She turns from where she been leaning on the stove to face me. The lightbulb glowing down on her in the greasy air. She shakes her rag head. I do hate her, because at St Ailanthus I had a future, I could see it, I can't now, not if she's my . . . my *anything*. A big water bug is crawling out from under the clock on the wall behind her, like yo! He's saying time to get shit straight, Granny! Time for Granny to start talking. But maybe she can't, maybe she's a for real nut?

"Who are you! Say something!" I holler.

"Who you hollerin' at!"

"Why I'm here! Who are you! What the fuck is going on, how I'm related to you. Who's my father, who's my mom? What kinda shit you walking around mumbling to yourself. I gotta stay in this house five years?" She walks over to the kitchen table slow.

"Nigger, you got it good. You got somebody. Whether you likes me or not. I ain' had nobody, nothin'. You hear me, nothin'. You got a place, food, you ain't got to do nothin' for it. I'm de only kin you got left—yo mama's dead, gran'mama, if dey'da brought you six months earlier, you'da seen her, yeah, six months earlier you'da seen yo' gran'mama, dat was my daughter, Mary. I'm yo' great-gran'ma, hear me, thas who I am!" She snorts. "Hmph! 'Who are you?'" she mimic me.

"Mary had stopped talkin' 'fore she died, eatin'—movin'. She hadn't been out de bed in years. It's not like I forgot 'bout her, but one day I jus' went in dere 'n, you know, she layin' up dere dead. Firemens had to get her out. Five hunert pounds, Lawh Awmighty."

I totally am not getting it. I think of Brother John talking about how the shopkeepers on 125th roll down the gray metal gates at night to keep their shit safe. Brother John say we got to do the same, the devil's a looter. Keep yourself safe, roll down the gates, hear no evil, see no evil, speak no evil. I feel the rattle in my mind, the metal gates coming down. But Mrs Washington say, *Humph! Do no evil and you won't have to worry about the rest of the mess. There's a time to see and hear evil.*

Yeah, what about Hamlet's father's ghost? Spoze Hamlet hadn't listened to his father's ghost? I've lost control again. Some big hand turns the kaleidoscope. It's awful. And whether I like it or not, it's a different picture. I don't get to choose. If it was me choosing, my life would be a *Cosby* rerun from the olden days. Someone who loved me would say, "Get up from here! You don't need to listen to this old witch darker than Shakespeare's shit."

"Yo' name Jamal, mean 'comely,' like Solomon in de Bible."

But this ain't TV or Shakespeare. "Comely"? How does she know what my name means? Ugh! On the table next to the salt shaker is a glistening roach egg sac I feel like when the chalk goes down the blackboard the wrong way, ugh, the creeps. Where did I get my kaleidoscope? I know I got my chess set from Mrs Washington.

"Say sumptin'? Oh, I like to talk, ha, ha, yes I do, only ain' usually nobody to talk to."

I forgot what Brother John said about the deers stopping in front of the oncoming cars, frozen in the light. Why they do it? Just stand there and get killed.

"You ain' stupid, what can I tell you 'bout yo' mama you don't know? You was wit' her every day of her life, damn near. If she evah let you outta her sight, I don' remember it. She didn't even bring you round, nothin'."

"She died of AIDS?"

"I don' know what she died of, know what dey say she died of. Shit, dey die of it too. Thas promised, death. I don' know what part of de Bible thas in, find it 'n read it for yo'self. You can read? Then you can find it. Taxes, death, 'n locusses, which is what dese roaches is. Locusses! So stop worrying 'bout dat, it's in de Bible.

"No telling what Fast Ass died of. I know it near 'bout killt her mama—between Carl Baby 'n Fast Ass, umph, umph, umph!"

I remember taking the kaleidoscope from Etheridge Killdeer, but I don't know if that's because it was his, I don't think so, I think it was mine, and I traded it for something, then didn't want the something and wanted my kaleidoscope back, that's fair.

Slavery Days ain't operating with a full battery pack. The hamburger was good, bigger than McDonald's but not as good. What I really need is fries. I look at the film on the kitchen wall, a coat of dust attached to years of grease. It ain't like this at St Ailanthus, it's clean there. Over the stove on the wall is a clock, not a digital, but a tick-tock, second hand moving. I don't make any answer to the woman (my . . . my what?) when she talks to me. It would make this whole shit real. Across from the table at the other end of the room is a door to a maid's room, Slavery Days said when I was looking at it one day. A long time ago rich people lived here in Harlem, had maids. That must have been a real long time ago. Slavery Days got to be around a hundred. I don't know if I am really going to live here—

I look down at my jeans. I need new gear, dance shit. I want money. How I know this arf-arf is gonna get ducats for me? I don't wanna hafta rob. I remember the pigs walking my elbows, that . . . that anticipation in their bones just radiating out, joy, if I give 'em a chance to kill me. I decide to die I'll kill my motherfucking self. I don't need no motherfucking NYPD.

"I knew you even though I nevah seed you befo'—"

Nevah seed? For God's sake! And, like, hello! Didn't the brothers or someone tell her I was coming? Who else could have showed up at her door?

"I was scared to say anythin' when you didn't show up after yo' mama died—"

Slavery Days sound like when you call and get an automated message, it's going, going but you know you not connected to a real person.

"See—"

No, I don't.

"'Cause I was, you know, keepin' care of yo' sister again."

Sister? broken pieces shake broken pieces of goddamn glass goddamn pieces of glass I'm only thirteen Miz Mary Mack Mack MACK all dressed in black My country 'tis of thee Now I lay me down to sleep Our Father who art in heaven hallow be thy name. As many times as you shake it, its picture change, who's crazy who's crazy? Sister?

Slavery Days walks over from the stove where she's been standing talking her crazy shit to me and picks up my plate. "Lemme git you some more meat."

St Ailanthus we had a microwave we could put our snacks in, cookies, nachos, half burrito with cheese, stuff like that. She gets another burger out the pan.

"I want some cheese," I mumble, a little embarrassed and leery at the same time. Leery because to ask for something is to give in to the situation and admit it exist, and this shit here does not exist for me.

She goes to the fridge and gets out a jar of mayonnaise and plunks it down on the table. Only one of her legs is swollen big, but both are bowed.

"Sister?" I echo when I realize she hasn't paused but is finished talking. Plop! A piece of the peeling ceiling paint drops. Suddenly I want to smash her!

"Yo' mama wadn't but twelve."

Twelve what? Size? Grade twelve? I'm thirteen, twelve, thirteen, twelve, thirteen, twelve?

"Shit, I had Mary when I was ten."

Free. Right now I'm free. I can't let them take my freedom. Ten? The date? What day is it today?

"She was retarded. She shoulda died. I kept care of her till yo' mama got her ass on her shoulders, den dey take her from me. I tell you I miss my record player more than I miss yo' mama 'n dat damn Mongo. But I took care her, only natchall I shoulda took care of you too."

Natchall? Only natchall? Only natural, she mean. She's crazy.

"You look like yo' daddy. Look like her too, same difference. You pretty like him. She looked like him too, only what's pretty on a man ain' so pretty on a gal, gal cain't get away wit' big lips can she, 'n being dark. People like dey meat dark if it's a man, light if it's a woman. But yo' mama looked like she was twenty-five at thirteen, sho did. You de same. But you ain't fat. You was spozed to come here after yo' mama died. Hear dat?"

What's she talking about? Then I hear the rain.

"Hear dat?"

I nod. I didn't realize we were on the top floor. It's raining hard. Hard.

"How did my father die?" Maybe he ain't dead. Maybe my dad is out there looking for me.

"AIDS, he had it. Don' know if thas what killt him. AIDS, nigger nevah give us nothin' 'cept his disease 'n three damn kids. Took, took, took! I tol' Mary from day one wadn't nothin' dere. I only saw him in de beginnin' when he was comin' round to court Mary's welfare check. Or whatevah he call himself doin'. Don' you evah feel like you de only one. Yo' daddy did his duty in many a pussy. You got brothers 'n sisters out dere. You jus' gotta go out 'n dig 'em up 'n you ain' got to do no deep diggin'!"

I feel like vomiting hearing her talk. Lie. Hearing her try to tear my father down like what happened to Alvin Johnson at school, but his father did love him, and his mother keep shit from him because she didn't get no child-support money.

I could call the social worker and tell her this is some wack shit, I can't deal, come get me, save me. And then what? Get put in a group home or some juvenile detention shit. I could just walk out of here, run away, live on the street, be a park boy till I get AIDS or killed or some shit. How come I can't just get a full deck like everybody else, why? Why?

First thing I got to get is a schedule. I'm used to getting up, going to school, and doing good stuff every day. I'm not a bum.

"She nevah even brought you by to visit. I nevah even seed you once. She act like her fast tail ain' de cause of a lot of what happened. Carl did it by himself? Twice? I don' think so. How old is you now?"

I'm not used to talking to people unless it's other kids. It's hard to describe, but she ain't really talking to me. Her talk is like a fog, every now and then she throw a question out of it. Now her crazy ass is . . . is what? Singing? Or trying to in a rusty voice.

> If an evah git away from a harvest
> I don't wanna see a rose grow

She's making like she's playing a banjo, stomping her feet, and stepping side to side. This is it, I guess she done dived all the way off the deep end.

"You know when I come here from Mississippi?"

"Huh?" Why me? Why is this happening to me?

"I said, you know when I come here from Mississippi?"

"Ahh, no."

"A long time ago."

Kill her, kill her! Just slap her old ass and stomp her brains out. What kinda life could I have here! St Ailanthus! *God, author of all heavenly gifts, you gave St Ailanthus both a wonderful innocence of life and a deep spirit of penance.* Now I lay me down to sleep—I think the life here, whatever happens to me here, is worse than if I went to jail. Then I think, chill, it's all a big mistake or . . . or I don't know. Brother John is probably working on this right now.

"You through?"

I look at the circles of stiff grease on the plate, shake my head yes. My head is a kaleidoscope. She gets up and with her dragging walk goes to put my plate in the sink. Looking at her gives me a sick feeling, the dream I had of Blondie her jar breaks in on me.

"I got a lot of stuff to do to catch up with my schoolwork and dancing," I tell her.

"My mama hadda been dere ol' Nigger Boy wouldn'ta got me. In fact thas how he got me, talkin' 'bout my mama—"

I mean what is this, is she on automatic, does she jus' sit up and talk to anybody?

"I was sittin' on a rock—"

And I'm sittin' on a chair at a table in a blue room where a piece of peeling paint has just fallen from the ceiling.

"Yeah, honey, I was sittin' up on a rock away from de picnic tables 'n de music. Lookin' down de road. Sky blue fluffy clouds, hog on de spit, good smell up yo' nose. Nigger Boy pluckin' de banjo. Banjo stop. Somebody start up on guitar. Black shadow cross me, Nigger Boy's pant legs. Hair on my arm stand up. 'Youze lookin' for yo' mama?' Nigger Boy weird. Sick. Let's face it, he ain' de only man stick his dick in a ten-year-old. I seed a lot, 'n it almos' ain' nothin'. But Nigger Boy weird 'cause, let's face it, back den every colored fella in de South a 'boy,' a 'nigger boy,' to de white folks. But Nigger Boy dat to hisself! Ask him his name 'n he'd tell you, Nigger Boy. How's dat fo' last week's gravy! Why I care what a man fuck me when I'm ten years old call hisself? I don'! Jus' when people find out he daddy my baby dey tell me—so, shit, I'm tellin' you!"

Gee, thanks. I need my jacket, I think. I look at her sitting at the table talking. I just feel cold inside and like I need to vomit, but like my mouth is sealed. There's a calendar on the wall from? Shit! Twenty years ago! Before I was born, before anybody I know was born except the brothers.

"You ain't talkin' to me," I tell her. "You talkin' to the air!" You know, like shut up! And stop wasting your breath. It's not getting in me.

"I know who I'm talkin' to. I'm talkin' to you, nigger!"

Nigger? She's crazy for sure, one thing for kids to be talking about nigger but a old lady like this—

"I ain' talkin' to you? You sho nuff is crazy! Who you think I'm talkin' to? You mine, my great-gran'son. Nigger Boy yo' great-gran'father!"

My mother died in a car accident, my father died in the war. I get up go get my jacket, but I come back in the kitchen.

"I had jumped up to run after Mama but Auntie slap me, hold me back till I cain't see nothin' of Mama goin' down de road. After dat I go sit on de rock whar I can see de road, weeks I go dere waitin', thinkin' like she went down de road, she be back, gonna come up de road. Thas whar I'm sittin' day of de picnic, on de rock off by mysef when Nigger Boy come up."

In seventh we were looking at the one-celled amoebae on the projection screen. *Isn't it fascinating, boys!* No! The seething blobs make my skin crawl. I want to tear the screen off the wall. I want to slap her. Why I gotta listen to this shit?

"Whatchu doin' ovah here by yo'sef? Ize waitin' fo' Mama. Come on, Nigger Boy say, let's go find yo' mama. I jumps up hold out my hand fo' Nigger Boy to take it. I'm walkin' wit' him into de woods ovah de little stream I ain' spozed to go ovah by mysef. I think, Mama ain' in no woods. You evah play house wit' boys? How he know? It a secret what me 'n Jonesy Boy do! Why a big ol' man like Nigger Boy want to know anyhow? We walk over to whar de weepy willow trees is. I'm scared of snakes. Nigger Boy jus' push me down off my feet like we kids playin' in de field or sumptin'. Den he take out his dick. I remember it don' scare me. I don' know what's comin', how could I? It's so pretty, really, a man's thang, his at least, shiny 'n black like a licorice. I sit up to see better, he push me back down, don' say nothin', spit in his hands rub on his dick. Is he gonna pee? He reach down pull my draws, such as dey was, off. Press his hand ovah my mouf. He stick hisself in a place I ain' know I had yet. I'm lookin' at de sky through de trees, it cracks apart in big blue pieces under de dark branches 'n green leaves. I go out today 'n look up, de sky dat same blue 'n I feel it start to crack apart again. Cry, what else you gonna do? Rest here a few minutes 'fore you go home, he say. Don' go back to de picnic, do dey'll know what you did 'n you'll git a whippin' fo' doin' it! Yo' mama find out what you made me do to you, she'll nevah, nevah come back. Nevah! When you hear de banjo start up to playin' again, git up go home, go to bed 'n don' tell nobody, nevah, you hear me, what you done done. Shit, I don' know what I done done. But 'cause he say it like dat I think of it like dat, dat I done done sumptin'."

Synonym for make you sick? Revulsion. Use that word in a sentence. I am revulsioned by this stinky bitch. No revulsed. Repulsion. I feel repulsion I might throw up. Nauseate. Some little insect is jumping around the lightbulb into the ceiling. The lightbulb is its sun. If some shit like that really happened, in broad daylight? A river, a river is with boats and people fishing and . . . and shipping, ports, commerce. Roaches, the opposite—they run from the light, I don't think I've ever seen a roach outside. Can they live outside? I don't feel like I'm cracking. I feel I have cracked. In two. I'm separate pieces. This kitchen is not dirty like no one has ever cleaned it or people throw shit and don't pick it up. It's grimy, grease and dirt stuck to stuff, but everything is in place, the dish towel is so dirty it's almost black, but it's folded neat hanging on a rack over the sink. What is she talking about? Who is she talking to? This is a worse mistake than the police station. Way worse. Like open the car door and

driver point to that pile of shit, *Hey, dude, this is you, your fucking relative.*
Get used to it? Fuck that!

"I don' know what to say when people point at my belly."

If this was a dream, I'd be done woke up already! I'm still standing
clutching my jacket, which I left the kitchen to get . . . what ? A minute,
second, a half hour ago. I sit back down press the jacket to my chest, sniff
it, start to rock slightly. Toosie? What the fuck!

"Daddy? Daddy of what! You git what I'm sayin' don'chu?"

She looks at me expecting something. I don't blink. She's acting mental like a homeless sitting up there talking to herself like she ain't all there.

"Dey talkin' 'bout Daddy 'n I ain' even hip to I'm pregnant. Chile,
chile, chile! Who you been playin' doctor wit'? I shake my head. Doctor? I don' know dat game. Come on now, we know it someone. Mama
Daddy? House? I nevah played house wit' nobody 'cept Jonesy Boy. Jonesy's Mama 'n Daddy ask him he de daddy. He say naw! Dey beat him to
tell de truth. He still say naw. Beat him some mo'. Tooth come out. He
tell de truth. Auntie Sweet who keep kids while folks is in de fields say
shame I'm in trouble so young. Trouble? Yeah, trouble, Auntie Sweet say,
youze knocked up. She walk me ovah to de hog pen."

Thirteen going on fourteen, a boy. The side of my face itches like hell,
the skin tightening as it heals? I want to scratch it. Scarred face, black,
Harlem—all that go together? Yeah, Jaime, I look like Denzel except my
face is scarred. Permanent. I ain't Crazy Horse. I'm a stupid kid, nigger,
like they say in public school, with a gash across the side of my face for
life, not Crazy Horse. No cheeseburger, I remember the quiche, spinach
and cheese, about to be chucked up with all the chocolate cake I'd eaten.
I crawl through the window over the ledge falling, falling down to 125th
Street. They'll all be sorry now. But I never got to the window, I just
threw up. I wish I had got to the window.

"Auntie Sweet point to Big Pink, who ain' even pink, point to de little
hogs suckin' at her tits. De tits pink. Look at de little one, Auntie Sweet
say, 'Member when dey was inside Big Pink? Yeah, I say, 'n now dey on
de outside! Well, she say, dat's what done happened to you, you got a little

one inside of you. Hog! I holler. No fool, a baby, a little boy or gal. How? Well, from you 'n Jonesy doin' de nasty, I hear it right. You ain' storyin', is you? Naw, I ain' storyin', I tells her. Storyin' is a whippin' fo' sure!"

I'm sitting at one end of the table near the door, she's at the other end of the table, her chair facing perpendicular to me so I'm looking at her silhouette rocking and talking crazy. She's hunched back, look like she don't have a neck. I just feel like the heebie-jeebies listening to her like when a roach scurry across the floor STAMP IT! I never seen a green refrigerator. Underneath some spots of the peeling blue paint you can see the walls was yellow, the color of old piss. Everything here is old, like from the 1950s or something, maybe the '70s, I'm not sure. When did people have shit like this? I never seen a hog.

"It was twins is what it was! Of course, I didn't know dat den. So hog, baby, whatevah it was, I knowed I was gettin' bigger 'n bigger every day."

She's like a movie, rocking, the green refrigerator behind her. Insect, I think, I step on her and throw her out. She's an insect. She ain't human. Her being human makes me ashamed.

"I be chewin' on sumptin' 'n a toof fall out. Or I wake up chokin' 'n it on a toof, roll ovah 'n spit it out. Dey was half gone when I got here. All gone now. Keep yo' teef, boy! Den it's like my bones wax, not my back like it is now, but my legs start to bend, like wax git warm, bend—I gits bowlegged whar I was nevah like that befo'. Auntie says thas what chile birfin' early do fo' you. But nothin' else change 'cept my body, I keeps fol-lowin' Auntie out to de fields every day. Evah git some chicken, Auntie say, eat de bones. Whar I'm gonna git chicken from, I live wit' her since Mama gone, she don't give me none. Eat clay, she say. I like the taste 'n it fill me up. Only time I filled up livin' down dere. Later Beymour tell me, thas wrong. You pregnant, shoulda drinked milk."

She looks at me. "Gon' git you some milk."

Broke-brain retard, what milk? I get up. The only doors I've opened since I been here aside from "my" room and front door is the refrigerator doors, ain't no milk. Like she could read my mind.

"Wadn't none befo', but de home attendant from de 'fare, she shop fo' me sometimes. I got to give her some of de food stamps, but I don' care, I don' hardly eat none no way. Gon' git some milk, it's milk 'n bacon in dere, biscuit mix, no tellin' what else. Clay's got lead 'n shit in it, ain' always good, Beymour say. He took me to de dentist when I got here. I'm in de field, I got my hoe raised, not high, you know, but I got it raised, you know, you chop 'n you step, chop 'n you step, like dat. Don' be wastin' no whole lots of energy raisin' de hoe all high, ain' nobody takin' yo' picture, you workin'! I grab de hoe so hard, screams Oh, OH, OH! Auntie put her hoe down, walk fast ovah to me. Ride it, ride it! she hollerin'. I pure dee don' know what de fuck she talkin' 'bout. If you'll excuse my French. Dis hurt more den Nigger Boy bustin' me open. Dis breakin' me. Feel like de bones in my back on fire. Shit! Den oohhh weird like a egg PLOP easy thing fall outta me, Auntie say later, fo' she could ketch it. She pick it up, Hush now, it's ovah. But I go to hollerin' again. Whatever it is she done picked up 'n done pulled out, it ain't movin'. She bite de cord, her teef strong, she ain't nevah had no kids. Hush, she say, it's dead. She soun' sad. I nevah heard her soun' like that befo'. Ahhh! I scream. Someone say, Ain' ovah yet, Auntie, sumptin' still up dere. Well, I wadn't jus' screamin' to be screamin', thas yo' gran'mother up in dere—"

I feel my head is swelling. What's going in my ears like air being pumped into a balloon.

"Yeah, yo' gran'ma up dere but don' nothin' come down. Sun past high in de sky when dey bring Mavis. Ninety-two years old, white folks call her de same thang dey call Auntie, 'n Auntie Sweet: Auntie. Only Mavis tell 'em, I ain' none of you people's auntie! Cain't call me Mavis, don' call me! But dey call her Auntie Mavis anyway. Master's first son, white doctor do him 'n forceps clamper his brain, after dat dey call Mavis. Yeah, she say, dey got to call ol' nigger Mavis! I don' call her nothin' at de time 'cause I'm layin' in de dirt in so much pain I'm jus' goin', Oh, oh. I'm sho' Ize dyin'. Bring me some water, Mavis holler, some water 'n hawg grease. I'm fidden to go up in her. Sumptin' up dere. I think of Big Pink 'n her little worm hogs, oh, no! Den I don' think no more. If my bones was on fire befo', they thunder 'n lightnin' now. I don' know whether it takes minutes or hours, but it feel like all de bones in me is bein' pulled apart. Den it's all ovah. Nevah to happen again. Someone say, Shucks, it got hair enough to braid! Big thang, Girl. I feel sumptin', not proud, but sumptin'. Dirt all ovah my shoulders, I remember dat! A boy 'n a girl done come outta me. Boy died."

A roach is crawling over the table. She pops the roach's back with her thumb. Splat. I push back from the table, but the leg of my chair sticks in a hole in the linoleum. She looks at me.

"You de first boy to come out alive."

My skin is crawling.

"I don' remember from dere. Somehow I musta got back to de cabin. Maybe somebody carry me, maybe I walks. I'm tired."

Shut up, I think, *would you just shut the fuck up!*

"I lay down on my blanket wit' de baby on top of me. I wanna throw up."

Shut up shut up!

"But ain' nothin' to throw up. Auntie look at me stretched on my pallet. It's in de dirt. What I hate 'bout back den—lyin' on de dirt, birfin' in de dirt. Auntie say, my name Mary. I look at her, you know thas nice, but I'm tired. Yo' mama ain' nevah comin' back. Why she tell me dat? Youze in my house, she say, why don' you name de baby after me? I hadn't thought 'bout it, but if I'd had a minute I woulda said, Dessa, dat was my mama's name. Make sense to name her dat. Auntie say again, Why don' you name de baby after me? Auntie? No, fool, Mary, my name is Mary. So dat's how Mary got to be Mary."

I feel like roaches is crawling all over me now. I want to scream shut up, shut up! Slap her. The balloon my head has become, every word, every word—pressure. I hate how her back curls over, the ugly hump, how she talk all country and shit. She's staring in front of her like it's TV, only turn around to look at me when she got something extra retarded to say, like hog babies or some shit. I unbutton top button of my Levi's. I don't know what she's talking about. She's talking roaches walking over me, feel crazy. OK, hog babies and all that shit, we so motherfucking crazy. Let's go crazy. I unzip my jeans take my shit out and start jacking off while she's talking. OK, the shit is equal now. Up and down up and down up down up down try to see the pretty colors in my kaleidoscope not hogs and country girl busted up down by some river I never seen. Ohhh, I can change the picture, um huh another one comes up instead of this dumb one, I see little blue lights, it's dark, the dark is smooth like the preemies, how smooth they skin like babies, how strong I am, how the white girl come to Imena's class looking at me, can't take her eyes off me, sitting on my dick now, she's telling me I love you, Papi, or whatever white bitches say I love you ohh shake shake kaleidoscope dick shake don't break me mirror explain this shit Oohh! to me, what I did to end up with this old bitch talking about Nigger Boys, hogs and shit. Jaime's asshole is like a velvet apple to my tongue, the smell like leaves from a tree. Ohh! I stand up my dick in my hand pumping now, I feel like a tower of light power like light is in me, not blood ohh ohh! I feel like a beautiful white girl is sucking me off! Shit my hand moving faster and faster and faster!

"Crazy!" she screams. "You fuckin' CRAZY!"

It come out like white light, divine goodness like Brother John said Jesus so loved his brother as he so loved himself, it is good to touch your-self oooohhhhhhh let Brother John see it go SPOUT OUT SPLAT! How you like that, you old WITCH! Running around talking all that weird old shit. I'm normal normal! Old roach bitch! I run my fist clenched down the shaft of my beautiful penis to the tip and then shake WHAP! Cum splatter onto the plastic tablecloth. Ha, ha, ha! She screaming how she gonna tell the social worker I'm crazy and shit. Let her! Who gives a fuck, I'm just spozed to listen to stupid shit? She ain't my relative. Maybe I find out my father ain't really dead or this bitch ain't my real relative, which I already know she ain't. I zip up my pants button my fly pull the chair out from the table, grab the back of it like it's a barre, it's the right height. First position! Tendu à la second, demi and up, demi and up, now demi grande plié and up. I'm in Roman's class when I really see myself, discover myself, in the mirror. My hand is on the barre. I'm looking at the flabby thighs and big butt of the white girl in front of me. The meat hangs off her arm between her shoulder and elbow like a dead bird's wing, her wrists break instead of doing like Roman says, *Extend in a straight line out from the shoulder to the elbow to the wrist like you is holding a giant beach ball*. She's looking at Roman to see if he's paying her any attention. I look at him too, then look straight ahead of me at the girl, at all the bodies lined up in front of her jammed in the same position, trying to execute the thing called rond de jambe, hardly anybody able to do it right like Roman had demonstrated. We're beginners. Everybody's anxious. I look to the side of me in the mirror. It's almost a shock, like I've never seen before the way the muscles of my thighs stand up and out as if somebody called their name, quadriceps, biceps, soleus, femoris? Quadriceps femoris? I want more books where am I going to get them from harder to steal from the library now that they got that sensor thing. I want to know the names of every muscle, everything in the body, period. Brother John found Christ when he was a little boy. I know here is the Holy Eucharist. Fuck God. The way my black tights are holes and raggedy like Jesus in a way makes my thighs look more perfect. I look in the mirror on the opposite wall, which reflects the mirror on this wall and is endlessly repeating my body! The mirror is magic! Giving yourself back to you over and over again.

We step away from the barre to center floor in front of Roman, who is standing in front of the mirror.

"Glissade, assemblé!"

I stumble. Someone giggles. At me? I'm flooded with humiliation. And determination. What I can't do, I will. Roman knows it. Fuck these people. Shake shake disappear, motherfuckers, like bits of colored glass rearranged into oblivion with my kaleidoscope.

"Assemblé!" Roman screams. "Like this!" And he shows me with his hands and arms what my feet and legs should be doing. I try again and again. "Leave it for now!"

Inhale, plié.

"Did you hear what I said? I said leave it for now!" Then with something almost like regret he says, "You'll get it. Don't worry, boy, you'll get it."

"I strikes out when I'm twelve! I had been done lookin' down de road every day—" she says.

I sit back down for now, exhausted, my barre a chair again.

"Wonder what could be down dat damn road! De road, de road! How far it go, whar it take my mama 'n what's at de end of it? Sumptin' pullin' at my bones. Heel hittin' de road, dirt 'tween my toes, barefoot in a blue dress same color as dese plates. I bought dese, not Beymour or Betsy, for de house seem like a hunnert years ago. I got dese at Klein's. I don' even know if dere is a Klein's anymo'. Dress same color as hour befo' night sky. Same color as my dreams!"

I look at her.

"Huh! I got dat dress off a clothesline, one of de missuh's children! Blowin' in de wind, like a piece of de sky, I thinked. I'm young I ain' nevah been afraid to take sumptin'. Beymour liked dat 'bout me. I got on de sky, dust 'tween my toes, little rocks under de bottoms of my feets. Ground feel different. Breathe in, air seem different on de road! Feel like I'm breathin' in some of Mama, breathin' out some of de lonely. I don' even hear Auntie come up behind me, slap me down to de ground, Gal! I get up start to run, she snatch me by de collar of de dress, rip it off. Whar in Job's name do you a think you goin'! Bap! You jus' like your nothin' mammy! Ize standin' dere in some drawers made outta a sack. Sun hot, I gits cold. Get dark inside, yeah, whar was I goin', no money food shoes. A blue dress. Dreamin'."

Passé fifth, passé fifth changement. Hmmm, then what did he do? Oh! Dégagé with the back foot. Fourth. Plié. *That's your preparation for your turn. Plié, turn—Jon and Sara, doubles. Paul, single. Not you, Abdul, passé relevé only. No turn.* But I will turn. *I said, NO turn!* he screams. *You listen or you get out!* I look at myself in the glass, see how I'm gonna be.

I look at the blue plate, empty except for the rings of thick white grease left by the hamburgers. What is it about plates? What did Miss Lillie say? This kitchen is a rectangle, the table pushed against the side wall. At Miss Lillie's the table was in the middle of the room, only one refrigerator and a cabinet full of plates. No orange juice, eggs sausage jam pancakes steak fries but plenty plates. *I got them out the washing-powder box. They used to give you something when I was coming up. You need something with a house full of leeches sucking the life out of your purse. I done had them plates longer than you niggers been alive!* White with red roses on them. Baked beans wieners. Batty Boy BAP! Then after that one ear different. Running Knife of the Sioux stabs Miss Lillie's scout to death. Scout masquerading as a dog! They cared about that! I hate dogs. What they do with Tyrese's finger? Forget about it, my mother says. I do. What a lot of people don't know is that the Lakota were the westernmost arm of the Dakota nation. I don't hate dogs. I want to cut myself. Or pierce, yeah pierce, something. Tattoo? I'm so dark would it really stand out?

"Chop-step, chop-step, de little green plants dat gonna be cotton gotta be chopped till dey 'bout dis much"—she raises her hands to her TV screen in the air, moves them about six inches apart—"from each other. Don', dey choke each other when dey grow. Step raise yo' hoe swing. Waste energy raisin' it too high, too low gotta do it again. We struck out wit' nothin'. Dis time I left in de middle of de night, wit' Mary. Not so much I wanted her honest to tell but I didn't want to be dragged back like befo', 'n she knew I was gonna leave her. She knew 'n wouldn't let me outta her sight. We lay down las' thang I see is her eyes starin' at me. She nevah let herself go to sleep first. When I wake up, she up. We walked. Don' let no one tell you bein' on de road is easy. We slept in ditches. I can remember snakes slidin' cross us. But better dat than de two-leg snakes. Seed a hangin' hear me. Hear me? I seed a lynchin'. Can still smell it. Like hair burnin' but worse. Mary get hungry I give her a rock to suck on. We ate dandelion, roots 'n all, clay. I worked fields, yards, a woman take me in her house to clean. Try not to pay me. I crawl back in a window 'n under de bed 'n get de money out her box. Fool had de key to de box hangin' on de underside of de bed leg. Hah! I seed it cleanin' on my hands 'n knees like dey like you to do, don' feel it's clean if you ain' crawlin'. People think you stupid 'cause you cain't read 'n all, I may be, but dese some fast fingers, hah! From dere we runnin' for our lives! If she miss it, we dead. Dey on wheel, we on foot, shotguns sticks, don' even need no badge to kill you back den. Dey jus' do it. We barefoot niggers. But I guess she don' miss it. I buy us bus tickets to New York City. After de tickets had five dollars, you gotta remember a shoeshine ain' even cost a dime, boy! A nickel was de fare to take you anywhar! We was rich to ourselves, ate chicken-fried steak at de rest stop—*at,* not *in* it. Dey hand you de food out de back door 'n you sit on de dirt or a rock or a garbage can to eat 'n be grateful to git it! Thas right, ate chicken-fried steak 'n dranked Royal Crown soda, RC! You cain't even git dat too much no more.

"Lookin' out de window, sleepin', lookin' out de window, stoppin' towns along de way. Cain't keep track of time, was we on de bus a week, two weeks? Or was it jus' days? One day we lookin' out de window 'n ain' no more cows 'n roadside diners 'n everythang git bigger 'n closer together, trees forget theyself in de steel 'n cement, cars is buzzin'! It's like a million parties goin' in yo' eyes. De driver holler. One half hour to New Yawk Citay! 'N we still a half hour from it? Everythang keep gittin' closer 'n closer, even in de daytime, lights! Now stuff is all in de sky, buildings reachin' up to heaven. Bus pull into a dark tunnel, den open into a long cement yard full of other buses 'n he holler, Last stop! New Yawk Citay! Port Authority, Forteee-second Street. Everybody off! Folks reachin' overhead 'n under de seats fo' cardboard boxes, grips, blanket rolls. I ain' gotta reach up, what I got is on my back 'n in de seat next to me, big ol' gal baby. I almos' hate her. I don' know why. She don' cry or ask for nothin'. De station is de biggest buildin' I evah seed in my life! So many lights look like dey done brought de stars indoors. People! Whew! More people 'n I evah seed, all movin' at once.

"I look out 'n see him. At least dat how it seem at de time, I jus' look 'n see him. Later I find out he seed me way fo' I seed him. In fact he been waitin' on me. Well, not me me, but someone like me. He done noticed I ain' got no luggage 'n I'm lookin' at everyone but not fo' no one. Some people on de bus had scraps of paper, envelopes wit' letters in 'em, dey take out 'n read ovah 'n ovah, a cousin, sister. He got pointed-toe shoes de color of sweet potato pie, tan suit wit' stripes, high drape pants, 'n a shirt de color of honeysuckle.

"You know what I remember 'bout dat day? He was so purty 'n shiny, I was thinkin', scratchin' my head 'n thinkin', Is he real? Is he like some kinda angel 'n is dis place heaven? He walked ovah to me 'n Mary. I remember he surprised she only five 'n I'm only fifteen. I guess both of us look older den we is. I'm not really ugly at all, but I don' find dat out till a few days later dressed up lookin' in de glass at Beymour's. But I'm gittin' ahead of mysef. Beymour Waycross. I don' know what he's talkin' 'bout, he say, I got a sportin' house in Harlem.

"Dat's good, I say.

"Yeah, I think so, he say.

What kinda sports you play? I only really know 'bout baseball 'n footraces de mens useta run on de plantation.

"He look at me funny. Where you goin'?

"I explain to him here is whar we goin'. We done walked 'n walked, slept outdoors, cleaned folks' house, chopped cotton, picked weed outta white folks' yard to git bus fare. 'N now we here.

"So ah, he say, where you goin' from here?

"From here? Dat's crazy-soundin'. From here? From here? I hadn't thought dat far. Pick up gold in de street? Whar to from here? We got no money, no place to go. Now what? My last ounce o' spirit had gone to gittin' us here. Now we was here, a million people 'n I didn't know a one, signs all around 'n I couldn't make out a one. I was fifteen years old, I coulda been five.

"He said, Come on, I take you uptown and you can get a feel for our little operation. If you like it, cool, if you don't like it, you can move on! Slavery's over! He laff at his own joke.

"Next thang I know, I'm in Harlem 'n I been here evah since."

Roman says Capezio canvas split sole are the best but leather slippers last the longest. *The split sole is best. You got nice feet for a black boy.* I'll get the Capezios.

Locusses! What kind of shit is that? I try to think of something, anything except what I'm hearing. The skin is tightening on the cut side of my face. The pain feels good, takes me out of here. I could tear my own fuckin' face off! I feel like I want to see my bones. I want to go back to St Ailanthus and stomp Brother Samuel. She's still talking!

"Shut up! Shut up! SHUT UP!"

What is she talking about? Roach-ass bitch! OK, I got the deal, I don't come from shit according to her ass? So she can shut up now. Just shut the fuck up! Not shit? I don't come from shit? Ugly freak, she freaks me out in her dirty dress, rags. Roach! Hah! I put my hand over my mouth to stop the giggle coming out. See the feelers coming out of her stupid head, her curved scaly back. Antenna wiggle waft stupid mouth moving. She don't need to be talking. I get up from my chair tiptoe across the room like she's not staring right at me, open the cupboard under the sink. Ajax, boric acid, ammonia, bucket, oh, there we go—Raid! Kills roaches with one shot! Ha! Ha! I snatch the aerosol can! Leap toward her horrible lying ass.

"RAID! RAID!" I scream, pointing the nozzle at her old ass.

"You done lost yo' mind!"

"YES!" And I'm getting ready to do a service to humanity like Brother Samuel said Hitler did. What Brother John say when I told him that? "Brother Samuel did *not* say that, and I don't want to hear you say anything like that about him ever again. Hear? Hear?" And *I* don't want to hear no more about hogs and Nigger Boy. I step closer.

"Shut up, Roach! Shut up, ROACH!!!"

Press the nozzle, hardly anything comes out. It's all used up like everything in this fucking house! I shake the can, flinging some drops at her. She screams. It feels like my chest is being squeezed into a little box. I try to laugh at her screaming, but it comes out as a sob. I'm sobbing and sobbing. I can see everything even though my tears is blinding me. I see her on her back in the dirt giving birth, giant playing the banjo, and hogs, hogs, ugh, like pink worms. If I had some gasoline, I'd pour it on her, watch her burn, then go around to St Ailanthus and burn that whole shit down! Yeah, burn! My grandfather played a banjo, was named Nigger Boy? Please! I'm only a kid. My head aches. I walk back to the table, sit down, lay my face down like we do in time-out at school, UGH! My head pops back up. Shit! I laid down in the damn sperms! Ugh! I cry some more. I've never cried like this. I look at her. She's wiping her face with the dirty dish rag. She hands the insecticide-smelling rag to me and like my looking at her was some kind of cue starts talking!

"Well, dis apartment was different back den, lemme tell ya! But dat subway was somethin'. Beymour say follow him. 'N we did. What else could we do? We stepped out in the street still light. Night was comin' though in mo' ways den one. You too young to know how dark it can really git! You don' know nothin' till you love somebody, nigguh! I was lookin' fo' my mama. I walked barefoot, I steal, mens take atvannage more den once. Know what atvannage mean? Mean you work all day in de field. Know what work all day in de field mean? Mean you ask dis person, dat person whar someone need a hand, show up whar dey tell you 'fore sunup. Be a man in a straw hat leanin' on a stick or hoe lookin' like a daddy point to some fields heavy wit' needin' to do. It's still mornin' dark. You standin' there with de locals, de live-ons, 'n de other drifters like yo'sef. You ain't de only one got a kid, but you de only one wit'out a bandanna or straw hat, paper bag or pail wit' some dinner. You work all day till you drop fo' so little, so little. Look behind you, you walkin' lookin' to git somethin' to eat, anythin' to eat, lay down, den hit de road again in de morning. You thinkin' which way north, but de nigger walkin' behind you, followin' you out de field, got yo' money 'n yo' behind on his mind. Ain' like TV, don' nobody save yo' ass. Surprise me after dat anythin' can scare me, but look like it de opposite, everythin' scare me, startin' with dat damn iron horse!

"It like Beymour pullin' us down inside de world's pussy 'n dat train come rumblin' out, bull eyes burnin' yellow, de cement ground shakin', I mean shakin', sparks was spittin'. Mary pee on herself. What is it? I ain' gittin' on it. Is you crazy! Make a awful sound when it stop. Doors open, de people jammed in like a bunch of maggots, but I do git in. De people pours out 'n Beymour pushin' hard pushes me in!

"We get out 145th Street, so long ago, so long ago. All de folks movin' so fast, so much cement, blacktop street, peoples dressed up like Sunday, like angels! Nothin's like Mississippi! I cain't keep my eyes off de women dressed up like dey white! Hair pomaded straight 'n shiny, high heels, stockin's—cinnamon was de tone back den, tight bright dresses. You, no, *I* never seen de like. Every other place we pass, Beymour nod his head. That's Hi Boy's Playhouse, that's Moore's Bar & Grill, piano combo Mon, tappers come in Tuesday, big name Friday and Saturday, jam session afterward, Thursdays hot, maids got that day off and they party hard soon's they git away from them white folks' nasty kids! You'll see, he promise. 'N he didn't lie. 'N after some of dese folks party, dey come to us! Baby, Harlem gotta fast lane 'n we part of it! It's a river flowin', de bedrock de music 'n de feets dancin' is de water. Life short, gotta live it! Pass a butcher shop, shoe repair, a man haulin' a cart on his back full of rags, den some little hole in de wall smell like a picnic! That's the best barbecue in town, chitlins, potato salad, greens, whatever you had back there, we got here only ten times, no a hunnert times, more!

"We git to 805 St Nicholas, I forgit de day, de year even. We wadn't big on countin' months 'n stuff back in de country. You look at a tree or yo' kids to see how dey done grown how ol' dey is to tell you 'bout yo'self. Jazz was big, blues in all de clubs, not dat banjo shit like Nigger Boy play but stuff wit' electricity behind it, damn near kill you to listen to it. But anyway we git to 805, doorman open de door. Shit, nowadays we hardly got a door much less a doorman! De floors shine like white summer sky, all dat white marble, de floors, walls, all marble. I nevah seed de like! Dere was a statue in de middle of de lobby of a naked person, I say I nevah seed de like. Chandeliers make de light look like a hunnert little candles burnin' all at once. Now, I ain' nevah been in a elevator befo', I still remember de feelin' inside my pussy when de door closed 'n we zoomed up, EEH! I'm so tired, though everythin' seem like a dream.

"When I walk in here, I think it's de mos' beautiful place, better den de white folks I had cleaned fo'. De floors was shiny as mirrors, even had chandeliers in de hall, yes indeed. Boarders stole mos' of our stuff ovah de years, but I tell you when I walked through dat door, I couldn't believe dis was a place colored people live in. Dis place finer den de white woman's house I steal de bus money from. How a nigger git a house like dis? I remember de floors mos'ly befo' dey got all covered wit' linoleum. Paisley 'n cypress pattern, man say when he come to put it in, I hated it, one layer wear out 'n dey put on another wit'out takin' de ol' one up. I hated it. Hated de way de house went down after Beymour. Beymour was a young man on his way up, you hear me!

"Beymour introduce me to Betsy first thing. Who is mo' like she got a magnet in her den dat she's so pretty. Yo' eyes jus' pulled to her in spite of yo'sef. She dark, daddy was Chinese, so she got dem eyes, big titties, little behind. Betsy look at me 'n Mary, den she look away, like one look is enough!"

She stops talking and gets up with the filthy rag in her hand and wipes up the blob of sperms on the table. She goes to sit back down without looking at me.

"Yeah, de way Betsy look at me 'n Mary make me wonder what I looks like to her. I don' think I evah thought nothin' like dat befo', what I look like to somebody. I look at Mary like I nevah seed her befo'. We been on de road almos' starvin' till de end, but she don' look it. She almos' up to my shoulder. Nigger Boy almos' de tallest man on de plantation. She bigger around de shoulders den mos' girls, coulda picked a lot of cotton. But she nevah worked a day in her life. Her hair so tuff it sit on her head in beads. I cain't comb it. Shit, didn't even comb my own. Like mos' babies got big eyes, she was nevah like dat, had little bitty shiny black eyes like bullets.

"They's just up from Mississippi, Beymour tell Betsy. Ain't got too much of nothin'. But this here is an honest girl tryin' to make it. Willin' to work hard, ain't ya? He look at me I nod yes. She look at him. Well, what you want me to do, Bey?

"Put her in the room Dolly useta work out of, figure out what to do with the crumb crusher. He reach in his pocket pull out a shiny brown leather billfold hand Betsy a bill. Git her what she need. Then hip her to the scam she don't get it already. Start her off Friday.

"Well, uh, first thing usses need to do is run some bathwater. Y'all got any clothes?

"Jus' what we got on.

"I got drawers and garter belts, but you need to get some stockin's from Two-Bit, she small like you. We'll get you a dress and some shoes today. What's her name?

"Mary.

"We'll find her something jus' so she can get out of what she got on. After tomorrow night you'll probably have enough money to go out and get her something. Come on, let me show you your room.

"Thas de room you in now. Back den it was somethin', at least to me it was. You gotta remember even in de white lady's house I make her bed 'n me 'n Mary sleep on a pallet on de floor. Back at Auntie's I sleeps on de floor, dirt floor. Dis room raggedy but everythin' in de same place it was when it was fine—bed, vanity table, mirror you done broke, little chairs, floor different, useta be shiny hardwood wit' white bearskin rugs, real fur. Das gone, white fur rug, de white 'n gold bedspreads 'n curtains, look like a movie when I walked through de door. 'N dat someone like me, a motherless chile, gonna rest my head on a bed. Thas somethin'! Don' fault me. People come rent de room out, mess up stuff, steal, rearrange shit, I push it right back. Finally I jus' stop rentin' out rooms, live off what dey give me, everythin' else is too much trouble. My eyes ain' what dey was but dey still good. I can see de colors all like mold on de inside of de garbage can. I don' know when dat wallpaper got put up. Locusses everywhere. Sign from de Bible us rushin' toward de last days 'n times. I thought 'bout you. You nevah thought 'bout me?"

She turns her head and looks me in the eye, it gives me the creeps!

I shake my head as some kind of answer, but I just feel sad and bewildered. It's like I'm sitting here trying not to listen. A part of me is standing, looking at me sitting here, and saying, this can't be my life. I feel sad, but mostly I don't feel nothing. Nothing. Except I've fallen down a hole there might not be a bottom to, and I'm trying to figure out what to do. But I know I'm too young, too young. Whatever this is talking at me, is it really happening?

"You talk 'bout dancin'?" she says. "I seed 'em all! Imagine! You cain't!

You cain't imagine all de people I done heard sing, de beauties I done seed dance. Dance? Thas good, boy, thas as close to God as you gonna git in dis world. Forgit church, every preacher in town damn near was a regular up here. But I seed em down at de club, Bubbles, Cookie, Honi, Chuck Green, big ol' dark fella dance like an angel. De tappers, den was de interpretive dancers. Dey was big names back den, young. I seed 'em come through too. One night Pearl Primus herse'f, yes indeedy. Dat woman jumped five feet in de air if she jumped a inch! Den she did a dance to some country blues near 'bout tear my heart out watchin' it. Made me think of de plantation, all what I escaped from, runned away from. Even all I been through, I still think it good I left. Josh White record playing while she dancin'. Everybody sittin' dere knowed what she was talkin' 'bout or was holdin' on to somebody dat knew.

"'N Chuck! Honey, Chuck step out sometimes to drums, piano, but most of de time ain' 'comp'niment, he *is* de music 'n he ain' no lil' faggot. He was a big guy like you, 'n when dem feets, heel toe, ra-ta-tat-tat-tat tap, slappa ball heel 'n I don' know all what else, but he don' need no drum, he is de drum 'n de horn too. It was magic. I nevah tried it, nevah even thought 'bout tryin' it. It seemed almos' mo' den my eyes could bear to really see it, hear it. Like love makin' or when a car comin' headlong fast 'n de dog or cat in its way—disaster. All dat rolled into one: love, disaster. When I watch him dance movin' his feet steppin' time over de top like dat, my bones hurt. I remember what I'm always tryin' to forgit, walkin' on dat highway, Mary like a wagon I'm pullin' like my own death, tryin' to keep it behind me. Heavy, dat chile was heavy. Ain' no nature to it. What go in go out! Shit, nothin' go in 'n she still big. I hate her almos' since she born. I remember all dat 'n I forgits all dat when I watch dat man dance. First time I see Chuck Green, my mouf fall open, you hear me! It's like a animal crawl up my back bite my head 'n crawl inside me. I feel like I got snakes in me, sex snakes! Beymour say, I like watchin' you watch. I think you see inside the music or whatever be up there. But it ain' all dat. He give me too much credit. I don' see inside, I jus' let it take me ovah 'n don' nothin' else exist outside dat man movin' up dere, man I ain' never gonna get, be. Dey only up dere ten, fifteen minutes, half hour at de mos'. So what's dat when it's de only good thang might happen to you all week. Times watchin' dem was de only time 'n people didn't try to make you feel like less. I knew what I was, what de lady at de drugstore knew when we came in to buy de catheters 'n quinine, de rubbers, Kwell 'n all dat, what de man at de liquor store know when we gettin' JB sent up by de case. Reefer man know it. You know dat song: Fancy women, dey de envy of de women 'n de rulers of de men! Maybe in de dark. I liked de night, in de night we was somethin'! De dancers too. Daytime dey got Ginger Rogers 'n Fred Astaire on de Hollywood TV. Ain' gonna let no big nigger like Chuck Green get his talent on in de light. I hated goin' out in streets big broad daylight. I felt everybody lookin' at me. Even people shit's stinkier den yo's turn away, make 'em feel good to have someone under 'em. Don' you serve dat function! But club people is our people! What we care 'bout what de Lady drinkin' or shootin', who give a fuck 'bout who got sent what place or other. All we cares is when is our music comin' back. Dey singin' 'n dancin' fo' us as much, shit *mo'*, den dey singin' 'n dancin' fo' de white folks crawl up here. By de time I got to New Yawk, all dat ol' nigger hebben shit was ovah, more stuff goin' on downtown den up here. Dey took de talent 'n left de drugs.

"Look I ain' crazy, I know you probably ain' gonna stay—don' make no difference, you grown. I don' care thirteen or fourteen. I had yo' gran'ma when I was ten, yo' mama had you when she was sixteen, Mongo when she was twelve. But I tell you somethin', lil' pop-up nigger, you forgit me you gonna die yo'sef. J.J.? Hush wit' dat shit. Abdul, dat's what yo' mama called you. Dis place useta be somethin'! You could stay here, fix it up, 'n it be yo's when I die. Put de lease in yo' name. Shit, you know I had my first tub bath in dis house.

"Come on, Betsy say. Let's hit the tub! You first, then the little one.

"I done cleaned a tub befo', but I nevah been in one myself. I tell Betsy dat. She say, What you mean? I tell her, I worked a white woman's house in Mississippi, cleaned her house, tub 'n all—

"She don't allow you in it?

"I don' even ask. Down dere you know what's allowed. I clean mysef in de kitchen wit' a bucket 'n soap.

"Well, get ready, she say. Ain' no hot water bill in New Yawk! She fill de tub wit' warm water 'n bubbles! When I sticked my foot in dat water, it feel so good I laugh. Feel like I'm in hebben warm water 'n bubbles all ovah me, up in my coochie, titties, back, perfume smell. Great oogla moogla! 'N I'm lookin' out de window see all ovah de city lights sparklin'. I nevah seed de like!

"Betsy say, We up on a hill in Harlem, plus de apartment itsef sit up on a hill. Nice, ain' it? I'm gonna scrub yo' back 'n wash yo' hair. I'll straighten it later.

"All I say is, OK.

"She's sittin' on de toilet stool paintin' her toenails. True what Bey-mour say? she ask me.

"Ma'am?

"Hush with that shit! Cain't call me Betsy, don't call me at all! She laugh at her fast talk.

"Betsy?

"Beymour say you ain't but fifteen years old, and he was downtown puttin' one of the girls on the bus for Vegas, and he come out and seen you standing in the station with the girl, and you followed him home. That true?"

"Only half true, but I say yes anyway.

"You ever worked in a place like this before?

"What kinda place dis is?

"It's a ho house.

"She come over help me rinse de soap from my head. Den she spurt some mo' shampoo in my head, lather it up, her fingers in my head de best thing I done felt, ever.

"What's a ho house?"

"She gits up 'n open de faucet, runnin' her fingers through my hair wit' de water.

"You got a nice grade of hair, long too—shoot! I done messed up my toenails messin' with you. Don't matter. She laughs. I didn't like that color no way! Give me a excuse to put on another color!

"Den she hold de sides of my face in her hands 'n look in my eyes. Poontang, pussy, coochie, sock, cunt, fish—we sell it here.

"Sell—

"Sell, honey. She pat her pussy. This here is a ho house.

"I git it now, she a fancy woman 'n dis a house of sin! She point to de washcloth, point to de soap, den rub her hands together. Lather up! All them places you couldn't get standing up on a dirt floor with a bucket, I know, honey, git 'em now!

"I rub de soap cloth tween my legs.

"Stand up and do it! OK, now you done done it good, sit down.

"Umph feels good! Soap smells good, like perfume.

"Girl, you sure got some bowlegs on you! Bowlegs and big feet. But you built up nice, titties don't look like you had a baby at all. Bet you can wear my shoes, a nine-ten? What do you think? I really don' know.

"Mens like bowlegged women, I hear tell.

"I look out de window.

"What's wrong? You don't like mens?

"What's to like? What I'm lookin' at, mo' lights den you can count, lights movin' on cars like glow eye of flies, streets, houses full of light. Dis what God see, I know it.

"I ask her question back to her. You like mens?

"She laugh. Honey, I dooze it wit' 'em, don't I!

"She fills a pot of warm water from de faucet 'n pours it ovah my head. I can't wait to get my hands on your head, honey! I love to do hair. When I get me enough moola, dat's what I'm gonna do, open me up a little salon, but that's a way down the line. Let me tell you how things go. We get all dressed up, sit in the parlor, one drink, that's all. This a class joint, best in Harlem, not the biggest but the best. Beymour run this better than a woman! So you know hair, nails, everything. The mens come in the door, walk down the hall, look at us. Go back and tell Beymour which one they want. Beymour settle the cash, walk the man up to us, safe, no funny stuff. This better than downtown. I been wit' Big Black awhile, downtown, Jersey, I been aroun'!

"What you do wif de mens?

"You do whatever they want you to do. Suck they johnson, dance around, talk nasty, let 'em talk nasty to you, suck you, if they pay for it, pee on you! They gets to come once in your pussy. Then push 'em off you. They wanna come again, spend longer than they time, they got to pay again! Don't be afraid to call Beymour 'bout nothin'! You here to make money not get all wore out! Understand?

"I nods my head."

As she says it, I nod too. I'm disappearing in her story. As if now don't exist, as if I don't exist.

"You know whar I first do it?" She's looking at me, but I don't blink, acknowledge. We're both watching a movie.

"Down de hall, dat room Mary useta be in till dey carry her outta here. Dey call it 'breakin' luck.' Well, if I evah had any—luck dat is—'n I don' remember havin' any, dat what it did—broke it! It's like a curse. Who wanna be a ho? Our whole life happen here. Seem like it end here too. Carl fuck Mary here. She ain' move over to Lenox till after yo' mother was born. Yo' room whar it happen. But Mary's ol' room, mine now, whar I first do it fo' money."

OK, do I need this? I haven't had enough, this bag of rags is a ho? I think of fire, if she was burning.

"I ain' nevah had my hair straightened befo'. OK, Betsy say. So dry off, rub some of this on your behind and let me get to that head of yours!

"You know I hadn't had dat done befo', always jus' wore my hair, come to think of it, jus' like it is now, braids! But Betsy grab it up, set me in a chair, I'm tellin' you she pull out dis big ol' jar of Dixie Peach, hot comb, 'n a curlin' iron. I didn't know mysef a hour later!

"De dress Betsy give me is orange silk, long on me but tight 'n shiny, show my hiney off good. Her shoes did fit, I got on someone else's brazzeer, 'n Betsy done got me a little white garter belt wit' little pink roses on it fo' holdin' up my first pair of nylons!

"It's not like I know what to do when I git in de room wit' de guy. I raise de dress Betsy give me ovah my head, drop it all orange 'n silky on a chair. I got on de white garter belt holdin' up off-black stockin's. I ain' got no drawers on. Hair on my bush thick as hair on my head back den. I look in de guy's eyes, don' see nothin'. I don' know what to do. I'm fifteen years old. I nevah been alone in a room wit' a white man befo'. So I walks over to de bed, lay down, 'n spread my legs apart. Stare at him hard. My name is John, he say. Now, I ain' been off de bus a week yet, so how I know his name ain' John, but I do. What's your name? He talk so proper like a king. Toosie, I say. How'd you get a name like that? I dunno, I tell him. I don' tell him dey call me Gal at La Croix. I hear Master Croix call his dog Toosie, he say it so nice. I want dat name, I think. Next time Auntie call me Gal, I say Toosie my name. Whar you come up with dat? Yo' mama ain' named you none of dat. What she name me? I says. Don' remember, but it wadn't none of dat. Yeah it was, I say. Auntie look at me funny, but she call me Toosie next day. I don' answer to nothin' else after dat. But I don' tell all dat to John. I jus' tell John I dunno."

A dog's name? She's what, the mother of my mother's mother? I ain't buying that, I don't see how, she don't look like me at all.

"So anyway 'John' walk ovah 'n sit down on de side of de bed wit' all his clothes on. He put his fingers in my coochie. Nice! he say. He bend down kiss my coochie! I ain' nevah had no one kiss me down dere befo'. Den he lick it. Ooowhee! Do you like it? Yeah!"

Then she hits the table with her fist, gets up and points at me. "You is de first boy born alive to us! I been waitin' on you since 1949!"

Since 1949? My mother wasn't even born then, I don't even know nobody that old. How I'm gonna make it? How I'm gonna live? Who can I tell this shit to?

"It feel so good! His hands on my nipples make my body feel like flowers growin' all ovah me. I start to breathe harder. His lickin' is pickin' me up! Yes sirree! Den he jump up like a snake bit him, unzip his pants, pull his dick out 'n start jackin' off. Oooh! Oooh! Oooh! he goin'. You fine black bitch! OOOH! You fine black bitch! Den SPURT! Right in my face. Drip down. Jesus, girl, you are something else! I'm wipin' all dat shit off my face. I ain' seed too many since shoot like dat! It done got in my eyes 'n all. Maybe I see you next week, Tootie, he say. 'N wipe his hands on a towel, fix his collar, 'n walk out de room. I feel like a flower dat someone is pullin' de petals off one by one. Thas de first time I hear de voice tell me to do things. *Git her.* Tell me to git Mary from behind de red 'n black Chinese screen whar she sleepin'. Betsy give her laudanum so she don' wake up durin' bizness. *Git her,* voice says. So I gits her. *De bathroom,* it say. De bathroom? Whar I tooked my first bath in a tub, two days ago. A lot can happen in one day, I tell ya! I know den when I hear de voice I had God's eye 'n could see, see life wadn't nevah gonna git no better period. *Dis is it,* voice say. 'N it wadn't wrong! *Window,* it say, *window.* I hear banjo, Nigger Boy playin' sho nuff! I walkin' down de hall wit' Mary knocked out in my arms. I looked forward to comin' up north. Up north! Up north! Whar everybody said Mama was. Back of Mama's legs black shiny wit' grease 'n sweat. Why I have to name my baby after Auntie? 'N what was my mama's name, I cain't even remember it now! De voice soft like it care 'bout me. Window open. *Drop her 'n jump! Drop her 'n den jump!* Voice, banjo all stirred together. I gotta put Mary down to git in de tub. Smell of reefers, cigarettes 'n another voice comin' in from de parlor. I'll jump wit' her in my arms, dat's what I'll do. Music from de parlor louder, voice comin' out de parlor, someone like me singin', someone flower petals done got pulled off too, I think. I hurt so bad, I've got Mary in my arms, ready to jump, but voice from de parlor freezin' me I cain't move, more hurtin' den I can bear, but de voice is bearin' for me. I can feel de night air comin' in de window, smell like pickin' strawberries clean 'n cold on my face. De voice from de parlor now fightin' in a way wit' de voice inside sayin' jump. De smell of reefers is strong.

"Whooaa! Little Mama, whatchu doin'! Beymour's arms is all around me grab me tight. That ain' no door, you go out that, Little Mama, you ain't comin' back!

"His arms, de voice on de records comin' from de parlor holdin' me mo' den anythin' I evah 'sperienced. Out de windows is a black sky full of stars.

"Who dat? I ask.

"What, Mama?"

"Who dat singin'?

"Ain't you something! One minute you actin' psycho and the next you actin' like we listenin' to the radio playin' poker or something! All I care 'bout right now is de voice singin'. I am dat voice. De other voice gone like it come. I let Mary go. She drop in de tub still sleep. Beymour hug me tighter breathe me in.

"Singin'? he say. That's an old one from Lady Day, I know that's Prez behind her, soun' like Buck on trumpet.

"*I'll nevah be the same there is such an ache in my heart.* Auntie swing de hammer knock ol' Pink out, tell me pick up de butcher knife cut her throat, if I don' I won' eat. Blood run.

"Yeah, Beymour say. That's Billie Holiday, she rule. Can't nobody touch her. Now, git out this fuckin' tub and git back to work!"

I grab my brown bomber jacket off the back of the chair, put it on, and walk back to "my" room. Slavery Days in the kitchen croaking. I guess she think she singing. OK, got my jacket on, my kaleidoscope, clown doll with china head, two pair of jeans, all these socks, no hat, no boots for winter. Last year I had those Timberland boots, too small by summer, still too big for Jaime. I end up giving them back to Mrs Lee to give to someone else. One pair of leather pants, black, backpack (recently borrowed). I hear her I look up from my suitcase—she's at the bedroom door.

"Give me some money. Give me some money," I repeat. She ain't crazy. She pay rent and shit, she got some kind of scam, hustle—something goin' on here. Shit, she got me here in this loony bin, roach motel. "I want some motherfuckin' money!"

"Fo' what?"

Because you got it. "I want to get some gear to dance in, OK. I want to get my dick pierced, OK," I sneer. What fucking difference does it make, you . . . you mummy!

"Betsy de one fix up de screen, de crib 'n all fo' Mary. Dis here"—she steps through the doorway—"useta be my room. Beymour let me have it, tell me thangs are gonna work out fine. He like me."

My mother died in a car accident, my father got killed in the war. I was an only child. My grandparents had died of cancer down in Virginia. Yeah, both of 'em. What kind? Of cancer, how would I know. I was just a little kid. I was put in an orphanage because I was Catholic. It was rough, but I worked very hard. My mother died in a car accident. My father got killed in the war.

"How much, I said."

She talking to me? "Huh?"

"How much you need to git yo'sef pierced up?"

Shit, I don't know I was just talking. "I . . . uh, around, a couple hundred at least—to get dance gear, then piercing, I don't know, it got to be sanitary and all."

"Shit, I wanna see it. I done seed a lot. But I ain' nevah seed dat. Beymour say he ain' no pimp. He a bizness manager. Tell me a guy name Big Black run dis house, one in Little Italy, 'n one in New Jersey. I manage merchandise for Big Black. I don't own nothin' or nobody. My job is to keep shit copasetic. I gets paid off the top. I keep the hos happy, Big Black happy, johns happy, got me? Gotcha! I would say.

"Something about Beymour you should know, Betsy say. Beymour done picked me out. As much as I like Betsy, she basically dress me in de beginnin' show me how I could put money in de bank if I want to, help me hook it up so Mary could stay wit' her auntie some weekends. But I'm a woman 'n I know enuff, even though I ain' but sixteen years ol', not to let another woman tell me nothin' 'bout my man. Honey, later I'll wish I hadda listened. Like you, mark my words, you'll wish you hadda listened to what I'm sayin'!"

She sits down on the bench in front of the vanity table where the mirror useta be. Shit, I been listening, and what is it? Scrambled eggs in my kaleidoscope. And she becomes a roach every time she opens her stupid mouth. I look at my jeans, two pairs in my suitcase, count my socks— twelve pairs, all them socks and no boots.

"But you cain't know now what you woulda known later or it wouldn't be now. Ain' dat right! So now Beymour is wit' me, not Betsy! He's lyin' on my bed! How he eat my pussy, how he screw is way out! Sol, one of de regulars, a musician, say dat, Way out, man! Like jazz—oo—blah—dee—dah! You mine, Beymour say. I was comin' out de bathroom, dat bathroom, down de hall. I'm comin' from takin' a bubbly bath wit' some of Betsy's bubbles."

I look at my kaleidoscope, my clown, lying neat on top of my jeans in my suitcase. Look like picture on Roman's bedroom wall. Did Picasso really say that shit, that he had black blood from the Moors, or was Roman just bullshittin' me? I look at the little chess set, I don't think I would like chess, too long sitting in one place. She gets up and walks over to where I'm getting ready to close my suitcase and get out of here. Just grabs my arm!

"DON'T!" she screams like I'm killing her. "Don' leave now, Abdul. I ain' finished—jus' sit down, sit down, please."

I plop down on the bed. She goes back to the bench in front the vanity table looking at the old dry wood like it's still a mirror. How long can I stand this?

"So I'm comin' out de bathroom—you know dis useta be my room. Did I tell you dat? You stay here you always have a home. I leave you everythin' when I die. Dis apartment rent-controlled, only person payin' less than me is Koch. Hee-hee."

Who the fuck is Koch?

"Anyway, how it start out, Beymour who has always been like a bizness person to me come up grinnin' stupid like one of de johns, talkin' 'bout, Let's take a bath. Beymour, I tells him, I done already took a bath. I mean together, he say. I start to ask what for, 'cause like a fool I'm talkin' to him like he got sense 'n fool of course he don'! Beymour was jus' tryin' to get some! But I don' know dat, you nevah know what's on somebody's mind—"

If I touch the side of my face, the jagged scar, it would hurt me. If she knew what was on my mind.

"So I'm tryin' to figure out why he want me to, why he wanna take a bath, when he done took one dis mornin'. I wanna say, Fool, you crazy, but Beymour is like de boss man in a way. I mean, he run de house, de money we git, Betsy, Eloise, Irene, Betsy's aunt, 'n me—come from him. But he don' act like no boss man—mean 'n stupid, like. So when he say, Get yo' fine self on back in the tub and run some water."

My mother's mother's mother? Synonym for crazy. Insane. No, that's the same as crazy. That's what a synonym is, same family same name? I ain't the same as a schizophrenic simple stupid mental-deranged cracked, shit, what else? OFF her rocker, bugging, bugged-out, motherfucking maniac. Antonym, yeah! What's the opposite of this motherfucking shit! Cool, good-sensed, rational. Intelligent. Normal.

"You know how big dat tub is 'n de window right ovah it. Look out forevah at New York! Beymour push his suspenders off his shoulder, undo his pants. By now I done seed so many men undress, it ain' nothin' special to me. Beymour so skinny his knees like doorknobs. I smile. What you laughin' at! I ain' laughin', I swear I ain', Beymour! Beymour pull his shorts down—Laugh at this! Lawd I got to give it to him. Beymour got something 'tween his legs. I look in de mirror—why you go 'n break dis here mirror, Abdul? Look at yo' face, you gonna hafta wear dat fo' life. But anyway my hair in paper-bag curlers, I got on ol' dusty robe Betsy give me. I'm useta meetin' mens in a nice way, all dressed up, silky dress, perfume, whiskey. Dis here—Beymour, knees all knobby, dick danglin', no music, whiskey, me in my duster, paper curlers—it don' seem natural! I wanna laugh at Beymour knobby knees, big dick, suspenders, 'n pants on his ankles.

"'N it ain' no fun in de bathtub! Stop! Jus' stop! I tell Beymour. My head bangin' against de tub, bubbles gettin' all in my mouth. This ain' gonna git it, Beymour. Well, what is? I push him off me, git his dick in my mouth, think of de closet empty dust a few months ago, all shine now wit' hot dresses, pink 'n orange, patent leather shoes. Underwears, I got mo' in one drawer den all de women on de plantation together. I likes this, I'm not Eloise, hate de men or like Betsy, I thinks likes de women. Mos' of dese guys nice people actually.

"He 'bout to come in my mouf, makin' little baby-bitch noises wit' his breath. You evah been in love? Den all of a sudden he push my head away 'n say real mean, That's what you want, ain't it? Huh? *I* want, I says to myself. What's wit' this man? You just wanna get me off so you can get it over with!"

Does anybody really love me? Brother John? Jaime?

"I think, well ain' dat de point? I don' know what to say. What about you? he say. Me? Where your feel-good come in? I remember first time wit' John how my body light up fo' a minute or two dere, but dat don' happen no mo' again. I jus' keep my mind on bein' . . . bein' fine, doin' it good fo' de mens. I ain't paying no bitch, but I wanna give you somethin' back. Oh Lawd, what he's talkin' 'bout I don' know. Let's go in my room, Beymour say. What's dat 'cept de parlor whar we drinks wit' de men? But when de tricks gone, de couch pull out to be Beymour's bed 'n don' nobody go in dere. Room his. Record player 'n radio too. OK, let's go in yo' room. What's dat playin'? I ask. Oh that's new Bird, baby, the latest! Sol's friend give him that, Boris jus' take the sets off the radio on his seventy-eight-RPM disc recorder. We git sounds ain't even in the record store yet! Honey, I don' know what Beymour talkin' 'bout, but I know de Bird sound good.

"Prez is playin' when he enter me, 'Lady Be Good'! Hah! That's a old one, but I like it, Beymour grunt. I done stopped tryin' to be good, or fine, or please him. I dig my orange-painted nails in his back not 'cause I'm hot but 'cause I want to hurt him, hurt him bad. Like I hurt standin' up in dat station nowhere to go. It's all black, dark, hate almost. But hate ain' in Beymour, he move off me 'n start playin' wit' me, suckin' my tittie, den it's like dat thang you got. Colors shakin', what you call dat?"

Huh? What . . . is she? She's looking at me like she want me to talk. I want her to talk now, finish the story. "Kaleidoscope," I tell her. "From the Greek *kalos* for 'beautiful.'"

"Beymour touchin' me jus' break me up inside. A wave roll through my blood so happy-feelin' I could cry. I do cry, it feel so fuckin' good! Then he go down on me. Dis Miss Billie Holiday's music in my body, a song I couldn't sing mysef. You make me feel good, Beymour. You ain't gotta say nothin' to me you don' mean. But I do mean it, I do. My body still goin' like it not mine. I give it to Beymour in pieces, big pieces, little pieces—black 'n white—of hurt. He give de pieces back to me in colors!

"Well, wit' all dat—music, kallyscope, gardenia flowers, it shouldn'ta happened. I shouldn'ta needed nothin' else. But when I opened I felt so good, but it would remind me I ain' nevah known nothin' but pain. I had hurt so bad, long, or maybe it wadn't none of dat. I don' know. I do know down de line when he ask me did I want some. I didn't know—I ain' even ask what 'some' was. I jus' said yes."

She stops and it's like she's nodding out. Can't be? All these . . . these fuckin' hours I been trying to keep her out of my ears, and now I'm really listening, and she looks like she drifting off to la-la land.

"Well?" I say.

She raises her head. "Well." Like she hadn't missed a beat. "One mornin' I waked up next to Beymour, we here in dis room, I tol' you dis useta be my room. Shake, shake, shake, Beymour don' wake up. Scare me. He breathin' but don' wake up. Scare me. What to do? Call Big Black, Betsy say. You got de number? I ask. She head to de parlor, ain' like nowadays folks got a phone in dey pocket."

I look at my suitcase, think that's next, a cell phone. I look at the windows, the one shade left dusty brown with age. Can I take this?

"Out de window I see a black Lincoln Continental pull up. Thas him, Betsy say. Well, Big Black a midget, a albino, big lips like liver. He walk in de room, up to de bed—Everybody out! Who he talkin' to? Ain' nobody in dere 'cept me 'n Betsy. Eloise at de door, but she ain' in de room. OUT! he scream. Betsy 'n Eloise walk down de hall. I stand dere a second outside de door, den sink down on my knees look in de keyhole. It's de weirdest feelin', like air down in Mississippi befo' a storm, emptied out 'n dangerous. I look see Mary 'tween de partin' in de panels of de Chinese screen. She standin' up. Don' move, don' say nothin', I wanna tell her. Keep yo' mouf shut! I guess she feel my words, 'cause she don' even breathe hard. Big Black pull de sheets off Beymour, turn him ovah so he face down in de pillow. Big Black take off his pants, I see why dey call him Big Black, his thang bigger den Beymour's, 'n it's hard. He climb on top of Beymour 'n start fuckin' him in de ass. One hand holdin' Beymour's head down in de pillow. Dis is crazy I think. How dis helpin' Beymour? Beymour cain't breathe, can he? How can Beymour breathe Big Black doin' dat! Now Beymour's whole body buck like a fish no water, den, I mean Lord Jesus how is dis helpin' Beymour! Beymour still now. I look over at de Chinese screen, don' see Mary standin' up, maybe she done laid down in her crib. Den I don' remember. Entirely. Jus' rusty kinda sticky smell of blood. All over everywhere.

"I'm already on my knees I stay down 'n start to crawl to Betsy's room. Inchin' hand knee hand knee hand knee. I'm soakin' wet shakin' as I crawl. Footsteps behind me. Get up! De floor so shiny I can see his shoes 'n pants legs reflected. I rare back to come up off my hands 'n knees jus' when his tan shoe is comin' dead in my face again 'n again. Beymour! Beymour! I hollers, but don' nothin' come out 'cept blood 'n tooths.

Betsy open her door 'n run up to me screamin', Stop! Big Black, STOP! I push mysef against de wall away from him. Big Black pull a razor out his pocket 'n slice it cross Betsy's throat. I nevah hear a scream like dat in all my life. I close my eyes, it's Mississippi fo' a second, sky blue. I open my eyes it's Big Black's hand comin' down steady like a hoe choppin' cotton, but it's Betsy he choppin'—again 'n down again 'n down 'n again 'n again.

"Blood everywhere. Later people tell me de screams I heard was my own. Betsy's throat cut past de bone die immediately. Guy say he heard me screamin' on 145th Street. He nevah heard no screamin' like dat befo', not sirens on fire engines, elephants in movies, not nothin' nobody.

"Dat was . . . oh, I don' know forty, fifty years, yeah forty, forty-five, fifty years ago. Super, he was startin' to be one of my regulars, tell de owner Beymour my husband. Dey let me keep de apartment, put a lease in my name. Dat was Rodriguez, he dead now. Blood was everywhere. Still smell it sometime."

It's like a movie only it ain't. I close my eyes, pictures, the pictures is screaming. All around me blood, Beymour, the brothers, Richie Jackson. Fifty years. I start crying. Rocking. Sorry. So sorry. I get up off the bed. I feel so sorry love her so much. She's noddin', someplace else, her story over. Water is rolling down my face. I take the kaleidoscope out of the suitcase and lay it at her feet. Bye, Toosie. Bye, Great-Gran'ma. I close the suitcase. Where? I don't know—I don't want to live like her, I don't want to *be* like her—I do know I'm outta here.

BOOK THREE

ASCENSION

... making me dance
Inside
Your love is king

—SADE ADU

ONE

Whenever I see anyone hauling one of those oversize cheap suitcases on the subway, I think about that day, me holding on to my shit for dear life, everything else gone. Slavery Days went off at 805 and never really came back. I had come from Roman's class that night with his card in my pocket, *"téléphone-moi"* on one side, *"CALL ME"* on the other. She was still sitting in roaches talking to herself, and I'm rapping to myself: My mother died in a car accident, my father died in the war. I'll work out the details later. I canNOT be related to somebody ate dirt—Slavery Days, Nigger Boy—No. Maybe in the movies or a book or some shit. Big Black? Albino midget? *He climb on Beymour.* NO.

The first night I went home with him was maybe the end of the second or beginning of the third week of classes. I don't remember. What I remember now is it was the end of his class at the Y, and I was leaning against the barre, and he walked over and said, "I have another class on the Upper West Side at Stride. If you serious about dance, you should be dancing every day. What other classes you is taking?" I told him about Imena on Thursday nights and Saturday afternoons. "That sounds good. If she's who I think she is, she's good. But whatever kind of dance you do, you need a strong foundation. Ballet is good for that. I like you, youze a hard worker." I was looking down on his shiny pink scalp and his hair that looked like it had been planted in neat little rows.

"What happened to the side of your face? You has such a pretty face."
My hand flew up like a girl's to the side of my face.

"It don't mess you up, you know," he says. "Roman just ask. After all, you is his pupil, isn't you?"

I didn't answer. My shoulder still hurt when I did port de bras, and the stitches on the top of my head ITCHED! When the cold hit my cheek, the whole side of my face throbbed. Pain. I was still trying to figure out what was going on with his hair. I had never seen implants before. Stride, yeah right, I thought, how was I gonna pay them double digits for classes at Stride? Stan had said Bureau of Child Welfare was paying for me at the Y through the City Arts for Kids Project.

"You was fighting with those boys uptown? Roman don't want that. You become a dancer, you got to let them things go. You know what I mean?"

I knew what he meant.

"You could be my guest at Stride. Just use another name so City Kids don't know. How old are you? Seventeen. Wait for me in front of Gourmet Fare."

"CRAZY HORSE! What kinda stupid shit is that!

"Stop being silly, you know what I mean. I mean something like Jim Jones, or Robert Johnson, or something like that. You is no Indian. I don't know where you get all that from. You boys need to come to France sometime and see. Abdul is no name for you either. You is no Arab. Where you get that name from— Hey! Hey! Where you going! Come back! OK, OK, no more. I'm just saying a nice name like John or Robert bring you luck. You is a beautiful black boy, like . . . like *art*, you is so beautiful."

I like the Upper West Side, it's easier to steal food. I shouldn't have let him see me pull a big Ghirardelli chocolate bar out my jeans, but shit, I was hungry. I had walked all the way from 150th and St Nicholas to 75th and Broadway to class.

"So you want to go to jail?"

"No, I wanted something to eat."

A red and gold leaf lands in front of my feet. I'm sick of this fucker already. I'll be fourteen in January. I got to survive my own life until I'm eighteen. I can do that being Crazy Horse, thinking these streets is hills and I'm lightning flying over them. I don't know if I can do that being some nigger named Jim Jones; sound like a body-bag tag to me. I can't stay at 805. I could roam, but not and study dance. Kick the leaf, I remember riding the bus upstate with my mother. She's so tired she's dozing off, but I'm nose to the window looking at the crazy-colored beautiful leaves. Every time she would wake up, she'd tell me, "Look at the leaves now. I want you to write me a report about *everything*." We went to an inn for dinner and sat near a big window and watched the sky turn dark. We walked back to the bus station and sat outside looking at all the stars. "Why are there so many more stars up here, Mommy?" "There aren't, it's just the air is less polluted so you can see them better up here." It was so cold, but my mother was warm and smelling of apple cider, clean sweat, and the sky was starry starry. We caught the last bus and saw every star in the world out the window on the way home. "Give your report to your teacher." *We See the Trees Be Different Colors,* I had written. "Turn," the teacher said, "*turn* different colors." Whatever, I think, kicking the leaf out of my way as if it was some big obstacle. I don't want to roam. Boys who roam end up weird, killed, or worse than killed.

Yeah, or worse, maybe that's why I'm following this butt sniffer home.

At his apartment on Riverside Drive I'm sitting on a cream-colored leather couch looking out on the river, watching the sun disappear, and the city lights come on like stars. I'm drinking cognac. I like drinking, it opens me up. Not like Jaime, he drink and all he wants is another drink and another, till he's fucking wiped out. I drink something and I am, umm, *more* . . . more nice, more funny, smart. I'm thinking about the McDonald's we passed on the way up here. I'm going to get three Super Value Meals, that'll give me three Quarter Pounders with Cheese, three supersize fries, and three sodas, all for almost cheaper than three regular-size meals. And some donuts. And some protein energy bars from the convenience store, cinnamon-oatmeal and the peanut butter ones. I wonder how much he's gonna give me, should I ask or just take it if he don't act right? Where is it? He pours me another glass of cognac. I like the glass; if I had a bag, I would take it. Where's the money, that's what I'm thinking when he appears like a nurse with all these test tubes, little sticks, and shit.

Brother John always gave me stuff—my jacket, Timberlands, the best jeans from the box—but no money. Brother Samuel never gave me shit. I was never a . . . a *kid* to Brother Samuel, maybe because I was almost as big as him, but what about the kids who were littler? Because I was black? Most of us was. I wasn't the blackest. Bobby, Etheridge Killdeer, *blue*-black, even though he was from Indians and had straight hair. Delete that shit! I ain't there no more: My mother died in a car accident, and my father got killed in the war. After that, I went to live with my grandmother. Then I got a job and started to live by myself. I'm a normal person I'm a normal person I'm a normal person just like everybody else just like everybody else *just like everybody else.*

I'm sitting on the side of his bed now, which is like ridiculous high, the mattress must be two feet deep or some shit. I think of my bed at St Ailanthus, plastic-covered black-and-white-striped mattress, number six under the window between Alvin Johnson and Malik Edwards. Who's sleeping in my bed now? Roman has a little timer on the tray with the test tubes and strips of paper.

"Nurse Roman," he says.

What's this all about?

"This is my little home testing kit for you, you know, the virus."

He can test for AIDS with this shit? The whole bedroom—walls, bedspread, furniture—is all the same white cream color as the couch in his living room. I never been in a room that's all one color before. The bedspread is like satin or something. All I have on is my jeans, still zipped up but the button above the zipper is undone. How do I look, my black chest against all this satin cream? What's he seeing? Brother John liked me because I was black, "You're the only one," he said. But I wasn't. I *saw.* It still confuses me, but I think I see it now, what excited him, but why?

He didn't excite me, Jaime excited me, but then he's not white, he's beige. The pictures of the girls like Britney Spears, one hand holding their tit and licking their nipple, the other hand spreading their pussy, excited me. Excited me a lot. "You like *that*," Brother John would say. "Well, take a look at *this*," and show me more big white titties, pink tongues, yellow hair. He would get hard watching me get hard. But Brother John was so doofy-looking, all them pimples on his butt. Maybe only white people in magazines is exciting.

"You know you too tall to be a ballet dancer. Too tall and too big. Balanchine used to keep all those tall guys around because of all those giraffes he had in the company. But no more. How tall is you? Six-five, six-six, I bet?"

I don't think so unless I grew overnight. Yeah, unless being told your great-grandfather's name is Nigger Boy, unless being lied on and getting your arm twisted to shit causes you to get taller overnight, I'm six feet. But I guess in this little dude's head I'm some kind of giant. Of all the kids in the class, he picked me. Or does he pick 'em all one by one? No, that's sick. I'm special.

It never crossed my mind I might be HIV-positive. I look at Roman fiddling with his tubes on the tray. We're kids, Jaime, Bobby, Malik, Richie, and us—thirteen, twelve, five, six. Kids don't get it. You see the skeleton-looking addicts that got it, walking around humped over canes and shit till they die. You could look at those shits and tell they got it—

Well, I was right! I ain't got it. Where was I going to get it from? St Ailanthus? We're Catholic people, the brothers, they're like priests, they don't be in the Village or doing dope. The kids? We're not homos. The park? I just unzip, pure vanilla, that's it.

Roman seems all happy as he walks out the bedroom with his little chemistry set. He has on pink ballet slippers; I guess that's how these types relax.

He puts on some dinosaur rap. I don't know why, but I'm starting to get mad.

"You must tell me what you like. I know you boys—"

I jump up. "Shit, how many of us is in here!"

"What?" He's looking all alarmed.

"You keep saying 'you boys' this, 'you boys' that." I dash to a door I guess is a closet, fling the door open. "They in here?" I feel like a fool for letting him give me that test. What made him think I would just sit still for that? He had me figured out?

"You gonna pay for that test," I try to growl, but my voice just comes out loud and high. Like a girl?

"Ah, sweetheart, do not be angry. Roman is trying to stop this dreadful disease that kills so many young boys and so many of your people. And us too. So many is dead."

Half the time he sound like some old movie actress with that "you is so beautiful" shit. Other times he's talking I hear something else, but I can't put my finger on it. What would Jaime think of this guy? I take off my jeans.

"Give me the cookies and a condom."

"Huh?"

"The dough, bread, *money*."

"But we have tested for each other."

We. I can't believe this dude. I'm a kid so I'm dumb? He better have some money, or I'll crack his motherfucking head open, take everything I can carry out of here, *and* show for ballet class in the morning. "You boys." Please!

I take the condom from him, it's weird to put it on, I never wore one before. Your dick is supposed to be hard? I see the white girl's hand in the video as she opens the square package and gives it to the boy, but I don't remember how they put it on, just that she points at the little peak left at the tip, room to come. Video is different from real life. Row row row the boat, roll it down the dick. Hah! I'm a poet. I can't let this old dude think I don't know what I'm doing.

"Let me lubricate you, dahling."

I'm rolling this shit, trying to get it on my dick. I know this hurts this dude more than if I stomped his head. He had his program laid out.

Wonder what he do with the "you boys" that test out shitty. He's pouting. I finish rolling it down. Revenge. Roman is different from the brothers. He ain't no man, dude. But then Brother Samuel wasn't no man with the pit bulls down at the police station. And Brother John disappeared. I look at the turquoise film of latex over my penis. Ha! I look at a picture on the wall in front of me. He turns to see what I'm looking at.

"Oh, Picasso! You know Picasso?"

"I heard his name before."

"You should know him. He's the most famous artist. You know he claim he have African blood."

"They said that about him?"

"No, the fool say it about himself! I don't mean he's a fool to say that, just he's a fool in general, how he treat all those girls, and his son, don't like gay people and all, but talking about his 'Moorish ancestors.'"

Moorish ancestors?

The white people called her Lucy, but the Ethiopians called her Dinquenesh. What does Dinquenesh mean, Mommy? *Baby, I don't know.*

"Where you is, boy?" He waves his hand in front of my face.

"Look we got to work this 'boy' shit out."

"You is a boy. How old are you? Tell Roman the truth."

"Thirteen."

"Stop lying! Making a fool of me!" He touches the turquoise.

"I told you I was seventeen, so why keep asking?"

"I is not 'keep asking.' I ask you once and ask one more time because I is concerned about you. OK, now when one is seventeen, he is a boy. He should go to school, not drink whiskey or go to *prostituée*. A boy need help, protection. A boy is not a man, even though he be a man one day. Don't no mens come here to Roman."

He has on a pair of faded jeans, one knee out and a fluffy pink sweater, like what ballerinas wear to warm up in, and leg warmers. When he takes off the sweater and the torn T-shirt he had on under it, his body is a shock. It's like Michelangelo drew his muscles for him!

"First position!" he barks, turning his legs out from his hip sockets, his bulging thigh muscles pointing to the side of the room along with his feet.

"I made this body! I was not you—look what you got! God is give you everything! You boys always crying racism, my mother, my father, the police! Nobody give you anything in this goddamn world! Suffer? I could tell you about what happen to my family in Europe, but you don't care. My family experience it all. You want to dance? You dance. You better built than Alvin or Arthur. I tell you I know them? I was very close to Alvin before her died. Arthur too. I could tell you stories."

About what, and who is Alvin, and I *don't* care about his parents and Europe. Maybe I'll get an order of chicken nuggets too. He's still standing in first position, looking more like a soldier than a dancer. So where was he born?

"You got more than three or four people put together! No one thought I would dance—bad body, short. But I did. Roman been around a long time. I run into some of them people every now and then, not many left, most of them dead, you know, the plague. Them not dead is fat, same thing, right?"

I think of the big girls in Imena's class dancing their asses off; I try to imagine Roman in that funky gym with no mirrors getting down in front of the drums. I can't. He turns his little legs back in, walks toward me. What I see now is me getting up, picking up the lamp on the table by the bed, and walking slow, like I'm walking through water, toward him— Then I see myself onstage, the corps lined up behind me. Holding my head up, I walk downstage, I port de bras, bow, the stage is bathed in light. People are screaming my name. I see the newspaper headlines: NOT SINCE THE GREAT SO-&-SO! Ladies are crying. I hear one lady over the roar of the crowd: "You dance like an angel!"

"You will let Roman suck you without thee con*dumb*," he begs.

Now that he's safe, he want to play hardball, "without thee con*dumb*." Fuck him. But I do get confused about head; you can't get AIDS from that shit. Chocolate, yes, vanilla, no. It ain't gonna be a thang even if he was thinking about riding, which girlfriend ain't. He's going to work on my nuts. *Testicles, Abdul.* His tongue playing me, feels good. My dick gets hard. *It's your body*— Shut up. It's *your* fault. I feel like crying. His finger touches my asshole, I flinch, forget it, Roman, I think of Brother John, Brother Samuel, at least they was *men.* He's kissing the inside of my thighs, ooh. He's also trying to roll the condom down. Ping! On the side of his head with my thumb and middle finger. He looks up all puppy-dog innocence. I wag my finger, playing but not really, even though I don't care about the condom, I don't want to give in.

"How much?" I taunt.

"Roman does not have a lot of money."

"Then what you gonna do?" I wanted my voice to come out way deep, but it squeaked.

"Roman wishes you was his boy. His big black boy. You could live here."

He reaches up, touches a cut on my chest from where a piece of the mirror fell on me.

"Who, your father beat you like that? Whatever." He doesn't wait for an answer. "You could be Roman's man."

He unrolls the condom, his tongue following it down, the air hitting me makes me shiver. The condom is a blue spot on his white carpet. He swallows me.

"You are a good clean boy. You like for Roman to take care of you?"

He swallows me again. I thrust slow in his mouth. Hail Mary full of grace. Eeee! Feels so fucking good what he's doing with his tongue, the Lord is with thee, on the tip, whoa! I keep thrusting. He's holding my booty. Blessed art thou among women, I'm breaking like firecrackers going off, fucking Fourth of July. Fucking Jesus Christ Holy Mary Mother of God! My skin is lighting up all over, I'm kneading my nipples, blessed is the fruit of thy womb Jesus! Thinking of Christ and the D train going across the bridge, me and my mother, January night the whole city cold and lit up, fireworks going off across the water like the end of loneliness. For a minute I'm who I was and who I will be, a little boy and a man, in the last inning and I'm winning, coming, it's my birthday, Mommy is bringing me ice cream and cake. Mostly ice cream down his throat. Oomph ump! Blow out the candles now make a wish on a falling star. I don't see a falling star, Mommy. Well, pretend you do! I wish I may I wish I might be the dancingest star in the sky tonight! Ha!

THAT WAS MY first night with Roman, how it began. Now I'm leaving.

"So what's with all the questions?" I ask.

"You is the one told me to move the stuff around to make room for your sneakers. I didn't go looking for nothing. They fall in my lap! Now, yes, Roman is curious."

"They just *fell* out of the suitcase into your lap? Yeah, right!"

"The suitcase wasn't locked. Stop being an idiot!" he snaps.

"Oh, I'm being an idiot now?" I snap back.

"You wanna fight rather than answer me. You mean you never read them? I don't believe you!"

"I don't have to lie to you." Fuck him!

"I can't believe I never know any of this before, all I hear about is this book, that exhibit, Herd, Basquiat! You never tell me any of this before!"

"You never *asked* before. You didn't *want* to know. You're asking now because . . ."

"Well, finish. You asking now *because*? Well, go on! *Because* . . . ?"

"Forget it!" I shout.

"You always do that, talking out the side of your mouth. You can't answer me in a decent conversation." He pouts.

Here we go again.

"I can't even finish a sentence, you ask me so many fucking questions."

"So finish the story," he insists.

"You keep inter—"

"Well, because I never hear anything like it," he interrupts again.

"And you ain't gonna hear nothing 'like it' if you don't shut up. I have a rehearsal in a little while."

"Don't get grand, dear. I know what you got. You forget who introduce you to those people in the first place."

"Introduce me to *who?*" I say.

"You meet Scott and Noël in my class; you don't think I remember," he says.

"I'm glad you remember something," I say.

"What's that supposed to mean?"

"Nothing," I say.

"See how you is," he says in his most injured voice. "Go on with the story, please."

"So anyway, I'd only been there a few—"

"Where's 'there'? I'm sorry, go on."

"So anyway, I'd only been there a couple of weeks or so and there was all this . . . this *confusion*. Some of the priests had been messing with the kids, and evidently one of them had moved on me—"

"Evidently?"

"Yeah, one of them *tried* to mess with me—"

"Ooohh, I wish it had been me!"

I glare at his stupid ass.

"It's a joke, silly. You has no sense of humor."

"It's all over the news now, but back then no one believed that shit. So here I am a kid in the hands of these . . . these *perpetrators*. They got custody of me by saying I was an orphan with no living relatives. But they tell that shit to me too—everybody's dead, you ain't got nobody, right? No, wrong! I had a grandmother, great-grandmother, some of my dad's people in the Bronx, a sister—"

"You has a sister?"

"Lemme finish! So I mean my mom and dad are dead but the brothers had x-ed the knowledge about the rest of my family. So they were, like, trying to make me the captive orphan sex slave. I mean really!"

"So the sister?"

"She died."

"How sad. So this was when I meet you, you never tell me any of this.

223

Sometimes you say 'brothers,' sometimes you say 'priests,' which one was it?" he asks.

"I don't know."

"So go ahead, this was when I meet you—"

"Yeah, just, so they got busted, I guess, and had to get rid of the kids who'd tell on them, so I got sent to live with my great-grandmother—"

"How they find her?"

"I don't know. I mean, they probably always knew where she was. She was thinking, I think, that I had gotten adopted by some rich Arabs. At least that's what she said. 'I thought de Cath'lics had give you to de Ay-rabs 'cause of yo' name—'"

"I never hear of Arabs adopting no colored kids."

"Well, whatever, old people say weird shit. So anyway, I ended up with her in her house. Everything's all old, nasty, and raggedy. She's . . . I don't know, maybe all old people is like that."

"What do you mean?"

"You know, just go off. So I had asked her to give me the 411, you know, the whole deal—her, me, the creepy crib, what's going on here? I'm thinking, despite appearances that state otherwise, she's normal, under-stand what I'm saying? I figure she's gonna respond, you know, normal. I mean, I'm a kid who shows up on her doorstep, innocent—"

"I remember how innocent you was."

"What's that supposed to mean?"

"Nothing. You getting distracted. So what happened?"

"Well, she just started talking, like she was crazy or having a nervous breakdown or . . . or high, or I don't know, like, like remembering herself being high. But, whatever, she was gone. She was sitting in the kitchen staring at the wall, or at something couldn't nobody see but her. And she's talking, just a-talking, loud too. Every now and then, she'll check me out, look at me or ask me a question. But why I say nervous breakdown or something is because this goes on for hours. I don't know, it felt like days, even. I mean, I would get up, go to the bathroom, and come back, and she's *still* talking."

"About what, Arthur?"

"Her life—Mississippi. According to her, she damn near walked to New York, and then she gets involved with some 'nigger boy' in the fast lane who gets killed. She never got over it. Then her daughter—"

"Ta mère?"

"No, my grandmother, this is my great-grandmother talking. You know, the whole bad-man story for generations—"

"She didn't try to find you when they put you up for adoption?"

"I wasn't put up for adoption."

"But you said you were."

What's *with* this motherfucker!

"No, I said, *she* said or thought I had been adopted—"

"But that's what I'm asking. Didn't she, *anybody,* say anything or try to find you or . . . or *anything?*"

This faggot is starting to get on my last nerve!

"I don't know. No, I guess not."

Is that what he wanted to hear?

"Well, don't get mad and stop talking. You do that all the time! It's not fair!"

The sound of his voice makes me sick. The accent, the lisp—*I never hear anysing like it. . . . You boys . . . you sink you cute! . . . I seen hundred of boys like you*—I bet!

"Shall I fix you a coffee or a protein shake while you staring off into space?"

"No thanks, I got to get out of here. I have a rehearsal."

"What else you got with that boy?"

"*Boy?* You make it sound like I'm fifty years old or something." He winces. Good, faggot, feel it. "They're all older than me downtown. And how do you know it's a *boy?*" Period, end of sentence. Let that sink in.

"When will you be back?"

"Why?"

"For God's sake, I just asked! I can't ask you nothing no more?"

Faggot! I hate him. "He wish it was him!" Joke, my ass. All of a sudden he's so curious about some damn notebooks, my mother, the priests—he doesn't care. He could have asked years ago, but then he would have had to deal with me being thirteen. He didn't want to know, goddamn it! He's panicking now. That's what the motherfucker's doing. He don't care about no damn dance either, "*la danse*." Maybe he used to, I don't know. I know all he care about now is wrapping his lips around some dick? He can forget about me, I ain't a "you boys" no more. Next faggot call me a boy is dead.

Walking down Riverside Drive on the Upper West Side, I turn my gaze away from the beautiful green and silver river snaking down the side of the city and look at the ugly black nannies pushing their pink babies on the sidewalk. Shit, what choices did I have back then? Slavery Days? Marcus Garvey Park—the bushes or the watchtower? Port Authority— the bathrooms? Central Park—the lake, the Meat Rack? Or Roman? I made a choice.

I think things are opening up for me downtown.

CPRKR, one of the pieces Scott set on Herd, has two screens placed on opposite sides of the stage. One screen shows a large vase falling off a kitchen counter, crashing onto a tile floor into smithereens. The other screen shows the same footage in reverse. The splashes of water unsplattering and coming back into the vase as the shards of glass unfragment and fly upward until the vase is on the countertop again. The DVDs are played over and *over:* falling, shattered, coming back together, rising, restored—again and again. And Herd is dancing downstage of the vases.

I only went back once after I left. "Tell 'em you put me on a train to Mississippi and my father picked me up at the station." That's when she gave me the notebooks. "I don' know what dey say, I cain't make out nothin' wit'out my glasses."

All I wanted was to get as far away from her as possible, forget, be . . . be the opposite—CLEAN, neat, leather down, cool city, Parker! Basquiat! Triple A—African American Artist. I didn't want shit to do with "dis and dat" or "you de seed" or "down in Mississippi."

I think of a piece of My Lai's we just did, "Suicide Seed." Behind the company is a still from "Sick: The Life and Death of Bob Flanagan, Super Masochist." The piece ends with a line from a poem by John Donne: "For Godsake hold your tongue, and let me love."

"That's *not* dance, it's not theater either—you is doing nothing with them idiots! Dance is not some assholes reciting a poem in front of some porn video."

Fuck him, if it ain't a dying swan, it's not dance to Roman's ass.

I left the notebooks at the pad. I need to swing back and get them. I should have known he was going through my stuff, or was he? It was my fault for telling him to put my shoes in the closet? I stop in my tracks and double back up Riverside Drive home.

Henri the doorman stares at me. I try to joke. "Nope, you're not seeing things, I just left."

But he doesn't say anything or smile; it feels like he's looking right through me. Does he believe I'm Arthur Stevens? Twenty-five years old? Four years I've never gotten any mail here or visitors. He's probably known something was up from day one. But I wasn't worth losing those hundred-buck gratuities over. Plus, I don't think he likes black people too tough. But that could be all in my head. He's never said anything; if he had, where would I be now? Where would Roman be? What difference does it make, it's almost over now.

Back in the apartment, I make a straight line to the closet for the suitcase I had the notebooks in. Where—okaay, one, two, three, four—where's the other one? His ass! Where could it be, he had to have taken it. I am going to throw these motherfuckers so far away. The longer they're lying around, the greater the, the *potential* for a mistake, that that shit will get into somebody's hands who will mistake me for that weird shit, think that's who I am. Jesus Christ, I ain't that! I don't know what I am, but I'm different from that. On the real, I'm different from everybody's expectations anyway. What's a nigger spozed to be any fucking way! Even PC motherfuckers like Scott and them got stereotypes. They're surprised when I say I was born uptown, and then they see I ain't no yo-hoodie-coupla-forties-welfare-baby-daddy or a shitball-eating faggot walking around, "Well, hello, *girlfriend*," and snapping my fingers like Roman. They can't figure me out. They ain't never been past Fourteenth Street. Who was I? Shit, man, I was who the fuck I had to be. But now, who am I *now*? Motherfucking Crazy Horse, that's who! But that's not real. I made up somebody to survive. I don't know who I am, but I damn sure know what I ain't. And I ain't this shit. I toss the notebooks in my backpack. My inheritance, I snort. Scott's ass is sitting on millions when his parents die. My Lai is due for mad paper too.

A sob shakes my chest as I drop down the subway steps remembering how easily I disappeared. Stan was supposed to take me to school that next Monday. I had started dance classes already but had missed nearly three weeks of school (now I've missed three years). Roman tells me again if I be his boy he will make me a dancer, feed me, and let me stay in his house, *and* keep me in leather and jeans and anything else I want. When I go back, Slavery Days begs me to stay. "You de seed." I don't know what she told them; I know I never picked up a milk carton with my face on it.

I never hid, I never ran, I never had to. All that shit—J.J., Crazy Horse, Arthur Stevens—nobody knew my fucking name. But the real deal was, nobody cared I was gone once there was no ass to eat or check to collect. I took two classes a day at Stride with Roman for free, no questions asked, took classes at the Y, came uptown and took classes from Imena every Thursday and Saturday afternoon. I didn't have to hide. I never existed for nobody, no way.

What's going to be hard is existing. Reappearing. This January I'll be eighteen years old. Get a job, Barnes & Noble, Starbucks, or Mickey D's, then take the GED and get in a college dance program, NYU or someplace? Just come on up like those boomer bombers in the movie, kaBOOM, we're back! I like that! They're like sixty now. Even though they didn't kill anybody, they blew shit up. What did I do? Nothing. Sometimes I wish I had killed somebody or something, then at least I'd be suffering for some reason.

On the train I look across the aisle at some babes giggling, their ears stuffed with sounds, one player between them and one earphone in one girl's ear, the other in her friend's. Friends. Looking up above the girls' heads in the train window, I see my reflection, and then it's like a ghost, the black leather hood Brother Samuel used to wear, appears with smoke wafting out of the eye- and earholes. It's smoldering like it's about to burst into flames. Scared, I jump up when the train screeches into Seventy-second Street and dash out the opening doors instead of continuing downtown to Fourteenth Street, where I was going to switch to the Number 1 to the Loft. I run up the steps just in time to dash in between the closing doors of an uptown Number 3. I want to spit in that faggot's face and tell him how he fucked up my life. Am I losing it? Why now? Can't you let it go? You got a rehearsal, suppose you get in trouble? Then I see the babes in my head, listening to the same song, sharing earphones. I never had that. He should die. Yeah, by my bare hands! I ain't thirteen no more. These four years been the beef years. I close my eyes shut but can't squeeze out the leather-hooded ghost, then it morphs into Brother Samuel's pink sweaty face.

I get off at 135th Street and Malcolm X Blvd. Shit, I spent most of my life here. On Lenox there's the funeral parlor where my mother was laid out, and around the corner on 135th, the recreation center where I started dancing.

Where's the security in this place? I think as I breeze through the front door of St Ailanthus and down the hall to the administration office. I used to put papers in piles here for Mrs Washington. I don't recognize the girl sitting behind the wooden stile at the desk, working on the computer. All of a sudden I'm out of steam.

"Can I help you?"

"I want to see Brother John."

"Who?"

"Brother John," I say, like when you're in one of those vintage stores downtown and you ask about some shirt you don't really want because you're nervous about the price of the pants you do want.

"He's been gone a while now, almost three years."

"I used to be in his earth science class."

"Brother John is teaching in South Dakota on an Indian reservation. Some of the boys still get letters from him."

I bet they do.

"Brother Samuel?"

She's looks at me weird. "Brother Samuel died two days ago."

So it *was* him.

"He committed suicide. Hung himself from one of the beams in the library. The kids found him like that, naked except for this . . . this *thing* . . ." She can't finish but draws her hands down the sides of her face.

The hood. Yeah, it was him, him on his way to hell.

As if the girl is some kind of witch or something, I back out of the door without turning my back on her and then run.

Hail Mary Full of Grace Blessed art thou among women and Blessed is the fruit of thy womb Jesus—

"Fuck him!" I shout to the sky. Let somebody else pray for his ass. I'm glad he's dead!

That night I dream one of the old dreams I used to have when I was a kid, flying over endless blue water. Flying and flying as if I'm some giant puffed-up bird, all-powerful. Nothing can stop me. Then I start to feel a little tired, just a little bit, not a lot, really. I look out over the vast blue water; some of the fun is gone, not all, just some. I'm looking for someplace I can land, except as far as I can see, water. But everything ends; there is no endless *anything*, except in dreams. If I can keep flying until the water ends, or I see some island, or I wake up . . . I'm scared, which gives me energy to keep flying. In the dream I feel so much sorrow. I think of how they killed Crazy Horse. I feel the knife through the centuries. It hurts worse than when they twisted my shoulder at St Ailanthus. I keep flying, I'm an Indian now, dead and crying, watching Brother John walk toward my great-great-great-grandchildren. I look at the full moon. *Shit, go for it,* I think, and I arch upward and start flying toward the moon!

When I get there, I see an old man with a straw hat on, his back to me, sitting on one of the glowing moon rocks playing a banjo loud and singing:

If I evah git from 'round dis harvest,
I don' even wanna see a rose bush grow.

Who is he? I want to see his face, so I run up on him. But before I can get in front of him and see his face, he stands up and shoots forward on beams of light like long gleaming skis. I try again; the same thing happens. Then I see some beams of light and hop on them, getting my own "skis," which turn out to be faster than his. I catch up with him and whip around on my beams of light in front of him to see who he is. But where his face should be is green vapor floating in the shape of a skull. A pair of eyeballs is staring out at me from the vapor as he plucks on his banjo, shouting:

If I evah git from 'round dis harvest,
I don' even wanna see a rose bush grow.
An' if anybody ask me 'bout de country,
Lord have mercy on his soul.

He keeps singing. I know who he is! He's groaning now and singing out words from another world. I'm getting scared. I want to go back to my own world, but I don't know how to get back from space. I wake up in a panic.

IN THE MORNING he's talking talking.

"Let's go for breakfast," he says.

"What time is it?"

"Eight o'clock."

I want to go back to sleep.

"Come on, sleepyhead, put something on and we go get some breakfast."

I feel like shit. Life should begin at noon. Plus, I don't want to go nowhere with him.

"What you is laying up there thinking? I never know what you think-ing anymore."

"But I know what you're thinking," I snap.

"You is become so cruel. You was not cruel when I take you in."

"I'm not thirteen anymore."

"You is always bringing that up nowadays. That, and those priests that molest you. Roman don't molest. You is bigger than Roman. I thought you was a man. You tell me you is seventeen. Who am I supposed to be-lieve? Then you tell me the truth after it's too late—we is already in love!"

We? This motherfucker is crazy. I got to get up; I got a rehearsal at ten.

"You want to go to breakfast?"

"I got a rehearsal at ten."

"We never go anwhere!"

"You know why that is as well as I do."

"Well, you is of age now. We can go out like . . . like other couples."

For shit's sake, "other couples." Please, if it had been me, a black man, fifty-, sixty-something years old, bringing home his little white ass, I'd still be in jail.

"I'm not hungry."

"So what, you need something, it's not good to dance on an empty stomach."

"Where's the other notebook?"

"I don't know what you is talking about."

"Forget it, then."

"No, what you is talking about?"

"No use talking about it if you don't know what I'm talking about."

"So what I *am* talking about is, it ain't good to dance on an empty stomach. You need to eat something. Let's go get a coffee and croissant. I have to teach at eleven-thirty, that advanced intermediate. What time is your rehearsal over?"

He has a ten o'clock advanced professional class. He's been telling me for almost a year I need to take a more advanced class than the advanced intermediate. It's true, but I don't want to take it from him.

"You taking class somewhere else?" he asks.

So this is what's up.

"Come on, I've always taken class 'somewhere else'!"

"You know what I mean." He pouts. "Ballet class."

"Hey, I don't feel like going into it, but if you must know, Herd decided we should all take the same technique class."

"That's silly! Each one is different, everybody has—"

"Look, it's just an experiment we're doing for a couple of months." I'm trying to sound blasé, but I ain't coming to the ten o'clock class, and I ain't going back to the eleven-thirty class or any of his other classes, ever. Never. We have a new girl, woman, I guess, coming today. Since that review in the *Voice,* a lot of people been calling to audition.

"You know, you so excited about that goddamned group. That's because you think you is the goddamned best or some shit. Or maybe they is so bad you *is* the best, and they let you get away with every kind of shit, convince you you is some kind of creative genius. Well, you not! You got a long way, long, *long* way to go before you is a real dancer!"

"I thought you liked some of what I was doing!" I hear myself whining like a little kid. I hate that. I close my eyes. I don't even hear what he says next; a wave of hate rolls through me so hot I could slit his throat and feel no pain, feel good, in fact. Old-ass faggot!

"Let me tell you one more thing—"

Before he can finish, I snatch the front of his neck with one hand. He can't even scream.

"I don't want to hear it!" I hiss. "And go get that other notebook before I wipe the floor with your faggot ass!"

I squeeze tighter like I'm gonna pull his pipes out of his throat.

"Get it!" I snarl, letting go and pushing him away from me onto the floor.

He's on the floor, gasping for breath. I never seen him this scared before. I look him dead in the eye then look away. I was scared for a minute too; if I hurt him, it's still like hurting myself. Every time I come in the building, a security camera takes my picture, every time I leave. Who cares about me? If I hurt him, *I'm* going to jail. Don't nobody care about what he did to me.

"OK, OK, I get it. I was not meaning to steal it from you only, only . . ."

He scurries away and back like a squirrel. I lean over and look at the clock; I got no time to do anything now. I put the notebook in my backpack, take a ho's bath, and head for the train.

I get off at Franklin Street and head for the Loft—because of Scott's money *our* Loft, really—where we rehearse. I know Roman is being an old douchebag, but it bothers me, him insinuating I can't dance or being in Herd is some kind of cop out. Fuck him, he's just jealous because I've made some friends. Well, not friends—how can you be friends when you can't even tell people your name?—but they're *something,* associates. Kids like me in a way, even though they're older, NYUers, downtownies, but fuck Roman! We're dancing! Not like some of those old motherfuckers in his class at Stride, twenty-three, twenty-four years old, still just taking class, not auditioning or anything, talking about one day when they're ready and all that shit. I mean, shit, when are you fucking ready! Leave it to bitches like Roman, and you're never ready or you're ready when *he* says you're ready.

Herd, it's five of us now since Rebecca and Bianca left: Scott, My Lai, Snake, Ricky, and me, and with the new bitch it'll be six. I think Ricky is on his way out, we'll see. With the new girl, if he does split, it'll be three-two, three men and two girls. That's good, too many girls changes things. Ricky's bringing the new bitch in, so you know that whether she can dance or not, she's cute. I never seen him with anybody ugly even though he's only five-four and looks like he crawled out of a cave somewhere with all that hair. He hates me, I can feel it. I never did anything to him except dance better; I can't help that. I ain't going to saw off my legs so he won't be threatened. My Lai says it's the Mexican thing—he's used to feeling superior to black. Hey, maybe he is, get on out there and go for it! What do I give a fuck about anybody being superior to me? He's mad at himself, that's what it is. Scott talks a good game, power sharing, blah-blah, but Scott's not moving over. Plus, Ricky's getting heavy, and it don't look too good.

Next month is when I break out. I have to, Scott told me, take my turn at maintaining the Loft. I love it, I *have* to. If he only knew. That's all I been thinking about 24/7. "You don't have to stay here if you don't want to, but the three months you're assigned Loft duty you're responsible for everything—shopping, security, cleaning, record keeping, *everything*. You may as well stay here, 'cause you'll be over here 24/7."

I can't wait. That's all I been thinking about, my own crib, even if it's only temporary, and *bitches*, scoring some pussy. Yeah, leaving Roman, bagging some pussy, getting some kind of job. I've never even had a job before. It's gonna be so cool to get in here. Three months rent-free, maybe longer 'cause no one else wants to do this shit. Maybe I'll take the GED, see if I can get in a college dance program, Snake says he has friends who been at NYU for years on grant money. How they get that shit? Now's the time to find out. Shit, I'll be eighteen soon; nobody can touch me. I'm tired of hiding. Well, I'm not hiding, but what is it if nobody knows your name, where you live, who you live with? Everything's been made up, my age, name, what else is there?

I glance at my watch. Nine-fifty, I'm on time.

When I walk in, everybody's already there standing around. The new chick is awesome, tall, blond, goddamn!

"This is Arthur Stevens, or Crazy Horse as he's also called. Arthur, this is Amy Ash," Scott says.

"Hi, Arthur."

"Hi."

She doesn't look no twenty-five to me. She looks really young.

"We were just telling Amy about Herd, how we got started and shit. My Lai was getting ready to break down the piece we're going to be doing that's evolving out of *My Lai 4*." Snake.

Amy looks like she wants to ask a question but is trying to be cool.

Ricky, who is picking at his beefy toes, asks it for her. "What's My Lai got to do with you?"

"It was like a war crime in Vietnam—" My Lai tries to explain.

"Yeah, like duh, I get that. What I'm asking is how does this have anything to do with *us*? You, even?" Ricky persists.

"Well, lemme finish, and maybe you'll get it."

Amy is looking at My Lai like she's from another planet. My Lai could care less. That's one of the things I found different from kids like My Lai and Scott, rich kids, they don't give a fuck. Kids like me are walking around wondering what are people thinking, gonna think—shit, what are motherfuckers gonna *do* to me?

Scott looks excited. "Talk us through what you want to do and how. You were talking last night about being adopted. How does that figure into this?"

"Hmm, well, the shit I was saying about adoption, I mean, who fucking cares? Are you bored already or not with the adoptee trope? I mean, everything you pick up in Barnes & Noble is some goddamn half-breed or immigrant adoptee blues. They're either grateful or resentful as hell. I was offering up the adoptee thing to you as *part* of a story. I want to go there to what this fucking country did, not just to me but to a nation, a *race*, why we ended up so poor, why our kids ended up on the adoption block in the first place. Why Vietnam? Why not Vietnam? Shit, I could be Vietnamese. That's what my dad blamed his drinking and shit on, Vietnam. Not like he even went, dig that, he didn't even go. He was *affected*. So then everything this asshole touches is affected, like forever. I want to use this." She pulls a battered paperback out of her backpack. "I got this out of the dollar bin at the Strand, *Bloods* by Wallace Terry. And this." She holds another book up. "*My Lai 4: A Report on the Massacre and Its Aftermath* by Seymour M. Hersh. I got it from the same place; it's a blow-by-blow account of the massacre—"

"Massacre?" Amy scowls.

"Massacre, honey. Business as usual by the motherfuckers your mama and daddy pay taxes to."

"I pay my own taxes," Amy says.

"Do you want to extract text directly from it? Can we use it?" Scott asks.

"Hell yeah, it was written in Vietnam times. This guy's dead or in a nursing home for sure," she says.

"Fossil," Snake chimes.

"So lay it on us," I say.

"Well, I think what I want to do is relive that day onstage. I don't know yet. There's text I definitely want to use. We can start by just playing around doing some improv with the video camera while I read from the text. It'll give me an idea of how you guys feel the text. I see us dancing with some documentary footage behind us or even center stage. There's been a lot, a shitload, of films, documentaries, and news archived about Vietnam."

"So when did you change your name to My Lai?" Amy asks.

"Legally my name is still Nöel Wynne Desiré Orlinsky. At this stage of the game, I try to avoid any conflict that would interfere with my monthly EBT."

"Come again?" Amy says.

"I don't have time." My Lai.

"That's it for this. Here's new rehearsal schedules," My Lai announces.

WHEN I LEAVE, I feel like these notebooks are a dead baby I'm carrying in my backpack. Where to ditch it? Ditch the smell of roach shit, the old bitch sitting in that chair and a roach looking like it just crawled out of her head as it scuttles up the wall. Ditch the sound of her: *Don't leave, youze de only boy born alive to us.* (Who the fuck is "us"?) *Youze de seed.*

I touch the line down the side of my face, it's fading but ain't never going to go all the way away. "Perfect face," My Lai says, except for that. Roman says, "You more beautiful because of the scar, like those ancient Oriental painters who mess up a corner of they painting to show how perfect the rest is." To me it looks like I got sliced in a street fight, but I didn't get sliced in a street fight, I did it to myself. Well, I ain't gonna do this to myself. These notebooks are some kind of indictment or . . . or judgment. They're not normal. Scott, My Lai—what would they think?

Kill these lies, burn 'em! I can't just start a fire on the street. I'm afraid if I put them in a trash can, someone will find them and trace them back to me. How? I don't know, but the thought squeezes my stomach, makes me want to vomit—vomit Toosie in orange silk her young self and her old stinky self all muddled up in my mind. *You beautiful, oh yez you is, not all big like you mama or pimple-face like yo' weak daddy.* Music is playing, I'm playing, doing big boy, smoking chiba, riding in cars, getting my dick sucked by girls who call it, like Toosie did, a "johnson," then cutting, blood rain, Billie sings: *I'll Never Be The Same.* I want to go back to some place before this scar on my face, to something clean. *I'll Never Be The Same. Good Morning Heartache.* You is so beautiful, like art. You is a fine black boy, different; his tongue goes down the side of my face neck tits navel thighs, johnson it feels so good so why do I hate it uhh! Sometimes I do vomit. Hit Mickey D's, the King, the Colonel, or Taco Bell and then upchuck, yuk! Nasty but better than being fat. I want to be muscle lean bone sleek. I want to vomit this shit. I can't be what I want to be with this, this shit, filth: *What dady do to me my lif not be what it shuld be cause mama an dady. My sun my lilte sun my lif his dady mine*

Hold fast to dreams
For if dreams die
Life is broken-wigged bird
That cannot fly
Hold fast to dreams
For if dreams die
Life is broken-wigged bird
That cannot fly

Whoever she is, fills up ten pages copying that over and over, each time misspelling "winged." It's not until the ninth page she starts writing "winged" instead of "wigged."

My mother? "My mother and father were married," I say out loud. And, unfortunately, my mother got killed in a car accident, and my father got killed in the Gulf War. I'm a good person. I never hurt anybody. The sun is up. Shining. Central Park, the reservoir? Nah, too many people out there running and that fence, anybody see you throwing something over the fence into the water, they might shoot you. And some of these shits are written in pencil, and water won't wash that away. Burn? Where? No, tear these shits in little pieces and throw them away. Let's go to the park and get this over with.

I have this fear like a nightmare: Roman is somehow there at 805 St Nicholas Avenue. The implants in his head are growing like geysers. He's looking at Toosie, who's standing there holding her coffeepot. "Now tell me everysing. *Everysing.*" He says. And she does. Then he gets in my face, "You wanna tell me this woulda been better than what I give you!"

Come on, feet! The park, I know what I want to do, and I do it. Sitting on the grass, the notebooks stacked beside me, I start tearing them page by page into tiny bits. I shred them over my backpack, scooping any pieces that fall on the grass up and into the pack. By the time I'm through, my fingers hurt. I put on my stuffed backpack and start to run toward the 103rd Street subway station. There's only two people, a professional-looking black guy and a white woman together. They could be police, but what am I gonna do? Litter, I never saw anybody get arrested for littering. They stiffen when I walk past them to the end of the platform, to the stinky hole where the train comes roaring out. My hands are full of bits of paper. The earth starts to rumble, the train is coming. COME ON, BITCH! I scream, and start throwing bits of paper into the black void. RUN OVER THAT, YOU MOTHER-FUCKER! I scream at the approaching lights, reaching down into my pack, scooping handfuls of paper again and again up into the air over the steel tracks. As the train comes closer, they fly everywhere, down, up, back in my face. Ha! Maybe they'll start a fire; they always say that, DON'T THROW PAPER ON THE TRACKS, IT COULD START A FIRE. Well, burn baby, fuck it! The train roars past me, stops, and pulls out again. I turn my pack upside down over the tracks, watch the last bits of paper drift down onto the tracks. Free. I stand back and wait for the next train. Get on.

WHEN I GET HOME, Roman is like a puppy. I can't even get in the door before he starts running his mouth.

"I was talking about you today."

"Gee, thanks."

"Why you have that attitude? It was quite good. Alphonse, his boyfriend is going to Columbia and is writing a paper on Jean-Michel Pasquiat."

"*Basquiat.*"

"OK, whatever. He asks me I ever heard of him. I go to the bookshelf, you has almost all his stuff. He say you is probably very smart young man. I say not probably, honey!"

"I'm really tired."

"Too tired to listen? That don't take no energy." He pouts.

Roman has the Whitney Exhibition book on Basquiat open on the coffee table. One time, talking to Snake, I found out he had read the whole book too, not just Greg Tate's essay but *all* the essays. My Lai and I read *Story of O* together. Roman had it sitting on his shelf, that and *The Thief's Journal*—wild French stuff Roman never even read, one of the "boys" left it.

I wonder how much money he really has. I know he has a safety-deposit box where he keeps his stock certificates and bonds and jewelry. He told me. "I got to, some of the boys used to come here is bad. Come to rob you. You different from the other boys." Not really. How did he get any fucking stocks and bonds anyway? Not teaching dance. Cash? Does he keep cash in the safety-deposit box? What's a bond anyway?

But you know what, fuck it! Fuck his money, put it out your head, it's the last thing tying you to this old douchebag. You're gonna make money! Hell, what did My Lai say? "Shit, you *are* money!"

"He asks me—"

"What are you talking about?" I snap.

"Alphonse, my friend. What, you wasn't listening? He asks me why you is not in school like his boyfriend if you so smart. I say I don't know, but it's a good idea. He says how old is he? I say twenty—"

"Why? I'm seventeen."

"Well, you is been seventeen so long."

He laughs. I laugh too, even though I half want to slap the shit out of him. But I don't, number one, because I know he likes it and two, because I'm tired of being mad.

"You want to go to college. It's all around here, Columbia, City College, right here."

"I know."

I look at the coffee table. How fucking weird; he has the book open to pages 88–89, *Acque Pericolose*. The reproduction takes up both pages.

"Let's go get some Chinese, OK," he says.

"OK."

We're standing on Broadway near Ninety-eighth Street in front of Hunan Balcony when I feel someone's eyes on me. I look up; it's Amy, the new girl. I look away, try to act like I didn't see her, like she didn't see me. You saw someone that looked like me, you stupid ho. My stomach contracts. Shit, me pretending I didn't see her don't change she saw me standing with this antique fag! I feel like killing myself. That's good and stupid, really stupid. Just because I'm walking down the street or standing on a corner with someone doesn't mean I'm *with* them. Come on, gimme a break! I'm a dancer. He's one of the best ballet teachers in the city. I'm a dancer, but hey, do I look like— Where is she? Let me explain. She's gone, of course she is, why wouldn't she be? The smell of sautéing garlic coming from the restaurant nauseates me.

"What's wrong with you?" Roman asks.

"Nothing. I'm tired. I'm going home."

"Going home? But you didn't eat nothing yet."

"I said I don't feel good."

"You don't feel good?" he echoes.

I turn from him. Now, I think, *now*. They can't put me in no group home or juvenile lockup. I'm a man, an artist, hanging out with people in their twenties! I head for the subway, the swish of his tight jeans and clip of his leather-heeled cowboy boots right behind me.

"What's going on here!"

What's going on here? Late in the day to be asking that shit. I run down the subway steps and lose the sound of his boots behind me on the subway stairs. All these *selves* are floating in my head as the train jolts out of the station, morphing into people with names like Arthur or J.J. I see myself doing weird shit, but I know I'm basically normal. That shit at St Ailanthus was some kind of Halloween psycho. But back then I thought I had been kicked out of some kind of paradise.

I was a child; now I'm a man. I'm not what they were—baby-butt-busting homos. Or maybe I am, maybe they came to me for that shit because I'm one too. Maybe I am a fag. I like getting my dick sucked. Would I like it with a girl? When I'm jacking off, I think of girls, J-Lo or a girl like the new girl, tall, blond, big titties. Scott told his parents he wanted to be a dancer, and they sent him to NYU, Merce Cunningham, the Graham School, Africa; *un*-homeboy been to Africa! Normal kids don't have to pay! Where would he be now if he'd come through foster care and then had to deal with this faggot with his pink-implanted scalp, Pilates class, and tanning salons—slurping on his dick damn near every night. Does what I did with the kids at St Ailanthus make me a faggot? What I did with the kids wasn't nothing they weren't doing already. Shit, I did what they were doing to me. I don't care what she was, I wish I could of stayed with my mother, my parents, dope addicts or whatever they were. My dad?

I don't feel sick anymore; now I'm hungry.

Some days, standing at the barre after two days of nothing but coffee and double chocolate cake donuts from Dunkin' Donuts, I come center and just jump straight up four feet in the air, my legs wide apart in second, or I come across the floor and jeté, my legs making a perfect split in the air, and I just hang there for a second. I see the envy on Ricky's face and the challenge in My Lai's. Shit, I am the one. I didn't ask to be. I worked for this shit. But shit, everybody works. The fuck if I knew what it was gonna be in four years. But I can fucking do this. I can. Whether I do or not is another story, but at least I *can*. What does Roman's ass have now? Nothing. He's old. It's way over.

"FOURTEENTH STREET, change here—"

Fourteenth Street? Where am I going? What'd I even get on the train for? To get away from him. Now back up there for the last time. I dash out the opening doors and leap up the stairs across to the uptown side.

Sitting down in an uptown Number 3 waiting for the conductor to shout out the stops. I look at the hole in my jeans, very chic hole, two-hundred-dollar jeans, that's over for a while, at least until I get a job.

Someone's— No, he's looking down now. I had thought the guy across the aisle was staring at me, but he's in his *Daily News*. I look back at my pants, but I feel, what is this, some kind of heebie-jeebies day? Someone's looking at me, jeez! When I look up again, the guy has put his paper down. It's . . . it's Richie Jackson! Ol' lying-ass Richie Jackson. I can see he ain't at St Ailanthus no more. He looks like a old homeless. I can smell him across the aisle. He pushes the paper off his lap to the floor and walks to the other end of the car. I hate nasty dirty people like that. He got tall but he can't be no more than thirteen or fourteen.

THIRTY-FOURTH STREET!

He shuffles off the train.

FORTY-SECOND STREET!

Maybe he's on the pipe, a lot of those ghetto types are. He probably got AIDS or some shit already. Most of the white people who don't get off at Seventy-second will get off at Ninety-sixth.

SEVENTY-SECOND STREET!

Now's the time.

NINETY-SIXTH STREET!

I get off the train, run west, and swing up Riverside Drive home, to Roman.

He's been waiting for me.

"Where you been?"

"I didn't feel good, so I took off."

"Just like that! You just run off. You rude, that's what you is!" he shouts.

"Look, I'm leaving."

"Just like that!"

I guess that's the line for today.

"No, not 'just like that.' I been thinking about it for a long time."

"Oh, just how long you is been thinking about this?"

An impulse to cry wells up in me, but I know I won't. I don't cry. I dance. Right now I got to get out, or I'll never get out.

"I been thinking about leaving since I was thirteen."

"There you go with that thirteen shit again! Why you always bring it up?"

"You asked me a question," I snap.

"Where you going?"

"The Herd loft."

"What, so I can call the police and tell them—"

He's gonna call the police? He's really crazy!

"So I can come back and kick your ass!"

"Oh, we is very violent these days. Let me tell you one thing, you is deluding yourself with those little girls in the Village. You is down there fucking around in those little stinky pussies, eating it all up. Let me tell you, you is more pussy than the fish you eating. You running! You just as much fag as me, and you be like me one day—you love a boy, take in a boy, and he break your heart."

He starts crying, big sobs.

"Thanks for the blessing." I mean, gee, old dude, that really makes me want to stick around, I'm going to end up like you.

"Well, I got some news for you, you is got so much for me," he says triumphantly. "You don't know this, but I been to the doctor, I tested positive for the HIV!"

Everything freezes in a flash like a locked-up computer screen, it's going dark. And then I realize he *wants* me to jump up and almost beat him to death so he can call the police, have me locked up, and then visit me in jail with the wham-whams and zoo-zoos. I'll still be his, a "you boys." I was playing myself, thinking I was more. I feel ice growing around my heart.

"Where you going?"

"To get my stuff."

"You hear what I said, this is serious for *us*."

Who cares? Number one, I don't believe him. Number two, I'm going somewhere and dance till I drop, whether it's tomorrow or fifty years from now. I ain't even kissed this faggot in four years, much less let him butt-fuck me. So if I got it from this midget sucking my dick, then I just fucking got it. He can see I ain't scared, that was his hold card, that and his retarded ass was going to call the police on someone.

"Well, hurry up if you going."

If—please, motherfucker! I flip open this big cheap suitcase I got on Fourteenth Street. He starts in with the sobbing again. It's really disgusting.

"Please listen one more thing."

"What, you been shitting in the coffee?"

"I'm sorry, I'm really sorry. I didn't want to ruin your life—"

"My life ain't ruined."

"Just you is so . . . so *ravaged*, I don't know if that's the word, when you got here, when I take you in. One thing, I teach you to dance, admit that."

He's crazy. T-shirt, jeans, roll 'em up.

"You never listen to me! This is the last thing I have to say, maybe ever. I been so depress—"

"Kill yourself."

"Listen!"

I flip the suitcase shut and shift an army duffel bag up onto my shoulder.

"Listen, it's not what you think."

All his little puffed-up triumph is gone. I don't care what he says, he can't bring me down. Or back. He sighs like it's killing him, his next little bomb. If he brings up anything in the notebooks, I'll crack his skull.

"OK, I'm listening."

"You is a very good dancer. If you want to keep fucking with Herd, fine, but start auditioning for companies—ballet, modern, all that. I never tell you before, you are a fine dancer, one of the best young dancers I see in my life—anybody woulda did what I did to have you. From the first day I saw you—"

"Look, I'll call before I come get the rest of my stuff."

"Take it now!"

Fuck him, if I come back here for my shit, he better, number one, have it, and number two, let me in.

"Bye," I say, and head toward the door.

TWO "We should call you Ice-T Number Two or something, you're so cool." She had laughed, flipping her hair with her hand the way white chicks do. All I had said was, "Sexual history? I think what we're really talking about is HIV, *oui?*" Then I raised my eyebrow in the way I had been practicing in the mirror and said, "Fuck sexual history. I mean, so what if I been celibate since the day I was motherfucking born and I *got* it, right? And so what if I been fucking sheep and sucking off at an AIDS hospice or some shit and I *ain't* got it. I think you got, or have, as you would say, pretty good sense and you want to protect yourself. And I don't know no way to do that except get the test, oohhh scary scary, that, and *thee condumb*. And hey, beautiful, I'm willing to go there for you, you know." She turned all red, but boy, did she look relieved. I was relieved too, very. I can go somewhere and get some fucking test and sit up in fake, or maybe real, dread. Yeah, I can do that, but sexual history? Ah, I don't think so.

Yeah, red but relieved, very relieved. Afterward she tells me she's on the pill, but for like a week I avoid her, like she's nuts or something, like what's up with you, nothing was ever going to happen, like she's just another person came into Herd and we never had a little sting thing getting ready to jump off.

I PAINTED THE walls of the sleeping space blue. The whole loft was supposed to be painted in two colors, flat black and this dead white. Black was for the performance space and white for the bathrooms (which Scott

247

wanted to paint black too). He had already done the walled-off sleeping space in black. What, trendy, hip? I don't care; I didn't want it. My Lai picked the color, and she, Snake, and me did it in a weekend: scrape, prime, paint, and paint—sky blue. Snake painted fluffy white clouds! Then we got some high-gloss black, not like the flat we used for the performance space and did the floor. Perfect.

MUSIC? CHARLIE PARKER. How I got so into him? *Bird Lives!* by Ross Russell. Billie Holiday? Well, with her, Roman, to tell the truth, and Slavery Days, she had the records! Then too I wanted to love what Basquiat loved, and that was CPRKR. Old old school, Tupac, I used to not be able to stand him, now I like that shit sometimes. Bach, Roman would put him on sometimes, I started to like its realigning my gray space. I don't have that much except clothes, some CDs, and my books. Roman wanted me to look good, but I'm cool in ripped jeans and a T-shirt. Everyone is getting or has phones. Who would I call? What do you need to dance? Classes and your body.

This is my room for now. I put a lock on the door. "All the time I was there, I never had a lock on the door. Who comes in here but us?" "That's you," I tell him. I want privacy. Shit, he owns this sucker, or his parents do. How's that for a start in life! My room. Scott said don't worry about how long. We're supposed to rotate, take turns with the maintenance, but nobody wants to do it right now except me. Snake's in love with his man, plus he already put in three months. My Lai already did it, "loft duty," as she calls it. Amy just got here and is sharing with three friends in the Village, and they totally love living together. So hey, I can stay. I need to get a New York State ID or a license, but I don't drive yet.

We were sucking java juice in Starbucks when Scott went to get a refill and Snake got up to go to the bathroom; My Lai had left to do some shopping. It's just the two of us, me and Amy, and she leans in. "So what's your color?" "Huh?" "You know, purple, emerald, black, burgundy, blue? For *la chambre*?" I'm not feeling it with her no more, I think, but I tell her blue. What shade? Umm, my second-favorite color: the color of the almost-night sky, a lot darker than we did the walls. Who cares, really, she's starting to get on my nerves. I kinda like being by myself.

Scott comes back with four espressos on a tray. Snake bounds out of the bathroom. "Nothing better than a good shit!"

Scott laughs.

"It's true, and you know what I love." Snake.

"No, tell us," I say in what evidently doesn't come off as sarcastic, because he keeps talking.

"How the people who are waiting in line when you open the door look at you like you're from outer space when they smell shit. Like, hello, folks, it's a bathroom!" Snake.

"Thanks for the coffee, Scott," Amy says.

"No thing."

I break off another piece of her Divine Fair Trade chocolate bar.

"Well, take the whole thing, why don't you."

At that, I snatch the chocolate and my backpack and dash up to the counter. They're laughing at the table. I smile back at them and stuff the rest of the chocolate bar in my mouth.

"I'm going to get you!" she shouts, shaking a fist at me.

I ask the guy at the counter, "You guys still hiring?"

"That's the manager," he says, nodding at a fat, red-haired guy who darts into the back and comes back with an application.

"Fill it out now or bring it in the next time you come in."

The chocolate is still in my mouth. I look at the wrapper, Divine, right on. What's divine? Dancing, chocolate, getting my dick sucked, getting in deep, reading, being able to lock the door to my room and read a book without hearing Roman lisp, "What you is reading?" What else? Ballet class, leather, ripped jeans, downtown, dancing in sync with My Lai. Can girls suck dick? That would be divine, to have someone I like make me feel like Roman did going down on me. To be good enough to be in a famous company even if I didn't stay in it, to just know my shit was phat enough to get in. Travel? Paris? Japan?

After rehearsal Amy hands me a plastic bag.

"Ehh, er . . . what's this?"

"A present," she says, and turns and heads for the elevator.

I pull two white seven-day candles out the bag and Tommy Hilfiger four-hundred-thread-count 100 percent Egyptian cotton sheets, king, cobalt blue. Like duh, she's ready. I'm scared. Maybe all that shit Roman said about me is true. Maybe she'll think I'm stupid if she ever really talks to me; Scott, her, even Snake's crazy ass graduated from college. How do you eat pussy? I know girls like that. Shit, just go ahead and wash the mattress pad and blankets you been sleeping on and put the sheets on the bed. The candles will be cool with the ceiling fluorescent off.

"ARE YOU GAY?" she whispers.

"No," I say, "and don't you ever say some shit like that again."

I have the white seven-day candles burning in the corners near the head of the bed.

"Why? I'm bi, Snake's another world! And My Lai says if it can walk—"

"I don't care what anyone else is. I'm telling you what I am, OK?"

"OK, OK, whatever. I . . . I don't care. I want to be your friend *whatever* the deal is. That's what I was really trying to say."

She leans over and kisses me. Inside, I'm trembling, but it's because I hear her asking again, even though her lips are on mine, *Are you gay?* I feel helpless, flat. She lifts her T-shirt; I see her breasts, get excited, and pull her toward me. I never noticed just how tall she was, she's almost as tall as me. She leans down and pulls her tights off and throws them on top of my leather bag in the corner. I grab her shoulders and pull her closer to me like in the movies, only in the movies the girls is hardly ever as tall as you. I run my fingers through her silky hair, beautiful like a chick in a magazine. She wraps her arms around my waist, squeezes me. You can hear the sounds of traffic on the street even on Sunday, that's Manhattan.

"We don't have to worry about anybody coming?"

"They can't get in if they do come. I've locked the elevator door. No one else has a key except me and Scott. And Scott, if he comes, ain't coming back here. This is my room."

I look at the poster, *L'Acrobate*. The gray and white figure distorted beyond being a body, that's how I want to dance, not like the acrobat but the way that dude paints. I grab her butt pull her closer. Touching her breasts excites me, heat surges through my body, I glide my fingers along her rib cage, the hair under her arms is blond, there's not a scar on her anywhere. I lean forward kiss her. Next to the heat in my belly is a cold gray something that feels like a little frozen pearl. Fear? She takes my hand and puts it between her legs. She smells hot, real good, it's like cheese or something; her hair is bristly, not soft like I expected. Her cunt tightens around my fingers, whoa! What girls got. I smile; her smell is all up my nose, making me hard. She's all white and blond. I feel a surge of what, power? I don't know: Joy? Power? This is the ultimate, ain't it? I wish there was a mirror here; I want to see our bodies next to each other, entwined. I'm getting more excited, I remember Brother John jacking off looking at the pictures of black men and white men together, and then he had pictures of these white women with enormous tits, I would jack off with him looking at me looking at the white women (but never any black girls). She pulls my briefs down; I wonder does she feel like I feel. Does my black shine fuck her up inside, turn her on. Shit, I'm gonna murder her with my dick! Feel fear, like that minute, millisecond in the park, you not sure whether you got a killer or vanilla. She touches my penis. Groan, go there, yeah, go there. It feels right, like Jaime only righter because it's a girl. She gets on her knees. Kisses it, opens her lips. I push my hips, thrust just a little, she gags. What's up with that? She stops rubbing my butt and legs, gets up off her knees, and walks over to the bed made up neat. I ain't no slob, see what they teach you in an orphanage, oh, shut up will you, get over it, you ain't there no more. She's laying on the bed now, her flat belly, her smelly good blond bush gleaming pink from the inside. Je*zus*! She's ready! I go lay on top of her, press my lips on hers, stick my fingers in her pussy, yeah! Pussy! Put my hands on her breasts. I'm grinding my pelvis on top of her. She opens her mouth, I don't like to kiss that much.

I kissed Jaime, no big thing, but I didn't like it, his tongue like hers, a fish trying to swim in my mouth, little teeth nipping my lips. Whew, it seems like I'm grinding away what little hard-on I had. And I know my shortie is ready. It had been a little hard back then when she was sucking on it. Now I feel like ice cream. Sweat is breaking out on me, but not from excitement. The pearl in my belly is a boulder now. I got to fuck this cutie good! She gots a banging body I want to walk down the street with. I lean over take her tight tittie in my mouth, suck, she starts to grind her pelvis, she likes that. She wants my dick in her! I want my dick in her. Ride this bitch. I don't know what's wrong.

"Turn over," I tell her.

"What?"

"Turn over," I repeat.

"What for?"

"Nothing," I say, and throw myself back down on her grinding. Pressing my lips to hers, getting no action. I know my dick would get hard if she would suck it or let me in back. I'm used to that. I lick the side of her face like Roman used to do to my scar. She giggles. Is she laughing at me? I feel like slapping the shit out of her. She pulls out from under me, pushes me over, and climbs on top of me. She's grinding on top of me, eyes squeezed shut. She don't want to look at me? I'm feeling her titties, feels great. I don't know what's wrong. God, please don't let this happen to me. You know I got mad equipment. Please please *please*. She leans down kisses me, then she starts to inch up my chest till her pussy is in my face. I . . . I feel kinda trapped. I try to lick my tongue in there a little. Cough. She moves back down, her eyes open now, she gets on her side, pulls me on mine, she starts kissing me and rocking; I'm rocking back, but I can feel myself just hanging there. I want to die. She's stroking me now. She stops. "Not in the mood," she says soft. I can't talk. I close my eyes, will myself not to cry.

SEXUAL HISTORY? How can I tell it except with my body as I move through space after space downtown in painted black boxes? I look at the latest re-

THE KID

view of us in *Downtown Voice*, the picture is of me naked, except for the black leather jockstrap, in arabesque. They call me what I've told Herd to call me, Jones—Abdul Jones: "... despite Jones's infiltrating power..." then they go on to trash Scott's choreography. "My name is Abdul Jones. Period. Shut up. I don't care what I told you yesterday, today it's Abdul. Get with that." The article doesn't mention Snake, or Scott, except by way of shitting on his choreography; My Lai's like fucking Oprah or something, everybody loves her: "Virtuosic line ... difficult intelligence opening into a cacophony of movement." Cacophony? They mean she's a fine-ass freak, but they can't say that, can't say, Hot. No one ever mentions Ricky.

Nothing about him should surprise me after the time we went out to bring back sandwiches and he refused to walk on the sunny side of the street, saying he was black enough. He's what color? Fucking beige! Shit, compared to me he's *white*. So why I'm surprised when he dumps on My Lai, I don't know.

"If she's Chinese and this is supposed to be a piece about identity, she should—"

"Well, number one," Scott had said, "*she's* right here, so you can address her directly."

But he didn't, he just kept digging till they both got nasty.

"Well, you missed a couple of meetings, but I'll explain as best I can. I'm not really dealing with that identify thing like you're talking about— you know: Chinese, Mexican, like, 'Whoop whoop-de doo, I here and I so happy to be here, just give me some scented toilet paper and a green card—'"

"What would you know about that?" Ricky snapped.

"Nothing, motherfucker. And I ain't Chinese."

"Well, what *are* you, then!"

"Listen." My Lai restarts, trying to be cool and calm. "The piece revolves around an atrocity committed by Americans—"

"That nobody knows about, that happened in another century." Ricky again.

"Well, Ricky, isn't that more the reason to do it?" My Lai.

"What about the politics of *now*?"

"This is now as far as I'm concerned. We got *now* because people fucking forgot *then*," Scott says.

"What's your real beef, man?" I ask.

"You. No, I'm just kidding. Look at what the strong companies in the city are doing. This shit we're doing is getting too politico for me."

"First it's not political enough, not about *now*; then it's 'too politico'?" This from Amy.

"Are you trying to say good-bye?" Scott asks.

"I said it," Ricky says, and grabs his bag and heads for the elevator.

"Later," I say.

"Yeah, man. The best!" Snake.

I look at My Lai. "Cool," she says.

Hey, my sentiments exactly. Fuck his barrel ass.

I want My Lai. She doesn't scare me. We get our heads shaved together at the four-dollar barber school on Tenth Street. One of these days, I'm gonna ask her to pierce me. I know she did Amy's navel. She usually wears a wide leather wristband; without it you can see the raised scars lighter than the rest of her skin on her left wrist. I nudge her with my knee, trying to get her to break the awkwardness of Ricky's exit and get us moving again.

"Here, everybody," she says in her director voice. "It's a packet of Xeroxes on the My Lai massacre and Vietnam. Read everything. And see you at ten Saturday."

I flip through some of it on my way down the elevator—Ho Chi Minh? I'm the youngest, but even so it's not just me—no one here is old enough to remember Vietnam or even know a Vietnam veteran; I mean, they are serious grayheads. I read the shit when I get back to my room. This shit is crazy, unbelievable, but at the same time you know it's true and, like Ricky said, long fucking gone. The world is on to the next thing, the new worst thing. Maybe Ricky was right, we should be too? Normal guys from normal families and shit did this—killed babies and raped girls, that's worse than any shit I ever did.

I look at the print I got at the Whitney exhibit *To Repel Ghosts,* 1986, but I seen the real thing. Can I live this fucking life? On the other wall I have *Undiscovered Genius,* 1982–83: In the right-hand corner of the painting, a drawing of a slave ship, sickles, forks, axes.

Q: are not princes kings? The Dark (then under The Dark, ~~continent~~ is crossed out) ~~BLUESMAN~~ (crossed out) versus the devil
Mississippi
Mississippi
Mississippi

meat   a man with a guitar
flour
sugar   (underneath written)
alcohol   UNDISCOVERED GENIUS OF THE MISSISSIPPI DELTA
tobacco
corn

Who's that? Muddy Waters, Robert Johnson? Modern genius, Jimi, Vernon Reid?

I looked at the painting, read My Lai's Xeroxes, it's not a lie. My Lai's wrist? I stretch out on my silky sheets courtesy of Amy. Fuck her, she's boring. I want My Lai. She gonna be my baby mama? Hah! Shut up, fool, don't no bitches want you, you polluted by Roman and the fags at St Ailanthus? You shit. What you gonna do, rape her? She don't want you. Maybe she don't like black boys, a lot of them don't. I look back at the painting and the blue wall above it. I see sky and a clothesline with one blue dress flapping in the wind on it and a teenage Toosie jumping up to snatch it. *That's* la danse! I think, springing off the bed and jumping straight into the air. And *that's* me. And *that's* why I'm gonna make it, parents or no parents, school or no school, loft or no downtown funky chic. I put on some sounds, *Bird Meets Diz,* and read some more.

Heroin, that's what he did; why don't I? I don't know, I don't feel to do it, I never been around it; what made them do it, I know I would never get hooked, but what made them do it, what does it feel like, I don't know nobody who does it. Snake said My Lai has; that bitch has done everything. Read some more from Greg Tate's essay in *Flybook in the Buttermilk:*

> If we want to compare him to anybody it's Thelonius Monk, who also devised a style of grand complexity out of infantile gestures. Bringing us to Basquiat the wild child, who will be remembered as an enigmatic junkie who pollacked Armani suits, but who cataloguers knew was productive if nothing else. From the documented evidence, doodling, drawing, image-making, and writing turned up early as an obsessive reflex in Basquiat's nervous system. Apparently, Basquiat drew images as frequently as everybody else was drawing breaths.
>
> If we want to prove Basquiat was a serious artist to an unbelieving world, talk of sheer productivity is not going to get it. Actually nothing is going to do it, they've decided he's worthless so why not say fuck 'em and be done with it. [That's what I say.] Okay, I'll try. So what is it that I want to respond to in his work? Why is it significant to me? Okay, some of his intellectual obsessions: ancestry and modernity, originality and the origins of knowledge, personhood and property, possession (in the religious sense), slavery. . . .

Why is it significant to me? I don't know; I don't have words like that inside me; when I think, it's with a contraction of my torso, or a leap like a fucking savage. Savage! OOga BOOga. I'm gonna be like those paintings, like everything I ever loved. I'm gonna *be* that. And that means off your ass and PRACTICE till you drop.

meat
flour
sugar

I'm gonna get some fajitas, around six, four, I don't know, lemme count my change, and some donuts, and then come back and work.

A **COUPLE** of days later, I'm at Astor Place Starbucks with Snake, and he comes out with this "what's your story" thing.

"Say what?"

"What's your story?"

I never think of my life as a story. I think of myself as a kid trying to make it. What fucking story? It ain't been written yet.

"What do you mean?" I ask.

"You know, where are you coming from, gay, straight, uptown, downtown, out of town."

I look at Snake. Shit, what do I know about him, what's this all about? What, he's the CIA now?

"I'm from Harlem, born raised. I'm straight. How about you?"

"Well, not so fast."

"Whaddaya mean, 'Not so fast'?"

"I wanted to ask you something else."

"Like I exist to answer your questions, man?"

"Wow, don't go hostile on me."

"I'm not, man, but whas up with the Q&A?"

Who the fuck does he think he is? I feel like slapping him.

"So where are *you* coming from, up down gay straight?"

Why am I even doing this? I know where he's coming from.

"I'm transgender," he says.

Hmm, oh well, I thought I did.

"So what's that? You going surgical?" I ask.

So why me, why is he telling this shit to me?

"It's like a wrong body-assignment type thing, so it's more spiritual than surgical."

Getting your dick cut off. Does he really believe that?

"So what does that mean for *you*, you like to dress up or what?"

"It's hard to explain."

"But you can ask me shit?"

"I don't feel like a man; I feel like a woman."

"So are you gay?"

"It has nothing to do with that, I guess."

"You *guess?*"

"Well, if I get . . . get . . . *go forward*, with the transformation, then, you know, I guess I'll be, like, straight. A man, I mean a woman loving a man."

"Yeah, I guess." Why is this making me sick? "Lemme ask you something, Snake."

"Shoot."

"You're going to get your penis cut off?"

"It's called sex reassignment—"

"Don't you love your dick?"

"I want to fuck like a woman."

"And what about kids?"

"Oh, I'll adopt if I get, you know, married. But man, that's way down the line. It's not that I don't love dick, it's just that I don't want to be one." He laughs.

I can't believe he thinks that's funny.

"Who wants kids anyway?" he says.

"I do!"

Wow, I hadn't even thought about it before, I just assumed no, I don't, hell no, but I do, I want kids, a girl, maybe a boy, I don't know about a boy.

Snake's not as tall as me, but he is definitely as—no, *more* ripped than me, and his chest is wider—where they gonna throw the silicone? Who does he become? Snake with some shit pumped in him and his dick cut off?

"Have you thought about how this would affect your dancing, man?"

"I'll keep on dancing."

"As a . . . as what?"

"As a dancer."

"Ha! I like that, man!"

"So, like, Abdul, I ain't trying to bend you over or no shit. So whas up with you, can't nobody be your motherfucking friend, mystery man?"

"No, it's not like that."

"I need a cigarette break, let's go outside."

So talk to me, he says, and squats down like you see kids and sometimes old Chinese on the subway platform. Sucking on his cigarette, he waits, and I sit down on the sidewalk, cross my legs in lotus position in front of Starbucks, and tell him how hard it was when my mother died of cancer, then my father right after that in the Gulf War, but my grandmother used to dance at the Cotton Club way way back in the day, and she was into me getting lessons and that's how I got in City Kids and Imena's class at 135 City-Rec, and I kept studying and studying, and then you know I came downtown and got with you guys and shit. I don't know why, but I decided not to open up to him, what did he really tell me about hisself, except he's going to no-man's-land? And I don't understand that world, my dick is my friend; shit, sometimes I think it's my only friend. He ain't trying to bend me over—like fuck he ain't. Well, I'm curious too. And since he's trying to heist me, I just go ahead and ask him, is he hitting Scott, and what about My Lai, has Scott ever been down with her?

"No, he ain't really gay, but I have fucked him, too much cognac and Ecstasy one night, but it's always a cool bonding experience for me with these straight guys, you know. He used to go with this black Dominican chick, but his sister's shit messed that up."

"I so don't get what you're talking about."

"Well, you know he's a PC machine, parents gave him all this training and shit, and he wanted to choreograph and I guess, you know, be like the next Bill T. Jones. So that's where he and Ricky and a whole lot of them got together with this deep abstract shit that didn't really mean shit, and My Lai was throwing down with him as far as the money too, and it was cool. Well, you know, you came on in."

"But what's this big mystery with his sister?"

"Nothing, if he hadn't been so square, he would have got in there with her, but, you know, his parents lied to him, and then he lied to himself, and then he stopped lying to himself, but he didn't know what to do except be who he was, which was square. But what the hell! We are dancing and getting work—"

"And you still haven't told me what the fuck you're talking about."

"The money, his sister wrote a book and made a movie called *Traders*. Underneath all their New England shipping-scion shit, they were really slave traders. That's how they made their money. And she challenged them, the siblings, to walk from the ducats. And none of them did. His thing was he was going to change the world with his art and he was going to use the money to right wrongs, yadda-yadda, you know how people trip. Don't be so hard on *un*-homeboy. He's trying to do right, but this has all been in the past year or so since the bitch went off on the family."

"Let's go, man, my ass is going to sleep sitting on this hard pavement." I laugh. *Wow,* I think, *that's some totally bizarre shit,* but I don't care, I wanna dance with Herd, get a job, get in a college dance program. . . .

I read in Stride's newsletter that Roman is getting some kind of lifetime-achievement award from some American dance foundation.

"WELL, GOOD NEWS, we got a commission and we're going to get paid to do My Lai's piece at Dance Theater Studio," Amy announces, hugging a clipboard to her chest.

It all sounds good to me, especially the money. Starbucks wanted a NY State ID or school ID, which I didn't have.

"It's not that hard, Abdul," Snake said.

"Look, go down to 125 Worth Street between Centre and Lafayette. Tell them you lost your birth certificate. I did it. They'll ask you to fill out a form with, you know, your mother's name, mother's place of birth, father's name, et cetera," Scott says.

She said she didn't know who my father was. He was gone and didn't ever want us, and that's the end of that, don't ask me again, ever. I hated her for that.

"I did it," Snake says.

"You got a valid photo ID?" Scott asks.

"No, I got a birth certificate. That's what he needs so he can get a valid photo ID." Snake.

"OK, My Lai did it—" Scott again.

"I think she did it in Connecticut." Snake.

"No, she did it here. He can too. You need two utility bills or letters from government agencies," Scott rattles off.

"What the fuck?" I say.

"No, listen, it's not that hard," Scott insists. "We switch the landline in here to your name. There's electric and gas; we can get it switched to your name or add your name to the bill."

"Do you have a Social Security card?" Snake asks.

"I know the number."

"OK, so it's all good," Scott says.

"Shit, people come over here from Russia and shit and have documents. . . ." First thing from Amy.

"Probably with your name on it." Snake laughs.

"Stop, Snake." Scott.

"But you know what he means. Shit, Abdul was born here, and he's walking around without documents?" Amy says, not backing down from Scott.

"OK, My Lai, you're back on."

I can't stop eating her with my eyes, the long legs, short torso, dark red lips. I wonder how old she is; even Snake doesn't know, and he's got a file on everyone. What he does know is she has money, constant cash, and her own crib. That can only come from parents, drugs, or hoing. And she's dancing 24/7, so she can't be out selling nothing.

"Did everybody have time to read the text? Good, so you saw the roles. Listen up. Amy, you're Lieutenant Calley and Sergeant Medina. Scott, you're the Vietnam Memorial."

"Say what?" Scott.

"I have this, I don't know, *vision* of a human, breathing wall that speaks the name of every soldier that died. Maybe you're assembling and taking apart your weapon, whatever the motion, you'd say the name on four, or maybe the eight count—"

"Or maybe something with a five count, then the spoken word would alternate: right-left. Mingus does that a lot." Scott.

"I was thinking *Ascension* by Trane. Have you heard that?" My Lai.

"But it doesn't have a rhythm *I* can count." Scott.

"If you can't come in on a beat you can hear, add a beat—come in on your own four or five or whatever." Me.

"Everything we do in this piece should speak. Every choice is a sign, something that can be read just like they're reading our bodies. Let me put some music on while you warm up." My Lai.

Who is Mingus? One more thing to find out, I think, as I stretch out in second, grabbing both ankles and pulling myself down until my stomach almost touches the floor.

"You are stretched out, boy!" Amy whistles.

"Hey, I worked for this day and night, years."

"Nobody said you didn't; I was just looking. Can't blame a girl for looking."

What's that spozed to mean? I raise up and stretch out in a split, yeah, I worked for this shit, I think, sinking down in my split, then rolling over on my back and pulling my left leg over my head while my right leg is stretched out on the floor.

"Who *is* that?" Snake asks.

"Lucky Dube, South African."

Never heard of him, but he's awesome.

My Lai reaches into a tote and pulls out a wooden spoon and a tin pie pan, which makes me laugh because I can't imagine her eating a pie much less making one.

"One TWO sound OFF, three FOUR let's kill some MORE! Charlie Company is mad frustrated, some of their boys have been hit, but they feel alike their hands are tied and they can't retaliate. Last week they enter a minefield, guy lost both his eyes—powie WOW! Boom bang thank you ma'am—if your life don't flash before your eyes, too fucking bad, 'cause nothing else in this life ever will. You're blind!

"SINGLE FILE! Come on up, one behind the other, this is the Mekong Delta. It's ninety-six degrees, eighty-five percent humidity. Here's your friend Two-Step Sam, a snake, you had welfare spam in a green can this morning—K-rations. They call that snake in front of you slithering in the grass toward you Two-Step Sam because that's how many steps you take after it bites you. Behind you is your platoon leader, who has a map he doesn't know how to read, a pocket full of heroin and 'Nam weed. You must step forward, there is no place to go back to, you must put your foot down on the dangerous earth."

I put my foot down on the wood floor, it feels like the hot jungle. I never really thought about walking before. Heel, ball, toes push forward activating calves and hamstrings? Or is it the reverse, the butt and calves activating—yeah, I think it's the butt, the muscles in the back of my leg and the glutes that kick it off, raise the leg, then the heel connects.

BAM! BAM! BAM! BAM! BAM! BAM! She slams the tin.

"Shrapnel explodes in your face, blood drips."

"OK, OK, everybody, come back, but don't lose that feeling, it was all over your body, I could *see* it, the fear and the doubt, not knowing what's next. Take a look at the 'scripts,' if you want to call them that, that I'm passing out. The wall, black G.I. Joe, Lieutenant Calley, and Sergeant Medina. Snake is going to be coming in and out as a musician and a dancer. He's got a harmonica and a, like—"

"It's a washboard."

What's he gonna do with a washboard?

"Don't worry, the main thing is listen to me; the text, the music is your backdrop, you hear it, see it, but you move to what *I'm* saying, go with it, whatever comes up. Don't focus on the cameras. Just move."

I look at the "script":

Duckwiser got his hooks on a couple of reels of stag films and we're watching those to get hepped up for the mission tomorrow. It's called Operation Muscatine and we're supposed to pacify a sector or whatever, which means shoot up the gooks, smoke their tunnels, and burn down the village . . .

I think Scott has the physically hardest part to be moving for forty, fifty minutes or however long the piece is. So, like according to this script, I'm every nigger that ever went to Vietnam and Lieutenant Calley rolled into one?

"One TWO sound OFF, three FOUR let's kill some MORE! ONE TWO SOUND OFF! THREE FOUR LET'S KILL SOME MORE! *Rape* that village! *Kill* that village!" My Lai yells.

She's crazy.

"Hear the tape, but listen to me! Miles is gonna run it down, then that'll fade into Hendrix's 'Voodoo Chile,' then Buddy Miles, and Hendrix will come with 'Machine Gun' rat-a-tat-tat-tat, and then I don't know yet.

"You're new to the unit; you're young, black, from Mississippi.

"Mississippi to Vietnam.

"It's another century.

"It's 1968.

"We start out early in the morning. You want to run, but you—"

—I step cautiously. Excited, scared, I'm going to kill. I have never killed anybody before (at least I don't think I have).

"So for now just improvise. We're going to tape it and see if we can get some stuff we can use to jump-start some choreography. For now I'm going to read some text. Abdul, do whatever you want to do. Scott and Amy are going to videotape you. Tomorrow you and Scott will shoot Amy."

It's just me now, improvising to the sound of My Lai's text, which she ripped from everywhere. I don't know if my movements match their intense words: *My Lai 4: A Report on the Massacre and Its Aftermath, Bloods,* and "Herbert Carter's Letter." I remember that man on a skateboard on the D train with a sign safety-pinned to his back, black guy, I used to see him when I was little with my mother, he'd be shaking this cup he'd pull out of his pocket. His hands in thick leather gloves propelling him along the subway train floor. The handwritten sign on his back: VIETNAM. Then he'd put the cup in his Levi vest pocket and he'd hurl himself off the skateboard with his big bare arms and his torso would hit the floor with a thud. He'd swing open the door between the cars, scoot his body out onto the steel floor between the subway cars, then open the door to the next car and swing his body that ended at his waist back up on his skateboard and be gone from sight when the door clanged shut behind him!

That's as close as I can get to feeling this shit. I'm not feeling no sick niggers or Vietnamese people from thirty, fifty, whatever it was, years ago.

"You're doing fine. Stop being a bitch, Abdul, and just go for it."

Except for the thing with Amy, I haven't been with anybody. I dream bizarre stuff, I'm fucking a dog with a big girl pussy—three times I had that dream, the last time I'm going in the dog pussy from behind and the dog turns its face toward me and it's My Lai, I wake up and I've cum all over myself. It makes me sick, ashamed even. I'm so scared of women I rather fuck a dog? Jimi Hendrix and Buddy Miles "Machine Gun" rat-ta-tat-tat-tat the sound of a machine gun. I pummel my feet on the floor trying to imitate the sound of automatic gunfire. My Lai says something about bush and I think of Amy's blond patch of hair, the juicy good smell. A well—Brother Samuel's eyes, I always thought they were a well. Dark blue danger, well. What about it? Oh, I come to a well. He was a farmer. I don't think I've ever even seen a well. *In places where ordinary table water doesn't reach the surface, the ground water is reached by digging wells into the ground.* Earth science! How long ago was that! Into the ground! In-to-the-GROUND! I pummel my feet harder, on Brother John's face, on his fucking earth science.

Rat-ta-tat-tat-TAT! BAM! BAM!

I tune her out, all this G.I. Joe–in–the–jungle shit is boring, My Lai, do you hear me; My Lai, honey, I'm bored. I want her naked on my bed, her black bush and buff nipples, taut body slick with sweat under me, umph! I thrust into her, she digs her purple-painted fingernails in my shoulders, umph!

My Lai shouts, listing more atrocities. "Good, Abdul!

"Let's stay with what you started—"

I started something?

"The call-and-response thing, you were getting in deep there for a minute. I would say something and you would directly respond with your body—great!"

OK, whatever!

"*'Somebody brought in an old man. He was a farmer; there was no doubt in my mind.'*"

"*'Grzesik questioned the man, quickly found that he had an identifi-*cation card. *'I told Lieutenant Calley I didn't think he was a VC.'*"

Why are we doing this? Does she think this is getting back at her parents? My Lai! Huh! Last week I was thinking about kids, a family even if it was a thousand years away, now I don't want to have kids. This is a fucked-up world, always was, always will be, FUCKED UP!

"*Hey! I don't think*
       didn't think
       didn't think
          he was
             was
          was a VC'

VC VC VC V-V-V-CEEE!"

"*'Why are you going to kill him?' I asked.*"

A tisket a tasket a green and yellow basket I *lost* it I *lost* it. I start to skip. Nip that skipping shit in the bud, Rhonda said. Why? she said. You know. No, I don't know, she said.

Mary Mack Mack Mack All dressed in Black Black Black

"*'Why why why*

Why are you
Going going going to— Why
are you going to kill him?'"

I remember his brother asked about the rings. The body was never found, only that finger at McDonald's. With no rings. Children? Like you was a child once?

"Calley told him to 'get moving.' But before Calley could fire, Herbert Carter moved forward. Carter hit the old man into a well, but the old man spread his arms and legs and held on and didn't fall."

Well? I freeze. Snake starts to blow harmonica, blues. Amy is beating on her thighs like quiet drums. Snake croons.

I start to thrash about the studio. I hear My Lai shout, "Get what he's doing now from both angles!"

"'Then Carter
Then Carter'"

Yemaja is the Orisha of the ocean. Imena said when an African woman wants a baby, she puts a bowl of water by her bed. Tell that to Herbert Carter, Imena! Is there an Orisha in the well?

"'Then Carter hit the old man
in the stomach with his rifle stock'"

"What he's doing now! Shoot him from the front and side, make sure all this is on the video!"

"'The old man's feet'"

Under the ground, permeable beds of rock layered between impermeable beds of rock can form a pocket, a "sandwich." When rain enters the permeable bed, it's trapped. Trapped rain! I remember the weirdest shit.

"'Feet
Fell
His feet fell
In the well
His feet fell in the well
But he continued
To hold on with his hands.'"

"Dance Abdul dance!" Scott shouts.

"Yes!"

"'Carter hit the man's fingers trying to make him fall.'"

Did you get up at all during the night? Do you usually get up to go to the bathroom?

Mary Mack Mack Mack All dressed in black black black.

My Lai waves for me to slow down. I start moving like I'm in water. She reads:

> Hey babe, just writing again real quick because I had to tell you this hilarious thing before I forget.
>
> Right now I'm sitting next to roadside that is totally full of dead gomers. It's hilarious. 1st Platoon totally wigged out, like LT just stood there and watched while everyone just was going buck wild. What really kicked things off was when this dude was just totally standing there with his cow out in the field and 2nd squad came around this hootch they were burning. The dude threw his arms up in the air like "hey" and Nichols lit him up good and LT didn't bat an eye. Verona was the funniest, there was this dude standing with his hands up and Verona just totally stabbed the dude in the stomach with his bayonet. The dude was wheezing and Verona just BAM right in the head. I was in tears. It got better though. Verona just grabs this old guy who was doing a loaf in his shorts and took out his 45 and shot him in the throat. I was like "haha-haha!" and then he freaking throws the guy in a well. I was totally on the ground laughing by this point and Verona just turned to me and gave me that cockeyed grin of his and he dropped a pineapple right down the well. KABOOM! Oh man, I tell you, these guys are like Bob Hope times ten!

I stop moving. Sweat's rolling off of me, I'm looking at Amy, My Lai, Snake, and Scott. Scott starts it, stamping his feet and clapping. My Lai is smiling, nodding her head, then she starts clapping and runs over to the windows, pulling up the shades. Light streams in the loft. Amy and Snake are whooping and stamping their feet as they clap. Crazy, man, crazy! Far out, far fucking out! Traffic sounds. Birds dart through the sky in front of the window.

"I'm so glad we had both cameras!" Scott says. "Do you remember what you did?"

"I did something?" I quip. But to myself I say, *I did something!*

He waves his hand and keeps talking. "I got most of it just straight on, Amy got a lot from the side and, it seems, a lot straight on. Am I right?"

"We'll see," she answers.

"Well, working off this or even re-creating this will be stronger if you remember." Scott.

"Shit, if the video is near as astonishing as what he just did, we can have a split screen, the Vietnam shots, then him on another screen, while one of us recites the poem." My Lai.

"You wrote that?" I ask.

"No, like I said, it's from some stuff by Wallace Terry and Seymour Hersh. I don't even know if they're still on the set."

"So what, motherfuckers like that got estates," Snake says.

"Well, whatever, we put the Vietnamese clips on one side, this piece, the well, on the other—" My Lai.

"That's a good title." Amy.

"'The Well'?" My Lai.

"Yeah, that's great!" Snake.

I go sit down next to Amy, who's moved to the bleachers. She kisses me on the cheek, her eyes wide. Hmm, something opening up I had thought was closed? Not sure, really.

"You were awesome out there! What's on your mind when you're dancing like that?"

"I don't know." I follow her down as she slips off the bleachers to the floor and gets in a lotus position. I lay my head down in her lap, breathe in her sweet pussy-sweat-perfume smell. My heart, which was ripping, slows down.

My Lai comes to sit by us. I stretch out my hand.

"Coffee?" Scott asks.

"I can get it." The coffeemaker is in my room; I should have put it back in the kitchen.

"Don't be silly." Amy eases me off her lap. Soon the smell of coffee fills up where her scent had been. I lean over to My Lai, playfully tweak her ear. I wanted to tweak her nipple, but we're working, and I don't know how she might react.

"I feel like the piece should end with My Lai's story." Scott.

"Yeah, you know, and something from this century," I say.

"Like the reconciliations?" Scott asks.

"That's too corny," Snake snaps.

"I don't think it's corny," I say.

In each hand Amy has a steaming mug of coffee, one of which she hands to My Lai, the other to me.

"If God made anything better than coffee and chocolate, he kept it to himself," Amy says with a sigh.

"Or herself," Scott quips.

"Or herself, Mr PC. And I'll have mine with milk, no sugar." Amy.

"Gotcha," he says.

The dark smell of the steaming coffee takes over my senses. I feel so peaceful now.

THREE   In the dream a tall, bald-headed man is struggling with a much smaller man. The small man pulls out a screwdriver. The bald man whips out a big butcher knife but right away realizes how superior his weapon is to the little screwdriver and thrusts his knife into the ground so the fight will be fairer. Straightaway the little guy picks up the butcher knife and starts to slash him, me, slicing open my scalp. I wake up clutching my bleeding scalp. I'm shocked when I pull my hands away and see there's no blood. I start to cry. I've done bad things, bad, bad things. And I'm not through. I fall back on the bed, my fingers tracing the scar on my cheek. I press my hand to my head again. My hand fills with glass splinters that are growing from my head. I rub my eyes, and my eye sockets fill with dark slivers of glass that fall and fall to the floor. I scream, and my mouth begins to bloom with glass shards. My tongue has turned to glass. I'm like the Tin Man, except I'm made of glass—mirrors. I'm made of mirrors! I'm on top of a grassy hill. People are climbing up the hill and starting to gather around me. They're peering at themselves in my mirrors. Then a little girl with yellow hair, four or five years old, tells everybody, "He can't move!" *What does she know?* I think. Then I try. I can't. My glass joints are totally frozen.

"He can't move! He can't move! Ha, ha, ha!"

She disappears down the hill and comes running back up with a baseball bat. She's turned into a little boy? She, he, cocks the bat up over his shoulder like he's on home plate. Terror floods through me. When he hits me, I think, *I'm dreaming.* Then I think I'm not really asleep! Let me hurry up and go back to sleep, go to another dream or something, anything but wake up.

My body and face are covered with ultramarine body paint. As I dance, I change colors, under yellow gels to green, under the orange ones I almost look like myself, brown. I slide into the split it took me three years to get. From my split I bend at the knee the leg that's extended behind me, catch my foot in my hands, and pull it up to my head. The pose of Shiva! Some white Hare Krishna trying to pull me one night I was sleeping at Port Authority, a night I couldn't take the sight of Roman one more minute, told me Krishna was so black he was blue. After that I started looking at Indian people, so far I seen *a lot* of them darker than me, some blue-black. I'm Lord Krishna—blue, I think, sinking deeper into the pose. SPLAT! Somebody threw something onstage. Shit? That's fucked! "Come on, get up!" "What's with the blue paint!" "Put some clothes on!" "Dance, nigger!" "We came to see you dance!" Who's saying that shit? "BOO!" "BOO!" "BOO!" Why are they booing me? I look in the audience; the whole theater is empty except the front row; there's some faces I don't know, white; then there's Ricky, Brother John, and sitting next to Brother John is my mother and Rita, and Scott, but he looks different, he looks like Amy. My Lai's there; she has on red lipstick and a black lace bustier. When I look again, Ricky is sitting on a toilet. He's shitting so he can throw more shit at me. But Rita says, "No, no! Not in this life, faggot!" and slices him with a razor blade. *This life?* I look at everybody. I can see through them. GHOSTS! They're ghosts! Except My Lai. My Lai is bleeding; blood is dripping out and down the front of her bustier. Did Rita cut her? I'm a little boy again: I'm mad at Rita; I'm mad at my mom. Why isn't she home? Her home is in the grass now. "Go home, Mommy! Go home, Mommy!"

Forget them; they're not real; this is a dream; when I wake up, they'll all be gone. I continue with my dance, but now I'm not Lord Shiva. I'm King Kong. I'm still blue, *Blue* King Kong, and instead of the white bitch and the Empire State Building, I'm rising from the jungle with the whole city on my back. King Kong! Columns of glass, concrete, and steel go down with me as I plié, then fly into the sky as I rise.

"Is it really paint?"

"What color is he really?"

That's all these stupid motherfuckers ever talk about is color, what color somebody is, how dark, how light, how big a nose. Here I am now coals burning, shining, dancing, and they're talking about "What color is he really?" I open my neck with both hands like my skin is a curtain, and a glittering blue cobra slithers up from my belly and out of my open throat, hissing and screaming—

Everybody starts screaming—

Screaming? Who's screaming? My Lai? Is it My Lai?

"My Lai!" I bolt straight up in a panic until my hand touches the soft skin of her back.

I shake her. "My Lai, I don't want to be alone."

"You're not," she murmurs, kisses my thigh, and goes back to sleep.

I'm scared about the show, about living here. At first I was all yeah, cool. How cool can you get—loft, lock on the door, hip, downtown. No, cool is what these kids got, their own. I need to get back to sleep; I got a busy day in front of me. I got that interview at Starbucks, then the Italian restaurant, La Casa. I never seen a black waiter in there, but we always go there, the lunch special is first-rate. An NYUer was sitting at the table talking to the manager while me and My Lai were eating lunch. I leaned over after the kid left and asked, "You hiring?" The manager looked me up and down and all around and didn't say anything for a few seconds, and then he said, "Come by tomorrow and fill out an application."

My Lai's eyes were shining when we walked out. "You go, boy!"

"What'd I do? I just asked if he was hiring." "You saw a possibility, a *sniff* of a possibility, and you went for it!" "Well, I don't know 'bout all that, I just need a job." "I see you with mad paper sometime." "Yeah," is all I say. When I do have bucks, I take everybody out. I don't want to tell her how I get papered, or the years with Roman, Brother John, so much to tell, or *not* tell, I should say.

I feel helpless, stupid, like Humpty Dumpty's ass sitting on the wall. I used to cry for Humpty Dumpty when my mother would read "All the king's horses and all the king's men couldn't put poor Humpty together again." I think that's why Scott's film with the vase got to me so much. Well, it's not his film, but the film he used. *This* is his. I glance around the room; there're no windows, and it's nestled in the back and center of the loft, so when you turn out the lights in here, it gets dark. I like that, I feel safe. I love fucking My Lai in here. I feel free, I can cry if I want to, scream if I want to when I'm busting inside her. I pretend she's mine, but she ain't *mine*. I ain't stupid. I want to own her, but I can't.

When she wakes up, I feel like I've been up for hours. The red numerals on the clock radio are glowing 6:10. Class at ten (just do the barre), then run down to Starbucks on Astor Place and then down to Mott Street to La Casa and be back for rehearsal at noon. Can do.

"Hey," she says.

"Hey yourself."

"You woke me up last night," she says.

"No I didn't. What are you talking about?"

"Sucking my pussy!"

"You are all the way crazy, how'd we get there?"

"Amy said you sucked her good when she had you."

"Had me?" Gee thanks, Amy.

"You like me as much as you like her, right?"

"Right."

"Why?" she persists like a fucking girl.

"I just do. I like how you talk, look, smell—you make my dick hard. Oops!" I reach for her.

"Oops my ass! Git off me and git down there, nigguh!" She laughs.

So, OK.

"Keep going."

"Well, let me know—"

"Shut up already, lick-suck, lick-suck, yeah, there you go! You got talent!"

She stops talking, and I keep working. So this is what it's all about. Now she's trying to pull away? Yeah? No? I keep sucking. This is strong, her clit is throbbing in my mouth, her whole body is throbbing, she's going off groaning, I never heard her do this shit before. This never happened when I was fucking her. She's cumming, *really* cumming! Shit! So this is why the girls like each other. I come up, kiss her, suck her tongue into my mouth while I slide my dick into her wet cunt and start to fuck her. Yow! Way to start the day!

WHEN I RETURN from ballet class, Starbucks, and La Casa, I've got not one but *two* jobs. La Casa wants me on Thursday, Friday, and Saturday, which I told him I got a show coming up. "So switch with the other guy and do lunch for those weeks." Starbucks wants me four hours a day, five to nine in the morning, that's actually going to work! Yeah, it's going to work out fine.

So it's all good, then here she comes with this shit outta nowhere, like water torture drip-drip: So you Mr All-Roun'-American kid? Ain't you sumthin'!

Shut up!

No, I ain't shuttin' up. Ain't that gonna be cute, little white apron makin' in a week what you could be makin' in five minutes. You even startin' to sound like 'em. 'Gee, that's cool!' If you'd ever been to any of they houses, you'd see.

See *what*?

See yo' ass pullin' up weeds 'n mowin' the grass, that's what.

Shut up! You're *useless*!

And you're *shit*, do you think anybody would want you if they knew what you did? Phony, phony, phony! You a phony-ass nigger! You may fool them little white kids, but you can't fool me!

Shut up shut up shut *up*!

I hate her, whoever she is, and she's *not* me. She's just a . . . a stupid voice in my head. She's in me; she's not me.

Shit, it's quarter to twelve; I got to get going. I want to tell Scott I got a job. He loaned me some cash when I was strapped. Let him know I'm going to be able to pay him back.

TURNING, EVERY FIBER of my leg muscles burning, I feel like . . . fuel, gasoline, or that scared sick feeling you get sliding on ice. Like that time I was with Snake in his trade's Ferrari spinning out of control. Lucky we didn't crash. I'm going to have a car like that someday. Well, maybe not no Ferrari, but something, I'm going to have something.

Oh, shut up, nigger! You don't know what yo' stupid ass'll have—you might end up with a bullet in yo' fuckin' skull, or a jail bid—

Don't talk to me like that.

Don't talk to you like that? Who the fuck do you think I is if I ain' you now?

Well, stop putting me down.

Stop puttin' yo'self down, stupid!

Fuck her ol' ass, I don't want her in my head, let me get back to my turns. Yeah, where was I? A Ferrari spinning on ice—intrepid, the ut-most, ur-ultimate—

"Ur-ultimate?" Where'd you learn to talk like that? You so fuckin' fake. Phony! You need to pony up, nigger, to what you really are—butt-bustin' ho, rapist, leech. Freeloader! You live off faggots and rich kids. You ain' shit.

They're my friends. I would do the same for them. Fuck you, leave me alone! I need to keep working on my pirouettes, tours en l'air, and where I'm really having problems, those damn brisse volés. Remember, remember what I overheard Roman say after Alphonse came to watch the class one time: "What I tell you, Alphonse! I has not seen no one turn like that since Baryshnikov."

"You're exaggerating," Alphonse had said. Then he paused and said, "But only a little."

"HEY, Y'ALL!"

That's Scott, whoever calls us in is who's running rehearsal, Scott or Snake usually and lately, since the Vietnam piece, My Lai. I've never run rehearsal or laid down any choreography for the group; I know I could—run a rehearsal, that is, shit, I could choreograph too. What are you doing when you're improvising but making up steps as you move? Choreography is just doing it without the total spontaneous thing. You *think* what you're laying down when you're choreographing. With improv you don't think, you do.

Something's up today. We don't usually meet this early on Sunday. Scott is a born-again Christian. He's usually in church the whole morning on Sunday. That's all, being a Christian, according to Snake, in direct response to him not wanting anything to do with his family (except the moola) since his sister's book.

I didn't think I was going to be gut-level gung ho with the Vietnam shit. I just couldn't cross that street until I read *Bloods*. Damn, when I read that—I felt, shit, a few years back in the day and some of those stories could have maybe been my dad's, or my dad's dad. The "loosie" story stuck like Krazy Glue: The guy's a burnt-out homeless, but to hear him tell it he was a Vietcong killer, cutting off ears, annihilating gooks in the jungle right and left. So homeless is going into the corner store to get a loosie for a quarter or whatever they cost, because he can't afford a whole pack of cigarettes. So he goes to ask the guy behind the counter for a loosie and WHAM! They have this instant recognition. The guy's VC from 'Nam, some guy he'd escaped from or some shit. He's Vietcong, North Vietnamese, over here, the nigguh's here *with a store* after having fought *against* us. And this stupid nigger is here with his broke-up brain and shattered-shit life, homeless after fighting *for* us. I mean, he has to feel like a sucker. I snicker, shaking my head—

"What's so funny?" Scott asks.

"Nothing," I tell him. Why is he so touchy? Sometimes he's cool, *most* of the time he's cool. But then he can get into his king-dick alpha-male routine. I ain't trying to be boss. I just want to do my thing, I don't care who's king of the mountain, as long as I get to dance. Shit, when I get good enough to be boss, whatever that is, I'll just leave. Why does leaving even cross my mind? I just got here. Shit is working for me.

"So what we're really doing this morning is listening to your performance piece," Scott announces, turning to My Lai. "Is that right, My Lai?"

"Yeah, raw material for my solo. And it *is* fuckin' *raw*. So yeah, for now. I just need you guys to listen." My Lai.

"OK, let's hear it." Snake.

"Well, I'm still not clear exactly what it is we're going to hear." Amy.

"Well, you could just listen." Snake.

"I want to know *how* to listen. I mean, is this her story, or is it some compilation of Asian women's stories that she's woven together as an everywoman thing—"

"Stop!" Snake shouts. "Let's make some coffee. I have a feeling we're going to need it."

"Fool!" My Lai. But the laugh that escapes her is relieved.

I run to the kitchen with Snake to make sure I put the espresso machine back in there. Yeah, it's there.

"Should we do coffee or espresso?" I ask him.

"Let's just knock out five espressos."

"My Lai likes coffee," I say.

"So why'd ya ask, idiot!"

"Ain't no idiot, number one—" Lately I'm constantly having to put this faggot in check.

"Well, let's just say you don't know enough to know this Bacardi and Happy I got will go better in the espresso—"

"Man, during rehearsal?"

"We ain't gonna be doing no dancing today."

"Well, whaddaya got? Tabs, powder?"

He pulls out a silver flask. And a plastic bag with some white tablets.

"So put it on the tray—"

"I like to spike—"

"So what are you, one of these drug-in-the-drink dudes?"

"I'm not above that—"

"You mean below, motherfucker!"

"Only way I ever got to bang a bitch!" He laughs. I can't help but laugh too.

"I was checking out your turns, Abdul, while you were warming up in the corner, man—whew! Way out, dude. Shit, man, you look good! Skinny but good. What you been doing?"

"Working, man. I stretch and do an hour barre before I even leave that room." I nod toward my room, mine *for now*, I note. "It's no thing, I just do it, man. It keeps me from going postal, you know what I mean?"

"No, what do you mean?"

"You know, if I just sit and think how far behind everybody I am, choreography- and technique-wise. My Lai's technique alone—"

"Look, they been dancing—no, not just dancing, *training*—since they were kids, man."

"I know, man, I don't want all the years and shit I put into my body to just go down the motherfucking drain. If you don't practice, all you're doing is maintaining, sometimes not even that. You know what I mean?"

"All too well, but still—"

"I want to rise," I say, breaking in on him.

"Well, that's why the man has you here."

"Who, Scott?"

"Yeah, Scott, who do ya think?"

"He never asks me to choreograph or run rehearsal, you know what I mean?"

"Shit, that's his thing, Abdul. When I do it, it's just to carry out his, you know, fucking dictates. He doesn't need you for that, man. He needs you for what you say you want to do, *to dance*. Milk it, man. Don't be stupid and get into a competitive thing with him. You need to learn to read people better. You know what I see, man?"

"What?"

"You know, it's good to work hard and all that, but watch yourself. To me it looks like you're burning the candle at both ends, as they say, like you are *wired*, and if you ain't taking nothin', that's even worse. You're gonna burn out for sure, man—"

"HEY, DUDES! Like, some coffee already!"

When we bring the tray of steaming espressos in with Snake's silver flask of rum and plastic bag of white tablets in the center of the five cups, everyone cheers.

Amy surprises me by breaking a tab in half and sharing it with Scott. Snake offers My Lai a tab. "No thanks." Then she changes her mind and pops a tab. I shake my head no. If I do, I won't sleep at all. I'm the only one here who has to get up in the morning.

My Lai's sitting in lotus position on the floor with her notebook in front of her. She takes a deep breath opens her notebook.

"I was about five days old when I was found in a shopping bag on the doorstep of St Dymphna's New York Foundling Home on the morning of Christmas Eve. By that night I was a fuckin' celebrity! 'Baby Christmas,' the news stations were calling me. They Hollywooded the story by saying I was wrapped like a Christmas present! Anybody who had a radio, TV, or read a newspaper knew about me. Motherfuckers were calling up news stations wanting to adopt me. As far as I can figure out, those are the *facts* printed in the *New York Daily News*, December 24, 19__, preserved on microfiche at the New York Public Library. But the truth comes in details clouded in curses when they're arguing, and they're always arguing, my mother and father. It seems strange to be calling them that. Does my being adopted make me theirs or just 'adopted'? It should have—like with a cake, put in the ingredients, mix it up, stick it in the oven, and voilà! Done. But inside, it was raw, runny shit. I never became theirs.

"'Cold,' she had said once. 'You are one cold little girl.'

"Her sister had told her, 'It could have turned out that way if she'd come out of you.'

"'Whaddaya mean?'

"'My Jeremy's like that, a mean little snit. I feel sorry for his wife if his dumb ass ever gets one.'

"But my aunt wasn't there that day when they were arguing (not that they care who's there when they're arguing). So the back story here is my grandfather has the real moneybags. (He can't stand the sight of me.) My father's mother, Grandma Dora, is Catholic; his father is Jewish. My father is nothing religion-wise (or any other wise except his money), but I guess he used to be Catholic, because he used to throw big bucks at St Dymphna's. So they're arguing in front of me as usual like I don't exist, which is how I feel most times, when he guffaws and tells me over his shoulder between shouting at her 'You went to the highest bidder, you little nigger!'

"'Are you crazy? That's nonsense. And stop calling her names.'

"'I didn't say nothing to her.'

"'I'm listening to you. You think I'm fuckin' deaf?'

"'Well, it's not 'nonsense,' it's true.'

"'It's not true. Stop telling that *lie*. Your fuckin' money, your fuckin' money. You fuckin' megalomaniac! We went through a *process*. They interviewed us, they came to our house, remember? I talked to psychologists, social workers, nuns—*then* we were allowed to adopt Noël. We did not buy her. You can't buy children in New York, this is not Thailand or some shit. You're sick, sick, *sick*—'

"'Shut up, bitch! We bought her. I bought an apartment overnight around the corner so we'd have a New York State address. We were living in Jersey, remember? I donated a hundred K to that fuckin' goy orphanage so you could have dibs on a newborn white baby girl, and you go sit up and see a goddamn newscast and got to have her—'

"'Shut up, she's not deaf. She's your *daughter*.'

"'I don't give a fuck what she is, don't call me a fuckin' liar!'

"'You're high. You're getting to be a regular old drug addict, aren't you?'

"'Don't try to change the subject, bitch. You don't think me giving them dried-up old bitches a hundred grand had anything to do with you getting little Miss Tokyo?'

"'You're evil, evil, *evil*! There's no end to your evil. How do you talk like that in front of your own child?'

"'She's not my child, and for that matter you're not my fuckin' wife. The marriage was a joke. My brother ain't no fuckin' rabbi. He can't marry nobody. We were pulling your leg, you knew that. Don't—'

"'You said we would go to City Hall afterward.'

"'*Did we?* She's not my child, and you're not my wife. Shit, I could pull one off here like that big-name movie director and run away and marry her. Shit, if I marry anybody, that's what it'll be, young pussy—'

"My mother opened her mouth, but no words came out, only a kind of croak.

"'Shit, you think I'm too low-class to have an Asian wife?'

"'I hate you,' she hissed as she dropped down on the floor as if her legs had buckled under the weight of his cruelty.

"'Stop the drama! It takes two to tango.'

"'What the hell does that mean?' she said from the floor.

"'What the hell does that mean?' he mimicked her. 'You're glad to get what you want when you want it, but you get mad when I remind you how you got it. Yeah, yenta, *how*. My money, megalomaniac drug addict—whatever you want to call me, bitch, *my money*. Everything we got, we got because I bought it, bitch.'

"'I hate you more than I've ever hated anyone!'

"'Anytime you feel enough hate to leave, you can leave, you stupid whore.'"

But she didn't leave.

"'Where would I have gone?' she'd said. 'We need him.'

"'No we don't.'

"'Yes we do. He's just drunk right now. Everything'll be alright in the morning.'"

But it wasn't. She could have left him, but you just don't leave money like that, she said.

"Look, he's all talk. If he ever really hit me or hurt you . . ." Her voice trailed off. "I wouldn't stand for abuse."

But he was a millionaire, the son of a billionaire, and she wasn't his wife. She had been his secretary. His "brother" who had "married" them went to jail later that same day for possession with intent to sell.

"Listen, I'm going to read you something from Ann Landers."

"Who's Ann Landers?"

"A nice lady in the newspapers who gives people good advice."

"How do you know it's good?"

"I know it's good."

"How do you get it?" I asked.

"Get what?"

"The advice," I said.

"You write a letter and put it in the mail, and she writes you back and tells you what to do. Some of the letters she puts in the *Daily News*, like this one I was talking about. Listen to this guy; he's writing Ann a letter to give her some information she can give to the rest of the readers."

A man gave his wife a million dollars. ("Like your father has, OK.") *He told her to go out and spend a thousand dollars a day. She did. Three years later she returned to tell him the money was all gone. She wanted more.*

He then gave her one billion dollars. ("Now, that's how much money Grandpa has!") *He told her to go out and spend a thousand dollars a day. She didn't come back for three thousand years.*

"Three *thousand*? That's longer than a dinosaur. Why would the lady want to shop for that long?"

"She wouldn't, honey. The man is trying to illustrate something, *I'm* trying to illustrate something. I'm trying to show you how much money Grandpa has."

But he's not my grandpa. He said, "Get *it* out of here now." A question occurs to me.

"How long could we go shopping with your money?"

"Huh?"

"If we were spending a thousand dollars a day of your money, how long could we go shopping?"

"My money? Honey, we'd never go shopping. Mommy doesn't have any money."

I need her; she needs him, so we can go shopping. He doesn't need us, he doesn't even *want* us.

dear Annlanders,

    I am having a problem with my Dad He calls me names like nigger even thogh I am not a nigger and Little Miss Tokyoe even thogh I am not Miss Tokyoe. He eats everything and is big as a house my mother says but hes not really big as a house or he wouldn't be able to fit in one. Hes rich. He has the millions you wrote about in your newspaper and can go shopping every day for three years with a thousand dollars a day. Rmember that you wrote that??? We can go shopping a lot. My father comes in my room and puts a finger in me and covers my mouth with his hand. I can't breeth I'm scared I'm gonna die when he does that.

    Pleas get the advice to me ASP

    Also I know you are not Santa Claus I know theirs no Santa Clause but I would like you to send me a skateboard I could prove to my mother there not dangerous for girls

Love Noël Wynn Desiré Orlinsky

PS Don't forget to write back in a hurry

Love Noël (again)

"I waited every day for it seemed like forever. I was sure she would write me back with good advice. Finally I realized that, just like Santa Claus, she didn't really exist."

Whatever it was Snake handed out, it seems like it's starting to take hold of My Lai, or maybe she's acting? But she closes her notebook and crawls on her hands and knees into the middle of the circle. She's holding up her hands as if she has something in them.

"I'm under the big table in the dining room. No one can see me because of the long tablecloth, which is curtains to my house. This is me and Barbie and Ken's house. My mother is outside on the patio having lunch with her club. I've crawled under the table to play Barbie and Ken." She holds up Barbie and then Ken. "I lay Ken on top of Barbie and move his plastic butt up and down as he sticks his dick in Barbie to make a baby. He's yelling at her like Daddy does Mommy.

"'You fine bitch, ohh! You sexy cunt, suck my dick, ohh! Ohh! Ohh!'

"Barbie hisses, 'Saul, stop. She'll hear us.'

"'So what, are we doing something wrong? In France the whole family walks around naked!'

"'You've never been to France.'

"'So fuckin' what, you low-class cunt? You trying to make me feel stupid? Anyway, what'd we get this fuckin' house for anyway? Privacy!' He answers his own question.

"Ken has all the questions and all the answers.

"'C'mere, you, get on down there. You're good for something.'

"'Wait a minute,' she says.

"I hear her footsteps walking to the door! I scramble to my feet and run down the hallway away from Mommy and Daddy and the thick smell of sex that had been wafting out the slightly ajar door of their hot room. But I've fallen asleep now under the table with Barbie and Ken. I wake up to the sound of my mother's voice and the sight of a pair of fat feet with stuffed into red pointy-toe shoes that are not my mom's. I turn my head to my mother's legs, crossed like a pretzel, her feet in shiny silver flats.

"'It was a punishment for sure. I was thirty and had had five abortions. *Five.* So I guess the Lord fixed me. I guess he said, "You hate the issue of your womb enough to kill it five times, well, I'll fix you good." It was my husband, he's such a mensch, who said, "Get over it, we can always adopt." That's when we got Noël.'

"'Is it the same?' Red shoes.

"'I mean, you walk into a store and they know you've adopted. But, you know, as far as it being the same, it is, I think. You feed them, clothe them, love them—you're all they know. They don't know they're not white. Noël fits right in.'

"'Plus, they're more intelligent than black kids.' Hot Pink Heels.

"'Well, she doesn't seem to be so far.'

"'How so?' Black Patent Leather Loafers.

"'All she wants to do is play ballerina. It's almost autistic or something.'

"'How old is she?' Black Loafers has a high nasal voice.

"'Four and a half.'

"'Well, for God's sake, what do you expect? Calculus? Leave her alone and feed her. She's too thin.' Red Shoes.

"'She hates for me to hold her.'

"'Get a nigger nanny.' Hot Pink Heels.

"'Don't talk like that!' My mother.

"'Don't be so sanctimonious, Sarah. You know what she meant. Get a good colored girl in here. That flip you got is depressed if I ever saw anyone depressed. You know, they think they're too good. You know, passing through until they finish cosmetology school or whatever. Get a good girl in here, and she'll stay put and help you with that kid. I'm telling you they're good with kids.' Red Shoes.

"'Asian kids?'

"'With *kids*, any kind of kids. What are you talking about, *Asian* kids? She doesn't know what kind of kid she is! You want her to be more social, you have to *socialize* her. Some of these foreign-born can be mentally ill from being in those orphanages. I read about it in the *New York Times*.' Red Shoes.

"'Oh, my God, Eartha, don't talk like that.' My mother.

"'It's true, they had an article in the *Post* too.' Hot Pink Heels. 'Where did you say she's from?'

"'She's Asian.'

"'I know that, I'm not developmentally disabled as they say now.' Hot Pink Heels.

"'Is that what they say?' Black Loafers.

"'What country is she from?' Red Shoes.

"'China?' Black Loafers.

"'I don't think so.'

"'What do you mean, you don't *think* so? Don't you even know where she's from?' Hot Pink Heels.

"'She's a domestic adoption. She came from here.'

"By now the words are crawling over me: *Asian, adoption, nigger nanny, that flip, colored, cosmetology school.*

"'Shit, excuse my French, she could be anything.' Hot Pink Heels.

"'You don't say? Domestic. I never knew an immigrant to give up a kid—' Red Shoes.

"'Yeah, kill 'em or ritually abuse 'em. Did you read that article in the *Post*—'

"'Please.' My mother cuts Hot Pink Heels off. 'Not now, Vera.'

"'It was in all the papers. Sarah, you can't just put your head in the sand. But back to what Eartha was saying. I didn't know you could get South American or Oriental kids through domestic adoptions. You know each child they have is another dollar on their welfare check. They call the kids anchors, because you drop 'em and they help you stay put. I guess they can't deport 'em or whatever.' Hot Pink Heels.

"'So they come illegally, pop out a few babies, anchors, and they're set for life.' Red Shoes.

"'I don't know if working sixteen hours a day as a dishwasher is exactly set for life.' Black Loafers.

"'Oh, quit the liberal shit.' Hot Pink Heels. 'You know what my husband calls them? He's a parasitologist.'

"'Well, OK already, what does he call them?' Red Shoes.

"'Chagas.' Hot Pink Heels.

"'What the hell is that?' Black Loafers.

"'A bloodsucking parasite that attacks your heart. It's from Mexico. Once you get it, you can never get rid of it. Bloodsuckers!' Hot Pink Heels again.

"'Are you projecting, Vera?' Loafers.

"'Projecting? What's that supposed to mean? What the devil are you talking about? Why would I be doing any damn projecting? What are you, Freud or something?' Hot Pink Heels.

"'What's going on here? What's this, the Ladies' Fight Club? We're supposed to be raising money, gals, not squabbling.' My mother.

"Chagas? Fight Club? Bloodsuckers? What's projecting? All these big feet. I have to pee bad, real bad. I can't come out; she'll get mad. I'm going to lay down and go to sleep. Some people die when they go to sleep. I'm going to die. She'll be sorry—

"'I smell something.' Hot Pink Heels.

"'Stop, Vera.' Red Shoes.

"'Yes, it's coming from under the table.' Hot Pink Heels.

"'Oh, my God! Noël! Noël! She's asleep!' Mommy.

"I open my eyes, feigning grogginess and confusion.

"'Come on, wake up, come to Mommy.'

"I crawled out from under the table, my child cotton drawers sagging and soaked with urine, my head swimming with new words—and nightmares of talking feet for years to come."

My Lai, who had until a few seconds ago been three or four years old and "under the table" on her hands and knees talking in a voice I had never heard before, turns back into now.

"I didn't understand most of what my mother said, except one thing I understood and was sure she'd made a mistake on—I wasn't 'playing' anything, I *was* a ballerina!" She laughs, sitting back in the circle with her notebook in her lap. She turns to look at me, "Yeah, but other than a ballerina, what *was* I?" Her eyes still on me, "At least you *knew*."

Oh, so now she's had it harder than me? I don't respond. I don't want to get in her shit. I feel a crackling in my brain, a noise, a clak-clak-bang-bang. I haven't felt this way in a long time, so angry I could spit. *At least you knew*, I mock her in my mind. But I'm not going to be dragged into this shit in front of everybody. She knows how I feel since "the incident."

We were rolling a couple of weeks ago, and she comes up with this wack shit. I'll never forget it. She's trying to live it down now, play high and all that. Fuck it for now. Let me hear this out, and I'll think on that later.

"So that's what happened: My mother listened to her friends and got me a black nanny. It was like a lot of stuff in my life, one of the best things that happened to me precisely because it was a total disaster. After my father got this Haitian woman—who barely spoke any English to them—pregnant, we were in real trouble.

"I was in my house under the table with Barbie and Ken one morning when they were talking about Eruzulie.

"'I'll tell,' she said.

"'Tell what, you stupid cunt?' my father snarled.

"'Eruzulie says you raped her.'

"'Fuck that nigger.'

"'No, fuck you, you bastard. You want her to press charges?'

"'She's lying.'

"'Have you ever heard of a paternity test, Saul?'

"'You're in it with that nigger.'

"'Saul, that *nigger* is going to have your kid, how do you like that?'

"'I like it fine, bitch. And don't try to blackmail me, you—'

"'I'm not trying to blackmail you. I'm trying to get you to act like a human being and take responsibility.'

"'Like hell you are. Arf-arf, dog-ass bitch. I'm not giving you one more dime.'

"'Yes you are. And you're going to marry me too. I have enough to put you away for the rest of your life.'

"'And I'll put you six feet under.'

"'No you won't!'

"'Try me, bitch.'

"'I'm not trying shit, Saul. We get married or I go with Eruzulie to the police.'

"'You *are* crazy,' he hissed.

"'That's not all I know, Alondra, the flip, her daughter, Saul! Her *daughter*—'

"His fat bare white hippopotamus feet flew across the floor and stepped in to her.

"WHAM! He slapped her.

"'I love you, Saul!' she screamed.

"I shot out from under the table as he punched her hard.

"'I love you, Saul!' I screamed. Is that what he wanted? Is that why she said it? Would it make him stop beating her? I would say it too.

"'I LOVE YOU, SAUL!' I screamed.

"'Jesus Christ.' He groaned like he was the one being hit.

"'Would you stop with the Jesus!' my mother screamed.

"'Would you shut up!' he said, and slapped her again. 'My mother's Catholic, I'm half Catholic, bitch.'

"'JEEZUS CHRISE JEEZUS CHRISE!' I screamed over and over, my head turned up to the chandelier's light glittering from the ceiling. He lurched toward me and grabbed me up by my braids.

"'I'll cut off your feet, you little monkey-ass chink. See how much dancing you do then,' he sneered.

"My eyes grew wide, wide enough to take in my whole little world and me in it with no feet. I could feel the hairs on my head separating from their roots as I swung from my braids in the grip of his big hands. His piss-smelling sweat was running down his arm onto me.

"'Put her down, Saul,' my mother begged.

"'I love you, Saul,' I croaked.

"When he dropped me, I collapsed on the floor, praying, 'Jesus please don't let him cut off my feet Jesus please don't let him cut off my feet.'"

"WE WENT TO BED that night, battered, me wrapped in her arms that seemed like warm clouds around me. But I knew that, like the clouds, they wouldn't protect me, and as I drifted off to sleep, I knew that she knew it too.

"In the morning clumps of my hair fell to the floor as I sat between my mother's legs on the pink carpet in my bedroom. I could feel hot tears on my back and shoulders. I felt cold toward her.

"A pungent smell told me she had opened a bottle of rubbing alcohol. I flinched.

"'Come on, be brave.'

"I screamed when the cold alcohol-soaked cotton singed my scalp. I wrenched my body away from her. My scalp burned where she had touched it. She still had a firm grip on my arm.

"'Mommy's going to wipe this all away and make it well. Don't say anything to anybody about Saul. He really loves us, OK? *OK?* I'm not going to brush your hair, but I have to pull it together to cover these spots, OK? We're a family, and all families have problems. No need to go blabbing to a bunch of people who can't help you. Mommy's gonna help you.'

"So she's trying to blackmail Saul into playing nice family or she'll send him to jail. He's calling her bluff and threatening to kick us out."

She opens her notebook to a section where a sheaf of pages has been stapled together by maybe a hundred staples.

"I'm not going to read this section, but this is where he finally rapes me, where he 'kills' me, where for a second I was like an animal with its nose in the wind, sniffing a good scent as the light from the chandelier seemed to shimmer down from the ceiling, the smell that raises the hairs on my neck, and then I realize it's blood. I'm smelling my own blood. The smell irons a flat place in my brain, guaranteeing I will be inconsolable. *Gutted,* he guts me. When I wake up, there's a different girl in my skin. Because I can't forget what he did but can't bear to remember, I make a different girl to hold the memory. I split. I create a girl who forgets; between the two of us, night girl and day girl, me and her, we're able to move on. Day girl thinks and thinks and thinks, reads and reads and reads, and practices and practices and practices some more. If I dream after that, I don't know it. Night girl knows the blob of slime he leaves behind, the rude, yellow stink of his piss in her toilet that he leaves like an animal marking his territory. Night girl trembles in the dark. She knows what's coming. She's even relieved when he cums, because at least the terror, the dreadful anxiety, is over, and afterward, when he goes, she can go to sleep, black, hard sleep that saves me.

"I don't think my mother lets herself know, but she must feel some-thing, because after the rape, if she goes to her mother's or her sister's house, she takes me with her. She doesn't leave much, though, but I don't think that's about me. I think she's afraid he'll forget they're 'married' and move someone else in. He's out of the house in the day. We're alone together in the house except for the maid. But it's as if a sheet of glass is always between us. My side of the glass is clear; I see through to her, but her side is a mirror, all she sees is herself.

"I had to find a way to break through. I was with her when she bought the purse from Bloomingdale's in 'the City.' A big white purse. I decided to write her a letter and put it in a bottle like the shipwrecked cartoon characters did. It was a plastic water bottle. I carefully turned it upside down to let all the drops of water drain out, and when it was dry, I put the letter in (too bad I lost the top). Then I put the bottle in the new white bag with the big gold clasp. Snap! It was done. For some reason I thought then for the first time in a concrete way about my real mother."

Dear mom.

He is molesting me. Daddy is doing it. You know what that means. Mommy make him stop

Noël (your one and only daughter)

"I'm devastated when she doesn't respond to my letter until one day it dawns on me, *she never got the letter.* How do I know that? I realize I've never seen Mommy with the white bag! I've never seen Mommy with the white bag. I'veneverseenMommywiththewhitebag.

The mountain of dark feeling her betrayal had been building inside of me comes tumbling down. Of course! It was so obvious, why didn't I see the light sooner?

"She's washing my hair in the kitchen. I'm full of the thought now, that as firmly as my despairing mind had believed *she knows* and doesn't care, my total organism now believes *she doesn't know* and that she's a true mother. My nose is full of floral-smelling shampoo. Her body, smelling faintly of sweat and grapefruit, is pressed reassuringly against mine as her strong fingers knead my scalp. She wraps a fluffy pink towel around my head and turns me toward her.

"'Mom,' I say, 'he does things to me at night.'

"'Who, the boogeyman?' She laughs.

"'No, Mommy, what I wrote you in the letter.'

"'What letter?' she says, toweling my hair. I WAS RIGHT!

"'I put it in your purse.'

"'I have a hundred purses.'

"'The white purse.'

"'I have a dozen white purses.'

"'Mom, he comes in my room at night and sticks his finger. The time you went away, he took me to your room and gave me vitamins and sex with me.'

"'*Sex* with you?'

"'Innercourse innercourse, Mommy, like the dog sticks its thing in, but I was laying down on the bed.'

"'I ... I ... I ...' she's stuttering.

"I'm afraid she doesn't believe me. I start to cry as if my heart is broken, because it *is* broken.

"She takes my shoulders and gently shakes me. 'Do you remember which bag?'

"'The white bag!' I sob.

"I try to stretch out my arms to hug her, but she's still holding my shoulders, her forehead gathered in thinking wrinkles.

"'The white bag with the big—'

"'Gold,' we say together. 'Clasp,' she finishes, and lets go of my shoulders.

"'Keep drying off. I'll be right back.'

"She darts out of the kitchen and up the stairs. When she comes back, she looks like the witch in my old Disney Hansel and Gretel book—all scrunched up and full of evil.

"'We can *use* this! By God, we will use this. That's as good as a wedding ring. We can get anything out of him now.'

"What's she talking about? Maybe she sees the confusion on my face.

"'He's not going to bother you anymore.'

"'He already did *a lot*.'

"'It's over. Believe Mommy, OK?'

"'OK.' But I'm not sure I believe her a bit.

"'Say, "OK, Mommy, I believe you."'

"'OK, Mommy, I believe you,' I parroted. And I did. What choice did I have? Believe her and be her child again or be an abandoned nestling and die or go crazy. I chose to believe. There didn't seem to be a place in between, yet. At least I was something; even a lie is something. I was a kid, her kid, somebody's daughter. Without her I was just the nighttime girl and what he said I was, taken-in trash, dusted off to be fucked.

"I was her girl now, maybe in the same way he was going to be her husband. She had something on him. I had something on her. I would use it. I figured out what I wanted, just like she did. I had paid for it already. And yeah, she's paying me and will be for a long time to come. Pampered rich kid? I don't think so. I think war crime, the *second* rape of My Lai. American moment. I call myself My Lai, and as soon as I'm old enough, that's going on all my legal documents, MY LAI."

My Lai holds the notebook pressed against her breasts as she talks. I see myself tearing another woman's notebook to bits in Central Park and throwing the bits in the howling subway tunnel.

Finally Scott breaks the silence. "It's amazing."

"Off the hook." Snake. "But way long, My Lai. We have to totally go for the heart."

"Yeah, I agree, and the essence, the heart, of the story is the voice of this child. I keep hearing the part 'I love you, Saul, I love you, Saul.'" Scott.

"What got me was the little you writing the letters." Me.

"The part under the table wore me out!" Snake.

"The part that I totally ID'd with was how dancing gave you a life in the middle of the abuse." Me.

"That's theater, baby!"

"OK, OK, the question is—"

"Why?"

"No, *how*."

I can't keep up with who's talking. I'm seeing My Lai under her dad being fucked; I'm half repulsed, half aroused, and totally enraged. These fucking perps, it's like they throw you down a well, that's how I feel, like that gook, like that little rice farmer, *man*, that the G.I. knocked down the well. I promise myself then and there if I ever see Brother John again to do that faggot death. I hold My Lai tighter; she's silent while everyone's chattering.

Scott looks at his watch. "Let's call it a day—night, actually."

FOUR   I'm at Starbucks looking out of the floor-to-ceiling windows at a man vomiting on the subway steps and the crazed effort of a college student to turn the huge black cube in the center of Cooper Square on its axis. The alcove I'm sitting in is on a slightly raised platform between the window section and the rest of the café; my back is to those tables below on the cement floor, and I'm facing the windows and the door, so I see the three of them, Snake, Scott, and My Lai, when they walk in. The exact moment they walked in the door, I could have hollered, *Yo, guys!* But I didn't. I don't know why. Tasting My Lai with my eyes, my blood swirls. Her nose is pierced again; she had it done once, and it got infected, and she had to let it close up. This time she went back in with fourteen-karat instead of silver, and it's doing fine. She has on tight black leather pants, high heels, and, even though it's no longer summer and starting to cool off, her gold lamé tube top. Snake and Scott are in jeans, Snake with a big silver cowboy belt; Scott even in jeans looks like he has on a suit and tie.

I turn my head and bend further over my book, *Nureyev: Aspects of the Dancer* by John Percival:

> . . . *It was not until he was eleven that Nureyev had his first ballet lesson. He was taken by one of the Pioneer mistresses to the Ufa Scientists' Club to meet an old lady named Udeltsova, then about seventy, who had been a member of Serge Diaghilev's corps de ballet. She still taught, not professional students but children.*

They've chosen a table on the floor right in front of my table in the alcove. Now would be a good time to turn around and say hi. But again I don't.

"What do you want?" Scott.

"I can get it?" My Lai.

"Let's just leave our stuff here and go up together." Scott.

"This is still New York. I'll stay here and watch our shit." Snake.

"So what do you want?" Scott.

"What are you guys getting?" Snake.

"Black Forest ham and cheddar, and a coffee." Scott.

"Americano and a chocolate croissant." My Lai.

"Bet."

"Bet what?"

"The ham and cheese with an Americano, room for milk." Snake, but I don't hear no shuffling of bills from him to My Lai or Scott. Snake has no problem taking.

When My Lai and Scott get back to the table, I turn my head a bit and sneak a glance out the side of my eye. Their three backs form a little semicircle opposite to my back. It's too late to say hi now; it would be weird. They're nattering on about My Lai's performance, whether it should be a solo (what else could it be?), finding a way to make it more central (I agree with that). Scott says transnational adoption is indicative almost always of a past colonial or conqueror relationship of the adopting recipient/buyer country to the child donor/seller countries. (So what? Kids need a home, that's my two cents!)

"How so?" Snake.

"I mean no people come from China or Africa to adopt kids in the U.S." Scott.

"I gotcha." Snake.

"It's not a judgment, just a fact. It would be hard for an African to come over here and adopt an 'orphan' whose father objected to him or her being adopted. I mean, it's not a probability." Scott.

"So how are we going to proceed with this?" My Lai.

"Well, we got a million little pieces here. You know we want to feed the story into a central place in the text and choreography. So we're making no attempt at passing off the finished product as a factual attempt to tell My Lai's biography. She becomes, as Amy asked if she was that first time before My Lai read the piece, an Asian everywoman-child."

"Bet, build power into the performance by having something that seems personal, *is* in fact personal, give flavor—" Snake.

"Added emotional valence—" Scott.

"Flavor, added emotional valence—same difference." Snake.

Sigh. Scott. (So what are they gonna do, change My Lai's story to make it like she's a Vietnamese adoptee or something so it complements the My Lai Massacre choreography? Interesting.)

They're talking about the opening-night reception. Should they have it before the show or after? After is my thinking. Then out the blue Scott says, "What about Abdul?"

"What about him? His section with Charlie Company at the well is one of the strongest parts of the performance." My Lai.

"And the video footage is gold." Snake.

"Well, you know the whole thing. Like, who is this guy? He came in with one name, now he has another one. Amy's not that into him—"

"She doesn't have to be *into* him to work with him." My Lai.

"Well, I'm not that comfortable with him *living* at the loft. It's supposed to be a rotating, *caretaking* position, and the dude has just moved in totally. I was going through the incoming mail last week, and he's getting mail!"

"Hey, man, why didn't you say that from the get-go? The loft is your digs. If you need him out, he's out." Snake.

"I didn't mean that." Scott.

"Yes you did." My Lai.

"Well, if you didn't mean it, you were getting around to meaning it." Snake.

"You know he's my man." My Lai.

"I know that. What's that got to do with anything?" Scott.

"Shit, would you want someone to bring up some shit like that in front of everybody about your spouse?" My Lai.

"Spouse? My Lai, that's pretty heavy. I didn't know you two were that hot an item. And since when did Snake become 'everybody'?" Scott.

"You just said you knew." My Lai.

"I mean when you said 'he's my man,' I knew already something had been going on between you two, so I responded, 'I know that.' But I didn't know it was all that, he's your *spouse* and shit." Scott.

"Look, spouse, house, louse, mouse! What the fuck! He's the strongest dancer we have, he's good, two steps from one day being great. If we really want Herd to get going, we need to pull in three or four more—"

"More what?" Scott cuts in on Snake. "Black dancers?"

"Scott! Man, are you *tripping*?" Snake.

"No, no, I didn't mean it that way, it came out all wrong. But it's like we . . . we have a concept and I don't want it to get . . . get taken. . . ."

"Taken over?" My Lai.

"No, no, you got me all wrong. Let's get off Abdul, we have too much to do together to be getting all convoluted. You're right, he's cool, and I *am* tripping, and I guess a little scared it's all going to—"

"*All* what, huh? All your daddy's and My Lai's mommy's financed company might really become a fucking real company you don't control." Snake.

"OK, OK, point taken. Now can we kill this and get back to what we were talking about before?"

Discipline, I tell myself, and *breathe*. Disappear into your breath, defuse your anger. Don't move except to lean further over and read from John Percival.

> She taught, not professional students but children. Nureyev was made to dance for her: a gopak, a lezginka and other folk dances. As he danced, the old lady looked stunned, and at the end she gave him the advice he had already heard from others: "Go to Leningrad, study there." But from her lips it meant something at last, and the

boy blushed. Besides, she was much more peremptory: "Child, you
have a duty to yourself to learn classical dancing."

When they get up, I feel wiped out, like that guy on that TV special on renal dialysis, as if something had just removed all the blood out of my body. I sit there waiting for whatever it is that's gone to come back. I mean, I knew he didn't like me. But why? Because I'm good, because I'm black? His "concept"! What is it with them, if they're sucking our shit, hip-hop or R&B or something, it's all good, they love love *love* us, can't get enough of that funky stuff, eat it up, cash in. Yet me being with Herd all of a sudden—well, it wasn't no all of a sudden. He's been scared from day one I'm going to "take over." Where's his fucking stupid head? Spozed to be so intelligent. Well, maybe he's right; before it's all done, I will take over. But not from his stupid ass. His "concept," fuck his concept! I feel tired now, rattled. None of my gigs pays me near enough to afford rent anywhere around here. I feel like I'm hurtling through dark space, like here we fucking go. I thought I was on solid ground, but it's just smoke, mirrors, and quicksand all over again. Well, suck it in, put on a hard face, don't let on you know shit. And shit, what do you know, really? Just get on out there and do the show, dance hard, harder than you ever danced. And when it's over, you figure out your next move.

I close the book, look at his muscular body in white tights and chest bared. He's on his knees, his arms muscular and sinewy raised above his head elegantly in fifth position. He has the face of a wolf, beautiful high cheekbones, smoky eyes, hungry lips. I look at him and know I have to be great while at the same time feeling I can't really be. The confusion makes me want to kill something, fuck up everybody, including myself.

I'VE HEARD THE MUSIC a thousand times, but because the wood floor trembles when I step like the walls around it are being consumed by flames and it will collapse at any minute, I mince my movement. I'm disgusted with myself; this is the third time I've missed the count where

I'm supposed to come in; then after I miss the damn count, I can't catch up and get on the beat, everybody has to stop. I think it's me trembling, not the floor.

"You know this piece backwards." My Lai.

"I've never seen you like this before. Pre-performance jitters?" Snake.

"Can we try it again?" Me. I haven't experienced this kind of disconnect between my body and my command of it since I started dancing in Imena's class in Harlem. I look at Amy, My Lai, Snake—I thought they were my friends. They're no more my friends than Brother John, and then I think that's not fair, not fair at all—

"Where's your head, Abdul? You are so not here today." Scott.

They're not my friends or they are my friends, so what! I'm a dancer; I don't need to like these motherfuckers to do my job. You think Nureyev liked everyone he danced with? Hell no, he hated some of them.

"Everybody has an off day—" My Lai.

"I'm not having an off day. Can we start over and do it again instead of yakking about it? I missed my cue, goddamn it, so what!"

"Bet!" Snake.

ME AND MY LAI are eating breakfast at a diner on Seventh Avenue off Sixteenth Street. My Lai is chowing down on a bowl of high-fiber cereal swamped with two orders of blueberries and nonfat milk. She's spooning the cereal into her mouth, trying to get as many blueberries on the spoon as she can. The perfect smell of bacon sizzling on the diner's grill brings tears to my eyes. I'm remembering Aunt Rita picking up a slice of bacon with her red-tipped fingers and holding it to my mouth. The greasy, salty pleasure of pork filled my mouth as I stared at the dark place between her breasts accented by her low-cut dress and hard black push-up bra. The bra I had thought was extra breasts when I saw it laid out on the white bedspread and buried my nose in the cups, drinking in her musky perfume smell. I get up and head to the restroom in the back of the diner, the tears almost spilling over. I head past the urinals for the one stall. Locked inside, I sob, seeing her leaning out a hotel room door as I trot down the hall to the bathroom, the floor always sticky-slick with piss, sometimes blood and needles, occasionally shit, no matter how she complained or cleaned. I couldn't imagine why she felt she had to stand watch; I was a big boy, nine years old, what could happen to me?

The urgent sound of piss surging in the trough outside the stall, a rap on the stall door, and a "Hey, buddy, I need to take a dump" remind me I'm in the wrong place to get gushy. I open the door, and there's a guy about four feet five and three hundred pounds at least whose face looks like one big pimple. Has he been listening to me cry, waiting for me to come out, because he can't, I mean, no way can he fit in this stall to take a shit or anything else. He's actually blocking my exit.

"Mind if I pass, buddy?" I say. He's fluttering a fifty-dollar bill between his thumb and forefinger.

"Oh, no, of course not," he says, still not moving and like a magician producing two more fifty-dollar bills out of nowhere. He looks up, I catch his eye, burn him. He flings his weight to the side and lets me pass.

When I get back to the booth, my pancakes are cold. I wave my hand for the waitress. "Could you heat this up for me?"

"Sure." She swoops down on the plate and picks it up as gracefully as she put it down. She does her job well, I think, watching her wide hips walk away from the booth, wondering what it would be like to ride them. And why am I thinking about the waitress when I got life sitting in front of me? Maybe I didn't get enough sleep last night, or maybe that's just how guys are, we can't help it. What Scott said runs through my head: *Like, who is this guy?* Fuck that dry-ass faggot. If it wasn't for My Lai, I'd destroy his fucking ass loft before I split, but it's not just her; I'm holding myself back because of me. I don't want that kind of karma riding my ass, plus Daddy's boy might call the pigs. I got enough dogs on my brain as it is.

"What are you thinking so hard?" she asks as I pick up a piece of bacon and put it down after one bite.

"I was thinking you're right, the best thing about bacon is how it smells.

It smells way better than it tastes—at least this stuff here does." I push it to the side of the plate and spear a forkful of buttery blueberry pancakes, which taste pretty good despite being nuked back to life.

"That is *not* what you were thinking." She pouts.

"Calling me a liar?"

"No, just saying you weren't thinking about no fucking bacon. You know, every time, half the time you feel something—"

"Which is it? You're contradicting yourself, every time, half the time—"

"Would you let me finish? When you feel something, you hide it from me."

She's pouting again, or at least that's how it seems to me. And what can I say? It's true. Instead of getting closer, I feel myself building a wall, or maybe I'm digging a hole.

I remember Roman's meddling ass and look at My Lai and think it's better not to know. I swear that ninny went through everything I had or brought into that apartment.

"You know, something is funny with you papers."

"Why were you even bothering with them?"

"Because you live here, you mine," he said, matter-of-fact. "I help you. So I want to know you."

It didn't register then, but I think now, if he had gone through that envelope, he had to know how old I was, fucking faggot. I hadn't even gone through the envelope myself except to glance in it when I left St Ailanthus. There was nothing in it could help me with the shit I was going through. It was just I didn't have shit, and whatever I had, I held on to. I remember Aunt Rita giving it to the white woman who took me away from the hotel, then Miss Lillie, then the Brothers at St Ailanthus, then they gave it to me, and I brought it from Roman's to the loft.

I don't give much thought to Roman's "something is funny with you papers." I figure it's a mistake like so much of my life. So I call 311:

"Hi, I need to get a copy of my birth certificate."

"Foster care?" She must could tell I'm young.

"Yeah."

"Aging out?" she asks.

"Yeah." In a way I wasn't lying—it *should* have been true; legally, I was still over there on 805 St Nicholas Avenue with my grandmother (only she wasn't my grandmother when I checked out my mother's shit!). "I know I was born in Harlem. How do I get a copy of my birth certificate for school and a New York State ID?"

"You can get it by fax, Internet, mail, or you can walk in and get it the same day."

"OK, bet, walk in?"

"To get it in person, you come to 125 Worth Street between Centre and Lafayette, Room 133, between nine a.m. and three-thirty p.m. Enter using the side entrance on Lafayette Street. It's fifteen dollars, credit card, debit card, check, or cash. We need your full name, your mother's name, father's name if available, and the reason for requesting the birth certificate."

"Reason?"

"You already gave your reason: aging out of foster care with no documents; just repeat that when you get down here. It's common, you ain't gonna have no problem. It's fifteen dollars, credit card, debit card, check, or cash. If the form is complete and payment paid, you should walk out with the birth certificate."

She was right.

I look at My Lai. "Ready to go?"

"I think I'm going to get a poached egg on toast, I didn't have any protein," My Lai says.

"Order me one too," I tell her, not even half listening to her go on about the evils of protein deficiency. I'm thinking about the birth certificate. The *mistake* is on this one too: My father's name is the same as my mother's father's name. What's up with that? It's another dog loose in my brain, a bad dog.

"To get in a college dance program I got to have what?"

"The whole shebang—Social Security number, you got to come up, dude; same thing if you want to get a driver's license, got to come up. Did you get your birth certificate?"

"I did. In fact, I actually already had one."

"So why the drama?"

"I . . . there was a mistake on the one I had."

"Mistake? What mistake? Did you fix it?"

"No."

"Well, what is it, are you you? I mean, ah, nineteen, AA, a man, I know you got your Y chromosomes," she teases.

"I'll tell you later."

"No you won't," and she stabs her egg with her fork. "Tell me *now*. Tell me now or get someone you can tell. I'm tired of being locked out. What do we have lately aside from you getting your dick wet regularly?"

"I'm . . . I'm in love with you."

"Then tell me."

I feel the hole getting deeper; I know I should say something, have to. She's serious. But something won't let me respond. At the same time, I can't stop the tears from rolling down my cheeks. I wish Aunt Rita was here, she would tell me. I hang my head.

"Don't leave me," I beg, sobbing.

"Abdul, I love you. I'm sorry. I didn't mean it. I was just being a hard-ass because I thought you were. Don't worry. I should have known it was . . . was—whatever it was, was *big*. Honey, don't, *don't*," she says, wiping my face with her napkin.

"IT WAS A good rehearsal, guys. I think, no, I *know* it's going to go off great. It's controlled where it needs to be and wild and free where it can be. We're on and off in fifty minutes. I'm saying the names, and the two screens are behind me, then when these screens synchronize with the helicopter scenes, My Lai, you're on. The Jenkins track doesn't come on until you're out there. Don't wait for it, because they're waiting for you.

Your cue is visual—those two screens synchronize and then merge into one screen center stage, and when we see that helicopter scene, get out there! The lights don't go down, there's no intermission or part one or part two—we've got to provide those divisions with our presence—and when the Leroy Jenkins track starts, My Lai, I want you to do like in rehearsal, *stalk* that music, eat it!

"So when My Lai comes offstage, the stage goes dark for a second, and you have Abdul center screen, it's superb, that—it's still mind-boggling that footage we got that day. So he's on one screen, and that's fully three minutes, and then the screen splits again, and he's on the two screens, and then, you know, I mean, you guys know all this, the images go on the ceiling, out into the audience, on the walls surrounding the audience, on the audience's bodies, so for a minute they're inundated with scenes from this dancing black soldier.

"The risks are real, this couldn't be rehearsed. What Snake said is true: We can't predict if this is going to have the same effect on a full house of strangers that it had on us doing it at rehears—"

"It was a great idea, Scott. What doesn't come off opening night, we'll tweak that shit and tighten during the rest of the run." Snake.

"Or leave it alone. The purpose of taking the images off the screen was to foreshadow the action that's going to come. To make them feel something for these guys who are going to do this horrible stuff. Whatever effect the bombardment has, I say let's go with it." Amy.

"Yeah, I agree, there's no way to 'tweak' this. We got to let it fall where it falls." Me.

"I was talking more about the tech." Snake.

"OK, then everyone's changed. Bare chest men, women dance bras fatigue material, everybody fatigue tights." Scott.

"Yoho! Charlie Company!" Snake.

"Bet."

"Bet."

"So tomorrow we meet before the show?" Amy.

"Here, the 'Bucks and walk over to the theater together."

"Astor Place?"

A chorus of "Cool"s.

"Nobody late, hell or high water." Scott.

"Gotcha."

"Gotcha."

"Bet."

"On it."

BOOK FOUR

DIRTY 4 DIRTY

He recalled it far more vividly in his
dream than he had done in memory.

—FYODOR DOSTOEVSKY,
Crime and Punishment

Is this a hospital?

ONE   Where are the doctors, nurses, other patients, telephones in your room, nurses' station, charts, thermometers, people coming with their flowers? Where are the other people, windows, interns, the nurses walking up and down? What's going on here?

How did I get here? Yeah, how did I get here, and how long have I been here? What *am* I? Whose body is this laying here? Where's my black machine?

"You ain' crazy. You lucky to be here," some punk in marshmallow-looking white shoes tells me. He knows I'm too full of the death he gives me to jump up and kill him. Here? Where's here? How did I get here? What *am* I? Is this my body laying here like a broken machine? How could I be "lucky to be here"? Unless someplace else is worse, but where could I be? When will I get out of here? Ever? I try to count the days, but counting eludes me like when I was little and used to try to grab goldfish. And where is it I used to do that? I don't remember.

I do remember My Lai. Where is she? We were in this together, together, that's all I remember, together after being alone so long. This is how it ends? What is the love shit they are always shitting you about? I don't know. I just think her. I want, oh, I don't remember what I was saying. I do remember leaping, jumping, that's clear. But that was when I was a dancer?

I feel like a drooling *lump*. It's so frustrating when I try to remember anything. I don't remember, let's say, dancing, but I *know* it. Every day

it's like my mind is a stolen wallet returned; I'm going through it, knowing shit is missing but not able to remember what. Every day it's pills
and shots, inhale this or swallow that. It might be fun if I didn't have to
do it. I look for names but don't see any; I don't remember eating or if
I even can, but if I could, I would. Even though I'm not hungry, I feel
a hunger to be hungry. They think I'm asleep, or do they? Who's *they*?
In a way I am asleep, even though I hardly ever sleep; it seems to me
that I just go someplace I forget in between being awake, which feels
like a nightmare, a quiet one but a nightmare just the same. You really
can't call this being awake or alive. What I want to do is remember
what turned me into a weird lump, so I can turn back into myself. A
bird. Hey, maybe I'm where the bird was? Is Basquiat here? Am I dead?
Is this hell? Where, where is here? Who is they? And why am I alone?
This is not supposed to happen. I remember the swans in Prospect Park;
we had gone to see Prince. And she said that's us, swans. We know our
mind, we're in this for life, we mate for life. Or is that something I read
and then thought she said? She said she would die before she would let
them—No, that's a movie I saw. But who is them? Is she here? This is
so hard. Everything is erased; I can make the outlines of words written
in my head, but there's no ink, only a raised white shape on white paper.
Maybe what braille is, but I don't know braille. If I could read something, move, write, move, if I could move, I would know. I wouldn't be
in . . . in . . . I can't be in prison. I can't be. It's the shots they give me. I'm
sure of it until I get a shot. Then I don't know. In biology they show the
white blood cells as wide white smiley faces with stick legs and running
shoes. And they run to whatever bad thing is in your body. I wish they
was in me now to eat the shots. They would dash out like smiley-face
Batmen and eat whatever was coming down the needle, because I'm way
too tired, dead, to do it. I can't even think of doing it. Yeah, I mean no, I
can't even think, much less fight.

"They must hate you, homeboy, 'cause you gittin' it old time. They
don't even do it like this no more. They want to see how your ass will
react. Why else? Watkins come check out Big Dick."

THE KID

"Shut up, you sick freak. What do I care about his dick? Bite down! Bite down!" Watkins, he's the devil.

Zip zip ZAAP! My body flip-flops—a fish, then it's erect and quivering under the restraints. My brain drops, an egg, on a hot sidewalk. FRY. Passersby SPLAT step spatter yellow.

Zip zip ZAAP!

Is this really happening to me?

My bowels empty with a furious ejection of putrid liquid shit, even though they already gave me an enema. My hands are strapped down. Are they afraid I'm going to kill myself or them? If I wasn't strapped down, I'd fill my hand with shit and smear the blind white wall. I'm tired to my bones.

THE CONSTANT SMELL of bleach and alcohol, alcohol wipes, wiping, scrubbing, the smell is so strong it's as if the ceiling was one big white alcohol prep pad sending fumes down throughout the room. The smell is so strong I know it can't be real. Sometimes the workers' voices come at me from underwater; other times they're sharp as firecrackers hurting my ears, or a hammer that could shatter my heart, which feels like an empty glass in my chest. I hear fat marshmallow shoes fluttering around me when my eyes are closed. Mean ghost heads filled with feathers that they fly away on.

Alone, hate is my friend. Hate kill God friend hate kill God revenge. My body is swelling. My body has swollen. I'm a whale, a whale with a rash. A rash that begins behind my knees creeps up my thighs into the creases where my arm bends at the elbow and breaks into hives and boils and pus that smells like a dead rat trapped in a wall and that feels like ants stinging when I sweat. The pus cannot challenge the smell of bleach and alcohol, but it tries to. I itch, but I can't scratch. I'm restrained. Tied up. Tied up restrained talked at. I feel soft, as if I'm beginning to melt, as if my bones are dissolving. Am I dreaming? Why won't I wake up? I seem to not know things, the central knowledge of my life, how old I am, what my name is, for God's sake. I feel sure here is a real place, that I'm not dreaming it. But I'm *not* sure. I ask one of the men in marshmallow shoes, Where am I, where am I? But my tongue doesn't work. The words don't seem to come out of my mouth. I'm in a hospital? A . . . a *where*? Something must have happened. Sometimes I feel within this dreaming, I am dreaming, and in that dream I'm someone with a name. My Lai is there. I tell my muscles, move. I command, speak. Nothing happens.

This must be hell. A white place without music, with lights that never go off. Just above my head is the devil, two fluorescent lamps, two long tubes, bulbs, in each fixture. Four bulbs on all the time, how is that energy-efficient? The long white lights never go off. I close my eyes to see dark, but the lights eat the darkness out of my head. Sometimes a needle goes in with some darkness, but it's fake. The lights overhead don't go off. This room is about, what? Eight feet wide, ten feet long. The way the ceiling is shaped, I feel like I might be on the top floor close to the roof. Have I heard the sound of rain above my head? There's no windows. The only furniture is the metal bed that I'm strapped in and a metal chair with a white plastic seat. The floor is white scarred squares of linoleum.

Lucky to be here? The meanest of the men in marshmallow shoes, I can't call his name. He stands out for being mean and blacker than the others and always chewing something in his purple lips. What time of day is it, *year* is it? Am I old, still young, sick, handsome, did I get something? AIDS? Or leprosy from the Bible?

"Be still." From ghost devil out of nowhere. "Be still," he repeats, though I haven't moved, and wipes some stuff on the side of my face. He raises a pair of clippers so I can see them. CLICK BUZZ.

"Don't move," he says. I have no intention of moving. The clippers feel good on my face, his fingers tilt my jaw, and then he moves to my head, black bits of hair fall on the white linen. Have they done this before? I don't remember. How old am I? Why am I here? The air feels good on my shaved temples. Is this a dream? Some kind of state I never learned about in catechism—purgatory two or something? Did I do something wrong? When I hear my own voice, it sounds like a retarded echo of itself. Am I fat, bigger, taller, finished growing, a grown-up? I can't fix my tongue to make all the words I am thinking. Why? I ask. I sound to myself like retarded kids we used to make fun of, like they are rolled up in my mouth. My tongue is a sack of cement.

"UH-wah-wah *why?*"

"What?" he snaps.

"Wh-wah wh-wh-why?"

"'Why?' Is that what you said, big-ass nigger?"

Why is he talking to me like that? He's black. Does everybody hate me? I've got to get away from here. In the dream, but it wasn't a dream. I'm on a ship, it *is* a dream. I can smell the salt water; usually in dreams I can't smell. I've still got to get away, water or not. I've got to try to swim back to shore. Everybody on the ship is dancing! Dancing like in the olden white days, they all, we, I'm one of them, have on breeches like from Shakespeare's or George Washington's time, gauntlet gloves, and embroidered shirts like from costume rental, dah dah dah, we do the mincing cinque pas. We're in the garden now. We're all light-skinned, white (except me!), sipping tea, in white ruffled shirts. The music sounds like it's played on a tin piano, a tin prissy sound. I stop dancing, and the whole court turns to look at me. I'm speaking in the carefully enunciated, elevated tones of a Shakespearean actor when I grab my sword—

"Look at you, you big drooling fool! You can't stay here no longer than a minute at a time. Can you? What are you talking about, shithead? 'Why?' Why what, nigger?"

His stupid voice kills the garden. Even if I could talk, I don't know what to say, or how to talk in his head like he talks in mine, not my ears but ringing in my head like a stupid bell bong bong bong "Why what, nigger?" He wants to know why? Why *what*? What does he want to know why about? I want to know why my tongue can't run or fly anymore. Broken bird. Hey, I remember that: *if dreams die life is a broken-winged bird that cannot fly.* Where? From my mother. He said I was lucky to be here. Let's talk about that. Why do you think I'm lucky to be here?

If you think I'm lucky to be here, you must know where here is. Where is here? I demand to know.

He grabs my arm, ties a tourniquet just above my elbow, make a fist. I don't. Smell alcohol, wipe, evaporates cool on my skin.

"Don't give me a hard time, motherfucker, you big-ass freak. You lucky to be alive after that shit you pulled the last time."

I don't know what he's talking about, if he's really talking. Pop. Needle plunges into my vein. *Shit you pulled?* I did something he didn't like?

Cool wipe of alcohol, another needle, he loosens the tourniquet. Blue clouds rush me wrap me in warm blue water and float float to a heavy gray place. I feel the Velcro wrapping me, and my bed grows wheels; wheels wheel me to another room, turn me onto a steel slab. Why? Why? No tongue. When my tongue comes back, I'll ask. Now I'm an animal. I smell hear see but without the sky colors. I remember in pieces, then not at all. I want to be left alone. Leave me alone. But the dark faces with marshmallow shoes and white jackets are all around me. One of them asks another one exactly what I'm thinking:

"Why are we doing this?"

"We just are."

"I don't understand why he doesn't go all the way under if he's gonna fry." A woman's voice.

"For Christ's sake, let's get this over with."

They pull straps on my feet tighter, stuff my mouth, attach silver things to my shaved head. Then I'm hit.

ZAP!
ZAP!
ZAP!
ZAP!

Paaaaainnn

Pain

pain

ZAP! ZAP!
ZAP! ZAP!
ZAP! ZAP!
ZAP! ZAP!
ZAP!
ZAP!
ZAP!
Paaaaainnn

Pain

pain

Then it's blank except for the smell of shit.

Then another shot no rush but the smell of chlorine, weird blue eyes the color of the bottom of a swimming pool I'm flailing grabbing at the water the bottom opens up panic rips my breath then the fall in black no thing.

I'M LYING ON a blanket at the beach, the hot sand warming my back as I watch white fluffy clouds floating by. As I stare at the clouds, they start to change, taking on shapes that look like children. They're round with big eyes but no arms or legs, just cloud bodies. Their big eyes are staring at me. Why? Do they like me? I don't like them. I want to get rid of them. This is no beach. I'm here, with nothing; why aren't they nothing too? Why can't I get rid of them? I want to get rid of everything.

Yeah, I want to get rid of everything and just keep the colors of things, the Charlie Parker sounds—these colors. The color of My Lai's clit pulsing like a heart alive in my mouth. Alive in my mouth like an animal or a curry. I licked her whole body with my tongue like a mother dog. I took her like she was my mama's tittie, I sucked her cunt like she taught me, diving into her black jungle hair. She taught me, she's a smart girl, *I* made her body scream, she'd be sweating, dripping because of *me*, her sweaty hips slipping in my hands like a fish, her long legs, toes, her whole body spasms of desire for me. Oh oh oh! That's how she'd come, thin, her body didn't scare me. She wasn't all fat and fluffy like Amy. I wasn't scared of My Lai. I fucked her so hard we bled. I smeared the blood on my cheeks and forehead like war paint. I want that . . . I want that . . . I want that. Why am I here? I want to get out of here. My Lai Desiré. I want to get out of here. I remember her nipples hard beasts, her big fishy tongue. Roman said, *No girl do you like I do.* He was wrong, anybody can suck a dick, My Lai blew me good. Roman? I had forgot about him. Does he have anything to do with me being here? He hasn't been in my head in a long time. It's so confusing here. She wanted me, I wanted her; what happened to our dance? Dancing? Blow me! Bloooow me! What are they doing to me? Why can't I move? Are they going to kill me and cut my heart out for some fat old white man like that story in the *News* about the guy who went to Pakistan and bought him a kidney; he didn't care that he hated the people he got the kidney from or that they hated him, he lived. Their asses got five grand, maybe. They won't care about me either. My body parts will be all over Long Island and the Upper East Side. They will eat me! Why can't I *move*? Do I have a name? Arf! Arf! Meow! Am I a cat, a nigger, a boy, a man? What's the difference between a cat and a nigger? And a man? Why is everything so bleary? Where is yellow? Pine-apple? Green? Trees? Ice cream? The pink bulb of My Lai's clit, her deep pussy, why isn't she here? If someone is yours, why don't you own them? If you're free, an American, why can't you leave when you want? I must be someplace else. Where the fuck is *here*? I want a mirror. Where's a mir-ror? Get these straps off of me. I'm tired of being strapped down like, like a . . . a prisoner of somewhere. I'm tired of being strapped down, wheeled around, blinking lights in my eyes, needles, brain fried. I'm hungry. I don't want a tube in my nose. I want some pork fried rice, real food, won-ton soup, some fried chicken and mashed potatoes. A WHOLE chicken, potato salad, two double Quarter Pounders with Cheese and large fries Dunkin' Donuts glazed jelly filled double chocolate cinnamon sugar I want to kill something and eat it, a baby, or a pig, kill and eat it raw, I want to run naked through the Amazon in . . . in wherever it is, I want to be free, grow long hair, and live in a cave like ancient white people in Europe, I want to be Jimi or Jean-Michel I rather die I rather *die* than this shit.

"Shut up, will you? I can't understand a word you sayin', you big faggot. What you doing with your nipple pierced?"

He's behind me, I can't really see him, but I can feel the weight of his body pushing me down a long hall under blinding lights. My back is cold lying against metal. If we kill anybody, I had told her, it should be these motherfuckers out here, these perpetrator faggots or the police, look what they did to that guy Diallo.

"No, fuck the police. I want him dead dead DEAD. I'm not doing anything with you ever again if you don't do it. You say you love me, I *told* you what he did to me."

I'm a good boy I can't do that. That's crazy, girl! Crazy girl, crazy. No one understands me. No one understands me—

He leans over in my face. "Stop grunting, *pig*."

Why does he talk to me like that? This must be a prison, if this is a hospital, where are the doctors and nurses? I feel my heart rising in my throat like it's an elevator inside of me. I suck in my cheeks, the flesh inside my mouth, between my teeth, and then I bite down hard. The blood fills my mouth. I grunt, and when he leans in to taunt me again, I spit blood in his face.

"Ah! Ah!" he gasps. "Nigger, is you crazy!"

The smell of blood, his fist splits my lip, more blood flows, ignites me like a match to lighter fluid. I want to kill him, then fuck him, I feel myself getting hard. His fist upside my head sends me to black.

THE WATER IS BLUE. I'm in a room, on a bed, looking out a window at a black woman, a native type, with a basket on her head, walking down a road toward the ocean. Or was the shade drawn, with just the smell of the ocean wafting in through the window screen? Yes, he would not have

319

had the window open. There's a picture on the wall; maybe it was another place or time. I remember now: the woman in the painting, her large feet, the basket on her head, the picture-book blue water. Brother John is blowing me on the bed. I smell something like ocean water. I'm eating popcorn at home with My Lai watching *In the Company of Men* on DVD. I'm at Kmart, crying, when Snake gets us both busted because he was shoplifting. They let me go; I cry some more. My mother is behind me, her hand is on top of my hand, which is on top of the computer's mouse. I laugh when she says, *Click click.* The scenes coming through my head like this confuse me. I know I'm not awake. I'm afraid I'm dying. Very afraid. At first I didn't think death could happen to me. How is it possible? I'm young strong beautiful. I felt that way at St Ailanthus that morning, how is it possible? Their white faces glowing like the walking dead in horror flicks. J.J.! J.J.! Leave the premises immediately! Huh? I liked it there. What else? I try to remember more, but it's like there was no time before there and no time after. But I know a lot of time has passed. I'm sure of that. I must be old by now. And My Lai? Where's my wife? I'm standing in a black pond. I know where my feet are, know they're wet, but can't see them, can't see what's in front or in back, can't see the next step. In the dream the black water is rising. I stop it. I don't want to dream that.

On Sundays at St Ailanthus, we have pancakes with butter and maple syrup, Spring Tree Maple Syrup Grade A Dark Amber. I know because when I had KP, I poured the syrup from the can into stainless-steel pitchers that I would put on a cart, and when the cart was loaded with pitchers, I pushed the cart to the tables and put a pitcher on each table. I was happy working. I was happy anticipating the taste of the pancakes, the yellow salty butter and the maple syrup all mixed up in my mouth.

Now I'm in a place with no taste except my blood in my mouth and the smells of alcohol wipes and bleach. No My Lai's onigiri-and-curry cunt, her mouth swallowing my balls. No Brother John like a sex father or little kids waiting like rosebuds to open for me. No food here no music no touching. I love touching people, pressing against them in the subway, sticking my nose in people's armpits, sticking my fingers in every curry pot. What did I do? No girl to drive my dick in, cupping her ass, smelling her juice, screaming me, the taste of her nipples, my big tongue, lips sucking home. Alone like this I feel dead, wiped away by the marshmallow shoes, voices like wind rustling the tops of trees in scary movies the moon frozen full in the sky the killer's knife coming closer and closer. So how do I get to be a boy again?

What's the opposite of death? Drums. Beat. House. African Latin heart beating like beat beat the drums in Imena's class Jaime I remember him tan boy I know he loved me but he cut me!

"What for!"

"You know what for!"

SLASH. I scream and try to take the blade from him, he cuts my hand one two three CUT CUT CUT. But . . . but I thought you loved me, I'm screaming. My blood is turning everything red as I wipe my face with my bleeding hands. "I hate you. I hate your black ass, you fucking gorilla! You raped me!" Behind the veil of blood, I see the girl he is performing for. She's looking at him. I recognize her look, she's wondering. He's come to me, to cut, to prove he's not a faggot, to prove he's man. Then out of what seems like nowhere, it's a bunch of them. They move in on me punching kicking. Shithead! Maricón! Motherfucker! You black motherfucker!

"For God's sake!" he screams like the bitch he is. "I was a little boy. You made me! You *made* me!"

Shit, I'm thinking, *they* made me. Then there's no more thinking. I'm all the way down. They're kicking me.

"What the fuck are you assholes doing!" It's like a old man's voice, one of the park winos. Everything halts. Indecision. Then one of them kicks me again.

The ice flick of a switchblade. "Come on, sonny boys, I'll git at least one of you spics!" Then running. Heave a sigh of relief.

"I didn't do nothin' I didn't do nothin'," I mumble through the taste of blood.

"Don't care if you did, dat's what we got coppers for. Need to get someplace?"

"Thank you thank you, no, no. I just want to go home. I can walk. Thank you thank you."

I had forgot all that. The scars fade away or into other hurts. The first thing I remember is how his little lips tasted, the skin of his belly, curly nigger hairs around his thing big like a man's, different from Brother Samuel's blue-veined red hair. He didn't have to do that; being in our world didn't make him a faggot, it was just our world, what else were we gonna do? The brothers had us, *me*, I figured; I thought he, the kids, loved me. I thought that was love. I remember his penis in my mouth my penis in Brother John's mouth My Lai's clit in my mouth my heart opens in my mouth her clit pulsing like a heart, *her* heart, in my mouth. She really loves me. She, we, danced; I thought that was love. Then why am I here without her?

"You don't know what love is. You find out one day."

Ah, yes. Roman. Roman said pussies could not be trusted. And they stink. He was wrong about that. My Lai doesn't stink; she taste good. I can't remember the last time I ate something. Is it dinnertime, lunch, breakfast? My mother used to fix me oatmeal with butter and a maple-sugar bear melting at the bottom of the bowl. Tears are starting to roll down my cheeks. I can't wipe my eyes. I feel cold shivery then hot burning up. My mouth's dry. I see my tongue crawl out my mouth like a pink slug. I eye it on the pillow. It looks back at me as if to say, How'd we get this way? Yes, you're crazy, it says, this is your tongue. It crawls up beside me on the pillow and starts to weep. I'm so lonely, it says, I'm so lonely I could die.

It's time to wake up if I'm asleep. I'm way drugged; this is something different than I ever had. Straitjacket, that's how I felt with Roman. Just be still, hold back, don't kill, just get through the shit, *endure* this faggot and he'll give me a life. And I was right, wasn't I? But what it took, what it took. And now this, what is this shit here? I didn't go through all that to end up here.

The door swings open. Black face, white coat, it's one of the ones who wheel me and stick me with needles.

"Get up!" he shouts, his voice turning to little black monkeys swinging from trees screeching Get up! Get up! Get up! They scare me. Anyway, I can't get up. What is he talking about?

"Get up, stupid. You ain' that high, you only had a quarter of what they been giving up."

Stupid? I'm not stupid. I may be bad, but I'm not stupid. Or did something change? Have they changed me with all their shit?

He kicks the bed. "You gotta shower, and we gotta clean that fucking bed."

What's he talking about? Is he crazy, not just peanuthead mean but wacko?

"Come on, man, you gonna make me really hate you, dude. I *said* get up. You ain' as crazy as you make out."

I jut my chin up, so I'm staring at the ceiling and the wall behind me.

"You got two minutes to quit the Looney Tunes routine and get up."

I can't get up; if I could get up, I would have gotten up a long time ago.

"I would appreciate your cooperation, you dumb motherfucker."

Dumb? I am a bright boy, my future is shining light.

"Come on, gorilla."

I'm a boy. Not a gorilla. Unless this is hell and I got turned into one. Did I get turned into a gorilla? I can't see for all the fog, yellow fog. I'm paralyzed in this body that is not a gorilla, maybe he sees a gorilla. Maybe that is hell, not being seen for who you are.

"Listen," he says into the fog.

"I—"

"I don't care about your fucking 'I.' *I* said get the fuck up. The doctor wants to see you."

He shakes the rail at the foot of the bed. "Fuck it."

He leaves the room, but the fog stays. I lay there. He comes back. How long was he gone? An hour, a minute?

"How long you gonna lay up and look at the ceiling, stupid?"

Am I high or crazy? How long *have* I been laying up, looking at the ceiling? My tongue feels like a boat sinking. Words sink down in me, their sounds disappearing—is this their dope or the new way I am? I want to flush myself away like a bowel movement. Look in a mirror and say I hate you I hate you I hate you.

You never talk you never talk you never talk, she says like a girl. Because she never stops talking, you are always talking I know everything about your childhood, your toys, tutors, and parents you hate. There's no room for my big clumsy thick words. My words feel like constipated hard balls of shit I keep inside me. Why don't these motherfuckers just kill me if I did such crazy shit I got to be treated like this? If this guy says one more word to me, I will, I will, I don't know what. Actually, I don't know why I'm raving. I feel better than I've felt in a while.

I look at the fool standing at the foot of the bed who thinks *I'm* a fool and say, "What time did you say the doctor would be here?"

"You fuckin' bastard! You motherfuckin' bastard!"

His hollering scares me, and I want to slip back to where I've been, silence, but I can't. Whatever's been making me android man, or whatever you call this state I been in, ain't flooding my brain no more. I'm still fucked up, but not paralyzed with their shit.

"So what is you, one of them idiot savants or some shit, only you don't draw bridges, you just come up with one intelligent sentence a year?"

A year? Jesus! Does anybody know my name? I'm going to kill you, motherfucker. That's gonna be my "next sentence." Without looking I can see him, big grinning skullhead nigger.

"Alright, nigger, I done tol' you, git up, the doctor's coming. You got to get cleaned up. We can do it easy or hard or, you know what, you dumb motherfucker, we can not do it at all. Jus' shoot you up and forget about your black ass, fast-track you to Harry Potter. Know what that is, stupid? Code for potter's field, you dumb motherfucker."

Squeezing my eyes shut, I see skulls floating around the room. I try to shit more. I can't. *Shoot you up.* I just want to give up. Why are they fucking with me? I thought I hated white people and faggots because of the brothers. But what is it with this shit here, these niggers? Now what do I hate?

"Look, stupid, I know you hear me 'cause they letting you hear—you ain't as high as you been. But we can have you swinging from the treetops again, motherfucker. I'm telling you, get up now or stay the fuck down, I mean that. Get up or stay down."

Who is he to tell me some shit like that, get up or stay down? He's a small guy. I could knock him down and leave here. Whatever, *wherever* here is. I don't have to know where I am to get out. Suppose you step out and it's the North Pole in the middle of a blizzard or a really big hospital spaceship. That's crazy, but ain't that what I am now? How do you knock someone out without killing them? Suppose I kill him? Shit, how do you knock someone out *and* kill them? Maybe I couldn't knock him out, maybe he knows karate or has a gun. Can I even get up? If I want to get out, I've got to get up. I'm scared. I'm scared I'm going to get up and my feet won't be there, or they'll be shrunk from voodoo powder sprinkled on them like Jaime said his grandmother did his grandpapi's dick, I had forgotten him. No, I had remembered him? What time is it? When does the doctor come, why am I scared of this little nigger, what does he have except his syringes, if I ever get a hold of one I'm gonna stick him see how he likes it, what have I done to be here, I deserve an explanation, hey I'm human why—

"Why?" I groan.

"Why what, motherfucker! I know you better get up, take those shitty clothes off, and walk your ass to the showers."

Take my clothes off, walk to the shower? Walk? The shower? That could be a million miles away. It could be like the Indians on the Trail of Tears. These people could be Nazis, I could be walking myself to the gas chamber, or hooks could come out of the drain and pull me down like in one of those Halloween horror flicks, dioxin could come out the showerhead or instead of water shooting out of the holes in the showerhead, *worms*! Tiny little threadworms that go up your nose, bore holes through your skin, swim around in your blood, and lay eggs in your heart, ahhh!! Stop! this crazy shit, I tell myself, and try to think like I have some sense, but it's like trying to nail Jell-O to a tree. What monkey seems to be telling me is someone is coming to see me, I been in a hospital, is this a hospital, for a year? Longer, less? How come no one comes to see about me? Where are my clothes, my jeans? I see blurred shapes, rats' feet whisper

whisper. Am I like Rip Van Winkle, I went to sleep young, woke up old? Maybe I am forty years old or some shit. I don't want no more needles.

I'm surprised to find my feet aren't shackled. Because my hands were, I didn't even try to move my feet. I felt paralyzed. The hallway to the showers seems like something out of a movie, blinding bright lights like I'm being filmed. I'm that guy in *Dead Man Walking*, being led to the electric chair, that song by Springsteen comes on and your heart is bursting, it's a moment of artistic genius, one like *I* wanted to make one day. Now I never will, not in here, not having *been* in here, even if I do get out. He didn't even get an Oscar for that shit. Maybe I did do something awesome before I got here. Maybe it was too far out, radical. Radical and far out. Maybe I'm a political prisoner and it's just a matter of time before voices around the world rise up on my behalf like one of those people Scott is always talking about, Saro-Wiwa or somebody like that. But no one knows I'm here. Anyway, for the people to rise up for you, you have to have risen up for the people. I never even had a chance to do that. I feel the tickle of a dry piece of something fall down and out of my pants leg. It's a dried piece of shit. I can smell myself.

"Eck!" from the guard. Guard? Executioner? Drone flunky drudge? I'm not a political prisoner being led to the gas chamber. I'm a little kid being made to take a shower, to wash away my filth. I shouldn't mind, but I do, what else do I have? Maybe I did that shit—shitting because I was crazy to keep them off me; in that case I wasn't crazy. But I think I was just mad. I don't know what has happened to me since I been in here.

"Don't stop walking, and when we get in there, don't think I'm wiping that shit off your big butt. You patients are crazy, man!"

Why do black people always have shit-ass jobs where you can't do nothing but hate them? I rather be a criminal, which I'm not, than do stupid shit fucking with people.

"Don't stop walking."

Did I stop walking?

"Turn left. Here's some soap, stupid. If I go take a piss, am I gonna come back and find you done killed yourself?"

What can I say to that?

"Not that I care, but I don't want to lose my job. Yuk-yuk."

An urge to totally break him surges up, send him home to his wifey crying. He's probably too stupid to have a wife. The urge goes back wherever it came from, and I hold out my hand for the soap.

"At least you don't have to worry about dropping it. Yuk-yuk."

The showers are in a room tiled in green from the floor to the ceiling, no stalls, everyone can see everyone, *could* see. I'm the only one here today, just me in a green room with eight showers.

"Hurry the fuck up!" he shouts from it sounds like somewhere way down the hall.

I smell cigarette smoke, hear a radio:

WBGO.FM every Saturday morning from ten till two, the Rhythm Revue with Felix Hernandez!

It's Saturday? Doctors don't come on Saturday, do they? Yeah, I guess, maybe, I don't know. I'm feeling confused now. What's gonna come out of the shower if I turn it on? I hope it is gas or anthrax or some shit. I don't care, long as it's not worms! Thin white threadworms that penetrate your skin and invade your major organs until you're a teeming mass of worms. Worms crawling out your nose, your ears, your mouth. Worms'll be coming out my dick, my asshole. "UGH!"

The sounds of the radio go down, the smell of smoke comes nearer.

"Ugh yourself! Motherfucker, I know you better turn that water on and get your ass cleaned up. Fool shitting on yourself. You ain' gonna aggravate me like you did Watkins. I'll come in here and do a midnight barbecue on your ass by myself, you fuck with me. I know you ain' crazy enough to like being fried. Is you? *Is you?* I know you better turn that water on."

It was December of 1964 that Billy Stewart wrote and recorded the song that crossed him over to the Pop charts. Regarded as a soul classic now, it went on to #6 on the R&B charts and #26 on the Pop charts. Here he is, Billy Stewart, "I Do Love You"

I do love you

Yes, I do girl

The sound of his voice is like warm hands on my heart. I do love you. Yes, I do girl. It's such a strong love music. He's singing from his heart. He means it. Whoever he is, he means it. He loves someone. I wonder what he looks like. He's black or a black-sounding white. No, 1964, the disc jockey said, back then white people hadn't taken it all yet. He's black! *(It's not you people is so talented or been through so much*—Shut up, Roman! *No, let me fucking finish. It's not you people is so talented or been through so much, compare what happen to you to what happen to us—you is like a bathtub we is the ocean.* I'll kill you, faggot. *You can't, I'm not here! What you got is wasted on you people, like being young on kids; we do you a favor to take it. You know what Roman think*—I don't care. *You should.)*

I do love you I pray for your love

The singing is bringing My Lai, her lips, slow dragging with her. I did so much for you, Roman is crying now. I never have a boyfriend who is not black. You know what they call fags like that My Lai said, dinge queens! We laughed. I turn on the faucet. Water! comes out the shower-head, too hot at first, then I adjust it. Warm, it feels so good, no worms but water and words from a song inside feeling.

I do love you.

When was the last time I felt good? The music gets louder.

PLOP! A wet washcloth lands at my feet.

"Use it!"

I do, vigorously rubbing the bar of soap into the wet washcloth, then rubbing the cloth under my arms, separate my butt cheeks, get the crack of my ass, the lather from the soap and the filth from my body run brown, then clear, down the drain. I make the water a little hotter and just stand there letting it run down my shoulders and back, I'm free from evil worms and pain.

"Hey, stupid! You been in there almost half an hour. How long does it take to take a shower? Come on out of there!"

When I get back to the room, the bed has been made up in thick white sheets, making it look like a mummy. The shower has worn me out. I climb into the bed and breathe in the fresh bleached-clean smell of the sheets. My head sinks to the pillow, and even before I fall asleep, I'm dreaming. Or did I really get up and creep to the door, look both ways, and, not seeing anybody, step out into the hallway, turn left, and start to walk down the hallway? The sparkling linoleum is white, clean, and cold under my feet. Cautiously, I open the first door I come to—a big sink, mops, buckets, and brooms. I close the door. Where am I? I can *feel* people. I know I'm not alone here. I keep walking and come to another door. I open it and enter a long white-walled corridor, at the end of the corridor there is another door. I open that door and step into a big room that smells like piss. The room is bright with high ceilings. Sunlight is streaming in from windows so high they almost reach the ceiling. I look up at the ceiling, then down at a row of beds lining each side of the room. At first I don't know what it is. The bright light obscures my sight. Then I see the people. Even though the smell is kicking me, I step closer. A man is lying in the bed closest to me naked on a bare plastic-covered mattress. He's curled up in a fetal position like a seed in a pod, hands tucked under his chin, toes digging into the mattress. Buzz-cut hair, large *Star Trek*–ish ears, his elbows and thin thighs hide his privates. There's no sheet or blanket on the bed, nothing, just him asleep in a puddle of yellow piss glistening on the plastic-covered mattress. On the bed next to him is a naked woman flat on her back, her flaccid breasts flopped down the side of her body, her hands curled like claws at the ends of arms bent at the elbows.

I hear a grunt, and between the first two beds a man is sitting on the floor, his back to the wall, one leg folded under him, the other bent at the knee, sticking out at a weird angle. It was like I was stuck in a dream or a movie with no sound track until he grunted. Now I hear low moans, wheezes, cough-cough, sniff, rattle, and groans coming from the twisted shapes in the beds, maybe fifty beds. What is this, a hospital? Well, where's everybody else? I don't know what it is, I know what it feels like, like I've stepped into a . . . a garbage can or something, a human landfill. I start to creep backward, away, step step. Then I turn and run to the door, fling it open, but the long white corridor is gone and I'm in another room. The first thing I see is a big television set hanging from the ceiling and people in wheelchairs, fifteen or twenty of them, their mouths gaped open like baby birds', staring at the TV. There's another group, maybe ten, sitting or laying on some benches. A commercial is playing on the TV. Tampons make a girl free from monthly worries or accidents, and she gets into an SUV and drives away. Then the TV shuts off, and one by one they turn their heads away from it and look at me. *Shit, I didn't do it!* I think, not say, because there's no speech here. One guy who'd been laid out like a corpse on one of the benches rises to look at me. It's Richie Jackson, lying-ass Richie Jackson! He's shrunken and twisted like he has polio or something. One arm folded to his chest, the hand curled over and useless-looking hangs from his wrist, bent. Only his eyes seem the same, big brown little-kid-looking. I hear a SKIRR-SQUEEEAK! and see one of the chairs start to roll toward me. It's Slavery Days!

"You know what you did to me!" She hikes up her skirt. She's flashing her old pussy.

Fuck her, she's crazy. I ain't did nothing to her. It should be the other way around, what she did to me!

"Boy!" she hollers. And like it was a command with her leading the way, all the wheelchairs start to roll and creak toward me! I turn around to run back to my bed, but when I get to where the white door leading to the corridor was, there's only a little blue door. I crash through the little blue door into the hallway, but once I'm back in the hallway, it's like either I'm getting taller or the hallway is shrinking. I stoop over and keep running until I can't anymore, because the hallway is getting smaller and smaller. I have to drop down onto my hands and knees. The hallway is a tunnel now. I hear footsteps behind as if someone is coming up to the door. Then I hear the door slam! I try to turn my head and shoulders to look back, but I can't; there's not enough room. My shoulders are almost touching the fishy-smelling wall of the tunnel. Disgust fills me as cysts swell from the walls of the tunnel and burst one by one, spewing tiny little worms that start to crawl over me. Ugh! The tunnel is touching my shoulders now. In front of me, a cyst super-swells like bubble gum until its glistening skin bursts, spewing dozens of tiny spiders. I'm sweating like crazy, and it stinks, sweat, fishy smell, and cigarettes. I have to keep batting my eyelids to keep the tiny spiders from crawling into my eyes. There's not enough room for me to crawl on my hands and knees anymore, so I contract my abdominal muscles, hunching my butt up to the top of the tunnel, then I contract my butt muscles and release my abdominals, propelling my body forward, contract butt release gut, contract butt release gut, inching along like a caterpillar. I'm scared the tunnel walls are going to crush me before I can get out. I can't wipe the worms or spiders off, and they smell or something smells like old garbage. My heart is beating so fast it's almost vibrating. Breathe *breathe*, don't hyperventilate, I tell myself. I look ahead of me, the light is brighter. Almost somewhere! Next thing you know, I'm coming out of the tunnel head and shoulders first. When my arms get free, I use them to pull myself all the way out of the tunnel. I tumble onto the black, rain-slick asphalt of a parking lot. I don't look back, because I know the tunnel is gone. A warm, misty rain is coming down. Lights from the parking lot shine down on the few cars parked here and there throughout the lot between gleaming white lines. I don't see any people. The blue-black sky is studded with blazing stars. If it wasn't for the parking lot cars, I could be in a Van Gogh painting. Ahead and to the side of me is a row of motel rooms in a U shape around the parking lot. The neat numbered doors are all shut against the night. The cars seem rooted. No one comes out of the rooms to get them, no vehicles from outside wheel into the lot. No noise, no sound coming from anywhere. Where am I? I don't know which way to go, what to do. I'm thinking I have to get back when a light comes on in one of the rooms. Number 6. I walk toward it.

I'm standing in front of the door, looking at the light coming from behind the drawn blinds, when I notice the blinds are *outside* the window. The blinds start to rise by themselves as I'm checking them out. I'm scared, and my bare feet are starting to get cold. I don't really want to, but my feet step closer to the window, maybe they are thinking about the warmth that might be inside? Inside the room there is a raggedy man in jeans who looks like he's drunk. His mumbled curses are the first sounds I've heard since I tumbled into the parking lot. He's standing in front of a TV screen. Whatever he's seeing is making him mad; wobbling on drunk legs, he starts screaming at the TV. I don't see anyone else in the room, and I can't see what's making him so mad, but he scares me with his drunk, defeated face. I got to get out of here. I can't stop trembling. My chest tightens. He's lighting a cigarette now. I don't smoke, I think, then think funny I thought that. He's smoking now. His room changes to a control room hung with dozens of TV monitors that look like the multiple eyes of a bee. Please, please, I rather not have no eyes than see this. I will myself not to see it. My chest really hurts now, I can smell the smoke from his cigarette, I start to weep, but my eyes are dry, No, no, I'm shaking my head and crying.

"Hey there, are you OK, friend?"

I open my eyes, sit up. I'm in my bed again and looking at a man who is flicking ash from a cigarette into an ashtray on the bedside table. Who's he? What's he doing in here smoking? I lurch away, falling flat on my back, squeezing my eyes shut.

"Open your eyes, Abdul."

Abdul? Who's calling me? All those places, has this all been a dream? Will I wake up and be home? Or dead? Or am I still here, in this place, this room, these stupid white walls, these stupid white clothes? If I am in this place, if it's not a dream, how do I get out of here? What did I do to get here? He's close. I can't hear his breathing, but I can feel him, *smell* him, cigarettes, coffee, and hospital. Is he drinking coffee? Where's the filthy man in the motel room? Maybe I'm still in the dream? No, I'm wide awake with my eyes closed. I don't want to open my eyes. He's moving. Coming closer?

"Well, are you going to open your eyes or not?"

"Why should I?"

"Well, it's customary when two people talk for them to look at each other."

"I'm not talking to you."

"Yes you are."

"No I'm not."

"Abdul, don't be ridiculous, you're talking to me right now."

"You know what I mean," I say.

"No I don't."

"Yes you do, liar," I insist. He thinks he's smart.

"Would you open your eyes, Abdul?"

This shit is getting tired. I'm not sure what to do; I just wish he would go away, but he isn't going away. That's obvious. The light coming through the skin of my closed eyelids is blood orange. I want music. I don't want this shit. What for? Open, closed, what's the difference? Shit sucks. But I want to get out. I really want to get out of this bed, this *place*, wherever it is. If I open my eyes, what? Blaring fluorescents, sheets, walls white. Hell is your eyes open? I'm starting to sweat. I want to wipe away the irritating beads of sweat I feel rolling down the side of my face. I want to go to sleep. I haven't done anything to anybody. I have a right to sleep if I want to. What can I think of to go back to sleep? In dance class we use deep breathing to relax: IN-2-3-4-5-6-7-8, OUT-2-3-4-5-6-7-8, *2*-2-3-4-5-6-7-8, *3*-2-3-4-5-6-7-8, Git your ass outta here *4*-2-3-4-5-6-7-8, *5*-2-3-4-5-6-7-8 . . .

I hear a chair moving, yeah, pushing back. Yeah, he's walking to the door? I keep breathing, it's working: 1-2-3-4-go back-5-6-7-8-where you came from. His footsteps are disappearing. He's gone. I open my eyes and prop myself up on my elbows.

"Come, come," says the man, standing just outside the doorway in a brown jacket and pants, with a white turban on his head. "Did you think I would be that easy to get rid of?"

I collapse back in the bed, turning my head away from his voice. I feel silly and dumb. Why doesn't he get his ass out of here? I squeeze my eyes shut, see a beach, a flock of seagulls rise up over the crashing waves to the shore caw caw caw—

"Come, come, Abdul, this is very time-consuming. I'm going to come back into the room and sit down in the chair. And I want you to open your eyes."

I sigh, you win, fuck me, give me some more shit to fuck me up so I can't think straight, talk, think, remember, get up; I don't care. Bring on your straitjackets, faggot motherfucker; it's your world, ain't it? All I want is to get out of here; do whatever you want, just let me out of here. Show me how much shit I have to eat, bring it on forever and all motherfucking time. I hate you and will murder your mother, your kids, I'll grab your kids by the feet and bash their heads in. I open my eyes.

"I'm going to walk back into the room now, Abdul, and sit in the chair next to your bed. I am not going to touch you in any way unless you want to shake hands with me, maybe you do, maybe you don't." He's walking as he's talking. And he's talking as if he's trying to soothe some volatile unpredictable crazy nigger. He sits down in a chair next to the bed.

"My name is Dr Sanjeev—Dr See from here on out if that's too big a mouthful. How are you today?"

Fuck you, that's how I am today. I don't take his extended hand. Where's he from, India? What's up with the turban? No doctor clothes. His jacket has leather patches at the elbows. That's pretentious. He's not riding no fucking horse. I remember asking Mrs Washington why do those guys need leather patches on their jackets? He's dark-skinned, not as dark as me, but dark, straight hair, a nice-looking guy.

"Mind if I smoke?"

"Bad for you."

"So you do talk."

I'm surprised myself. I was starting to forget how I sounded. They say their shit out loud, and I answer in my head. But everything in me is so fucking *in* it's disappearing.

"This is the first time we've been formally introduced, although I've actually been in here several times talking to you. Do you remember those times?"

"What do you want?" Let's get to it, dude.

He smokes Marlboros. He has his own little beanbag ashtray. Was it in his pocket?

"Can I have one?"

He gives me a hard look, takes a drag, and snuffs out his cigarette. "Not right now."

I just said the first thing out of my mouth. I feel the opposite of how I been feeling, drowsy and spaced, or at least I want to feel different, want to speed, or maybe it's just that I want my own adrenaline back. I feel like maybe they got me on something making me up, but it ain't enough!

"What do I want? Well, I want to talk to you, get to know you some, and see if I can help."

He already knows me if he's been in here checking on me and shit. He knew my name, he probably knows how old I am, for sure how long I been here, what the fuck is wrong with me, why I got put in here, or whatever the fuck happened. Should I let him know how much I don't know, yesterday, what, nothing! It's like a thick coat of dust on a picture, wipe some away and what you see is that particular part. Yesterday I don't even remember what I was seeing. But today all I can think of is St Ailanthus: Mrs Washington's face, the brothers, my dorm room, clean and empty, the beds made up tight: Bobby Jackson bed number one, Richard Stein number two, Angel Hernandez number three. Omar Washington number four, number five Malik Edwards, and number six me. Then Alvin, Louie Hernandez, Billy Song, Etheridge, Jaime, and at the end Amir. Bacon and eggs on Saturday, prunes and oatmeal with brown sugar on Monday. Am I in New York? I know I'm in America from Watkins and his radio, I *think*. Amir loved oatmeal with brown sugar and butter. Art class, Amir was the best, head bent over construction paper, scissors moving, hands shining. I had forgotten about him, those guys were my buddies. Amir had AMIR THE ARTIST written on his notebook.

He pulls another smoke out, fingers it but doesn't light up.

"And you, Abdul, what do you want?"

I want to know how old I am, how long have I been in here. Oh, fuck him. Fourth position, I prepare, pull up plié and pirouette! One two three four five six seven—the audience gasps, I'm still turning, I can't stop. I'm shaking; I'm hungry in a weird way, like in my brain, like my stomach is dead or something. I squeeze my eyes shut and scoot further down under the covers.

"Hey, hey, where you going, man?"

Figure it out. Then I think I want something. "Music."

"Huh? You want the radio?"

Good doctor. I'm shaking so much my teeth are chattering.

"That was nice, wasn't it, Smith's radio. There are plenty of radios around here. I'll see what I can do."

I don't say nothing else. I'm not being mean; I really am going like fetal, shaking bad. I can't control it. I have to curl up in a ball to stop it. I press my clenched fist against my forehead. I feel the rough cuts crossing my wrists and open my eyes to look at them.

"Abdul? Do you remember that?"

I stare. The left wrist looks uglier than the right.

"You came in in pretty bad shape. You've been under observation and in isolation. I'd like to see you moved to another part of the complex, a ward with other guys, and see where to take it after that. What do you think?"

What do I think? I don't want to be in no fucking ward. I don't want to be here period! Are you crazy? That's what I think. I want to get the fuck out of here. My anger stops my body from trembling.

"Sanjeev? What kind of name is that?"

"It's my first name, actually, but I use it as a last name in this country."

I'm trying not to get chatty, but words keep coming out my mouth. "Why?"

"Well, it got made into a last name when I came to this country. You know, for example if your name is John or Ibrahim and people are calling you Mr John or Mr Ibrahim. What difference does it make? The village where I came from, people didn't have last names. I was Sanjeev until my family—"

Oh, la-di-da, I don't want to hear about your fucking family, you fucking whatever kind of nigger you are.

"You mentioned music. What kinds of music do you like to listen to?"

I'm so fucking sleepy right now. This dude just does not get it. What kind of music do I like? Hey DJ, how about some Coltrane, "A Love Supreme" or—

"Charlie Parker."

That's who I really like, and Erykah Badu, is he hip to her?

Something is coming down now, sleep a river. I'm in another white room, water is running, who's banging on the door screaming? I'm really nervous, too nervous to be dreaming, but I'm dreaming now. I can't see how I'm going to get out of this. I take the plastic party knife and start to slice and slash, and sob hard, then harder. It's me screaming. I sit up in the bed; sweat stings my eyes, I put my arms around my knees, hugging them to my chest. I look in the doctor's dark face. I'm angry. My heart is closed, but my mouth opens with a mind of its own.

"I remember."

"What do you remember?"

Nothing, sucker, not a goddamned thing, homeboy. I lean back, stretching out in bed, then roll over onto my side, rubbing the twinge in my shoulder that is turning into an ache. A reminder of the last time I trusted anybody. Them rushing toward me, blank white faces, long vestments swishing like black knives, their voices coming at me, light pouring through the windows shining like Christ! I'm rising toward them; I always remember that—not running away but walking toward them. I was theirs, wasn't I? A child who had found my way home. They didn't really send me away to lose myself in the forest. Like Hansel and Gretel. Then they grabbed me, twisted my arm, and took me down. I thought my arm was going to come out of my shoulder and just fall off my body, it felt like my shoulder was just sitting in napalm, burning. It hadn't broken me when they sodomized me, pinched my navel with nail clippers, alienated me from the other kids and myself. We'll take care of you, you'll always have a home at St Ailanthus. All that shit they did, and I never told on them. My heart is in my shoulder, a soft-tissue injury that will never totally heal, breaking, it's just breaking.

"Abdul, you were getting ready to say something?" Dr Sanjeev.

No I wasn't. Go away, I think, and will myself to sleep. The last thing I hear is the chair move back and his footsteps disappear.

WHEN I WAKE UP, I can't move my arms, they've been restrained. I'm on my back, looking at the long annoying tubes of light stuck to the ceiling. They never turn the lights off. Did I miss something, or is it just when the fuck they want to strap me in they strap me in?

"Abdul?"

I feel the weight of drugs in my body. What's the purpose of this shit? I'm waking up after being out for five minutes or five hours or five days? How much time has passed? Time worries me like a mother.

"Abdul?"

Why be bothered with his voice if the end result is being strapped down and shot up?

"I just wanna dance."

"Well, ah, well, there's no law that says you can't dance in here if you want. I certainly don't care."

I feel his warm hands on my skin, hear the Velcro ripping open. But now that I can move, I don't. How much of what I remember is yesterday or the distant past? What's the last memory I have outside this place? I don't think it's a real memory but more like a fact: I was walking, like I did a lot, and I was young and strong. I don't know if that's how things really were or what, but they *must* have been at some point: walking, strong and young, having what I want, having what other people want. Yes, but when, where, *who*, even? Is that me anymore? I can't figure it out. I turn over onto my side, pull my knees up fetal, I want to go back to sleep. I almost am anyway; whatever they gave me has me on extreme slo-mo. I don't want to move. I close my eyes and see Roman's face, but it's a young face, younger than I ever knew him. He's saying something I can't hear. A lot of times in my dream, I can't hear what people are saying.

"He's saying something I can't hear."

"If you *could* hear him, what would he be saying?"

He's gone, good. Am I talking or sleeping now? Talking, sleeping, dreaming different things?

"One day we were all hanging out—"

"Who is 'all'?"

"Me, Amy, Scott, Snake, and My Lai, so we're all hanging out having fun, and Jaime walks in."

"Where's this?"

"Starbucks, Astor Place. And Jaime, he's like nowhere now, but for a while he was trying to dance and shit. He didn't really have it in him, and he was so small; that might be a plus for a bitch, but it's a minus for a man. So we're, like, talking, laughing, and into our lattes and so on, and he just invites himself to sit down. Well, OK, wrong thing to do, but if you were going to do that, just sit your ass down and shut up. But no, he starts in with all this shit about St Ailanthus. I just look at him like he's crazy when he starts that 'remember when' shit. Scott used to take, maybe he still does, Imena's class in Harlem; that's how Jaime found out about Herd, not from me. He wanted to be a part of Herd, but you know it wasn't happening.

"'Remember that time at St Ailanthus when Brother Samuel flipped your ass and body-slammed your ass and you peed all over yourself while he had you pinned down? No? What about the time Brother John, Brother Samuel, and Brother Bill kicked your ass?'

"I, like, totally ignore him, raise my eyebrows like, Is this dude crazy or what?

"'Well man,' he goes, 'what *do* you remember?'

"My Lai is feeling me, raises her eyebrow, and looks Jaime's pitiful ass dead in the eye and says, 'Why don't you shut up, bitch, and get the fuck out of here.'

"'Yeah, *whatever* this is, this is not the place for it.' Scott.

"'You don't remember trying to rape me when I was a little boy.'

"'Little boy! Motherfucker, you're older than I am!'

"This has an effect on everybody, like who is this hairy-ass mother-fucker?

"Amy who's, like, been in stunned mode says, 'Well, that is . . . is some-thing. How old are you, Jaime?'

"'Twenty.'

"'Abdul is only nineteen,' My Lai comes in hard. 'So when did this shit happen? Not like I really fuckin' care or want to know. I mean, like, dude, you *always* been older than him.'

"'You're not going to get away with this.' Jaime.

"'You're crazy,' I scoff, 'totally wrecked, man. If anything, it was you pulling the creep on us younger kids.'

"'Your coffee is cold, dude, and your shit seems kinda tired, maybe you should go home and get some rest, you know.' My Lai. Then she says, 'You know,' again.

"He doesn't get she will fuck him up.

"'Like, leave, dude, you're not welcome here.'

"He gets up with her staring him down, and I don't see him anymore for a long time."

I'm tired of talking. I take the skin of my wrist into my mouth and bite down hard, hard as I can. Blood fills my mouth drops down cherry red onto the white sheets.

"Oh no, Abdul! Oh no!" he groans.

Oh yes, I think. Who do you think you are? You just walk in here with your fucking turban black ass and start talking shit to me. I ain't crazy don'tcha know who I am? Who we are, My Lai said we were dancing death—more powerful than life. I miss her—voices are rushing down the hall in white padded shoes. It's the nappy-headed assholes coming to tie me down and inject me. Watkins and his crew! Well, come on, mother-fucker. He busts into the room. Ah, I leap out of the bed, slam him dead in the jaw with my fist dripping with blood. Down that black mother-fucker goes. Ha, ha! Then he's up, screaming. Everybody is screaming. The doctor and the marshmallow-shoe crew is holding back Watkins, who got up screaming.

"You black motherfucker! I'm going to kill you!" Watkins.

"Watkins, get back, he's not dangerous!" Dr See.

"He's not dangerous, he just hit me!" He breaks loose, they get him again.

"He's bleeding—"

"Fuck that shit, his ass is going to die or wish he was dead."

I already wish I was dead.

"Get out, Watkins!"

My blood is all over everything, the white-suited little black flunkies, the sheets, the white walls.

"Get out of here right now!"

"What do you mean, 'Get out'! I have the right to defend myself, you Arab motherfucker."

"I mean it, get out of here! And if these boys don't get you out, I'll call security. And if I have to do that, *that* will be your job!"

"Are you crazy, I was doing my job. I don't have to be hit by nobody! Ain't *nobody* gonna hit me and I don't defend myself, motherfucker!"

"You are not defending yourself now. The boy is not moving, he has backed off. You are trying to retaliate, and you don't have that right. Look, if you don't get out of here, I will have your job."

"And I will have your ass."

"Please!" Dr See claps his hands like a sultan and says to the crew, "Get him *out* of here."

They drag him out still frothing at the mouth. I lay back down on the bed, pull the bloody sheet over my head, even though I know it's too late to act like nothing's happened.

"Why did you do that?" he shouts.

"I'm going to keep on doing it."

"Why?"

"He was going to hit—"

"Why did you bite yourself!"

"It's my body!" I shout.

"Oh, great, that makes a lot of sense."

"Is that why I'm here, because I make a lot of sense?"

I hear feet in soft shoes coming down the hall fast, an army of them, ten twenty thirty faces like black death masks. Dr See gives orders, a cold alcohol wipe, needle sting, then *plunge.* It gets dark in me, then outside of me, and I leave.

PLIÉ STRAIGHTEN RELEVÉ, tendu into second, plié, straighten, I really get off on opening out into plié, pressing my muscles, antagonist agonist, to open my thighs as I bend my knees. They don't want to open, the muscles, tendons, ligaments want to stay closed, be comfortable, not hurt. But I press on and out.

Roman says, "Bend, open wider. Put your heart into it. Everything you do, put your heart into it. You as strong a dancer as your plié is strong. I seen a few dancers who is not got good deep pliés, but not many. You got a good body; work on putting something into it, saying something. Every time you move, you should be saying something. People look at you and read your story like a book. Did you know that? That's all we have is our bodies, dancers, and you can't hide or lie. If you do, nobody want to look at you. You hiding, Abdul. Show me your heart. Don't worry about fouettés, so what are you going to be, the swan in act three where she does thirty-two fouettés? The black swan?"

I don't know what he's talking about, I had never seen *Swan Lake,* but I kept that, "the black swan." That's what I was, no more ugly black duck! My Lai hated him because he liked me. She hated the way he taught his class, his accent, she made fun of how he walked. She was so mean sometimes. I fell in love with her body, her smell, her juice way before I fell in love with her. First it was just the way the bitch *moved,* then the tough pieces of her cunt hair, her briny cunt, hips, and tits—so hard it was like sucking a lollipop. I grooved on that, I never even knew I wanted to do that before, suck a girl's tits. She would start to writhe and arch.

"Put your finger in me, put your finger—no, go like this, yeah, in an' out like you're fucking me, don't stop sucking my tit, stupid! You gotta do both at the same time. This is way cool," she panted, cumming on top of my fingers. I felt for her what I think Roman felt for me, desire and terror, but I didn't have what he had. He had control. My Lai had the money. I loved her, love her. But I don't know if she loves me. She only said it once, and that was when she . . . well, whatever. I don't want to think about that. I call up the picture of her in my mind laying on my bed her thighs open as a baby's, to ask my own thighs in class to open past that point where my body thinks it can go. I pretend her body is mine and push my legs open; my legs believe the picture in my head more than they believe their own almost-hard-as-steel tendons and tight ligaments. When I'm fucking her, she cums in heaves and spasms; I feel like a volcano, rock outside and liquid on fire inside. She taste like water, tears, piss, curry powder sometimes, not like how Roman said she would, "Stinking pussies!" He hates girls, and how would he know if their pussies stink? "I like how you taste," I tell her between catching her clit in my lips till she screamed. I don't feel alone when I'm slamming. I ain't afraid to die when I'm slamming. Tombé pas de bourreé, tendu, fourth position, plié TURN TURN *TURN*!

Mornings intermediate advanced ballet, afternoons contemporary jazz, evenings we have rehearsals. For a while it's like having parents: not having to worry about money for classes or clothes, dancing on scholarship, living off handouts from Scott's and My Lai's parents. Restitution, My Lai called it. Freeloading? Where'd bucks like that come from? Endless, no fucking bottom, how could they afford to just give and give to their kids, while me, Amir, Jaime, Etheridge, and the rest of us little shits lined up in front of our pee plastic mattresses in our striped jailhouse pajamas like we were in Siberia or some fucking place? Shit, if we'd been in Siberia, we might have been better off, we would of maybe had a chance of getting adopted. Who knows, and what fucking difference does any of it make now?

We went to DKNY, me and My Lai. Of course I had seen credit cards before—what do you do, hand 'em to the clerk, they swipe, you sign? I never paid any attention before, because that wasn't me, I didn't have one. (Hey, hey, I'm the cash underground!) So I'm hanging with My Lai, waiting for her to go in, do her shopping so we can go get some sushi and fuck. And she digs in her bag and hands me this gold AmEx card with my name on it, talking 'bout ten grand.

"Go head, motherfucker, get dressed."

My mouth falls open, it doesn't compute as they say. She's giving this to me? Total, new experience. With Roman, he had, but I had to ask all the time, half of the time I would just do without rather than ask, and I wasn't going to go shopping with him, fuck that.

Humiliation, what I felt at the donut shop on 125th Street comes back to me now. Me thinking I was gonna grease on a dozen and the perv hadn't given me a ten but that crumpled one-dollar bill, a hot feeling rising up in my chest when she put the donuts back. Rage, humiliation. I felt so stupid, such a sucker.

The same feeling with Brother John.

"Leave it!" Brother John shouts.

Leave the *books*? Pussy-face hypocrite, could he hear himself telling me books are our friend and how his life turned around, how he would have been like any of those guys out there nodding if it wasn't for books? "Books took me from the crowded foster home on 155th Street." Then the foster brothers, four dead, two in prison, he escaped. I always hated that story. I hated it for the missing parts, did he fuck *them*, did they fuck him, is that why he fucked me, us? Or is it some, some *magnet* in us?

He's crying all over you, licking your butt, all the time talking in his nigger voice. I convinced myself I was special. Shit, if I ever kill anybody, it would be— *Have* I ever killed anybody? Maybe that's why I'm in here! Did I kill Brother John that day? That's what I had gone up there for, to save my own life by killing that fucking faggot. But maybe something else happened. Sometimes I think I'll go to look in the mirror and I'll see him there, that they made me, *made* me, be them. I'll ask Dr See when he comes back. My thoughts are racing now, remembering in a hole full of colors and sounds, deep but not connected to the next thing. Dr See will know. I want to talk, but my mouth is dry cotton. I try to move my tongue. No happenings. Whatever they gave me put me on the opposite side of speech, like we're boxers in separate corners. I have not shit in how long? I sat on the toilet and stuck my finger up my ass circling around hard pebbles of shit, pulling them out my ass one by one till I farted and finally some shit came out that wasn't rock hard. I don't dream much, but just now I dozed off and was dreaming, at least I think it was a dream. I can't tell you because I don't know if you're really here or you're in the dream.

What happened?

I was uptown somewhere, maybe walking along St Nicholas Terrace, that little lane behind the college that winds along the little cliff above St Nicholas Park and looks down on green grass, giant granite boulders sparkling in the sun, the playgrounds and wide black street below. You never know where you are in a dream, really, and I was dreaming, I think. But it was one of those days I was broke and just didn't want to ask My Lai or Scott to hold me over till I got my next check from Starbucks; they didn't care, but I did. I don't want to be dependent on those motherfuckers all the time. So when he drove past me, crawling, then turned around and came back, older white guy, maybe some professor at the college or some white shirt, yeah. He was driving a black BMW, freak-ass car, you know, the kind of car I want to have someday. So he rolls down the window, I can feel the cold air from the air conditioner out where I'm standing on the curb.

"Want a ride?"

I look over my shoulder.

"We could go anywhere. It doesn't have to be around here."

"Where?"

"Take the Henry Hudson to the Bronx?"

I look around again, I could just be giving a lost white guy directions. The door opens. I get in. He is a medium-build old guy, forty-five, fifty, sixty, what's the difference? They all look alike, losing hair, bellies with glasses.

"What's your name?" he asks.

I look at him. Probably from the burbs; if he isn't a professor, he's a broker or a dentist or some shit.

"What's *your* name?"

"Oh." He like almost chokes. "Martin, Martin Wilson. I'm a teacher."

He's driving faster now. Good, I don't want anybody to see me with this old white motherfucker. Not that I know anybody around here that much.

"You didn't tell me your name."

"Martin, my name's Martin too," I say.

"You're kidding me."

"Why would I do that?"

"I've got some good videos. You like videos?"

"Yeah," I say.

"Movies?"

"Yeah, sure," I tell him.

"You'll like these movies, and we can have a little fun while we watch." His laughter is all nervous.

"Yeah, sure." I hope this motherfucker doesn't think he's going to keep me up there all day, watching no fucking porn with his tired ass.

I forget the street, the exact area, the name of the bridge we crossed. But I know we crossed a bridge to get to the one-story flat white motel. It could have been anywhere.

"I'll be right back. I'm going to pay for the room, and then we get the equipment out of the trunk and have some fun. Are you an athlete?"

He's looking at me like I'm a package of Ding Dongs.

He comes back and then sure enough goes and gets all this shit out of the trunk—tripod, camera, video camera, videocassettes. He's got one of those silver fold-up screens and lights.

"I thought you might want to take a few shots, you of me, me of you, just for fun. What do you say?"

I don't say. He ain't mentioned coins yet—I want at least two bills—and he *ain't* taking no pictures of me doing nothing. He motions for me to take the key sticking out of his fat shirt pocket. I make him put the stuff down and open the door himself. The room is no surprise. Bed: box spring and mattress pushed up against a permanently-attached-to-the-wall headboard. Two thin pillows on top a dreary bedspread with geometric designs and a VCR on a dresser. And next to the VCR an ice bucket and two paper-capped glasses. He starts setting up his stuff and pops a cassette in the VCR. Two black boys appear on the screen, twelve, fourteen, maybe sixteen at the most, on their hands and knees fucking each other doggie. And that's what they look like, skinny black dogs. Is this supposed to be turning me on? The picture opens up to show him, or someone who looks like him—chunky oldish white guy—sitting in a chair, no shirt, pants unzipped, whacking off. I hardly ever go to the Bronx, what happens up in Boogie Down aside from this shit, and house fires, drug shoot-outs, or shoot-downs like Amadou Diallo? Someone like that taken off the count for believing in a dollar and a dream and having a cell phone, and this guy is riding around with a kiddie-porn home industry in his car like it's nothing at fucking all.

"I want to get the camera set up, OK?"

"Let's just go on and do what we gonna do. I don't feel like taking no whole bunch of pictures right now."

"You think I came all the way up here and rented a room for that? We could have done that in the backseat."

Man, he's like nasty!

"OK, give me two hundred." Fuck it, who's gonna see some shit like that? I mean, how many people can he show it to without going to jail?

"I don't have two hundred."

"You wanna take pictures?"

"Look, I—"

"No, you look. What kind of money are you talking about?"

"I've got twenty dollars."

"Twenty dollars?"

He yanks out his wallet, snatches out a twenty, and thrusts it at me. "I had to pay for the room in cash. I don't carry around a lot of cash. . . ."

I'm just standing looking at him, his voice trails off. He's scared. I snatch the wallet out of his hand. I could stick a fork through him, hold him over boiling water like a tomato, skin him alive. It's like a fire in my brain. He brought me all the way up here for twenty motherfucking dollars? I open his wallet and see a bulge under a Visa card and pull out a wad of bills.

"One hundred, two hundred, three hundred, four hundred! Now we're talking," I say in a triumphant voice.

"Oh, please, I got to get my son's bicycle from the shop."

"Use one of these." I point to a row of plastic cards.

"It's his birthday. The guy who's customizing his bike for him only takes cash."

I put the four bills in my pocket and step into him and slap him as hard as I can. The slap knocks him onto the bed on his back, but he bounces up again like a jack-in-the-box. I hit him in the face with my fist, hard, all my weight behind it. I hit him again and again, then snatch him up off the bed and throw him on the floor. He's groaning, his face is covered with blood. I kick him in the stomach. Wish I had boots on. I look around the room for something to smash him in the head with, although a little voice in me is saying stop, enough already. I pick up his camera and throw it at his head. He jerks as the camera bounces off his head to the floor. I look at my hands—hitting his stupid ass has broken the skin on my knuckles. My right hand is covered in blood. I don't know whether it's mine or his. There's blood on my right shoe. I go to wash my hands in the bathroom; even with the cold water, my knuckles are still bleeding. I grab a towel. How should I do this? I wipe the blood off my shoe. What should I do with the towel? Take it with me, it has his blood; leave it, it has my blood. I start to stuff it in my pocket, then see how big the pool of blood is getting around his head. He's groaning? I don't believe it, maybe it was my own voice. Just drop the towel in his blood? No take it with you. Take it and get the fuck out of here.

Where am I? Way the fuck up around Van Cortlandt Park. Slow down. Train train train. I gotta find a train downtown. Stroll, walk slow. I locked the doorknob lock from inside and pulled the blinds tight, then drew the curtains over the blinds. Either he'll wake up or they'll find him, him and his kiddie porn. OK! Number 1, Van Cortlandt Park station. After 225th Street, Marble Hill, we go over the bridge. I step between the cars and let the bloody towel drop. Swirling down toward the water, it looks like a white wounded bird.

I switch to the A train at 168th in the Heights. I look down at my feet. I didn't get rid of all the blood on my shoe. So cut these motherfuckers up in little pieces for landfill, yeah, everything I got on. Twenty dollars! I should have cut his dick off!

It's Dr See's deep "Hmmmm" that lets me know I've been talking and at the same time stops me from talking. Dr See is sitting by the bed.

"Tell me, do you *dream* like that often?"

"I don't know."

"Abdul, can you tell me about the dream that brought you here?"

"I don't remember most of my dreams," I tell him, and it's the truth. Not that I owe him the fucking truth.

"If you could remember, what would you remember?"

He's fucking with me. I got this shit figured out; he's in me, he's my mind. I'm going to die. They're experimenting on me with all these drugs, and they're never going to let me out. They're going to kill me or. Or *something*. What the fuck is going on here? If I don't remember, why doesn't he? Shit!

"If I don't remember, why don't you?" I ask.

"Say what?"

"Don't you know what I remember?" I ask.

"How would I know that? That would be to know who you are. Who are you but what you remember?"

"But you know why I'm here," I tell him.

"Even if I knew everything about you, I still wouldn't know what you remember. Even your DNA couldn't tell me what you remember."

"I want to go to sleep."

"Am I stopping you, sitting here?"

"The lights."

"They're a problem. Shall I get you something to help you sleep?"

"No, yes, let me see," I mumble, drifting in the whiter light like polluted foam down a stream. I reach out my foam hand for things: my name—just had it, but it passes me by. I can't hold on to nothing with my foam hands. Things are drifting past me again, how old I am, where I am, did I ever know? Of course I knew, I had to have known, but like a bar of soap in the shower it slipped out of my hands. How long *have* I been here? If I knew that, I could figure out how old I am, maybe. If I'm normal, what am I doing here? I feel death trying to rub up on me. And the guy across the hall, Watkins and another nigger are talking. ". . . Piece of Velcro wasn't did, letting another piece of Velcro to be undid, 'n he got loose! And hung himself from the side of the bed." "Close the door," one says. "I ain't closing shit," Watkins taunts. I see across the hall. I can smell shit piss. It's not like the movies, no stretcher or wheeling the bed away. Watkins and the other guy roll his body onto a long piece of black plastic and then roll him over and over again in the plastic like he's a tamale they're wrapping in corn husks, and then they kick his body onto a long piece of canvas and drag him BUMPETY-BUMP out the room. It's like they ain't going to fuck up their back carrying the nigger.

So that's it. No more nothing. The end. That scares me. I feel darkness under all the light and air turn to bricks that are impossible to breathe. Dr See is just sitting there. Why doesn't he turn the lights out and go, so I can sleep? I look at a tube in my arm and wonder when it got there and who put it there; the next thing I see are horses. I'm standing with them in a green pasture, and the air is balmy but the sky is cloudy. I can smell the ocean even though I can't see it. I follow the smell to the top of a hill, which turns to a cliff where the surf is crashing against the rocks below. A tall woman on a pretty silver horse is riding toward me. The horse stops abruptly, then picks up again with a gallop toward me. I step closer in its path rather than away from it. The long silver hairs of its mane brush my face, leaving the smell of an ocean breeze in my nostrils.

I know the horse is coming back for me without the woman.

"Why?"

Am I talking?

"It will be like . . . I don't know, dying, the silver horse is death, don't you think, Dr See?"

"Actually, that's not what I think. But what do *you* think death will be like?"

"I think it will be gray and cold. I'm tired of talking about it."

"Don't you dare," he says. "Every time I bring you out of the fog, you run right back in."

"You think you control everything." Mindfucker, I hate him, and I hate myself for sounding like a fucking kid talking to his daddy.

"What you're doing is not control; it's not even resistance, if you're fooling yourself into thinking that. You're not a child whose tantrums are going to get him what he wants. You're an adult turning the key that's going to lock you in."

It's the truth socking me in the jaw! I feel like I've been hit by lightning or found God. I sit up rigid with fear and a raggedy little piece of hope.

"So we need to talk."

"About what?" I ask.

"Your mental state. Look, boy, I'm not angry at you or tired of you, though perhaps I should be or could be. I don't know which. What I do know is this is about it for me and therefore in some ways about it for you unless I have something to put in my report on Friday."

"Friday?"

"Friday is my last day."

Last day? Last day? *Day?* I don't even know what year this is, and he's talking about day. I don't say anything. My chest muscles tighten.

"Yes, I'll be leaving to work for Big Pharma. I'll be doing the same thing I do here—"

"Huh?"

"Run clinical trials—"

"Dope?"

"*Director*, medical director. I could never do that here."

Here. He's leaving? He can't leave without telling me my name, how long I been here, why I'm here, how old I am. My mother, my dancing? He's chitchatting like, like this isn't my life, like he's talking about his grocery list.

"You can't leave without telling me who I am. I deserve to know why I was brought here. You can't just lock people up for no reason and then say, 'Friday is my last day' and—"

"Well, let's get one thing straight: You were locked up for a reason. And basically when you end up in the position you're in, we can do whatever we think is necessary."

"The man across the hall?"

"Nobody *did* anything to him. He did it to himself. But you're right to ask, because that could have been you."

"Isn't this a hospital? Aren't you supposed to help people?"

"Do you want help, Abdul?"

What the fuck, am I talking to the devil here? What's going on? Weird, weird. I sink back down in the bed.

"Come on, sit back up, look alive, Abdul. We don't have much time unless you want to stay here for a very long time."

"I don't want to stay here."

"On Friday I will hand in an evaluation on our sessions together."

"What sessions?"

"I will write up all those times you pulled the sheets over your head and turned your back on me and pretended you were asleep or bit yourself and spewed blood on the walls—"

"They got it off, all of—"

"Yes, they're—*we* are, I guess you could say that, good at getting rid of things. As I was saying before you interrupted, those sessions, that's what I get paid for, I'm a psychopharmacologist."

"I couldn't talk on all that shit. Why—"

"Talk now. Talk now, Abdul. Talk."

"I don't know what to say."

"Stop whining, Abdul. What's on your mind? You can always start there."

"How old am I? What's my name? How long have I been here? Where, *what*, is this? Who am I?"

"You know, this is interesting, but to be honest with you, there are certain things I need to hear. That's if you want to leave here. I can't write a recommendation for you to leave here if you're going to be running around telling people you don't know your name. What is your name? Let's start there. What is your name? I asked you a question, Abdul. Don't you get it yet?"

"I'm not sure." What's with this guy?

"What is your name?"

"Abdul Jamal Louis Jones."

"OK, that's not exactly what I have written down here."

"Yeah," I say re-remembering. "That's not exactly what I have 'written down' either."

"So what exactly *is* your name?"

"Abdul Jones, period. I dropped the rest."

"Why?"

"I don't know, it felt like dead weight. All I need is Abdul and Jones."

I so don't trust this guy. I thought he was different from Watkins and those niggers. Yeah he's different, but the same. Or maybe he isn't the same, maybe he is my friend.

"The name I have is Abdul-Azi Ali. How old are you?"

"I don't know."

"Why don't you know?"

"Well, I don't know how long I been here, how many years, or whatever."

"How old were you when you came here?" Staring at me hard.

"I don't know. I don't remember coming here."

"What *do* you remember, Abdul?"

"I don't. I just woke up one day and I was here strapped down getting shot up."

"You know you're not delusional. Maybe you have some depression or posttraumatic stress, maybe. And that's not so strange, considering what you've been through."

Like he's not part of what I've been through.

"Abdul, I don't want this to become a battle of wills—"

"I'll lose?"

"You already have, if you're here. Like I said earlier, I'm leaving at the end of the week. You could wind up staying here for a long, long time, you know, doing, oh, say, testing meds for these people, locked down, strapped in. I've seen it happen before. Or we, *they*, I mean, damage people so badly they can't let them out, and then they leave enough Velcro loose so they take care of themselves. I'll ask you again: How old are you?"

"I told you I don't know."

"What is the last age you remember being?"

"Um, I think nineteen, twenty, maybe eighteen."

"So what makes you think you're not nineteen or eighteen anymore?"

"Well, that's how old I was when I came here, but I'm older than that now by the years I've been in here."

"Years?"

"Yeah."

"How long do you think you've been here?"

"Shit, I don't know, *you* know. Why don't you tell me?"

"I will, Abdul. You've been here for twenty-one days, exactly to the day."

"Twenty-one days? You mean, I . . ." What's he talking about? I can't—

"Yes, that's exactly what I mean. We had to keep you—"

"*Why?*"

"Well, maybe *how* is more like it and or more useful. You were incapacitated. They slapped a label on you as a threat to yourself and others, and if you were Abdul-Azi Ali like we thought you were, then it was not just a threat to others but a *lot* of others.

"So you just drag me here, lock me up in a room. *Who?* Who said you could do that? What did I *do*? I have rights? Why am I here?"

"Good question, Abdul. That's one I'm going to ask you to answer, because I don't know."

"I had to have done something. I couldn't just get locked up for nothing."

"You never heard of people getting locked up for nothing?"

"Yeah, trash people, hoodies, and rapists and shit, or . . . or in China or someplace. This is America."

"Where have you been, boy?"

I'm stunned. He's Watkins in a jacket with leather patches on the elbows, a pipe. He needs a pipe and a fireplace. This is madness.

"Where have you been, boy? Where have you been?"

"I dunno."

"You need to find out, you really do."

"What if I can't?"

"You could be here a long time, oh, declared this or that by the state, insane displaced person paranoid schizophrenic. They'll come up with something, and you would end up fodder—"

"Fodder, dried hay for horses."

"I'm not giving you a vocabulary quiz, Abdul. Don't you understand what I'm talking about? Watkins, our minimum-wage sadist, *every day,* how's that for a life? Not so nice, I think. Then wake up, kid, I asked you a question."

"Honestly, after all that, I forgot what that question was."

"You were going to tell me why you were here. What do you remember?"

J.J., when I first saw the devil it was an abyss, a straight drop into blackness. And, J.J., that's when I understood Hopkins! That's when I understood the great holy blinding light was the same as the devil's dark, the very same, the exact very same.

"Abdul? *Abdul?* What's going on in there?"

"I wake and feel the fell of dark, not day.
What hours, O what black hours we have spent
This night! What sights you, heart, saw; ways you went!
And more must, in yet longer light's delay.
With witness I speak this. But where I say
Hours I mean years, mean life."

"Who taught you Shakespeare?"

"It's not Shakespeare," I say.

"Who is it?"

"It's Gerard Manley Hopkins, a Jesuit priest. He observed a lot of natural phenomena—flowers, trees, rock formations. So my earth science teacher, Brother John, had us read his poems and memorize them. That's one I memorized. When you said, 'What do you remember?' that's what came out."

"Sounds like you got it perfect there."

"Not perfect. Why did I get shock treatment?"

"Good question, and we'll come to that. But remember our focus is getting you out of here. If you get mad now, it won't happen. So I need to assess your current state of mind—"

"Why?"

"Well, think of me, you're doing me a favor. Suppose I authorize your release and you go kill somebody."

Shit, he's serious. If he's not *the* devil, he's *a* devil. Maybe I can talk to him.

"So what is it about the Jesuits?"

"Nothing really. I was thinking about how after that, when I was seventeen—" I say.

"What about it?" he interrupts.

"Well, nothing really, just hitting this guy."

"Who?"

"Roman, a guy I know. It was funny. After I hit him, he was screeching on and on, but later he claimed I broke his jaw. How was his jaw broken if he kept talking?"

"Why did you hit him?"

"He was trying to stop me from going. I had come back to get some books, and he didn't want me to go."

"You were leaving what?"

"His house, I was living with him, since I was thirteen."

"Was he a friend, a lover, a relative?"

"What relative would act like that?"

"It's not so uncommon."

"I mean normal relative."

"So go on, why was he so upset? Why did you feel you had to hit him?"

"He's such a faker, I don't know, but I guess he was in love with me."
I'm not lying, I realize. I didn't know shit about him, really.

"Were you in love with him?"

"No. I was thirteen. I needed a place to stay. He took me in, trained
me as a dancer—took care of me. In love? I didn't even *like* him, but—"

"But what?"

"But I admired him in a way."

"How so?"

"His skill, the guy was a virtuoso. He said he would teach me everything he knew, and he did but—"

"You hear the back story yourself, don't you, Abdul? 'But.' But what?"

"But I wasn't gay. But it felt good getting my dick sucked. I felt like
he had me in a cage lined with money. I couldn't get out even though the
door was open. That made me feel even more trapped, because it was
like I was choosing to stay. I didn't know what to do. I felt polluted, yeah,
polluted. I didn't think I could get a girl and be normal, because I *wasn't*."

"Did he force you?"

"No, it was that to get what I wanted, I knew what I had to do. I felt
like I had no choice. Of course I did: be homeless, go to a group home jail
where I'd probably *really* have gotten fucked."

"Say what?"

"Roman, all he wanted to do was blow me. It was not like he ever even
tried to fuck me; it just wasn't part of his program. But . . . but I hated the
feeling, like now. I feel it now, like I don't have any rights or choice—you
got all the power. Do I have any rights?"

"Did you?"

"No, *do* I?"

"What do you mean?"

"Do I have to do this shit, talk to you?"

"No, you don't have to do anything. But I suggest you choose to. Think of this as getting your 'rights,' as you call them, back. So finish telling me about this guy. It sounds like he played the role of parent and teacher even while sexually exploiting you."

"He didn't see it that way, as exploitation. He saw me as his 'boy,' like a husband or some shit."

"So you're angry, understandably, at being used. What most kids get for free, you had to pay for—"

"Exactly! And later I find out this faggot is whaling on me and he got HIV!"

"When did you find that out?"

"The day I was leaving."

"So today do you have anyone, a boyfriend or girlfriend?"

"I got a girl. Or did have."

"Did? What happened?"

"You tell me, you're the one knows why I'm here."

"Is this your first girlfriend?"

"I never had one before. I used to look at pictures and stuff."

"And stuff?"

"You know, jack off."

"What kind of pictures?"

What a fucking creep, why am I talking? "Britney, Lil' Kim, mostly Britney but—"

"But?"

"But when I finally hook up with a Britney bitch, I couldn't do nothing." I'm still embarrassed.

"That's called performance anxiety."

"I thought it was the brothers at St Ailanthus fixing me. Like what happened to my grandmother in Mississippi. Someone fixed her and she was never happy again. Roman said I was more of a pussy than the ones I be sniffing after."

"Did you like relating sexually to guys?"

"If they paid me. Anyway, that's all I knew before My Lai."

"My Lai?"

"My girl." I'm surprised at the pride in my voice. What do I have to be proud about?

"Did you initiate sex with men?"

"No, but, I mean . . . I mean, I didn't have to, they came to me. But—"

"But?"

"I did with the kids."

"How old were they?"

I think of Richie Jackson. "Um, six, seven." Actually, he was five.

"How old were you?"

"Thirteen."

"Little girls?"

"There was never any of them around."

"Did you ever think of why you did that?"

"It felt good."

"Better than Roman and—"

"I was in control and having fun with the little kids."

"Fun? What about them?"

"They were having fun too. They loved it!"

"Are you sure?"

He's getting on my nerves. "Yeah, they loved it, and me. They loved me. I was like a . . . a *father*."

"The girl you're with now? Is she a 'Britney bitch'?"

"My Lai, hell no. She's a . . . a woman. She's real. She's the first person I was ever real with. She's no *picture*. She farts. We get down together. I'm her man." Yeah, I remind myself, I'm a man.

"Did you ever hit her?"

"It never crossed my mind."

"You were telling me about this guy."

"Who?" I ask.

"The guy at the motel."

"I already told you."

"Tell me some more, Abdul."

359

"I want to go back to sleep." All of a sudden I'm in a funk.

"Abdul, I told you we don't have time for that. Wake up, Abdul."

"In the dream she asks me to kill him."

"*Who* asks you to kill *whom*?" He's leaning forward now, interested, real interested.

"In the dream My Lai wanted me to kill her father. All this time I thought she, maybe, really just loved me, but she wanted me to do that shit. She's no different from anybody else out there."

I turn away from Dr See. Fuck him. I can, and *am*, going to sleep.

"Do you dream like that often?"

"No. I mean, sometimes."

"Abdul, can you tell me about the dream that brought you here?"

"I don't remember my dreams anymore," I tell him. "I told you that before!"

"And I asked you before, if you could remember, what would you remember?"

He's fucking with me again. I feel like I only have a few seconds where my mind is mine before they take it back. *He* remembers.

"You know what I remember," I insist.

"How so?"

"Don't you know what I remember?"

"I told you before, Abdul, I'm not in your mind."

He's lying!

I can't tell the difference between dreaming and being awake in here. Didn't I just go to sleep, and here he is again talking to me and I'm talking back again, which is the shocker.

"I just wanted to think she loved me, that I was her man, the big cheese, the king or something. And all she wanted was to use me like everybody else. And also like I'm crazy or some shit, I'm just gonna go out to Connecticut and kill her fucking parents, two people I ain't never seen, who are basically supporting her, *us*, 'cause she's kicking me coins when I need 'em—I'm just gonna go kill them for *nothing*."

THE KID

"Her father raping her was 'nothing'?" Dr See asks.

"You know what I mean."

"Maybe I do, maybe I don't. You have an understandably bitter view of her request, but I don't know if that means she doesn't love you."

"You don't?"

"It was wrong. It was evil—I guess there's a time to use that word. But she did see you as the 'big cheese,' as you say. She wanted him dead. You love her, she loves you. You're her king, you should slay the dragon. That it's the wrong thing to do, that it would've destroyed her life *and* your life, as well as her father's, she obviously didn't have enough . . . enough *sense* to figure that out."

"She's very intelligent."

"I didn't say she wasn't. Sense and intelligence aren't necessarily the same thing. Whatever sense she had, her emotions ate up. Millions of people survive child abuse and go on to live life. She got twisted up in revenge and hatred."

"I forgot something."

"What would that be?" he asks in his sickeningly cool voice.

"I told her something about the brothers. Well, the brother who molested me, Brother Samuel, and, kind of, Brother John. I told her I went up there and confronted Brother Samuel in his room, where he had raped me when I was a kid. And I killed him. And then I climbed out the window and ran away."

"Did that happen?"

"No, what really happened was, I went up there to confront them and Brother John had been transferred. And Brother Samuel had committed suicide."

"So, it's not *so* unreasonable that My Lai would see you as capable of riding out to Connecticut and killing her parents."

"It still hurt."

"Have you ever forgiven anyone?"

"No."

"You ever thought of telling her the truth?"

"Of . . . of what, that I didn't have the heart to just kill?"

"Or, that you had too much heart to 'just kill.'"

THE PICTURES ARE DREAMS, or I'm dreaming pictures: My Lai floating in a see-through beige leotard; then myself, nothing on, charging across the floor, a tiger taking her like an animal from behind, sinking my teeth into her neck, busting her open, *I* open. We collapse when we're through. Free. I see Richie Jackson, Jaime, like dreams, bad. Jaime bad. I started to hate him. He wanted to kiss me, I wanted him to stay little forever, a child, and me the . . . the king father like Brother John. Not him screaming like a bitch, "Papi!" Ugh!

I'm on the D train coming out of the tunnel. Aha! The surprise, no matter how many times you see it, of the dark sky and the city lights dancing on the water beneath the bridge, wires me to another surprise: the vision of myself—step step jeté! We're coming across the floor, one by one, step step leap. I'm strong, like Roman said, I have ballon, but I've never had the stretch to be able to open my legs in the air in a split before. But when I turned my head to look in the mirror, I was doing a perfect split in the air! What I had thought was going to take another four or five years had crept up on me while I was stretching and working and practicing. I looked like the people I had been envying. My own beauty shocked, like just now coming out of the tunnel onto the bridge, seeing the lights glowing and sparkling on the water. Yes, Roman, I want to be the black swan. So what am I doing laying up here swollen with drugs, constipated, and pretending I'm asleep dreaming. Or was I really asleep dreaming?

I am asleep now, eating bagels at St Ailanthus. Thursdays we have bagels, as many as you want, whole wheat, jalapeño, poppy seed, everything, salt (my favorite), cinnamon raisin, pumpernickel (ugh!), cream cheese with: scallions, or lox (my favorite), or vegetables (ugh!), or walnuts and dates. Orange juice. And cereal with milk for kids who don't like bagels, I eat both, bagels and the cereal. I'm on another subway car now; Slavery Days is sitting next to me. I'm hungry. She knows I'm hungry, tries to give me her fried ham and grits, but what first looks like jelly in the middle of the grits turns out to be blood pulsing from the hot white center of the grits, covering the plate that I let drop with a SMASH!

I get off at DeKalb, cut across to McDonald's: fries, fries, fries, four Mickey D baked apple pies, and a quadruple cheeseburger I eat there. I turn to the side and there's Slavery Days again! She says something, but it's like when the Mexicans or Russians are lost and they come up to you on the street, their mouths open with a language that surrounds you but doesn't penetrate your brain. Their words flying around like red arrows from cupid. When I was at P.S.1_, me and my mother made a Valentine's Day card for everyone in my class, even the kids I didn't like. Each card had a big red lollipop taped to it. Everybody in first grade loved me. Slavery Days is her young self now, Toosie, dressed up in her orange dress singing old blue songs: "Good Morning Heartache" as I wake up.

I wake up hungry. "I'm hungry," I said. I repeat, but louder, "I'm hungry."

"OK, OK." Dr See. "Someone is going to come within the hour with some food. In the meantime don't leave this room, OK? *OK?*"

"What if I have to use the bathroom?"

"Go out, turn right, the first door is the WC."

The WC is a toilet and sink. Fuck, I say to myself. I can make words with my mouth now, *talk.* For a while it seemed like I was a fighter in a ring and in the opposite corner was my tongue, swollen and paralyzed from the waist down. I haven't shit in a long time. The last thing I ate was two baloney and cheese sandwiches two days ago. If I had anything else, I don't remember. I sit down on the toilet and stick my finger up my ass and with a groan start to pull hard little balls of shit out one by one till I'm able to pass shit that's not rocks. I'm still washing my hands when I hear the rattle of a cart that's probably got food on it.

I get back in bed and lift the tray onto my lap and immediately attack the hot, fluffy mound of scrambled eggs, the bacon strips, and the buttered whole wheat toast. When I finish, a woman in whites and marshmallow shoes comes in with a pot of joe and a cup.

"Coffee?"

I shake my head affirmatively and thank her while she's pouring and again when she's through pouring. The smell of fresh coffee is good music. It carries me away. By the time I notice the chalky residue at the bottom of the cup, I'm already drifting away under the fluorescent lights, feeling too good to get mad. I do think *why*? Then I'm dreaming, a mugger running down a dark street, the buildings growing taller and grayer, the street dirtier and dirtier, until I run out of it like a tunnel, onto a sunlit green. Herd, we're all there. My Lai is hopping around like Rumpelstiltskin, shouting, "I want him dead! I want him dead!"

I've killed him and set the house on fire, and she's still screaming, "I want him dead!" Everyone's looking at me, not her. Scott comes up with his pointy, surgeried nose and blue breath. "Hey, man, you just sold it to the junkman." I know it's true. I look down at my offending hands. Warts and worms are wriggling from them. I shiver at my life, at what love has done to me. I want to choke My Lai, but my hands won't obey. Everyone backs away from me, even My Lai. "I did this for you!" I shout, enraged. "I did this for *you*!"

Bitch doesn't care! Chinese whore! "Yellow *bitch*!" She's laughing at me. My hands are a useless mass of wriggling worms and warts now. I'll bite her throat out, that'll shut her up. I lunge for her, yeah. If I can't strangle her or beat her, I'll tear her throat out. AHH!!!!!!!!!! I'm so angry. All that shit, pretending she loved me, and she just wanted me to be her slave.

Suddenly we're on their lawn; it's like a pretty park, green grass, sky blue with white puffy clouds. All this for one famly? White statuettes on the lawn remind me of the grave markers in cemeteries. This is how people in magazines live, I think. I notice people, a lot of people, like it's a party or something. They seem to be moving; maybe they're leaving this party and going to another party, or home. I start moving across the green, but the people are moving away from me faster than I'm moving toward them. When I get to the other side, it's just Scott, Snake, and Amy and a bunch of Herd groupies standing there. Snake's taken off all his clothes and is wading into a pond that's in front of us.

"You're making it hard for all of us," Scott says.

"Me?" I shriek. "What about him!" I point at Snake, whose hair has turned into thick, red curls that are smoldering like they're going to erupt in flames.

"Same difference." Scott, dry as stale bread.

When I do meet My Lai's father, the guy looks straight through me. Big fat motherfucker, he's taller than me, so he's way over six feet. He smells like dog shit. His gut is hanging over his belt, and he has bags under his eyes that look like balloons filled with water. She wants me to kill this? He's already dead.

"You know, a word in her defense—"

"Poison Oasis."

"Poison Oasis?"

"Yeah, it's one of my favorite paintings by Basquiat. There's a man, and on one side of the man is a green snake coiling upward. The snake has big, sharp white teeth; the man has a square splash of paint on the side of his penis, setting it off. He's skeletal, a lot of brown paint. On the other side of him is the carcass of a dead or dying cow, and flies, flies big as birds around the cow— What made me think of it? Well, My Lai's parents' mansion in Connecticut and here, this place."

"You're quite articulate."

"Why wouldn't I be?"

"What did this painter mean to you?"

"He's great. He did his thing. I wanna do mine. He lived his life out—"

"He's dead?"

"Yeah."

"When did he die?"

"I don't know exactly, a while ago."

"How old was he when he died?"

"Twenty-seven."

"Twenty-seven? You call that 'living his life out'?"

"If you a black man, yes. Living long is not our forte."

"I don't think I've ever seen a young person as cynical as you."

"Is that why I'm in here?"

"Tell me about this painting. Where did you first see it?"

"I don't remember, but I got a poster of it on my wall at home."

"Where is home?"

"I don't know anymore. There's a tree with a big line through it. The guy is outlined in white paint like . . . like—"

"Like?"

"Like chalk around a dead body on the sidewalk. My mother grabbed my hand, pulled me away, saying that would never happen downtown. They would never leave a body laying in the street that long downtown. You know, since when do you leave a body, fuss, fuss—she's fussing. But I'm little, I didn't really understand it, until I saw a fly buzzing in his open mouth. *That's* dead. I knew that fly was like torture and, and he would stop it if he could. And he couldn't. It was my first whiff of death."

"Yeah?"

"The man's—"

"The man on the street?"

"No, in the painting. His hands are crossed over his chest like, like my mother's were."

"What else?"

"He's . . . there's a patch of blue above the cow, but he's standing in red."

"Blood?"

"Yeah."

"What are you thinking now?"

"Really?"

"Yeah, Abdul, really."

"Right this minute I was wondering if you were gay."

"Why?"

"I don't know, whenever a man is . . . is nice to me, or sympathetic toward me, you know, it's never . . . I don't know, *pure*. The next thing I know, they'll be trying to crawl on my dick."

"What about your father?"

"I never had one. I guess that's what got me about My Lai. She had all that, and . . . I don't know, her own crib—really cool pad, credit cards, she could *drive*. They had her hooked up! So he stuck his finger in her cunt. Even Scott didn't have the kind of training she had. She went to, *lived* in, a ballet conservatory, breathing it in for a year, day and night. For a *year*. And—"

"And?"

"And I didn't have shit. I mean, everybody gets fucked one way or the other. At least she got paid."

"That's your philosophy?"

"That's reality!" I insist.

"That's reality, period?"

"Period!" I shout.

"OK, OK, I didn't mean to make you angry, but you know it's OK to be angry. But if that's life, yadda-yadda, and everybody's getting fucked, why are you so upset, if that's just the way it is?"

"'Cause I'm still getting fucked! When is it gonna be my turn!"

"But you got something out of it, as you say too, with Raymond?"

"Roman, you mean."

"Yes. He used you sexually, but like your girlfriend's dad, he provided—"
I interrupt him. "Yeah, provided and *paid*."

"Come again?"

"Well, he paid me, and he paid too."

"What do you mean, Abdul?"

"I'd come, and then, you know how after you come you want to piss. Well, he'd be swallowing my load and then try to draw his head back, but I'd hold him there and piss in his mouth and then all over his ass. I'd do shit like that all the time to show . . ."

"To show?"

"I guess to show he wasn't totally ruling the situation. And I think because I hated him and couldn't really show it."

"Then you knew how My Lai felt."

"I couldn't understand why she couldn't just play the game."

"Well, why couldn't you have just hung in there and played the game with Roman?"

"I did, but he kept wanting more and more. Plus, I'm a man, I'm not supposed to have to put up with that shit!" I shout.

"You say he kept wanting more and more—you mean sex?"

"No, he wanted to, like, be in love and shit."

"You couldn't be in love with another man, is that it?"

"Well, I *wasn't*, just say that. And I couldn't be! I couldn't be in love with that old fake-hair faggot! He could have been my goddamned grandfather! It's alright because I'm a nigger—"

"What's that got to do with it?"

"What's that got to do with it?" I mimic his stupid accent. "When was the last time you saw a nigger walking down the street with a white underage? Huh? My Lai said Woody Allen would never have gotten away with his shit if the girl had been white and he had been Asian."

"I have no idea what you're talking about."

"You never heard about Woody Allen marrying his girlfriend's daughter?"

"Ah, maybe vaguely."

"Where you been?" I taunt.

"Well, obviously in some place where I haven't been able to keep up with every tabloid story that comes along."

"My Lai was obsessed with that shit, adoptees this, adoptees that. She never saw any shit like where I come from, little kids, five or six years old, lined up in front of steel cots in striped pajamas, like they're in prison or some shit. Little kids who know they're gonna be wards of some charity until they're grown and probably have to pay with their little booties every step of the way! Good luck is some foster home where someone sucks a check out of their ass till they're eighteen, and they age out on the motherfucking streets, homeless!"

"So, pretty hopeless, no escape, just get—"

"Fuck you, I'm tired of your stupid-ass questions, or whatever it is you're trying to pull. You just say the same shit over and over. I'm tired of talking! I WANT TO GET OUT OF HERE!"

"Abdul, I'm curious about the man in the Bronx, at the motel."

"So what, you're curious? I already told you about that. Anyway, that happened a long time ago."

"I don't think it happened that long ago."

"How would you know?"

"It happened after you left Roman and before you came here. I can see how that might be a long time to a young person, but a few years is not really a long time. Is that the first time you did something like that?"

"Like what?"

"Like set upon someone?"

"You're forgetting what he did to me."

"No I'm not. I'm asking you a question. Did you beat up other men who picked you up, or tried to pick you up?"

"Yeah."

"How often?"

"I don't remember." I'm starting to hate this Arab-ass nigger, or whatever he is.

"Why?"

"Why? Why was their nasty asses out crawling in the gutter trying to cream kids' asses for ten dollars or a hamburger? That's what one guy asked me: 'How about a Whopper?'"

"What's a Whopper?"

"A hamburger from Burger King. You know, like you so zero you spozed to fuck these motherfuckers for a hamburger and whatever change they got in their pockets."

"At what point did you begin to beat these guys? Do you remember?"

"I usually only beat the cheap ones."

"The *cheap* ones?"

"Yeah, if they get up off the coin and didn't act too stupid, I'd let them suck me off or I'd fuck them."

"Were you ever picked up by women?"

"Sometimes."

"I asked you earlier, what would make you decide to attack?"

"Number one, I don't like that word. But I didn't decide, *they* decided, you know, when they start pulling out them ten-dollar bills and start talking about 'Why don't you dance for me?' or any other of their weird shit, it's like they writing themselves a ticket."

"What weird shit?"

"I rather not discuss it."

"Did you ever attack the women?"

"No."

"Do you know why not?"

"They were usually drunk ladies pretending to themselves all they were doing was giving me a ride. Then they give you all the money in their purse—one lady tried to give me her mink coat to sell. I wouldn't even have known how to do any shit like that. They weren't like the guys, trying to get something for nothing."

"How long would you beat these guys?"

"Back to that." I'm so not into this shit no more.

"Yeah, how long did you beat these guys, Abdul?"

"It would depend."

"On what?"

"On when they stop moving. I beat them till they asses stop moving."

"After that?"

"Nada."

"Why not? A lot of people do."

"I ain't no 'lotta people.' You know, mission accomplished, I'd take the cash they owed me and tip. I ain't trying to kill nobody."

"What were you trying to do?"

"Disable, you know, render inoperative, a few of these perpetrators."

"Did you ever think you might have killed one of these guys?"

"No, I never killed nobody."

"How do you know?"

"I know."

IN THE DREAM she doesn't move.

"Get out of here!" she screams at me. "Get your crazy ass out of here."

The can of charcoal lighter fluid next to her could explode. The fire is growing. I've never seen fire before. It has a mind, a soul, a burning mission to eat everything. I grab her. Her resistance shocks me. She's standing staring into the fire, mesmerized. I pick her up and start to run across the lawn with her in my arms. A BOOM from behind knocks me down, and I hear flames roaring like lions. I've fallen on top of her.

That's how they find us, laying on the lawn, me on top of her, the house a wall of yellow flames behind us.

"Wake up, Abdul, and listen to me." Dr See.

"Huh?"

"You don't have time for 'huh.' It's time to go."

"Say what?" I know this is a dream; only in dreams does the same exact thing happen over and over.

"I hate you." It's the first thing that springs to mind. I don't know why I said it.

"Forget about hating me. In fact, forget about everything. It's time to go."

"Spoze I don't want to go?"

"I would say you were still lost in a dream or that I had really misevaluated you and you are a sick, sick boy. But I didn't misdiagnose you, and you don't *not* want to go. You want to have some control of your life so you don't feel totally crazy. This is hell for you. I wish we had more time to talk, but we don't. Come on, let's go."

"What happened here! Why was I here!" I'm screaming at him.

"You need to forget about what happened here, forget *here* period. Forget or drive yourself crazy."

"I don't want to forget. People like you fucking with people's heads is what drives motherfuckers crazy!" I'm yelling at his quietness, his something-is-wrong-with-you voice.

"The brothers did this to me. I hate you. I'm gonna get you!" I growl.

"Abdul, your revenge fantasies are nails in a coffin. Yours."

"Why am I here? I want to know what happened! Not just good-bye, get outta here, forget we beat you, electroshocked your butt, stuck a hose down you, and needles all—"

"Abdul, we *wanted* you here. That's how people get into this facility. If you want to stay, we can, albeit grudgingly, accommodate that wish. I'm going to close the door and smoke a cigarette. Abdul, you're not crazy, you're not delusional or dissociated. So you tell me. You've been walking around like a gene-spliced, fiddled-with mother chicken afraid to sit on an egg. You've got a minute, since you 'don't want to forget,' to remember. Tell you? No, you tell me. Tell me what happened that got you taken out of your life and brought here."

"I told you, I don't know! You know, you're the one who knows. I just woke up one day here with you crazy people!"

Doctor? What kind of doctor is this asshole? He strikes a match. I watch the flame touch the tip of the cigarette and flare red when he sucks in the smoke.

"I don't remember," I sigh.

"Try."

"I just remember there was a kid at our after party. I remember the way it was dressed I couldn't tell if it was a boy or a girl at first. He wanted some grapes. He couldn't reach them. Then he wanted to go to the bathroom. I offered to take him. 'Come on,' I said.

"Then?"

"Then nothing. He was Amy's little cousin. So she called him. I said, 'I'm just taking him to the head.' And the three of us walked to the bathroom, me and her chatting while the kid's in the head. But . . ."

"But?"

"But, I don't know, it was weird. A whole other scenario, a punishment, was flashing fast, in like nanoseconds, through my head, me and the kid. He's a girl, he's a boy, he's a girl. He's Amy, pink and white with yellow hair, but a child, I'm in there with him, her. I'm licking the drops of urine off his little penis, I'm Brother John and me, then it's a pussy and my dick gets hard, and I slam her up against the wall, I smell blood, that excites me even more, and I start to thrust my dick in her, hard. And the first scenario—me there chatting with Amy—with *this* scenario in my head, is gone. And I'm on one side of the door, and she's on the other, kicking it. Then I hear the little pop of a credit card against the lock and the door springs open. She and Scott are staring at me, their light-colored eyes burning with hate.

"'I knew it! I knew it!' she screams. Scott scoops the little boy (I thought he had disappeared a long time ago) up in his arms. 'You just flushed your life down the toilet!' Scott says.

"Then it's like the dream was only a fleeting lapse of consciousness, like getting elbowed in the head on the basketball court. I just shook my head and kept on playing. There was nothing even to repress or for-get like sometimes happens when I wake up, because . . . I don't know, just because. But what did happen was, I got a terrible headache, a *crushing* headache, like how people describe a migraine, but I wouldn't know if it was that, because I've never had a migraine before. I ask Amy if there was any aspirin anywhere. She says sure, she'll get me some. My head hurt something terrible, and it was getting worse, like a big noise in my brain that nobody could hear but me. Maybe I was having a stroke. In spite of it I smiled, because I could see headlines in my head along with the noisy explosions that were breaking my brain as I walked toward the table with the food. I picked up a plastic knife—it was the same color as the plates and napkins, silver—then I cut a slice of the stupid Death by Chocolate Floating in Raspberries Cake, downed it and a glass of champagne. I took the bottle of aspirin Amy had brought to me, and the silver knife, back to the bathroom, where I realized that nothing really had happened but was going to happen now. I'd never even dreamed about cutting my wrists before, but I did it now, almost perfectly."

"After that?"

"I don't know anything after that," I tell him. It's the truth.

"After that," he says "the police, who had posted an APB for a young man thirty years old, Abdul-Azi Ali—"

"That's not my name!"

"You didn't know your name—"

"That's no reason to do what you did!"

"It may not be the reason, but it's part of why. The obvious reason is, we could. You need to not forget that."

"You pump me with every drug in the book, torture me—" I can't speak anymore. I bounce up in the bed, then stand up on the mattress, and jump straight up, hitting the ceiling lights with the crown of my head. My head shatters the fluorescent bulbs, which spray glass and white stuff all over the room.

He gets on the phone, and as quick as he can speak, the marshmallow-shoed feet descend on the room.

"Ward Two?"

"No, pick him up so he doesn't get cut, and get him out of here!"

"Ward Two?"

"*No,* downstairs. Get the glass off his ass, get his clothes or find something that fits him, get him dressed, and wait for me." He takes my face in his hands and pulls it close to his face. "Abdul, fifteen minutes from now a door is going to open, and when it opens, you *go.* Hear? *Hear?*"

"I hear," I said.

ACKNOWLEDGMENTS

Nobody does it alone. Many people and institutions need to be acknowledged in the bringing of this novel into the world. I'd like to thank United States Artists Prudential Fellowship for support when I needed it most. I'm grateful for residencies at Yaddo, Headlands Center for the Arts, Künstlerhaus Schloss Wiepersdorf, the Mabel Dodge Luhan House, and The Writer's Room where parts of this book were written. Different colleagues and friends read parts or all of this manuscript in its various incarnations over the years. Very special thanks to Amy Scholder and Tracy Sherrod in this area. I also want to extend thanks to Brighde Mullins, Elizabeth Bernstein, Eve Ensler, Fran Gordon, Michelle Weinstein, Robin Friedman, and Jaye Austin William, who also read and gave valuable feedback on my novel. Sylvia Hafner provided me with valuable information about inner city youth I would not have had otherwise. DoVeanna Fulton, Neal Lester, and Elizabeth McNeil spearheaded an academic study of my work that encouraged me to dust off my "kid" and move forward with it, if for no other reason than to let them see the next step in my artistic development. Lee Daniels quite simply changed my life with the making of *Precious*. Teachers Marie Ponsot, Pat Schneider, and Natalie Goldberg provided light and the example of a writing practice as a means of generating hope when I had despaired of ever finishing this book. Meeting with writing buddies and friends like Constance Norgren and Lena Sze kept me immersed in reading and writing literature even when I was not publishing work. Friends like Patricia Bell-Scott, Brighde Mullins, Beladee Griffiths, Nicole Sealy, Linda Susan Jackson, Pamela Booker, and Leotis Clyburn kept me grounded and reminded me I was more than a writer but had value as a friend, confidante, and hang-out partner even if I never published another book (which for years it seemed like I might not!). My family, especially James, Beverly, and Rachel, made me feel unconditionally loved.

I want to thank my agent, Melanie Jackson, for putting me in touch with a daring I didn't know I had. I would not have made this leap without her.

I would also like to thank Benjamin Platt, my editor's assistant at The Penguin Press, who put in time and effort with me and this book. And I would like to acknowledge and thank Maureen Sugden, just the best copy editor ever, period.

And finally I would like to acknowledge and thank Ann Godoff, my publisher and editor at The Penguin Press, for her laser insight as an editor and for having the courage to take on *The Kid*.

A PENGUIN READERS GUIDE TO

THE KID

Sapphire

An Introduction to
The Kid

In the opening pages of *The Kid*, the follow-up to Sapphire's bestselling novel *Push*, Precious Jones dies of AIDS, leaving behind her nine-year-old son Abdul. With no immediate relatives to offer help, the disoriented child is placed in foster care. Abdul isn't there for long—vicious beatings at the hands of a fellow foster child land him in the hospital severely traumatized.

Abdul is then transferred to a Roman Catholic boarding school for orphans. At St Ailanthus, he's called J.J. and develops an interest in Shakespeare and science. With a good education and the encouragement of his teachers, Abdul plans to apply for a scholarship to college. When he's not studying, he wanders the streets of New York and at one point stumbles on a nearby dance class that captures his fascination.

Yet St Ailanthus is no safe haven. Abdul is sexually abused by the brothers who run the school. Longing for affection, closeness, and a sense of personal power, he replicates the abuse he has experienced on his younger and smaller classmates. When it happens, Abdul often dissociates and denies his actions to himself, and sometimes sees the events as dreams, as if he only imagined them. When outside authorities get word of the assaults, the brothers throw him out of the school and he is sent to live with his great grandmother—whose existence had been basically ignored by some members of the school—in her seedy, roach-infested Harlem apartment. Abdul has no tolerance for the filthy accommodations or for the old woman's shocking and frank stories of her own childhood of extreme poverty and abuse and her life as a prostitute in New York.

Violent and angry but desperate to still make something of himself, Abdul settles in with Roman, a gay dance teacher, who agrees to shelter and support him in exchange for sex. When Abdul is seventeen, he leaves Roman and joins an avant-garde dance troupe downtown and befriending the college-educated artist-activists who founded it. His talent is lauded by the press and he starts a relationship with one of the dancers, but even as his life seems to be coming together, Abdul's troubled past catches up with him.

Told through a virtuosic first-person narration that weaves together fantasy and memory, Abdul's harrowing tale chronicles a brutal cycle of violence and emotional devastation. Through Abdul, Sapphire has wrought a deeply conflicted protagonist whose own self-deceptions belie his remarkably persistent hope. Shocking, painful, and real, *The Kid* is simply unforgettable.

ABOUT THE AUTHOR

Sapphire is the author of two collections of poetry and the bestselling novel Push. The film adaption of her novel, *Precious* (2009), won an Academy Award for Best Screenplay and Best Supporting Actress. In 2009, she was awarded a United States Artist Fellowship. She lives in New York City.

A CONVERSATION WITH SAPPHIRE

The Kid *is, in some sense, a sequel to* Push. *What made you want to continue writing about this family?*

First, the question of a "sequel": *The Kid* is not a sequel in a traditional sense in that we don't enter into and follow up on the life of Precious Jones. It is a sequel in that we are looking at the life of Precious's child, Abdul Jones, who is now an AIDS orphan. And it is a sequel in the sense it continues to look at the profound and devastating effects of AIDS on the African American community. One "character" that we are

4

introduced to in *Push* is the AIDS epidemic. At the time I was writing *Push*, gay white activist Andrew Sullivan declared that if there was to be a triage concerning antiviral drugs (and it seemed there might be!), these drugs should first go to gay white men who have contributed so much to society, and not to poor blacks who were so stupid they didn't even know what had hit them. Conversely some black activists and many church leaders labeled and stigmatized AIDS as a "gay disease" and denied and hid the extent of the AIDS epidemic in the black community. These two forces, racism and the homophobic stigmatizing of AIDS as a gay disease, conflated and created a situation where African American women like Precious, who were diagnosed with AIDS in the late '80s, were many times more likely to be dead within a couple of months of their diagnosis than white men who were diagnosed at the same time. Precious Jones represents the last and least served, due to the combined effects of racism and homophobia, when it came to receiving medications that might have saved her life. Precious's death in *The Kid* is as much an effect of these forces as it is of the abuse she suffered as a child. One reason I wrote *Push* was to show how "precious" those blacks *who didn't even know what hit them* might be if given the opportunity to live. *The Kid* resonates on many levels and has many reasons for being, and indeed one of them is to show the continuing impact of the loss of our precious one(s). Precious's death and the forces that contributed to it are the backstory with which we enter an entirely different character's life and circumstances.

So, while *The Kid* is not a sequel in the usual sense of the word, in that we don't follow the life of Precious on to further developments, it *is* a sequel in the sense it continues to look at the profound and devastating effects of AIDS on the African American community. And we *do* see Precious again! We see her through the pained and often distorted memories of her baby boy. He has been her pride and joy and the center of her life. The reader sees the triumph of a devoted motherhood in a child who at the age of nine reads better than his mother did at eighteen—in a child who has great expectations that are, despite repeated pitfalls and abuse to come, never entirely dashed. The readers see a boy who clings to the words of a mother who told him he could and would be something, and strives as hard as any middle class or rich kid to do so. So while in *The Kid* we see the triumph of Precious Jones, we also see the tragedy, as her child is left alone and helpless on the occasion of her death and is repeatedly failed by the institutions of his city, state, and country—institutions that should have been in place to support him after his mother's death.

In answer to the second part of your question, "What made you want to continue writing about this family?" I felt Precious's ancestors, namely Toosie, and her descendant, Abdul Jones, were wonderful characters in and of themselves. I also felt they were excellent vehicles to explore such compelling social issues as nature versus nurture, the modern legacy of slavery, the crippling effects of poverty, the continuing AIDS epidemic, the ability of art to transform and transcend those situations, art's limitations to transcend or transform (think of Abdul's ballet teacher, who is an accomplished dancer but not so accomplished a human being). I also wanted to look at the situational aspects of mental illness. Critics and readers have often commented on Abdul's psychological adaption to racism and sexual abuse as a form of mental illness; some have, but most have not, looked at racism, negligence, and the tide of sexual abuse children are subjected to, and the subsequent denial of the culture that allows it (think Sandusky/Penn State), as forms of a societal psychosis. Perhaps Abdul's "mental illnesses" might indeed be important, though tragic, adaptive survival mechanisms.

Abdul's world, like his mother's, is a bleak one, and it's clear that his chances for survival are limited from the start. Where do you personally see redemption, if any, in his journey?

When I think of redemption I think of the saying by Carl G. Jung that, "One does not become enlightened by imagining figures of light, but by making the darkness conscious." There are possibilities in this story for Abdul if he deals with his shadow and the huge shadow that's been cast upon him—just as there is a tremendous benefit to the society as a whole when we see our hidden landmines and our potential for devastation, as in Rwanda. Abdul takes the reader on a journey through the full cycle of abuse. It is a devastating and debilitating circle, but a circle that is broken, as he is broken down. And with that break we have the possibility of a spiral out. There is a Zen saying: "When my barn burned down I was able to see the moon." By the end of the book Abdul is released from the hell that the actions of others, and *he himself*, have landed him in. And he, even if nobody else does, knows his name.

One of the most powerful scenes in the novel is when Abdul meets his great-grandmother and hears her story about how she came to New York. He has a violent desire to reject that history, but she continues on, forcing him to listen. What did this scene mean to you and what made you include it in the story?

Yes, as you said, she *forces* him to listen. In the allegory of Eloquence in Durer's *Kuntsbuch*, the persons who follow Ogmios are linked by chains that run from the god's tongue to their ears and can pull them into the underworld. This is what Toosie does in a way. She drags Abdul under and back in time. She herself is a Miss Havisham type character, in many ways arrested and defeated by the past, but not totally defeated in that she remembers the past and can construct a "story" from it. Although she is the first person outside of his mother who genuinely gives to Abdul (food, money, etc.) and expects nothing in return, it is this story which is her true gift to him. She knows for Abdul to be free, it will be necessary for him to reckon, to listen to his past, to his-story. He must listen to her or remain, despite his intelligence and fine body, without a history—a non-entity without the spiritual strength or necessary tools to become an artist.

One book I referred to before and while writing *The Kid* was *The Penguin Dictionary of Symbols* when talking about the symbolic meaning of the ear notes: "In Africa ears are always symbols of animal nature. To the Dogon and Bambara of Mali the ear is a twofold sexual symbol, the external ear being a penis and the auditory duct a vagina. This explains the comparison of words with sperm, both being verbal equivalents of the fertilizing water poured out by the Supreme Deity. . . . [The word] flows in at the ear, as sperm flows in at the vagina, to go spiraling down into the womb and make it fruitful" (*The Penguin*

Dictionary of Symbols, pp. 328–329). Of course Toosie's words are metaphorically "impregnating." Abdul's defense against this penetration of his ear is a dead literalness to her intense and vital words. But it is after his conversation with her that we see the first crack in his selfish and narcissistic armor. He who has lost almost everything—mother, toys, home, innocence, chance for a formal education—and has almost nothing of material worth, gives to his great grandmother one of his treasured possessions: his kaleidoscope, his "image maker." This happens for two reasons: one, because she has given him something more valuable than an image—she has given him, whether he likes it or not, "the word" (and he does *not* like it); and two, for the first time since his mother died he is on the same page with another person; he *hears* her.

The sense of hearing as an authenticating sense (as opposed to sight: mirrors, fashion, physical beauty, etc.) is an important theme throughout the novel. Abdul, despite his perfect body, fails at times to hear the beat in dance class; even his mother tells him as a child that he is hardheaded and doesn't listen. And of course it is his hearing that is damaged by the attack at the foster home. The one thing Dr. See demands of Abdul at the end of the book is, "Hear? *Hear?*"

Abdul's physicality—his pleasure from sex, his desire to dance—is central to his identity. Can you talk a little bit about how you developed this aspect of his character?

In one of James Baldwin's essays he criticizes black writing in general, Richard Wright in particular, for an empty space, a hole really, where sexuality should be (or could be) discussed. And while numerous heterosexual black male writers and critics have bemoaned the portrayal of a one-dimensional portrait of the black man as a victimizer, few have been interested in or had the courage to explore the obvious other end of the stick: the black male victim of sexual abuse.

In *The Kid* we see Abdul as a multifaceted sexual being. We see him attempt an equal and healthy relationship with his dancer friend; we see him as a coerced, but still willing, collaborator in his own oppression with an adult male, Roman—despite the problematic nature of a child making a "choice," Abdul chooses in some degree to be with this man, and enjoys—in a limited way—sex with this "sugar daddy." We also see Abdul as a helpless victim of sexual violence, which he neither invites nor wants, and can't control. We are *in* there with him as his brain is being warped. And we're with him when, in the coldest turn of the novel, he appropriates the behavior of his perpetrators and becomes a sexual predator himself, who takes what he wants as it has been taken from him.

But Abdul's sexuality is not a series of sexual *acts*. Abdul's sexuality—his "anima," or soul, if you will—is positive, pulsating and *strong*. Nothing totally daunts his joie de vivre, his charisma, or his optimism (and of course the flip side of that optimism—his denial). He tells us he's "happy to be a boy!" He likes how he looks (unlike his mother, he likes and accepts his skin color) and he revels in his strength and intelligence. He can read and he does; he's awestruck by art and creativity in general. All this is part of his sexuality.

In this book I raise some questions about who these man-children, who populate our African American communities, are. What do they bring to us from their various places of incarceration: prisons, the bad dreams of childhood, mental hospitals, and their after-school programs with the Jerry Sanduskys of the world? J.J., Abdul, who is he? Why do we have the highest rate of HIV infection outside of Africa in the world? These are questions that can't be answered in an effete, sexually conservative, and "proper" fiction, or by nationalistic ranting about what the white man has done to the black man, or even by black feminist male-female dichotomizations. *The Kid*, among other things, begins an accurate portrayal of what happens to many young males who have been abused, and their sometimes hideous responses. Over the top? Maybe, maybe not? True? Absolutely.

The narrative, because it takes place inside Abdul's head, skillfully drifts along his stream of consciousness. How do you achieve this effect in your writing? Is this the way your prose naturally flows or is it something that comes with the draft process?

A lot of what happens in *Push* happens in community, in conversation, in a dialogue journal—it is the story of a woman who more than anything wants to belong. Her faltering sense of self-esteem makes her take great strides and great risks to be accepted. That is not the case with Abdul. While Abdul seeks love and acceptance, he has absorbed the fact that he was loved and is a unique individual; his vital sense of self demands expression. Abdul's quest is to individuate, to "become somebody." His mother searched for people and community to affirm her self-worth; Abdul has goals. Part of the reason he is loyal to the Brothers at St Ailanthus, and doesn't tell anyone about the abuse he suffers, is because he feels his perpetrators will further his goals to be *somebody*.

Abdul's interiority needed to be expressed not through dialogue or third-person reflection, but as the propulsive thoughts of a brilliant man-child. I followed his flow to create a stream of consciousness narrative. I let that knowledge of him dictate to me as I created him.

Everyone is flawed in this book, including those who purport to be on Abdul's side. How might a person like Abdul ever find unconditional support and a more positive sense of self when surrounded by all of these negative influences?

Abdul, a flawed person himself, takes the best these people have to offer: Roman, a racially obsessed gay man (a dinge queen) teaches him the art of dance; the brothers at St Ailanthus give him a good education that sustains him and without which his future autodidactic impulses would not have been nearly as successful. He finds positive role models in flawed people, transferring his feelings of persecution to heroes like Charlie Parker, Jean-Michel Basquiat, and Billie Holiday. And like most lonely children, he seeks healthy and nurturing relationships through reading. In a biography of the ballet dancer Nureyev, Abdul finds a touchstone, one he doubts he can ever touch, but a touchstone nonetheless. He seeks out work by the African American critic Greg Tate. He finds modern-day equivalents of Charlie Parker and Billie Holiday in musicians like Jimi Hendrix, Vernon Reid, and the outré R&B/jazz singer Eryka Badu.

This story goes into some excruciatingly dark places. What was your emotional experience in writing it? Were there moments when you wanted to back away from the intensity of Abdul's life, and if so, what brought you back to the page?

I almost saw it as a political responsibility to go to this intense, dark place. No one else was doing it. We, the black community, were suffering intensely because of denial and a lack of certain kinds of examination and introspection. I wanted the text to be more than a catharsis. I wanted to show the domino effect of one person's hurt.

Being an artist means mapping dark and unknown territory often with no light but your own. Carolyn Forché wrote a poem called "The Colonel" about, among other things, the repressive regime in El Salvador. In the poem, the colonel spills a bag of severed ears onto a table in front of the poet. With this rendering of experience we are forced by Forché to focus on something that, were it outside the realm of art, would be more than most of us could bear. I believe this is what art is capable of: allowing us to see (and bear) what we might not otherwise be able to. I studied with Carolyn Forché in 1989. I came away from her workshop affirmed with the idea that art had a job and it wasn't to describe the sunset.

Abdul is ultimately hospitalized and declared insane in a Kafkaesque turn of events, but he finally has a chance to tell his story. The end feels like a cliffhanger. How did you arrive at this particular ending for the novel? Any plans for a sequel?

Actually, I don't see the last chapter or the ending as a cliffhanger, though it's not a happily ever after or he dies or is doomed, etc. The reader goes through a dark night of the soul with Abdul in a real or imagined place of ever-lit and blindingly bright darkness. With the help of Dr. See, Abdul confronts the only part of the vicious cycle of abuse he has total control over, that which he does to others. We never know what is the truth and what are his guilt-ridden, tortured imaginings. But a confession of sorts emerges, whether it is real or whether the events of his past have filled him with a need to construct a false reality in which he has the power to be as brutal to others as

11

they have been to him. We know, for instance, that he lied when he told his girlfriend, in a moment of bravado, that he'd "offed" someone he'd never touched. Here, Dr. See shows him how his lies might have alienated him from the one person he's been able to establish a real bond with since his mother's death.

Too much happens at the end of the book to talk about right now, but Abdul is freed from the real or imagined hell he finds himself in. One of his last acts before he is freed, inadvertent though it was, is to shatter the artificial lights (and those could symbolize almost any of the false gods he's been oppressed by) that have cut him off from nature, his own and the world's. When the book ends he's free to really be an artist—or anything else he wants to be—something his great grandmother "Slavery Days" and his mother never had a chance to do.

A sequel? Maybe. I'm working on something very different right now, but like the readers who have asked, I too would like to know what Abdul does with his life when that door opens for him.

QUESTIONS FOR DISCUSSION

1. *The Kid* is divided into four parts and follows the narrator from age nine to age eighteen. How does the writing style or voice evolve to represent the different phases of his life?

2. The narrator's name changes several times during the course of this story. What are his names and why do they change?

3. How does Abdul get lost in the social welfare system? What goes wrong? What could have been done differently?

4. Abdul seems to dissociate from reality during certain moments and can't distinguish between real life and his dreams. Why does this happen to him? As the reader, how did you interpret this part of the story? Did you believe him one way or another?

5. So many of the adults in Abdul's life play an ambiguous role—the people who claim to be helping him are often hurting him. Were there any adults whose actions surprised you? Were there any who could have truly helped him?

6. What is it that disturbs Abdul about his great grandmother? Should he have stayed with her? Why or why not?

7. The characters in this book have complicated and conflicting attitudes toward race—there's Brother John, the white priest who grew up in a black neighborhood; the teacher Roman, who fetishizes Abdul's blackness; and the young dancers who have their own liberal-minded prejudices. What is Abdul's own relationship with race? In what ways is it positive and in what ways is it negative?

8. What do you think about the novel's title? Is it fitting? Why do you think Sapphire chose this particular title?

9. Abdul is drawn, almost instinctively, to dance. What is it about this art form that attracts him and what does it allow him to express?

10. In the end of the book, Abdul seems to get one last chance to regain control over his life. What do you think he will do with it?

To access Penguin Readers Guides online, visit the Penguin Group (USA) Web site at www.penguin.com.